CW00684227

# LEGACY

## A SEVENTEEN SERIES NOVEL

# A.D. STARRLING

# COPYRIGHT

**Legacy (A Seventeen Series Novel) Book Four**

Copyright © AD Starrling 2015-2018. All rights reserved. Registered with the UK and US Copyright Services.

Fourth print edition: 2018

**First published as Ashstorm: A Seventeen Series Novel: Book Four in 2015**

www.ADStarrling.com

ISBN-13: 978-0-9572826-9-8

The right of AD Starrling to be identified as the author of this work has been asserted in accordance with the Copyright, Designs and Patents Act 1988.

All rights reserved. No parts of this book may be reproduced in any form or by any electronic or mechanical means, including information storage and retrieval systems, without the prior written consent of the author, excepting for brief quotes used in reviews. Your respect of the author's rights and hard work is appreciated.

Request to publish extracts from this book should be sent to the author at ads@adstarrling.com

This book is a work of fiction. References to real people (living or dead), events, establishments, organizations, or locations are intended only to provide a sense of authenticity, and are used factitiously. All other characters, and all other incidents and dialogue, are drawn from the author's imagination and are not to be construed as real.

Editors:

Invisible Ink Editing (www.invisibleinkediting.com)

Right Ink On The Wall (www.rightinkonthewall.com)

Cover: Deranged Doctor Design (www.derangeddoctordesign.com)

## DEDICATION

*To my Muse. Thank you for the ongoing inspiration, camaraderie, and occasional graphic threat when I procrastinate. FYI, 4 am is not a great time to drop by. Neither is the shower, you perverted entity.*

# THE IMMORTALS

The Crovirs and the Bastians: two races of immortals that have lived side by side with humans since the beginning of civilization and once ruled an empire that stretched across Europe, Asia, and North Africa. Each possessing the capacity to survive up to sixteen deaths, they have been engaged in a bloody and savage war from the very dawn of their existence. This unholy battle has, for the most part, remained a well-guarded secret from the eyes of ordinary humans, despite the fact that they have been used as pawns in some of the most epic chapters of the immortal conflict. It was not until the late fourteenth century that the two races were forced to forge an uneasy truce, following a deadly plague that wiped out more than half of their numbers and made the majority of survivors infertile.

Each immortal society is ruled by a hierarchy of councils made up of nobles. The First Council consists of the heads of seven Immortal Sections: the Order of the Hunters, the Counter-Terrorism Group, Human Relations, Commerce, Immortal Legislations and Conventions, Research and Development, and Immortal Culture and History. The Head of the Order of the Hunters is the most powerful member of the First

Council. The Second Council, or the Assembly, comprises the regional division directors under each Head of Section, while the Congress of the Council is made up of local authority chiefs.

Though they have been instrumental to the most significant events in world history, religion, and culture, the Immortals' existence is known to only a select few humans, among them the political leaders of the most powerful states on Earth and the Secretary General of the United Nations.

# PART ONE: FROZEN

# PROLOGUE

**JANUARY 1599. POLAR URALS. WESTERN RUSSIA.**

THE IMMORTAL BIT BACK A CURSE AS HIS BOOTS SANK IN A snowdrift. He struggled out of the icy clutches of the land and carried on climbing, his eyes never leaving the dark shape moving between the trees above him. The figure suddenly stopped and turned. A flash bloomed in the gloom of the ever-green forest.

The immortal heard the crack of the pistol's discharge a moment before the lead ball thudded into the trunk of a birch, just inches from his head. He dropped to the ground, wood chips raining down around him and the sulfurous smell of burning gunpowder tainting the crisp, cold air. A further bang drowned out the agitated barks of the sled dogs in the outbuilding next to the log cabin at the bottom of the rise. The second shot smacked through the tightly-packed snow next to his hand. He swore and rolled behind a cluster of bushes. He rocked to a stop and peered around the edge of the snow-laden branches as the echo of the blast died down.

His prey was disappearing into the shadows beneath the canopy.

The immortal jumped to his feet and gave chase once more, his breath leaving his lips in white plumes. A bitter wind whistled down the flank of the mountain and stung his frost-crusted eyes and exposed skin. Down below, the sled dogs started to howl. The immortal clenched his jaw against the burning pain in his lungs and legs and willed his body forward.

Dazzling light greeted him at the summit of the rise. He staggered to a halt in calf-deep snow and squinted in the glare. His stomach lurched.

The forest ended abruptly on the edge of a rising ice field. Beyond it, a glacier rose to the summit of the peak, a white scar spread across miles of jagged, dark rocks. Sunlight reflected off towering cliffs and precipitous valleys, the shimmering brilliance masking the deadliness of the hostile landscape. Some hundred feet ahead, barely visible in the blinding radiance, the man he had been hunting for nearly two centuries scaled the treacherous incline.

The immortal removed the musket rifle strapped to his backpack, his gaze locked on the running figure. He shouldered the weapon, cocked the hammer, and carefully sighted down the barrel. Blood pounded in his ears as he held his breath and pulled the trigger.

Flint struck steel. Sparks flared as gunpowder ignited. The lead shot erupted from the muzzle of the gun and flashed through the air, its path straight and true.

The man he was chasing jerked and cried out. He stumbled down to one knee and clamped a hand to his right flank. He swayed for a moment, pushed himself up, and turned to fire his weapon once more. The shot whistled harmlessly into the treetops. He threw the pistol to the ground and started to climb again.

Rage darkened the immortal's vision. He had waded

through thousands of miles of godforsaken wilderness before finally tracking down the man who had killed his lover and who posed the greatest threat the immortal societies had ever known. Having lost precious moments dispatching the body-guards who stood watch over the remote hideout in the Urals, he had come within seconds of killing his enemy when the man escaped his grasp once more, rescued by the same uncanny luck that had been his savior for the last two hundred years.

The immortal shoved the rifle into its straps and headed over the ice.

Despite the wound, his prey accelerated and angled for a black outcrop rising out of the glacier to the far left.

Cold air seared the immortal's throat as he pursued the bleeding figure. He had just reached the crimson trail staining the pristine snow when a distant boom reached his ears. He stopped and looked up.

Movement on the slope some six thousand feet above him caught his gaze. A wall of whiteness slowly detached itself from the face of the mountain.

The wounded man froze in his tracks. He stared at the approaching avalanche before moving once more, his legs pumping awkwardly through the snow as he raced for the shelter of the spur of rock.

The immortal followed, despair sending a fresh burst of energy through his body. *No, not now, not when I am this close!*

The deluge rushed inexorably closer, a tidal wave of death dancing gracefully down the incline.

The immortal staggered after his prey, his resolve unshaken, air leaving his body in harsh gasps. The land rocked violently beneath his feet. He floundered and lost his footing. A thunderous explosion tore the air as he fell to his knees. A large crack appeared in the glacier in front of him.

The immortal's eyes widened. A cold blast knocked him sideways and sent him tumbling along the incline. He rolled and slid to a stop on his stomach some twenty feet down the slope. The roar of the approaching maelstrom of snow and ice echoed against the looming peaks and vales. The fissure lengthened. He blinked and saw a jagged line dart inches past his right hand before snaking toward the distant tree line behind him.

He scrambled backward as a dark crevasse opened in the ice sheet. The ground crumbled beneath him. His stomach dropped. He yanked his sword from the scabbard on his back and stabbed the blade frantically upward.

It sank into the edge of the ice just as he started to fall. He dangled from the hilt for a shocked moment before slowly looking down at the yawning darkness between his legs. His breath froze in his throat, the fear that gripped him almost paralyzing in its intensity. He gritted his teeth and reached up with his free hand, his flailing fingers searching desperately for purchase. They closed on the lip of the widening chasm.

The avalanche became a deafening howl that eclipsed the rapid drumbeat of his pulse. He looked over his shoulder.

His prey had reached the rocky outcrop and was crouched beneath it, his body braced for impact. Their eyes met through a thickening mist of fine snow. The wounded man smiled, his gaze full of dark triumph.

The immortal closed his eyes. Despair formed a tightening band around his heart as he steeled himself for what was to come.

The white torrent washed over the crevasse, pounding him with a cold, deadly weight that knocked the air out of his lungs. A rock smashed into his fingers, breaking skin and bone. He choked back a cry and swallowed a mouthful of snow.

The sword shuddered in his grasp. He let go of the edge of the chasm and clung to the hilt with both hands. Blood made his grip slippery. Another crack reached his ears. He looked up through the gray haze and glimpsed the fracture tearing through the ice holding the blade. It collapsed a second later.

He fell into the abyss, sword in hand.

Wind whistled in his ears. White walls rushed past him. The light faded as the deluge followed him into the gulf.

Soaring cliffs of black rock replaced the walls of ice as he fell through the crevasse into the very bowels of the mountain itself. Then the rock disappeared.

He had a vague impression of a gaping, empty void before he struck the ground.

Pain exploded through his consciousness, blocking out sight and sound. He felt his bones shatter. The earth shifted beneath him once more. Icy liquid suddenly flooded his throat. He gasped and choked. As freezing numbness engulfed his body, dulling the agony searing his senses, the immortal blinked and registered the clear waters surrounding him in dull incomprehension.

Darkness descended from above. The rest of the avalanche crashed down around him.

His fingers slowly loosened on the hilt of his sword. His final thought before darkness and silence locked him in the icy grave of the underground lake was that no one in the immortal societies knew of the danger that was still to come.

# CHAPTER ONE

**JUNE 1969. SAN ANDRES MOUNTAINS. NEW MEXICO.**

*OH SHIT, NOT THE FACE!*

Ethan Storm steeled himself as the soldier's fist sailed through the air and smashed into his left cheek. He staggered back a step. The heels of his boots struck a rock wall. Chains jingled above him as iron cuffs bit into his wrists. He shook his head, spat out blood, and directed a crooked smile at the man who had hit him.

'Is that all you've got?'

An ugly grimace distorted the soldier's features. He snarled and pulled his arm back once more. His companion stepped in front of him.

'Enough!' barked the second soldier. 'Our orders were to capture the guy, not beat the living shit out of him! Besides, you know those scientists will complain if we make him bleed.'

The first soldier scowled and slowly lowered his hand.

'They probably won't notice anyway,' he said with a grunt. 'I don't know what the hell our government wants with all these bastards, but I've never seen people heal so damn fast. It's fucking unnatural is what it is!' He glanced around uneasily, his eyes alighting on the shackled figure on the far side of the cell. 'That asshole was a mess when they finished with him the other day. Now look at him! I can't even see a scar where they cut into him!'

Ethan blinked. He was finding it difficult to concentrate on the soldier's words; the narcotic they had given him had still not worn off. From what he could gather of their conversation, it seemed there were other immortals locked up in this infernal dungeon with him. He raised his head and squinted at the prisoner on the other side of the room. All he could make out through the drug-induced haze clouding his senses was a man with a long, filthy, matted mane and matching beard.

The stranger sat on the floor with his head bowed and his back against the wall, arms resting loosely on his knees. His wrists and ankles were locked in stout manacles and fetters. A metal collar bound him to an iron ring in the floor. The stench of human waste filled the room from a hole in the ground.

Anger surged through Ethan. He was damned if he was going to end up like that guy. He flexed his fingers and focused on the cuffs holding him to the wall. Tendons bulged in his neck while he concentrated on the metal. Sweat broke out across his forehead. His vision flickered.

Ethan gasped and sagged, the chains tinkling above his head as his legs almost gave way. Alarm flared inside him. Did they know of his ability? Was that the reason they had sedated him?

The soldier who had struck him looked around dismissively at the jangling noise before crossing the floor to the silent figure on the opposite side of the cell. He stopped a couple of feet from the chained man.

'Hey! What the hell *are* you?' he demanded.

The prisoner remained silent.

The soldier stiffened. He drew his foot back and kicked the

captive man viciously in the leg. 'I asked you a question, asshole!'

'For fuck's sake, Eddie, stop it!' hissed his companion. The man's eyes grew round with horror. He took a step forward. 'Eddie, no!'

The soldier called Eddie had taken his gun from his hip holster. He leveled it against the mute prisoner's head and cocked the hammer.

'Maybe I should blow your brains out. See if you survive that, you inhuman piece of shit!'

The bound man's hands rose so fast Ethan almost missed the move. He snatched the pistol from the soldier's grasp, removed the magazine, and dismantled the weapon in a blur of motion. The clatter of the parts hitting the floor was the only sound that broke the frozen silence that followed.

The soldiers gaped. Ethan bit back a snort. The prisoner's head rose. Teeth gleamed above his matted beard.

Eddie lost it. It took a further two guards to drag him, cursing and struggling, from the chamber. By the time they left, the prisoner's face was a bloodied pulp.

He had not made a single sound while the enraged soldier punched and kicked him.

Ethan's fingers cramped from fisting them in the tight iron cuffs. Frustration gnawed at his insides as he considered the helplessness of their situation.

'Hey, you okay?' he called out weakly to the still shape on the floor.

Footsteps echoed somewhere outside the room. The prisoner slowly pushed himself up to his elbows and mumbled something through swollen, cracked lips. A key rattled in the lock.

'What was that?' said Ethan, his eyes shifting briefly to the cell door.

'I would worry about your own self, boy,' the prisoner

repeated in a raspy voice. His piercing, blue-green gaze locked on Ethan's face.

The door swung open on thick hinges. A tall, distinguished-looking, middle-aged man in a white coat walked in. He stopped and stared at the bleeding figure on the floor.

'And what have we here?' he murmured, his tone unhurried.

The prisoner froze. Unbridled rage blazed in his aquamarine eyes. He jumped to his feet so quickly the movement startled Ethan and charged toward the man in the doorway. The chains stopped him short a second later.

A choked grunt escaped the prisoner's throat as he strained against the metal collar digging into his windpipe. He clawed the air inches from the silent figure's head, his face reddening while the metal links binding him jangled and shook around the iron ring in the floor.

The stranger in the coat turned his back on the enraged man, his expression unperturbed. His hooded eyes alighted on Ethan's face.

'Ah. You're awake.'

The man reached inside his pocket and walked leisurely across the floor.

Ethan tensed when he saw the capped needle and syringe the man withdrew from his coat. He stared at the clear liquid inside the glass tube with rising panic and started to struggle against the chains holding him captive. Veins throbbed on his forehead as he focused his mind once more on the iron restraints around his wrists.

The cuffs trembled above him.

The man in the coat paused. 'Now, now, we can't have you doing that, Mr. Storm.' He uttered a disappointed tut-tut. 'Not after all the time and resources we spent finding you.' He took the cap off the needle.

Ethan clenched his jaw and concentrated on the shackles. A

buzzing noise filled his ears. His knees suddenly collapsed beneath him.

Cursing the drug dulling his senses, he shook his head dazedly and pushed himself up just as the man reached him.

'No!' Ethan shouted. He stepped back until he hit the wall, shocked at how weak his voice sounded and the shudders of exhaustion racking his body. 'Get the hell away from me!'

He kicked out at the man in the coat. The stranger side-stepped smoothly.

Steely fingers closed around Ethan's throat. He found himself lifted off the floor and choked on the tightening band across his windpipe, legs thrashing feebly midair.

The man in the coat held him aloft and studied him coldly. 'Things will go better for you if you cooperate, son of Jared.'

Before Ethan could make sense of the stranger's cryptic words, he felt a sharp prick in his neck. The man depressed the plunger on the syringe. Cool oblivion washed over the immortal.

It was dark inside the cell when Ethan came to. He opened his eyes and blinked.

He was lying on his side on the cold stone floor. A rock wall swam into focus a couple of feet in front of him. He stared at it for a moment.

Hope welled inside his chest when he realized they had unchained him from the wall. He pushed up on his elbows. Metal clinked in the gloom. He looked down.

His heart sank when he saw the cuffs around his wrists. He raised a hand to the heavy collar around his neck and followed the iron links leading from it to the ring on the floor.

'Shit,' he muttered.

There was movement to his right. He turned and met an intense blue-green stare a couple of inches from his face.

'What the—?'

Ethan scrambled backward awkwardly.

'You're awake,' said the bearded prisoner.

Ethan clutched his chest. 'Jesus, man! You almost gave me a heart attack!'

Chains jingled as the prisoner sat back on his heels.

'Somehow, I suspect you will survive such an attack of the heart,' he professed calmly.

Ethan studied the man with a frown. 'I take it you're also an immortal?'

The man cocked his head and eyed him shrewdly. 'And what makes you say that, pray tell?'

The prisoner had an old-fashioned, cultivated way of expressing himself that Ethan had not heard in some time.

He scowled. 'Well, apart from the obvious clues from those soldiers, your wounds are healing pretty damn fast.'

The prisoner raised his fingers to the scabs on his face. 'Ah. Yes. I suppose there is no hiding that fact.'

A wave of dizziness suddenly struck Ethan. He shifted on the floor, pressed his back to the wall, and dropped his head between his raised knees. He concentrated on his breathing until the sickening feeling passed; he was evidently still under the influence of the latest injection.

He clamped down on the panic threatening to overwhelm him and raised his eyes to the bearded prisoner. 'So, what the hell gives?'

The man looked at him blankly. 'I am afraid I have no knowledge of such an expression.'

Ethan bit back a curse. *Seriously, what is wrong with this guy?*

'What's going on?' he rephrased with as much patience as he could muster. He indicated the interior of the cell with a weak wave. 'Why are we here? What do these people want with us?'

The immortal watched him for a beat. 'If I may ask, how exactly did they apprehend you?'

Heat flooded Ethan's cheeks. The subject of his capture was a source of great embarrassment to him.

'They put something in my drink when I was in the company of a...lady.'

He still felt chagrined for having fallen for the oldest trick in the book. A day after he had finished his latest assignment in Los Angeles, he had travelled to Vegas to enjoy the hard-earned cash that had been wired to one of his accounts. His suspicions should have been aroused when an attractive brunette bumped into him in the lobby of his hotel, spilled coffee down his shirt, and invited him for a drink in the bar as an apology. Had he not already consumed a fair amount of alcohol before the flight that brought him over from LA, he would have been in a better state of mind to smell the obvious trap.

The woman had been exactly his type, with dark hair and eyes, and all her curves in the right places. Ethan would have pondered his uncanny luck if he had been in full possession of his faculties. And he would have noticed the men watching them from various discreet places around the bar while he and his companion drank and flirted with each other.

It wasn't until he took the woman up to his room that the penny dropped. Halfway through undressing her, the bed started to spin alarmingly beneath him, much more than could be explained by the alcohol he had imbibed. A moment later, four men burst through the door, pinned him to the mattress, and jabbed something in his arm. The next thing he remembered was being lifted off the back of a truck in a large, brightly-lit hangar and being dragged through what felt like half a mile of underground tunnels to the room where he now found himself chained.

All this he haltingly related to his cellmate.

The other immortal leaned toward him, eyes glittering

intently in the gloom. 'This place you saw before they brought you here, can you describe it to me?'

Ethan hesitated. 'You're not gonna mention that I was an idiot for being so easily deceived?'

'Of course, you were a complete fool for falling prey to your baser animal instincts.' The prisoner shrugged. 'There is, however, no point weeping over shed milk. Now, about this place you spoke of.'

Ethan's jaw sagged. '"Weeping over shed milk?" What are you, an old lady?'

The prisoner's eyes narrowed slightly. 'There is no need to be discourteous, boy.'

'I'm starting to find "boy" slightly insulting myself,' snapped Ethan.

There was a flash of teeth in the dark. 'That's because you are but a child in immortal years.'

'Oh yeah? And you're like what, four hundred or something?'

Ethan could feel strength flowing back into his limbs. Arguing with this irritating guy seemed to be doing him some good. He almost missed the pained expression that flashed across the other man's face.

The prisoner dropped his head back on the bare rock wall. 'What year is it?'

Ethan stared at him, nonplussed. 'Year?'

'Yes. Jonah and his men have taunted me with so many half-truths in the last decade, I don't know what to believe anymore.'

Ethan wondered at the undertone of bitter dread in the man's voice. 'It's 1969.'

The prisoner went deathly still. Muscles worked in his throat.

'Then I am seven hundred and thirty-nine years old, boy,' he finally whispered in a tortured voice.

Ethan startled. 'You don't look a day over four hundred and fifty!'

The prisoner's knuckles whitened where his hands rested in his lap.

'What the hell happened to you? Were you frozen in time or something?' said Ethan.

The older immortal stiffened. 'You are correct.'

Ethan blinked, perplexed. 'What?'

'You asked if I had been frozen in time. The answer to that question is yes.'

Ethan shivered at the expression in the older immortal's eyes. The latter looked like someone who had survived the very depths of hell itself.

He looked away from the intense gaze and studied the manacles around his wrists. Wondering if he had enough reserves left to get himself out of this mess, he tugged at the cuffs. The iron was old and thick. He took a deep breath and concentrated on the locking mechanism.

'Jonah referred to you as a son of Jared,' said his companion. 'Who is Jared? Is he a member of your special Crovir ancestry?'

# CHAPTER TWO

ETHAN'S HEAD SNAPPED UP, ANY NOTION OF MANIPULATING the metal fleeing his mind. He lunged toward the older man and groaned when the cell reeled around him. He collapsed on the floor and swallowed the bile rising in his throat. A shudder racked his body.

'What the hell do you know about that?' he spat out once he could lift his head off the ground.

The other immortal reached for something in the gloom. There was a clink and a faint slosh. He passed across a wooden ladle full of water.

Ethan grabbed the handle and swallowed a mouthful of the cold liquid. Some of it spilled over and dribbled down his chin.

'From what I witnessed earlier, and our captors' persistence in keeping you under the influence of some sort of mind-altering substance, I can only surmise that you are an Elemental,' said the man. His gaze dropped to the birthmark on the back of Ethan's left hand. 'I have only ever heard rumors of your kind. You are a rare breed indeed among the Crovirs.'

Dismay flooded Ethan at the man's words. With it came a

familiar rush of anger and sadness. He flopped down, his cheek pressed against the chilly, wet stone.

'You don't know how rare.'

He felt the other man tense.

'You are the last of your kind?' his companion asked harshly.

Ethan closed his eyes and sagged on the bare rock under a fresh wave of exhaustion. 'I believe so.'

When the other immortal spoke again, a trace of compassion tinged his tone. 'It seems Jonah has been looking for you for some time. You did well to stay out of his reach for so long.'

Now that the drug was slowly clearing from his bloodstream, Ethan could no longer ignore the deep-seated fear that had plagued him ever since those men burst into his hotel room. More than a century after they had ripped his family apart, the invisible enemy who had been chasing him all over this godforsaken world had finally tracked him down.

In the wake of the terror that gripped him, Ethan was surprised to discover a reserve of rage. His nails bit into his palms. He sat up slowly, the face of the man in the white coat swimming in his mind.

'Is Jonah the name of the guy who stabbed me in the neck?'

'Yes. His true name is Jonah Krondike, although currently he appears to be using the alias Jonah Resner. He is a Crovir noble.'

'What does he want with me?'

The older immortal drew his legs up and rested his arms on his knees. 'I believe he is intending to use your body for some sort of experiment.'

Ethan stiffened. 'Experiment? What kind of experiment?'

His companion hesitated. 'That I do not know the answer to, boy.'

Ethan narrowed his eyes. He could not help but feel that the older immortal had just lied to him. 'There seems to be some kinda history between this Jonah Krondike and you. How do you know him?'

'It is a long tale and one I am afraid I will not have time to relate.'

Ethan arched an eyebrow. 'Why? You going somewhere?'

The immortal nodded. 'Yes. We both are.'

Ethan gaped at his fellow prisoner. 'Huh?'

'We are about to escape from here,' explained his companion. 'It has been twelve hours since they gave you that medication. They will be back to administer another dose soon.'

Ethan felt blood drain from his face.

'So, how are you feeling, Elemental?'

There was a clink from the chains as the older immortal rummaged around in the dark.

'Like shit, now that you ask,' mumbled Ethan.

'I meant, how are your immortal powers?' his companion asked patiently. 'Do you think you can use them?'

Ethan took a deep breath and stared at the cuffs around his wrists. He concentrated on the metal. Blood thundered in his ears. A grunt left his lips.

There was a faint noise from the locks.

He gasped and bent over, alarmed at how much the act had taken from him.

'Not bad,' said the older immortal. 'Now, see if you can open them all the way.'

Ethan panted where he crouched on the floor. He turned his left hand over and slowly extended his middle finger at the other man.

'There is no need for that kind of gesture.' There was a dim noise outside the cell. 'I would hurry if I were you.'

Ethan detected a glint of metal in the shadows as his companion placed something on the ground. He swallowed the lump of panic clogging his throat. 'What's that?'

'It is a shot from that idiotic infantry man's gun.'

The immortal maneuvered the handle of the ladle into the base of the wall behind him and carefully extracted a piece of rock the size of an orange.

From the marks around it, Ethan suspected it had taken the man weeks, if not months, to carve out the lump of stone. Despair swamped him at that thought; he did not want to end up locked in this hellish dungeon for eternity.

A low mumble of voices reached him from the other side of the cell door.

'It is the change of the guards,' said the older immortal. His eyes shone in the gloom. 'Are you getting anywhere with those fetters?'

'No. At least, not fast enough for it to be of any use.'

Beads of sweat dotted Ethan's brow and pooled at the base of his throat as he centered all his energy on the metal bands binding him. Had he been in full possession of his senses, he would have been out of them in seconds.

'This might help,' said the older immortal.

Ethan looked up. 'What—?'

His companion slapped him forcefully across the face.

Ethan's head snapped to the side. He turned and gaped at his cellmate. '*You bastard!* Why the hell did you do—?'

The immortal lunged toward him.

'Use that anger! *Focus!*' he hissed inches from Ethan's face.

He struck him again.

Ethan's ears rang from the second blow. Numbness bloomed on his cheek. A wave of fury flooded his body.

The older immortal made a satisfied noise at the back of his throat and shuffled backward. He lifted the rock above his head and brought it down sharply on the rim of the bullet. Sparks flared in the gloom when stone met metal. He raised the rock and hit the base of the cartridge a second time.

There was a flash and a loud bang as the casing exploded.

An alarmed curse sounded outside their prison above the

dying echoes of the detonation. A key jangled agitatedly in the lock. The door slammed open, spilling faint, yellow light across the floor.

A guard stormed inside the room, rifle in hand. He flicked the switch on the wall and blinked as brightness flooded the space.

'What the fuck was that?' he barked.

He raised the weapon stiffly to his shoulder, the barrel swinging between the two prisoners. A sudden clatter made him jump. His gaze moved to the iron shackles and collars lying open on the floor. His eyes grew round.

Ethan smiled savagely. The rage blazing through his veins had burned away the last vestiges of the narcotic in his system and allowed him to unlock the restraints holding him and the other immortal captive.

The guard swore. His finger moved on the trigger. Ethan zeroed in on the gun. With his mind clear, it took but a single breath for him to perceive the structure of the metal. He altered it.

The barrel of the rifle twisted sideways with a tortuous creak. The guard gaped at the buckled weapon. He cast it aside and reached for the army knife on his hip.

There was a blur by Ethan's side as the older immortal bolted to his feet and dashed across the room. He reached the soldier just as the latter raised his blade, ducked under the swinging arm, and drove his shoulder into the man's chest. Air whooshed out of the guard's mouth in a harsh grunt as the immortal tackled him to the ground; the knife fell from his hand and skittered across the floor as he landed heavily on his back.

The soldier lay stunned for a heartbeat before struggling against the man atop him. His eyes darted fearfully toward the half-open door and he opened his mouth to scream for help. Ethan tensed.

The soldier barely had time to utter the beginning of a cry before it became a choked gurgle; the immortal had straddled his body and was digging his thumbs into his windpipe. The man's face flushed to a deepening red as he punched and pulled at the prisoner's rock-steady arms, body bucking futilely beneath his attacker's weight and heels kicking at the ground.

The immortal remained silent, his face a study of fierce concentration and his knuckles white where they lay against the guard's neck.

It was a matter of seconds before the soldier stopped struggling.

Only when the man lay completely still, bloodshot eyes staring unseeingly at the ceiling and limbs relaxing in death, did the immortal finally move. He sat back on his heels and dropped his hands to his sides, his posture rigid.

Ethan released the breath he had been holding. Mixed with the growing admiration he felt for his companion's tenacity in the face of the odds stacked against them was a sliver of fear.

The older immortal had been a survivor for a lot longer than Ethan. And he was evidently not afraid to kill.

Hooded eyes turned to him. 'You did well.'

The immortal rose, stepped past the body of the soldier, closed the cell door, and removed the key from the lock.

Ethan climbed shakily to his feet, his heart hammering inside his chest. 'Now what?'

'We wait.' His companion glanced at him. 'What is your name, boy?'

Ethan hesitated. 'Ethan. Yours?'

'Asgard. Asgard Go—'

The sound of footsteps rose from outside. Ethan stiffened. The footsteps grew closer and stopped on the other side of the door.

Asgard brought a finger to his lips, turned off the light, and melted into the shadows. Ethan slipped into a dark corner of the room just as a key turned in the lock. The door opened.

A woman in a white lab coat walked in with a metal tray in hand. She started to reach for the switch on the wall and froze when she spotted the body of the guard in the pale beam of light washing across the ground from outside. A gasp left her lips. She took a step back and reached inside her pocket.

Asgard came up behind her and kicked the door shut with his heel. Darkness fell inside the chamber once more.

'Hello, Marilyn,' he hissed as he clamped a hand over the woman's mouth and locked his arm around her body, trapping her.

The tray fell from her grasp and clattered noisily on the floor. Ethan saw the woman's eyes shrink into slits. She stamped on her captor's foot with the heel of her pump and slipped something out of her coat. He made out the shape of a handgun as he moved toward the struggling pair.

A low noise escaped Asgard's throat when the woman bit down on his hand. The barrel of the gun moved erratically toward Ethan.

'I don't think so, lady.'

He raised a hand.

The weapon crumpled in the woman's grip. Her eyes rounded with horror and fluttered closed a second later when the man holding her captive struck the back of her neck sharply with the edge of his hand. Asgard lowered her limp body to the ground and moved to the dead soldier.

'We haven't got much time.' He started to strip the man of his clothes and boots. 'They will come looking for her.'

Ethan stared from the syringe that had fallen out of the tray to the woman's pale features. 'Who is she?'

Asgard grimaced. 'She works for Jonah.' He glanced at Ethan. 'Take her coat.'

They found the keys to the shackles on the dead guard and

chained the unconscious woman in the metal restraints that had previously bound them. Minutes after the soldier had stormed their cell, they were standing outside their prison.

An empty corridor carved out of bare rock stretched out on either side of them. The bulbs dotting the ceiling shed a subdued light on the metal doors lining it.

'Should we get the other prisoners out?' Ethan whispered. The woman's white coat stretched uncomfortably under his arms and across his back.

Asgard finished locking the door. 'No. The few that remain are too diseased to travel far. They will only be a burden.'

Despite his time in captivity, the older immortal had retained his brawny build; the guard's clothes barely fitted his broad-shouldered frame. He had tucked his unruly mane under the soldier's military cap and tugged the shirt collar up to mask his beard.

Ethan frowned. 'Diseased? How?'

Asgard's face darkened. 'The experiments Jonah and his associates have been carrying out on them have taken their toll on their bodies.'

# CHAPTER THREE

ETHAN INHALED SHARPLY.

'But they—they are *immortals*!' he stammered. 'As is he!'

'Jonah doesn't care about such things,' came the bitter reply.

Ethan's hands fisted by his sides. That his kind had suffered and died in this hellhole in such wretched and brutal circumstances, at the hands of one of their own, was a terrible truth to swallow. He suppressed the black thoughts filling his mind about the possible fate of his own family and indicated the corridor with a jerk of his head.

'Where to?'

'This way.'

Asgard headed right, his steps swift and confident.

Ethan went after him and glanced uneasily at the cells they passed. He thought he heard someone moan behind one of the doors. A shiver danced down his spine. He quickened his pace.

'It's a shame about those guns,' said his companion up ahead.

The older immortal had taken the guard's knife and slipped it under the cuff of his right sleeve.

'Yeah, well, not getting shot was kind of a priority at the

time,' Ethan muttered. 'Besides, it's not exactly as if I could have magicked it out of their hands.'

Asgard glanced at him. 'I don't know much about Elementals' abilities, but could you not have made the weapons soar in the air and come to you?'

Ethan stopped dead in his tracks and gaped. 'Who do you think I am, freakin' Houdini?'

Asgard stared at him blankly.

Ethan bit back a sigh; he'd forgotten this guy was locked in some kind of time warp. 'Never mind.'

A junction came into view. They approached it slowly and peered cautiously around the corners. The adjacent passages were deserted.

Ethan eyed them warily. He had been stripped of his watch and wallet after his capture. Although he had no idea of the exact time, the empty corridors indicated that the hour was late.

'Do you know where you're going?' Ethan said.

'Yes. I was always conscious when they removed me from the dungeon to take me to Jonah.' Asgard turned left. 'This should lead us away from the labs.'

Ethan quelled the grim images the other man's words evoked and followed in his steps. They cleared another pair of silent passageways before they came across the first guard.

The soldier stood in front of a steel door set deep in the rock wall halfway down the otherwise vacant corridor.

'Stay behind me,' murmured Asgard when they started down the passage.

Ethan kept his eyes focused on his companion's back as they came abreast of the guard. A low rumble travelled from the other side of the steel door and a faint vibration danced up the soles of his boots when they walked past. He sneaked a peek at the sign above the doorway. It said "Generator Room 4."

The soldier barely glanced at them.

'They brought me into the dungeon through there,' said Asgard when the guard was out of earshot. 'There is another passage beyond the chamber with the thunder devices. It leads to a cave where they keep the metal carriages with no horses.' He hesitated. 'From the little I remember, it was heavily guarded.'

It took a second for Ethan to figure out that the "thunder devices" were the generators powering the underground facility. He made a face. 'By "metal carriages with no horses," I take it you mean automobiles?'

'I know not their names, but I am certain they are the devil's own work,' grumbled his companion.

They crossed paths with four more guards as they negotiated a succession of identical, dimly-lit tunnels. At first, Ethan was surprised no one stopped and questioned them. When he registered the way the men ignored the older immortal and avoided looking at him, he realized the white coat was the reason they had not been challenged thus far.

The soldiers looked scared when they saw it. A quiver of apprehension darted through Ethan when this fact sunk in— that this Jonah character and his scientists could instill such fear in these battle-hardened men was unnerving.

The tension that had been building up inside him since they made their daring escape from the dungeon rose to fever pitch as he wondered what would happen if they came across someone who wasn't a simple foot soldier. Though he had smudged the photograph on the female scientist's badge with some dirt, it would not take long for somebody curious enough to take a closer look to figure out that he was not Dr. Marilyn Davies.

Five minutes later, Ethan was convinced they were lost. Though the occasional discreet plaque on the wall seemed to indicate their location, the cryptic lettering and numbers were of no help to him without a map. He was about to voice his concern to Asgard when the latter came to an abrupt halt. Ethan stopped and looked around, muscles taut and senses on alert.

They had reached yet another intersection. A steel door stood at the end of a short passage to the left. The sign plate on it read "Staff Quarters." Asgard turned and moved toward it.

'Hey, what the hell are you doing?' hissed Ethan.

He hurried after him.

Asgard stopped in front of the door, his lips pressed in a hard line. 'If this leads to the lodgings of Jonah and his underlings, we may find useful information within as to their goals.'

He reached for the handle, twisted it, and pulled. The door did not budge. Undeterred, he removed the dead guard's keys from his pocket and tried them one at a time.

None of them worked.

Ethan hesitated. Although he wanted nothing more than to get the hell out of there, he had to concede that the older immortal was right; uncovering their captors' intentions was crucial if they wanted to evade them in the future.

'Here, let me try,' he muttered.

Asgard nodded and moved to the side.

Ethan touched the lock. The internal mechanism appeared in his mind's eye. He twisted it with the faintest flicker of his fingers.

There was a soft click. Asgard grabbed the handle and opened the door. A gloomy corridor appeared on the other side.

A man in a white coat was striding briskly toward them, his gaze locked on the file in his hands. He looked up and faltered when he saw them. Confusion dawned on his face. He glanced from Ethan to Asgard.

His eyes widened in shocked recognition. 'You! How—?'

Ethan glimpsed a glimmer of metal to his left.

The knife left Asgard's hand and whirled through the air. It sank into the scientist's throat with a soft, fleshy thud.

The man choked. Frothy blood bubbled past his lips as he raised his hands to his neck, his pupils expanding dark circles in his pale face. The folder fell from his grip and spilled its contents across the stone floor. His body landed next to it a second later.

Asgard lowered his arm and straightened from his crouch. He ignored Ethan, closed the door behind them, and walked over to the dead scientist.

Ethan followed slowly. 'I take it this is another one of Jonah's goons?'

The nametag on the scientist's coat said "Albert Spiers."

'Yes,' said his companion between gritted teeth.

From the expression of hatred on the immortal's face, Ethan concluded that Albert Spiers had not been a kind man.

No cries of alarm or pounding footsteps broke the silence around them. The corridor remained deserted.

Asgard picked up the scattered, blood-stained papers on the ground, looked at them briefly, and shoved the entire bundle inside his shirt. He patted the scientist's clothes next. Metal jingled under his fingers. He removed a set of keys from one of Spiers's coat pockets.

They moved the dead man to a nearby janitor's closet, wiped the traces of blood from the floor, and headed deeper into the lodgings.

'It sure is quiet down here,' murmured Ethan after they passed an empty kitchen and a dining room.

'Jonah has his people working twenty-four hours a day,' said Asgard. 'Marilyn and Albert must be on the late shift.'

A minute later, they came to a corridor ending in a cul-de-sac. From the nameplates on the doors on either side, they had found the private accommodation of the scientists. The older immortal moved silently down the passage.

Ethan fell in behind him. Faint strands of classical music drifted from one of the rooms as they walked past it. He joined

Asgard in front of the last door. The sign on it said "Jonah Resner."

A muscle twitched in the older immortal's cheek.

Ethan raised a hand to the escutcheon plate surrounding the handle, made out the internal locking mechanism, and manipulated the metal gears open.

The room on the other side was cold and clinical. A naked bulb in the ceiling shed a drab light over a range of gray, army-issue furniture crowding the stone floor. The entire space was curiously bereft of pictures and personal touches. Ethan frowned. Jonah Krondike's quarters barely looked lived-in at all.

Asgard drew a breath in sharply. Ethan followed his gaze to the wall above the narrow army cot on the right.

A beautiful, double-edged, steel arming sword bearing a cruciform hilt and a silver-embellished pommel lay suspended on metal brackets a couple of feet from the headboard, below a leather scabbard with a steel locket and tip. An inscription glimmered faintly on the blade, just beneath the cross-guard.

'Armistad,' Asgard breathed in a voice full of heartfelt emotion.

The immortal crossed the floor and reverently took the sword down from the wall. 'My old friend, it is good to see you.'

He stroked the length of the weapon with gentle fingers before pressing the pommel to his forehead and brushing his lips against the blade.

Ethan averted his eyes from the strangely intimate scene and headed for the desk and filing cabinet opposite the bed. Asgard sheathed the sword and joined him. They started to go through Krondike's workspace.

Moments later, Ethan's hands stilled on the bottom drawer of the filing unit. He stared. Something about it looked odd.

He took out the folders he had examined and ran his fingers carefully along the inside edges of the drawer. His lips curved in a small smile when he felt the notch near the back. He hooked his little finger under it and lifted the metal panel.

The hidden recess beneath the drawer came into view. It contained a thick, brown envelope printed with the words "US Military, TOP SECRET" in maroon ink.

'Bingo.'

Ethan lifted out the package.

Asgard made an approving noise. 'How did you know there was a secret space in that very location?'

Ethan hesitated. 'I see this kind of thing a lot in my line of work.' He rose and tucked the envelope inside his shirt. 'Are we done here?'

His companion glanced around the room. 'I believe so.'

'Good,' said Ethan. 'I vote we get the hell out of here.'

As they headed for the door, he spotted a sheet of paper stuck to the back. He grinned and ripped it off on his way out of the room. It was a map showing the fire exits out of the facility.

With the keys they had taken from the dead guard and Albert Spiers, and the floor plan in hand, they soon made it to a crawlspace hidden behind a trap door in a storage room to the west of the complex. Thirty feet in, they came to an angled shaft carved out of the bare rock. Metal rungs screwed into the wall rose vertically in the gloom.

They climbed some five hundred feet to a round metal hatch in the roof of the borehole. The circular handle turned with the faintest creak in the Asgard's grip. He lifted the panel an inch, studied the exterior surroundings for a moment, and carefully pushed the whole thing open. He slipped soundlessly from the passage.

Ethan blinked at the bright stars studding the inky sky as he scrambled out after him.

The shaft had opened onto the side of a cliff. A cool breeze brought the smell of pine and juniper from the copses scattered along the flank of the mountain above them.

In the distance below, bright spotlights illuminated a large, fenced area blockading a road. A pair of guardhouses manned by armed soldiers framed the steel gates that faced the narrow ribbon of asphalt winding down toward a far-off valley. Though he could not see it from the angle where they squatted, Ethan suspected the men were guarding the entrance of a tunnel leading inside the facility. He was about to voice this thought when his companion clamped a hand over his mouth and motioned to the right.

Ethan's pulse quickened when he spied the soldier sitting inside a small, timber observation post some forty feet away. He nodded slowly and followed Asgard as he headed in the opposite direction. It was thanks to his associate's uncanny instincts that they avoided another three guard posts.

The fifth soldier came out of nowhere. The two immortals had just passed what they thought was an empty security station when the man stepped out from behind a tree, a cigarette glowing faintly at his lips as he fastened his pants.

For a frozen moment, guard and prisoners stared at one another.

The cigarette fell from the man's mouth at the same time that he let go of the zipper and reached for his gun.

Asgard grabbed the soldier's wrist and forced it upward, the weapon waving wildly at the sky. The guard kneed him in the stomach. The immortal let out a low grunt, tightened his hold on the soldier's arm, and jammed his forearm in the latter's throat. The man choked.

Ethan came up behind the soldier and stabbed him in the neck with the syringe Marilyn Davies had intended to use on him. The man went limp. They caught him before he fell, took his gun and knife, and propped him up on a chair inside his guard post.

By the time the first alarms sounded and searchlights stabbed the darkness around the mountain, they were more than three miles from the army base.

They reached the summit of another massif just before dawn broke across the land. The noise of the manhunt had long since faded behind them, thanks in no small part to Asgard's ingenuity. Much to Ethan's amazement, the immortal had located some mountain lion dung in the darkness and they had liberally smeared themselves with it to get the search dogs off their scent.

Ethan dropped down on a ledge and leaned forward with his arms on his raised knees. He had discarded the white coat at the bottom of the escape shaft. Despite the cold air whistling around the mountaintop, sweat had soaked through his clothes and ran in rivulets down his face and neck, and his limbs shook from exhaustion. His companion's pants beside him echoed his own rapid breathing.

Crimson fingers stabbed the gray horizon ahead, drawing his gaze. They bled to orange and gold as the sun rose on a new day.

Ethan closed his eyes against the dazzling brilliance and savored the warm light fluttering across his skin. Relief stabbed through him, the emotion all too sharp and sweet; he was a free man once more. He turned to the older immortal.

'I think it's about time we introduced ourselves properly, don't you think?' he said in a voice ringing with gratitude.

The other man watched him silently.

Ethan extended a hand. 'Ethan Storm. Professional thief.'

The immortal hesitated before shaking his hand. His grip was warm and strong. 'Asgard Godard. Bastian Hunter.'

~

# CHAPTER FOUR

APRIL 2013. BEAR RIVER MOUNTAINS. UTAH.

THE NIGHTMARE STARTED AS IT ALWAYS DID.

*She was standing on a low hill and looking down at a bloodied battlefield. Hundreds of mangled corpses stretched out before her, a motionless tangle of severed heads, limbs, and torsos that turned the desert scarlet. Carrion birds circled in the reddening sky, their guttural cries echoing ominously against the neighboring sand dunes.*

*On the other side of the war zone, an immense army stood amassed before a burning fortress. Flames licked the rooftops of buildings and the base of the defensive wall around the fortified city. The giant, metal gates guarding the entrance to the stronghold lay open, their buckled, distorted forms silent witnesses to the ferocity of the recent conflict. The spiraling smoke wreathing the air had given birth to a shimmering black haze that darkened the horizon to the south. The shrill screams of women and children could still be heard in the distance.*

*Olivia was aware of movement behind her. She looked over her shoulder and saw the second army gathered on the shallow elevation.*

*Though substantial, it was but a fraction the size of the enemy's factions facing them across the crimson arena of war.*

*She stood in the line of figures that headed the contingent of battle-weary, grim-faced men and women. They were dressed differently, with gilded armor and weapons that marked them as the commanders of the smaller force. She counted five on either side of her.*

*'Are you ready, cousin?' said someone on her right.*

*Olivia turned and saw a beautiful woman garbed in a gleaming breastplate overlying a short, chain mail dress. Leather elbow guards and greaves reinforced with polished bronze plates protected the figure's slender, toned limbs. The woman had dyed her black hair red, the color matching the stains streaking her sweat-slicked skin and the two trident daggers clasped tightly in her hands. A broadsword was strapped to her back. Pale, gray eyes moved from the battleground ahead and focused on her face. The expression in the silver depths sent a shiver down Olivia's spine.*

*'Yes,' she heard herself say in a confident voice she did not recognize.*

*She looked down and saw that she was clothed in a similar suit of armor. She was clutching the hilt of a bloodstained, double-edged blade between her fingers. A pair of sheathed daggers rested snuggly against her thighs.*

*'Let's go, sister,' said someone on her left.*

*Olivia beheld a handsome man with blue eyes and a short beard standing next to her. His teeth flashed fiercely in the fading sunlight. Something twisted inside her chest at the sight, the feeling both joyous and melancholic. She nodded.*

*In the next moment, she was racing down the incline and onto the battlefield, the savage sound tearing from her throat mirrored by the hundred others around her as they charged the enemy rushing toward them. Then, she was inside the melee. And the cries of terror and pain started anew.*

Olivia Ash sat up with a start, a silent scream choking her throat. She clasped the bed sheet to her breasts and squeezed her eyes shut. Blood roared in her head and her breaths came in short, sharp pants, the sounds filling her ears.

It was almost a minute before her racing pulse started to settle. The cotton nightdress she wore clung unpleasantly to her clammy skin, the silver crucifix on the chain around her neck cold against her flesh. Olivia blinked and looked blindly at the shards of moonlight streaking through the fluttering curtains opposite the metal bed.

Of all the nightmares that had plagued her since her eighteenth birthday, this was the worst. Whereas the others felt like she was an observer of distant events, a detached witness of things that seemed to barely touch upon her existence, she knew herself to be an active participant in this particular dream. She could feel the lives she had taken with her bare hands, the streams of human consciousness extinguished by her unrelenting, focused rage. So vivid were the images and the sensation of her blade piercing flesh, she was surprised she had never woken to a blood bath.

A sigh left her lips when her heartbeat finally slowed to a normal rhythm. The abbess would no doubt pick up on the fact that she had had yet another restless night. The elderly nun had uncannily shrewd powers of observation when it came to her oldest ward; after all, she had known Olivia from her infancy.

She reached for the carafe on the nightstand with trembling fingers and poured herself a glass of water. The liquid sloshed around as she raised it to her lips. She had just taken her first sip when a faint sound reached her ears. Her hand stilled. She looked up. The noise came again.

Olivia's brow furrowed. She hesitated, put the glass down, and slipped out from under the covers. She padded barefoot to the window.

The abbey where she had lived all of her life was located on two hundred acres of rolling farmland and forest at the head of a valley deep in the Bear River Mountains. It overlooked Logan

Canyon to the west and was surrounded by the Wasatch Range stretching out toward Idaho to the north. On a clear day, Bear Lake was visible from the summit of the ridge to the east. The only way to reach the isolated estate, home to the community of sixty souls who formed the cloistered Benedictine order of The Eternal Life, was with a four-wheel drive, up a steep, winding dirt road.

Her room was in a corner of the attic of the main house. Whereas the nuns and novices shared the dormitories and rooms on the first and second floors of the old Victorian mansion, Olivia had been given sole occupancy of the chamber under the pitched eaves for as long as she could recall. With its exposed beams and the commanding views it offered from its dual aspect windows, it was her favorite place in the whole abbey.

Tendrils of unease rose within her as she stared out across the moonlit landscape. The wind had fallen and a heavy hush shrouded the abbey grounds and surrounding evergreen forests. Beyond the trees to the south lay the fields and farm where they grew crops and tended to animals that provided for their self-sustained existence. Not a single breeze stirred the branches and leaves in the orchard next to the manor house. Even the owls had fallen silent.

Olivia had never seen the place so still. It was as if the whole world was holding its breath.

A familiar feeling suddenly blasted through her consciousness. She gasped. The hairs rose on her arms.

*No, not this again!*

Panic churned her stomach as the unwelcome precognitive aura prickled her skin and drenched her body in a cold sweat.

It had been six months, two weeks, and three days since the last "incident."

Olivia had but a handful of seconds to steel herself before the visions swept over her with the force of a storm. She backed away from the window and started to hyperventilate while a barrage of horrific images flashed through her mind. She was barely aware of the backs of her thighs striking the metal footboard of the bed. She closed her eyes tightly and willed the vivid pictures away, her nails digging into her palms. They continued unabated, each more shocking than the previous. A kaleidoscope of figures with frightened expressions danced across her sight.

Olivia froze when she finally registered what she was seeing. A whimper escaped her throat. Tears blossomed from beneath her eyelids and spilled unbidden down her cheeks.

The faces were those of the nuns in the abbey.

*They are going to die. They are all going to die this very night!*

Gunshots shattered the silence.

Olivia jumped, eyes slamming open. It was starting.

She fell back heavily on the mattress. Her breath hitched rapidly in her throat as she listened to the volley of blasts from the floors below. The screaming began a second later. Unable to stop the violent snapshots and sounds of death overwhelming her senses, she keened and rocked on the bed, her hands pressed hard against her ears and her chin tucked against her chest.

In her mind, she saw the nuns fall one after the other, women she had known her entire life looking bewildered and helpless in the face of an invisible enemy who showed them no mercy, terror painting their final moments crimson.

Her head snapped up when an achingly-familiar figure suddenly came into focus. Mother Margaret Edwards, the abbess of the order, stood on the doorstep of her cottage. She raised her hands in a placatory gesture while she addressed two men clad in dark uniforms.

Olivia felt the blood drain from her face. *Oh God! No, not this, please not thi—*

In her vision, the abbess jerked as if she had hiccuped. A

dark hole appeared in the middle of her forehead, an unsightly blemish on her pale skin. A trickle of blood bloomed from the gunshot wound and ran down the bridge of her nose, a scarlet line between her staring eyes. She folded gently to the floor.

Agony filled Olivia's heart and squeezed the air out of her lungs. The images subsided.

She rose and ran to the window.

Votive candles flickered behind the stained-glass windows of the chapel to the right of the mansion. Next to it, the abbess was opening the door of her cottage. Her white nightdress glowed in the night as she faced the men who appeared before her. She took a step back and lifted her hands. Her lips moved, forming words Olivia could not hear.

*'No! Get away from her!'* screamed Olivia.

She leaned out of the opening and reached blindly toward the woman who had been a mother to her through all the years of her existence.

The first man raised his gun and shot the elderly nun in the head.

Olivia stopped breathing. A buzzing noise filled her ears.

The second man turned and looked in her direction. He grabbed his companion's shoulder and gestured urgently toward the mansion.

There was a noise right outside her room. The door slammed open at the same time that a scrambling sound came from the rooftop.

Olivia remained rooted to the spot, her brain still trying to process the unthinkable event she had just witnessed. She watched, trance-like, as three figures in blood-splattered, olive army fatigues stormed her bedroom and headed toward her.

The man in the lead grabbed her arm, pulled her across the floor, and threw her down onto the bed. Air left her lungs in a shocked gasp that jolted her back to the reality of the moment.

Something cold and hard touched her brow. Mind-numbing

fear gripped Olivia as she stared past the barrel of a gun to the man holding the weapon to her head. The assassin's eyes were dark and fathomless, his face a passionless mask. He climbed on the bed and straddled her body, his fingers closing in a vice-like grip around her throat. His companions grabbed her feet and hands, and pinned her to the mattress.

Bile flooded the back of Olivia's mouth when they tore the nightdress off her body. She choked on a scream. The men holding her limbs ignored the sound and started to run their fingers roughly over her slender form and her plain cotton underwear. Their leader cocked the gun and pushed the mouth of the barrel into her skin. The hand around her neck tightened.

The buzzing noise returned as her oxygen-deprived brain started to falter. Black spots dotted Olivia's vision. She was faintly aware of the men squeezing and pawing at her flesh.

An unfamiliar emotion suddenly stabbed through her fading consciousness, white-hot and as incandescent as a ray of sunlight. Olivia blinked at the alien sensation. It took a few seconds for her to realize that this feeling was anger.

It grew until it flooded her entire being, making her blood sing with fury and sharpening her dimming senses as effectively as a bucket of icy water would have done. The blackness receded. Her fingers curled into fists.

Olivia scowled. *I will not die here!*

She started to struggle against her assailants with every fiber of her being, her body arching off the bed while grunts of effort rasped through her windpipe.

'There, on her hand!' one of the men exclaimed.

He yanked her right wrist back sharply and forced her fingers open, making her wince. The lead assassin went still. A triumphant expression blazed on his face as he studied the birthmark on her palm.

His icy gaze shifted to her eyes. 'Found you, little girl.'

His fingers relaxed around her throat. Olivia coughed and wheezed as air filled her starving lungs. She glanced at the flesh-colored gloves on the nightstand, the ones that usually covered her hands and hid the unearthly blemish on her skin. The sound of distant shots reached her dimly above the rush of blood in her ears. They had come from elsewhere in the mansion.

The man above her stiffened. He looked toward the open doorway of the bedroom. 'That wasn't one of ours.'

He climbed off the bed, his gun in hand. His subordinates released her and reached for their own weapons.

A muffled thud drew everyone's eyes to the ceiling. A tile tumbled past the window and clattered down the slope of the gambrel roof before clanging against the guttering. Someone cursed outside.

A shadow eclipsed the ambient moonlight as a man sailed feet first through the opening and landed heavily on the wooden floorboards in a low crouch.

Olivia gaped.

The stranger rose to his feet. Teeth gleamed in the gloom. 'Good evening, assholes.'

His voice skittered down her spine and raised goosebumps on her exposed skin. Olivia was suddenly conscious of her near nakedness. She grabbed the bed sheet and held it protectively against her body. A precognitive tremor rippled through her mind as she stared at the stranger. His gaze flicked briefly to her.

'Who the fuck are you?' said the man who had held the gun to her head, his tone unruffled.

'I'm your worst nightmare,' the stranger replied.

The assassin cocked his head to the side. His lips parted in a mocking smile. 'I don't have nightmares.'

He raised his gun. His companions followed suit.

Olivia whimpered and hunched over, hands rising to cover

her ears as she pressed her eyes shut. In the breathless moment that ensued, she heard a series of faint crunching noises. She blinked and peered up when gunfire failed to erupt across the room.

The stranger at the window was grinning. The curtains fluttered behind him. A shaft of moonlight danced across his face, highlighting his steel-blue eyes and strong jawline.

One of her assailants dropped his gun, the weapon clattering noisily onto the floorboards. 'What the—?'

The gun was a twisted mass of metal. She looked at the other men's firearms. Their weapons were in a similar state.

Recognition flashed across the face of the lead assassin. 'The Elemental!'

He drew a long, curved dagger from a sheath at his hip. His men yanked similar blades from their uniforms.

There was a slick noise of metal sliding against leather as the blue-eyed stranger pulled a pair of short swords from under his jacket. The smile slipped from his face. He rushed the three assassins.

Olivia scuttled back against the metal headboard, heart thudding wildly as she watched the four figures clash.

The stranger blocked the attacks to his head and body, the swords blurring in his grip. A fist glanced off his jaw. He ducked and twisted, his movements fast and fluid. One of her assailants cried out and dropped his blade, his hands rising to the deep slash across his gut. Blood spurted from between his fingers. Another whimpered and gripped the wound carving his leg from thigh to knee.

Her rescuer slipped under a high-kick aimed at his head by the leader of the assassins, spun his swords as he came up, and stabbed her injured assailants in the chest, a frown of concentration darkening his face. He was too late to avoid the knee thrust to the small of his back. A harsh grunt left his lips and he sagged on one knee.

The dark-eyed assassin smiled savagely and brought his dagger around toward the stranger's neck in a double-handed chopping motion. Olivia lurched forward, a cry of warning on her lips.

There was a sharp clang. The assassin bared his teeth; Olivia's rescuer had trapped the dagger between his swords and stopped the blade a mere inch before it kissed his skin. Veins bulged on the assassin's face and neck as he strained against his opponent. The blue-eyed stranger dropped to the ground and rolled out of the way of the falling knife.

The assassin attacked, body whirling in a series of rapid kicks and jabs while he thrust and slashed with the dagger. The stranger danced nimbly across the floor and shifted the swords to deflect the flurry of blows and strikes.

Olivia stared at the fighting men, mouth dry and body frozen to the bed. She gasped when the assassin slipped past her rescuer's defense and struck him hard in the mouth. The blue-eyed stranger staggered back against a dresser.

'*No!*' she shouted as the assassin raised his arm, the dagger glinting in the moonlight.

Shadows shifted to the right. Olivia turned and beheld a frightening figure with a beard looming in the doorway of her bedroom. Aquamarine eyes met hers for a fleeting second. Even through the paralyzing fear gripping her senses, she saw shock reverberate through the stranger's gaze. He raised a long-barreled revolver and fired a single shot.

The bullet struck the assassin in the chest, the impact lifting him off his feet before slamming him down onto his back. He slid across the polished floorboards and rocked to a standstill beneath the window at the opposite end of the bed.

Olivia's rescuer slowly straightened and wiped his bloodied lip with the back of his hand.

'What took you so long, old man?' he asked the bearded figure.

'I was otherwise engaged, boy,' came the gruff reply.

Olivia's rescuer muttered something under his breath.

Her gaze moved to the dark pool spreading out from under the motionless assassin. The reality of all that had happened started to sink in. The images of the dead nuns rose before her eyes. She saw the abbess in her final moments once more and started to shake uncontrollably.

The two men moved toward the bed. Olivia retreated against the headboard, eyes widening in panic, the metal bars digging into her back. They froze in their tracks.

'It's all right, child,' said the stranger with the beard.

His unruly brown hair curled slightly at his nape. He reached out toward her, his expression oddly gentle.

There was a noise from the window. Olivia looked around and froze.

The dark-eyed assassin was up on one elbow. An ugly expression distorted his features. Metal glimmered in his fingers.

'*Dammit!*' cursed her blue-eyed rescuer.

He raised his left hand toward the man on the floor. Olivia caught a glimpse of a star-shaped mark on his skin.

The dagger left the assassin's grasp and hurtled through the air toward her.

Time slowed.

As if in a dream, Olivia saw the blade crumple a few feet from her face. A shadow blocked her sight.

The knife glanced off the skin of the bearded man before thudding onto her lap. A sliver of blood stained a sharp edge on the distorted lump of metal where it had cut him. Crimson bled into the white sheet.

The bearded man lowered his arm from where he had raised it protectively in front of her, swung the revolver up, and shot the assassin in the head.

Flesh and bone crumpled beneath the bullet. A dark spray peppered the curtains behind the falling figure.

Something wet flicked across Olivia's face as the assassin's body thudded onto the floorboards. She wiped her cheek with a trembling hand and stared at the red smear on her fingertips.

A loud ringing filled her ears.

'She's gonna faint,' one of her rescuers warned. She thought it was the man with the steel-blue eyes. 'Hey! Stay with us!'

They were the last words she heard before darkness claimed her.

# CHAPTER FIVE

'I DON'T THINK THIS IS SUCH A GREAT IDEA.'

Ethan Storm dragged his gaze from the dirt track visible in the headlights of the jeep and glanced over his shoulder at the unconscious woman in the back of the vehicle.

They had covered the nun with a blanket and strapped her in securely with the seat belt. Her head lay against Asgard Godard's coat, the thick padding cushioning her face from the window. Her skin remained deathly pale under the ambient starlight streaming through the glass and her chest moved almost imperceptibly with her breathing.

Ethan had rarely seen anyone so fragile-looking. The nun looked like she would shatter if he so much as touched her.

It was three in the morning. Less than an hour had elapsed since they had fled the scene of the mass killing at the Benedictine abbey deep in the desolate Utah peaks.

A muscle jumped in Ethan's cheek.

The massacre of the nuns was one of the most singularly gruesome acts of butchery he had witnessed since he and Godard had started their covert mission against their enemy over four decades ago. Following their deadly clash with the soldiers who had committed the atrocity, Godard had dressed the sole survivor of the carnage in a plain summer dress he had found in the dresser of her bedroom, under the eaves of the Victorian mansion. He had cleaned the blood marks from the unconscious nun's face and insisted on carrying her slender form to where they had hidden their four-by-four in the forest, a mile from the estate. Ethan had not objected; the expression on Godard's face more than discouraged further discussion. If what the Bastian had told him proved to be true, his connection with the woman was incredibly significant.

'We could not leave her there,' said Asgard. 'She does not possess the skills to survive on her own.'

Ethan observed his companion's brooding face with a frown before turning his attention back to the trail. 'Okay, so we take her to the first safe town we find, give her money and a new ID, tell her to keep her head down, and go about our business.'

The lack of response from the man beside him unnerved him like few things could.

In the forty-odd years since he first met the Bastian Hunter, Ethan had come to learn some hard truths about his immortal associate. His extraordinary history aside, Asgard Godard was a scarily good tracker, an excellent shot, an astounding swordsman, and an incredibly stubborn bastard. Considering they had both been lone wolves before their fateful encounter in New Mexico all those decades ago, the Crovir immortal was surprised at how quickly and deeply the bonds of fellowship grew between them. It was the second longest relationship he had ever had with another living being in his one-hundred-and-eighty-odd years of existence. Still, there were times when he found himself curbing the urge to shake some sense into his friend. Like now, for instance.

'We've always left the others we saved to fend for themselves, Asgard,' Ethan said in a hard voice. 'It's tough enough doing what we do without having someone like her tagging along.' His eyes shifted to the rearview mirror and the still figure under the blanket. His tone turned accusing. 'I know there's a bond between the two of you. That only makes matters twice as dangerous. Jonah is bound to be aware of the link.' He hit the steering wheel with his fist. '*Dammit*, Asgard, you know as well as I do that she'll only be a liability!'

The older immortal rubbed the back of his neck and released a rueful sigh. 'She doesn't even know who or what she is, Ethan. And yes, I have no doubt that Jonah will try to find her again.' His voice dropped to a low murmur. 'She will not be lucky twice.'

Ethan changed gears as they came to a turn. The land fell away to the right. Moonlight bathed the forested canyon beyond in muted shades of gray.

'She won't be able to keep up,' he countered. 'We'll have to watch our backs *and* hers, constantly.'

'She might surprise you,' Asgard retorted. 'If she possesses even half the talent of her forebears, she will be a force to be reckon—'

The jeep rocked and juddered as they hit a pothole. Asgard cursed and steadied himself against the dashboard.

Ethan clenched his jaw. They had taken one of the secluded tracks that wound its way up and over the mountain. From the state of the trail, it was only ever used by the rangers who patrolled the forests. The rough terrain was proving to be a challenge, even with the suspension on the jeep. A quick look at the map on his lap showed that they were still ten miles from a main road.

The skin on the back of his neck prickled. He looked at the mirror.

The nun was staring at him.

Ethan stepped on the brakes, startled. The jeep skidded some fifteen feet across the exposed dirt before sliding to a halt in a spray of gravel.

Asgard slammed back against the headrest with a harsh grunt. 'What the devil—?'

'She's awake.'

Ethan's gaze remained locked on the figure in the back of the jeep. He could not have looked away if he had wanted to.

Asgard turned in his seat.

The woman blinked and shrank back under the blanket. Ethan felt the dark pull of her presence wane. It was only then that he realized he had been holding his breath. He inhaled shallowly and ignored the strange fluttering inside his skull.

'Olivia?' Asgard said gently. 'It's all right, child. You're safe now.'

The nun's expression did not change. Her gaze darted to the inky landscape outside the window.

'We're headed out of the mountains,' Asgard explained. 'We need to lie low for a while. They will come after us—'

For someone who had recently been the victim of a life-altering trauma and passed out, the nun could move pretty damn fast. She unclipped the seatbelt and slipped out of the vehicle in the blink of an eye.

'Olivia!' Asgard shouted.

He flung the passenger door open and ran into the night after her.

'Shit!' Ethan hissed.

He grabbed a flashlight from the glove compartment, yanked the handbrake on, and jumped out of the four-by-four.

The vehicle had come to a stop on the verge of a steep drop. The Crovir immortal paused at the edge of the treeline and listened intently for a couple of seconds. The noise of something crashing through the undergrowth rose from the left. He headed that way.

Tightly-packed trunks and dense vegetation materialized in the dancing light of the flashlight as he slid and staggered down the incline. The dead leaves and decaying matter covering the forest floor made the ground even more treacherous and he lost his footing twice, landing hard enough on his ass to bruise.

He reached the bottom of the slope, staggered to a stop, and looked around wildly. The trickle of running water reached his ears above the sound of his harsh breaths. He swung the flashlight around and caught the glitter of a mountain brook carving a shallow gully ahead and to the left. Asgard's voice came faintly from farther down the creek. Ethan bolted toward the sound.

The channel gradually widened. He slipped and stumbled over the moss-covered rocks strewn across the embankment as he aimed for the Bastian immortal's location. A shout rose in the distance. Alarm darted through Ethan at the fear lacing Asgard's voice; there were very few things in this world that could scare the battle-scarred Bastian immortal. He accelerated, suddenly conscious that they had left their weapons in the jeep.

Two figures came into view in the bed of the stream seconds later, frozen in the beam of the flashlight.

Ethan lurched to a stop. His stomach dropped.

The nun was standing on the brink of a yawning chasm. Water flowed over her feet and tumbled into the gaping black void behind her.

She had lost one of her shoes. Tiny cuts and grazes dotted her arms and legs where the underbrush had slashed her skin. Her hairband had come loose, releasing strands of long, light blonde hair that framed her flushed face.

Asgard stood stock still some five feet to her left, his body rigid with tension. 'Olivia, don't. You'll fall.'

His eyes flicked to the gulf behind her. The rush of a fast flowing river drifted up from far below.

Ethan took a step forward. The nun's head snapped around. She fixed him with a wild stare.

His mouth went dry at the blind terror in her green eyes. *She's not thinking straight. She can't even see us.*

'Olivia!' he barked.

She jumped, startled, and took a step back. Her heels came to rest bare inches from the edge of the ravine.

'Goddamnit, boy!' Asgard ground out. He scowled at Ethan. 'What do you think—?'

'Who—who are you?' said the nun in a tremulous voice.

She blinked rapidly, as if waking from a daze.

Ethan felt the odd fluttering inside his head once more. The sensation was akin to a ripple dancing across his consciousness. He shook his head slightly and glanced at Asgard.

The Bastian immortal gave no indication that he was experiencing a similar feeling.

The nun suddenly gasped and paled.

'Mother Margaret,' she whispered in a tortured voice. Her hands rose to her lips. Tears shimmered in her eyes. Her gaze shifted between Ethan and Asgard. 'Did that really happen? Are they all dead?' Her voice rose to a shrill, desperate cry.

Asgard hesitated. 'Let's get back to the jeep. We can—'

'*Answer me!*' she yelled. '*Are they dead?*'

Ethan blinked and rocked back slightly on his heels. He saw Asgard shift out of the corner of his eye and exchanged a startled glance with his friend.

This time, they had both felt it. An invisible force had just pushed lightly against them, like a gust of wind.

Asgard straightened and squared his shoulders. A muscle worked in his cheek. 'Yes. I'm afraid they are.'

The nun went still. Her fingers dropped to the silver crucifix around her neck. She closed her eyes and clasped the thin cross tightly, as if it were her anchor in a world gone mad. A single tear spilled over and trickled down her cheek. She took a shuddering breath. Her eyelids fluttered open.

'Who are you?' she asked once more, her voice hardening.

A bittersweet expression washed across Asgard's face. His gaze remained locked on the woman's face. 'I am your uncle.'

The nun's eyes grew round. She stepped back unconsciously.

Fear squeezed Ethan's chest in a vice-like grip. He opened his mouth to shout out a warning.

The nun's right foot slipped over the brink of the gorge. A shocked sound left her lips.

Ethan felt his body move.

Asgard dove toward the nun and reached for her flailing arm. 'Olivia!'

*We won't catch her in time!*

The thought barely had time to form inside Ethan's mind before he raised a hand toward the slender form drifting silently into the void. It was an impulse borne out of desperation.

The fluttering returned ten-fold inside his skull. With it came the sharp, metallic taste of someone else's fear and a frantic, faint cry.

*Help me!*

A roar filled Ethan's ears. He gasped as heat exploded inside his chest. He felt his powers surge through his entire being and thought he saw his birthmark shimmer.

The nun screamed.

～

CONSCIOUSNESS RETURNED SLOWLY. THE FIRST THING OLIVIA noticed was the jolting. She blinked.

A dark roof swam into focus above her. She studied it dazedly for a couple of seconds.

She was in the back of the jeep again. Someone had covered her with a blanket and placed a coat under her head.

She pushed up on one elbow and touched her forehead. A headache throbbed between her eyes. Voices registered faintly through the rush of blood pulsing through her ears. She looked toward the front of the vehicle.

Two men sat in the front seats. A heated conversation was taking place between them.

'For the last time, I don't know how the hell I did it!' hissed the driver.

It was the man who had rescued her from the assassins who had stormed her bedroom. The glow from the vehicle's dashboard highlighted sun-bleached strands in his short, brown hair. He changed gears and gripped the steering wheel with white-knuckled fingers, muscles jumping in his toned, tanned forearms. She spotted faint dark lines making up the star-shaped mark on the back of his left hand.

'Are you certain?' said his companion doggedly.

Olivia recognized the bearded figure who had claimed to be her uncle.

Memories flooded her mind. The brutal events at the abbey rose before her eyes once more. A wave of blind panic threatened to choke the air from her throat.

An unexpected surge of anger suddenly cut through her rising fear. Olivia gritted her teeth and concentrated on her breathing; she could not afford to let terror overwhelm her once more.

It was almost a minute before the calming techniques drilled into her by the abbess pushed the last of the gory images away. Those techniques were the only way to stem the aftereffects of her curse. She licked her lips and glanced out of the windows.

They were traveling at high speed down a dark road. An undulating, barren landscape stretched out to infinity on either side of the asphalt. The grayness of the sky up ahead highlighted distant hills. Bar the moon shining down on them from behind a bank of clouds, she could see no other lights.

Olivia ran a trembling hand down her body. She recalled her brief conversation with the bearded man while they stood in the middle of the stream, deep in the woods she had run into blindly. The last thing she remembered was the paralyzing dread that had filled her body as she started to fall, followed by the equally shocking sensation of being snatched back sharply from the abyss. Apart from the superficial scratches and cuts she had received as a result of her wild race through the forest, she detected no other injuries.

The bearded man sat back in his seat. 'It could be your powers are still evolving,' he murmured. 'Or your training is paying off.'

The younger man grunted. 'There's the other thing.' He glanced at his companion. 'You felt it too, didn't you? That wave of pressure, back at the creek?'

The bearded man hesitated. 'Yes.'

She was wondering at their words when the Jeep's driver sighed loudly.

'Hey, you just going to sit there?'

His hand dropped to the gearbox as they came to a shallow drop in the land. His eyes met hers in the rearview mirror.

Olivia blinked. Had he heard her move above the sound of the engine?

The bearded man turned in his seat and observed her with barely masked relief. 'Hi.'

His voice was low and gravelly.

Olivia gulped. 'Hi.'

He passed her a canteen. She straightened in the seat and took it with a small, grateful nod. Her fingers shook as she twisted the cap and brought the rim to her lips. A tiny groan left her throat when cold water flooded her mouth. She drank greedily until her thirst was quenched.

A ripple of awareness suddenly raced across her skin, raising goosebumps in its wake. She looked up and caught an amused stare in the mirror. Her rescuer with the steel-blue eyes was smiling faintly.

'You must have a lot of questions,' said the bearded man.

His voice broke through the strange daze she found herself falling into as she gazed at the reflection of the man in the driver's seat. Olivia dragged her eyes away and wiped her lips with the back of her hand. Although trepidation still thrummed through her veins, she felt oddly at ease with these two strangers. They had already saved her twice, during this one night that had turned her entire world upside down.

She dipped her chin in acquiescence.

The bearded man gazed at the lightening sky on the horizon. 'We're not far from a town. I shall tell you everything you wish to know once we're in a secure location.'

Olivia hesitated. 'Your name?'

'I am Asgard Godard.'

Her eyes flicked to her blue-eyed rescuer in the driver's seat.

'Ethan Storm,' the younger man muttered.

Their names meant nothing to Olivia. She raised a hand to the crucifix at the base of her throat, her fingers closing around the reassuring weight of the metal once more.

'Who were those men? What did they—?' She swallowed past the lump in her throat. 'What did they want with us?'

The two men exchanged guarded glances.

'Not "us,"' said Asgard Godard finally. 'They were after you.'

# CHAPTER SIX

A FREIGHT TRAIN RUMBLED PAST IN THE DISTANCE, THE NOISE faint through the heavy curtains covering the windows. Sunlight filtered through the bottom of the drapes and added to the soft glow of the table lamps on the nightstands.

The motel room was clean and cheerful. The walls were a pale pastel, with a flowery border meeting the ceiling. Twin beds took up the middle of the floor and a rollaway cot lay tucked up against one wall. An internal door led to a serviceable bathroom. There was a small fridge and a table holding a microwave and a coffeepot next to the TV.

All of it seemed shockingly mundane to Olivia in the face of what Asgard Godard was telling her. His words buzzed around in her skull, their meaning so extraordinary and far-fetched they beggared belief.

He spoke of two races that had existed alongside mankind for thousands of years, influencing the course of human history through the ages. Of battle-hardened beings with superior fighting skills, accelerated healing, delayed aging, and the capacity to survive up to sixteenth deaths. Of crows and ash. And of the fourteenth-century plague that dramatically reduced their numbers and led to the end of a savage war that had raged for millennia. When he started to talk, hesitantly at first but then with increasing fervor, about a secret branch of the US Army hunting immortals, a different kind of fear gripped Olivia.

*Have I been saved by men more dangerous than the assassins who attacked the abbey?*

She was aware of a heavy stare from across the room. Ethan Storm leaned against the wall next to the window overlooking the motel parking lot, long legs crossed at the heels and sinewy arms folded across his chest. His left hand was tucked under his armpit, the pentagram birthmark hidden from view. He watched her silently, his gaze so intense it almost bore under her skin.

She stared at the third eye symbol on her right palm. She wished she had her gloves to cover the unsightly birthmark staining her own flesh. It seemed to mock her, its lines stark against her pale skin, its existence a mute condemnation, if the man claiming to be her uncle spoke the truth. Which he couldn't be. No one in their right mind could even begin to swallow the impossible reality his words evoked. She curled her fingers until the mark disappeared from view and raised her head. Asgard's features blurred as angry tears welled up and threatened to spill down her cheeks. She wiped them away briskly.

Despite her best efforts, Olivia could not mask the tremor in her voice. 'Do you really expect me to believe what you've just told me?'

Asgard sighed and ran a hand through his hair. 'Look, I know how crazy this all sounds—'

A bark of laughter escaped her. It seemed to surprise the two men as much as her.

Olivia knew then she could never return to the innocent existence she had led in the safety and isolation of the abbey walls. The events of the last six hours had irrevocably changed her, to a point where she barely recognized herself. As she registered this harsh truth, the loss of her peaceful life and the brutal deaths of the nuns who had been her family made her want to weep once more.

The face of the abbess rose in her mind. It cut through the wave of grief and self-pity threatening to drown her. She had to be strong, if not for herself then for the woman who had raised her.

'What Asgard told you is the truth,' said Ethan in the awkward silence. 'You are an immortal, like us.'

His gaze moved briefly to her hand. Olivia stared challengingly at the two men, her nails digging into her palms.

'You were abandoned at the abbey when you were just an infant,' said Asgard. 'Your parents must have thought they were in great danger at the time. They chose to leave you in the care of someone they trusted, in a place where your chances of being discovered were almost non-existent.'

Olivia went still. Although she wanted to discount everything these men were saying, she could not help the sliver of hope that burst into existence inside her. Her past was a mystery that had occupied her waking moments for as long as she could remember.

'How can you possibly know this?'

Asgard shared a guarded look with Ethan. 'We found records back at the abbey that corroborate our information.'

Ethan pulled something from his jacket. Olivia gasped. It was a collection of thin diaries, tied with a gauze ribbon. She recognized them instantly. They were Mother Margaret Edwards's journals.

She shot off the bed and stormed across the floor, barely conscious of her movements. 'Where did you get those?'

She reached for the diaries.

Ethan raised them above his head. 'Uh-uh. Not until you

listen to what we've got to say. And there's more where this came from.'

Olivia scowled and rose on her tip-toes.

Asgard sighed. 'Olivia—'

A frustrated sound passed through her gritted teeth. Despite the extra height afforded by the sneakers the men had purchased for her in a store in town, she still couldn't reach the precious items that were all she had left of the woman who had raised her. She stretched up farther, lost her balance, and stumbled against Ethan.

'Whoa!'

He reached down, his arm wrapping firmly around her waist.

Olivia froze in his embrace. His face was inches from hers. Up close, his eyes were even more startling, steel specks dotting his irises like the constellations that graced the skies above the place she had once called her home. She could feel his fingers through the thin cotton dress. They scorched her skin.

Heat flooded her face. She struggled out of his hold and backed away, feeling strangely short of breath. 'How did you know about the diaries?'

Ethan shrugged. 'I didn't. I checked the cottage before we left and found these in a safe behind a wall panel.'

'You mean, you *broke* into Mother Margaret's private quarters?' squealed Olivia.

She realized how ridiculous her accusation sounded the moment the words left her lips. The abbess was dead, murdered mere hours ago. Robbery was low on the magnitude of the crimes that had been committed that night.

Ethan grimaced. 'If you recall, the bad guys did that first. I came in after the fact. So, technically, I was just scouting the place.'

Olivia looked at the diaries. For as long as she could recall, Mother Margaret Edwards had kept a journal. She had always wondered what it was the older woman wrote about, often late into the night, by the flickering light of a candle. She had suspected some of the chapters might have been about her.

'I didn't know there was a safe,' she said accusingly.

'Yeah, well, safes are kinda my specialty,' Ethan muttered.

She was wondering at the trace of embarrassment in his voice when Asgard spoke again.

'Part of the journals are a chronicle of life at the abbey and the personal reflections of the woman who wrote them. The other, more significant portion concerns you.'

Olivia whipped around. Had he read her mind?

'I flicked through them while you were sleeping,' Asgard explained at her reproachful glare. A sad light dawned in his eyes. 'I believe she wrote those journals for you. I think she intended to give them to you when the time was right. When you needed to know the truth the most.' He paused. 'She started the first one in 1913. It was the year she met you.'

Alarm flared through Olivia. She took a step back. What did these men know of her history?

'Mother Edwards was an anomaly in the human world, as are you,' said Asgard. 'She was the descendant of the offspring of a pureblood immortal and a human, a half-breed blessed with none of the abilities of true immortals except for a degree of delayed aging. At the time of her death, she was nearly three hundred years old.' His gaze drilled into her, bright, beautiful, and as hard as diamonds. 'You are one hundred years old, Olivia.'

Olivia backed away until her thighs struck the bed. She sat down heavily on the mattress, heart pounding a wild beat while she struggled to articulate a coherent response to his statement. She wanted to deny his words, to shout that he was wrong. Except that she couldn't, for it was the truth.

She wanted to yell that although the abbess and she were the same, both aberrations of the natural order of this world, it was not their fault. That they could not help the way God had made them.

'Mother Mar—Mother Margaret and I were ill,' she stammered, flushing under the usual wave of guilt and self-disgust that assaulted her whenever she gave this subject any thought. 'We were both afflicted with a rare condition.' She looked beseechingly at the silent men. 'The doctor told me there was no name for the disease. Both he and Mother Margaret said it was—that it was quite likely at the opposite spectrum of Progeria.'

They looked at her blankly.

'Progeria is a syndrome that causes children to age rapidly in infancy,' she explained haltingly. 'It's a disorder resulting from a genetic mutation. The doctor said our condition was likely caused by a different mutation in the same group of genes.' Her hands fisted in her lap. 'There is no cure for it. And no one knows how it will...progress,' she added, her voice dropping to a whisper.

'Was this doctor's name John Kincaid?' said Asgard after a short silence.

Olivia started. 'Yes.'

'Did you ever see him at the hospital?'

Olivia shook her head. 'No. He came to the abbey on several occasions, at Mother Margaret's request. He examined me and took a blood sample.'

She could not help the defensive note that crept in her voice. The two men were studying her with a trace of pity, yet she saw no accusation or distaste in their faces, reactions she felt she justly deserved for being a monster.

'John Kincaid was not a real doctor,' said Asgard. 'He was an impostor, another pureblood immortal-human half-breed hired by Mother Edwards to lie to you.'

Olivia stared open-mouthed. A hot wave of resentment

poured through her in the next moment. *Who are these men to question the abbess's integrity?*

Asgard's expression softened. 'I did not mean to insult the woman who raised you, child. She did what she had to do to protect you. For that, I will be eternally grateful to her.'

Olivia swallowed the angry words bubbling up her throat.

'Her journals do not lie,' Asgard continued. 'You will see for yourself when you read them. The truth she speaks in those pages is for your eyes and yours only. They are both an explanation and an apology for the century-old deception she subjected you to.'

Olivia's pulse thrummed rapidly as his words sank in. Though she remained skeptical about the information they had relayed to her thus far, something inside her was urging her to believe these two men. It was the same feeling she had experienced when she had come around in the Jeep the second time. Despite their extraordinary revelations in this more than ordinary motel room and despite the storm of emotions she had lived through since she awoke from her nightmare what felt like a lifetime ago, she felt safe in their presence.

'What proof do you have that Dr. Kincaid is an impostor?'

'We have our sources.' Ethan's eyes glinted dangerously. 'It is also thanks to this particular source that we found out Jonah had discovered your whereabouts and was hot on your trail.'

'Jonah?' Olivia repeated.

'Yes. Jonah Krondike,' said Asgard with a stiff nod. 'The Crovir noble most likely behind your parents' disappearance and your abandonment. The immortal ultimately responsible for what happened at the abbey tonight.'

Olivia's gaze shifted from Asgard's grim expression to the third eye birthmark on her palm once more. 'If what you say is true, what does this Jonah person want with me?' She raised her head and gazed unflinchingly at the two men. 'What am I to him?'

Something flitted across Asgard's face. For a moment, she thought she had imagined the tortured look in his eyes.

'You're not just any immortal, Olivia, but very likely the last of the Ashkarovs, a family of pureblood Bastian nobles.' He hesitated. 'Your mother was Natalia Ashkarov. She was the twin sister of my wife and soulmate, Sara Ashkarov.' His hands fisted by his sides. 'She was also the last true Seer of your bloodline. As such, she would have been a priceless target for Jonah's experiments. As are you.'

Olivia froze.

'My name— but my name is Olivia Ash!'

'It may be the name you were given by the abbess, but you are an Ashkarov. I knew it the moment I saw you.' Asgard's gaze moved briefly to her right hand. 'And your birthmark tells me that you've inherited your mother's abilities.'

She noted Asgard's white knuckles almost absent-mindedly as his words scorched a blazing trail through her mind. Her gut reaction was to deny the veracity of his statement. Her curse told her otherwise.

The first time she experienced a vision was shortly after her eighteenth birthday. When she came around after the incident, she found herself lying in the abbess's bed, the elderly nun reading calmly by candlelight at her side. Even then, Mother Margaret Edwards had seemed strangely prepared for what had happened.

She never asked Olivia what it was that she "saw" that day. At the time, Olivia had not even been aware that she had *had* a vision. When they heard of the earthquake that destroyed the city of Napier in New Zealand, two months had already passed since the dreadful tragedy. By then, Olivia had experienced a further three visions. News of the Nicaraguan earthquake did not reach them for another six weeks. It was much later that year that her third vision became a reality, when the largest natural disaster ever to hit China came about, with floods that claimed the lives of thousands, if not millions, of souls. While the Chinese death toll was still rising, the hurricane struck Honduras.

Over the decades that followed, Olivia watched as almost every single one of her visions came true, from natural calamities to man-made disasters, from the deaths of presidents to the massacres of millions in wars that ripped through entire continents. She devoured the news with near-morbid fascination, first through the papers, then a small radio someone had gifted to the abbey, and finally with the aid of the computers that made their way into the communal area of the main house. On the few occasions she contacted the authorities, her warnings were ignored as the ramblings of a mad person.

In addition to the distressing visions that plagued her, the nightmares also began. At one time, she was confined to the abbess's cottage, so loud were her screams when she woke from her dreams, her body slick with sweat and her limbs shaking. Throughout it all, Mother Edwards was there, her peaceful presence and calming words the only things that stopped Olivia from losing her mind.

It was a while before she realized that her nightmares were visions of the past, of bygone eras and people who were no longer of this world, of events disconnected from her present existence. Thanks to the abbess's rigorous training over the years that followed, Olivia achieved a degree of control over the aftereffects of her curse. She even reduced the number of visions and nightmares she experienced, both of which she came to realize were often triggered by stressful situations.

The third element of her affliction was so shocking that she had never spoken about it to anyone, including Mother Edwards. It developed well after her eighteenth birthday and occurred so rarely now she sometimes forgot its existence.

Over the years, Olivia realized that she could hear others'

thoughts. Not only hear them, but also influence them, somehow.

The first incident was with a young novice who joined the abbey after the end of the Second World War. It was a cool, autumn day and they were working the vegetable plot outside the farm in companionable silence. An hour or so after they started planting seeds in the freshly-turned soil, Olivia heard a whisper just beyond her hearing. The novice knelt a few feet from her, her eyes focused on her task, dirt-covered fingers busy. There was no one else around.

As Olivia resumed her chore, the murmur came again. Then, like echoes in the chapel, the words reached her, distinct and inflected with a rainbow of emotions. She knew instinctively that she was witnessing the private reflections of the novice who squatted a short distance from her. When she registered the meaning behind the younger woman's contemplation, Olivia flushed.

'Harry,' she breathed before she could stop herself.

The novice startled, head snapping up.

'What?' she said, the color draining from her face.

Olivia could only look at her mutely, chagrined. The novice had been thinking of her dead lover, a soldier who had perished in the war. More specifically, she had been reliving their last night together before he left to join his company.

'Nothing,' Olivia mumbled, her ears hot.

The novice stared for several moments before getting back to her task. This time, Olivia sensed anxiety and discord from the other woman. Flustered and fearful of provoking one of her visions, she unconsciously drew on the meditative techniques she had learned to calm herself. Within seconds, she felt the novice's agitation settle, the cadence of her emotions smoothed like the waters of a pond on a windless day. When Olivia looked at the young woman, she was working calmly, her expression unflustered and showing no evidence of her recent shock at hearing her dead lover's name.

Over the following months, Olivia experienced similar incidents with nuns she had known her entire life. Strangely enough, she never heard Mother Edwards's thoughts.

At first, she physically removed herself from such situations. Fear that she would stumble upon private matters was her primary concern. Remorse and mortification at being responsible for influencing her companions' behavior were her others. Eventually, she learned to shield her mind with the same techniques she used to cope with the visions and nightmares.

And then there was the final element of her curse.

'Olivia?'

Asgard's voice broke through her chaotic thoughts and brought her sharply back to the moment.

'You said my mother was a Seer?' she said, her mouth dry.

'Yes. Natalia's powers evolved after she reached physical maturity. Although Sara was her twin, she only possessed traces of Natalia's abilities.' A melancholic smile flashed across Asgard's face. 'She was good at hunches.'

'Was clairvoyance the only gift she possessed?' said Olivia.

She was surprised at the eagerness in her voice. Her fingers flexed unconsciously over the symbol on her right palm. 'Was she—was she marked in the same way as I?'

Asgard cocked his head and watched her shrewdly. 'She could also see the past through her dreams. And she possessed no unique marking. No one in the bloodline did, as far as I am aware.' He paused. 'I take it from your expression that you have experienced both visions and nightmares?'

Olivia nodded mutely. Relief and excitement filled her in equal measure, shocking her in their intensity. She had never been able to speak of these matters freely with anyone other than the abbess.

'They started after I turned eighteen,' she admitted shakily. 'Could my mother also hear other people's—?'

The vision came without warning. Instead of the sick feeling that normally preceded one of her prescient episodes, images suddenly filled her sight. She rose from the bed and gazed blindly in front of her.

Asgard took a step toward her. 'Olivia?'

His anxious voice came to her from far off, drowned by the roar of blood in her ears.

*Cars raced down a dusty main road, flashing lights atop their roofs. They screeched to a stop next to a long, low, one-story building sitting on a parking lot, their tires burning tracks of smoking rubber on the hot asphalt. Uniformed men with pistols and shotguns jumped out. In the bedlam that followed, a man in a familiar, olive army fatigue leaned across the hood of a black four-by-four and sighted down the barrel of a sniper rifle.*

She returned to the present with a jolt and stared at the two men, her pulse racing with fear. 'Run!'

# CHAPTER SEVEN

THEY CAME WITH SIRENS MUTED AND ENGINES SCREAMING. As he sprinted out of the front door of the room behind Asgard and Olivia, Ethan glimpsed county sheriff and state trooper cars sliding to a stop in front of the motel.

*Great, the cavalry is here!*

He scowled and gripped the duffel bag on his shoulder, his blades clinking under his jacket. At least they'd emptied the Jeep before they went inside their motel room.

Asgard pounded the blacktop to the south, his fingers clasped around Olivia's hand, a bag strapped to his back over his arming sword. They stayed between the building and the scattering of vehicles lining the parking lot. To her credit, the nun was keeping up.

The first gunshots shattered the sleepy stillness of the morning seconds later. Ethan rounded the corner of the building after the running immortals and felt stone chips strike the back of his legs from the bullets peppering the asphalt. He glanced over his shoulder, identified three shotguns, and focused on the weapons. Colorful cursing rose to the clear skies. Metal clattered to the ground in the distance behind him.

Ethan grinned and bolted onto the vacant lot at the back of the motel. Asgard and Olivia were halfway across it already.

Rust-stained silos rose above a concrete manufacturing plant to the north of the deserted parcel of land, the aluminium roofs of the main factory building glowing blindingly under the blazing sun. To the east and south, silver-colored, cylindrical storage tanks on steel struts dotted the perimeter of the plot. Beyond them, the ground dropped to a shallow basin.

The two immortals were headed straight for a gap between the tanks. Ethan put his head down and accelerated.

He was twenty feet from the running pair when he heard tires squeal on his left. A patrol car came into sight on the dirt track next to the motel. It veered wildly, bounced onto the empty lot, and barreled toward them.

Ethan skidded to a stop and scowled at the officers behind the windshield. His gaze dropped to the hood of the vehicle. He perceived the steering column in his mind's eye, raised his left hand, and flicked his wrist.

The steering wheel spun violently between the driver's hands. His companion braced himself against the dashboard and the roof, mouth opening on a scream. Their panicked shouts were barely audible above the shrill whine of the engine as the car pinwheeled on its axis in a cloud of dust and gravel.

'Ethan!' Asgard barked as the vehicle skidded to a screeching halt.

Four state troopers and two county sheriff officers emerged from the side of the motel. Ethan twisted on his heels and raced after the immortals.

Olivia suddenly staggered to a stop. Asgard grunted and stumbled. The nun ignored him and looked around wildly, her eyes frantically scanning the landscape.

Asgard tugged her forward. 'We have to go!'

Ethan saw her stiffen and followed her frozen gaze to the arid, brown hills rising beyond the rail tracks and the river east of the basin. Something glinted in the distance. The nun grabbed his wrist as he reached her side, pulled on Asgard's hand, and dragged them into the shadow of one of the storage tanks.

Silent shots pelted the ground where they had stood a second ago. The state troopers and county officers stopped in their tracks and gazed around in confusion. Further shots thudded into the ground next to them, raising small puffs of dirt. The men dove behind the cover of the stationary patrol car in the middle of the lot.

A bullet zinged off the driver's side mirror. The next one pierced the window and struck the policeman's left temple. He thudded onto the steering wheel, eyes wide open, his slack jaw striking the horn. A high-pitched blare tore through the air. His companion opened the passenger door and stumbled out of the vehicle, gun in hand.

'Shit!' hissed Ethan.

They were directly in the line of fire of the officers sheltering behind the car. He was wondering whether to disable their weapons when more bullets struck the dirt close to where the three immortals crouched. One pinged off the strut of the tank.

He turned and looked into Olivia's eyes, his heart thundering inside his chest. 'Sniper?'

She nodded, her fingers biting hotly into his skin. 'It's—it's the same men who were at the abbey!'

'Jonah,' growled Asgard.

Olivia's hand flexed unconsciously on Ethan's wrist. He felt a faint quivering inside his skull once more, as if a butterfly was touching his consciousness with its wings. He turned his arm over, grabbed her fingers, and yanked her toward him.

'Is that you?' he asked harshly, inches from her face.

She gasped. Her eyes turned to jade, dark pupils dilating with shock.

Asgard's hand landed heavily on Ethan's shoulder.

The older immortal was glaring at him. 'What the hell—?'

A bullet struck the body of the tank, making them jump. Liquid splashed onto the ground a couple of feet away, pale and viscous. Dread filled Ethan as he watched the growing puddle darken with dirt. He recognized the pungent, sweet smell of the fluid.

'That's naphtha oil!' He rose, yanked Olivia and Asgard to their feet, and urged them toward the southeast border of the plot. 'Go!'

Further shots whizzed by when they cleared the shelter of the storage tank. They ducked behind the next reservoir and skidded to a stop behind its hulking shape. Ethan moved to the back of the structure and peered around the contoured edge. A faint breeze stirred his hair when a bullet sang past his head.

He pulled back sharply. '*Dammit!* This bastard has us pinned. He'll shoot us like fish in a barrel if we go out there!'

Asgard was staring at the patrol car in the middle of the vacant plot. The state troopers were in the midst of an animated discussion, fingers occasionally pointing in their direction. The blast from the car horn stopped abruptly when they pulled the dead policeman off the steering wheel. Distant sirens broke the sudden silence. They had called for backup.

Another sound rose from the north. Asgard dropped flat to the ground and squinted between the tank's supporting struts.

'There's a freight train coming,' he said after a few seconds. He rose to his feet and dusted off his hands. 'That's our way out of here.'

Ethan looked from him to the tracks some five hundred feet on the other side of the shallow valley separating them from the hills. The train horn came again, faint but unmistakable.

'How the hell do you propose we get on it without being shot to pieces?' he said.

It was Olivia who replied. 'You can manipulate metal?'

Although her voice shook, she was studying him with a singularly focused expression.

'Yes,' said Ethan with a faint frown.

Her gaze shifted to the distant hills. She bit her lip. 'From how far?'

He blinked, surprised. 'I don't know.'

She squared her shoulders and seemed to reach a decision. 'Let's find out.'

She raised her right hand and hesitated for a heartbeat before gently cupping the side of his face. Her fingers trembled when her third eye birthmark came to rest against his skin.

Ethan froze. A shiver skittered down his spine as something alien glided across his consciousness. 'What—?'

Olivia closed her eyes, brow furrowed in concentration.

In the next moment, brightness flooded Ethan's sight and obscured his vision of the nun. He blinked when the dazzling brilliance coalesced into a kaleidoscope of colors and fragmented images. A wave of dizziness made him stagger back a step. The nun's hand flexed on his face. She stayed with him, never breaking contact.

Ethan swallowed down bile. The ground he stood upon appeared beneath him and unfurled rapidly, as if he were somehow flying above it. The valley flashed past at a dizzying speed. The rail tracks and the river followed. Then, the hills were looming before him, brown slopes rising to a pale blue sky. A black spot appeared on the arid ground and rapidly grew in size, a target in the middle of his view.

It was a SUV with tinted windows. A man in an olive army uniform leaned across the hood of the vehicle, a sniper rifle fixed to a tripod under his chin. His eye was glued to the scope atop the weapon. Another figure stood behind him. Ethan inhaled sharply.

He recognized the second man.

'Focus,' whispered Olivia.

For a moment, Ethan was unsure whether she had actually spoken or if he had heard her voice inside his head. He gritted his teeth and centered his attention on the rifle.

The soldier's finger moved on the trigger. Time slowed.

Ethan saw the shot leave the suppressor a second before the barrel crumpled into a twisted ball of metal. The soldier jerked back behind the scope, his expression startled.

The bullet struck the dark pool at the bottom of the punctured tank forty feet away. The liquid ignited.

Olivia dropped her hand from his face. Ethan rocked back on his heels as his consciousness slammed back inside his body. He blinked at the nun. Sweat beaded her forehead and she was panting unevenly. Her eyes gleamed with a hint of triumph.

Flames rose up the flowing rivulet of oil in a blazing roar. Asgard swore, grabbed their shoulders, and pushed them toward the lip of the basin. They stumbled and broke into a run. The tank exploded just as they reached the edge of the drop.

Searing pressure slammed into Ethan's back and lifted him off his feet. He heard Olivia cry out, reached out blindly, and wrapped his arms around her body just as they were flung clear of the brink.

They were suspended in midair for timeless seconds before gravity sucked them to the ground. The landscape spun sickeningly around Ethan. Air wheezed out of his lungs in a harsh grunt when they landed heavily on a gravelly slope. He tucked Olivia's head instinctively to his chest as they slid and rolled roughly down the incline. A rock sliced the skin on the back of his hand. Another ripped a hole in his jeans, gouging his leg. He ignored the stinging discomfort and tightened his hold on the woman in his arms.

They finally came to a stop at the bottom, Olivia lying atop him.

Ethan lay still for a stunned moment. He blinked at the

plumes of black smoke rising toward the sky above him. A buzzing noise filled his ears and muffled all sound. Olivia's heart fluttered madly against his chest, her rapid breaths warming the skin at the base of his throat. She raised her head and looked down at him.

The immortal felt as if he had been sucker-punched.

Her hair framed her face in a halo of gold. Her eyes were a green, hypnotic pool, her pupils a dark abyss he feared he would drown in. Self-preservation kicked in and sent a sudden burst of trepidation coursing through his veins. He gripped her shoulders to push her away.

A wave of dirt and gravel heralded Asgard's arrival. The older immortal rolled to a standstill a few feet from them and uttered a choice curse word in Czech. He spat out a mouthful of earth before crawling unsteadily to his knees.

'You two okay?' he asked hoarsely.

Olivia blinked.

Ethan found that he could breathe again. 'Yeah, we're all right. I—'

A shadow passed over them, cutting him off.

The burning carcass of the oil tank dropped from the sky and crashed some fifty feet from their position. Another detonation rocked through the twisted, metal remains. The ground trembled.

They scrambled to their feet as smoke from the conflagration washed over them. Police sirens wailed shrilly from the direction of the motel. Asgard looked to the north. The freight train had rounded a curve in the land and was a growing yellow shape on the horizon.

Asgard jerked his head. 'Let's go!'

Patches of wild woodland dotted the ground separating them from the tracks. They entered the cover of a coppice just as a horde of squad cars screeched to a stop at the top of the incline. Shots shattered the air above their heads a moment later.

Heat scorched Ethan's throat as he sprinted over the uneven terrain. Up head, Asgard had taken hold of Olivia's hand once more. Although she stumbled and nearly fell a couple of times, the nun stayed the course, her stance resolute. They navigated past a large pool of stagnant water and emerged from the shadows beneath the trees into the blazing sunlight bathing a wide patch of barren land.

The freight train was half a mile away and closing in rapidly. The scream of engines and the harsh sound of tires grinding on gravel reached Ethan's ears at the same time as the growing peals of sirens. He looked over his shoulder and spotted four patrol cars racing down a dirt track toward them.

'Shit!'

He glanced from the approaching train to the running pair ahead of him, gritted his teeth, and slid to a stop.

'Keep going!' he yelled at Asgard as the older immortal started to slow down.

Asgard hesitated before nodding, a muscle jumping in his jaw. Olivia gave Ethan a frantic look over her shoulder as she followed her uncle.

Ethan turned and focused on the vehicles coming at him. He took a deep breath, closed his eyes, and raised both hands, palms facing out.

There was a series of loud bangs. He heard a crash and blinked in time to see the vehicles smash into each other. He had popped their hoods, effectively blocking their windshields. The patrol cars juddered to a halt in a billow of dirt, a mass of buckled bodies and entangled metal. The shouts of the officers trapped inside echoed faintly in the hot, dry air.

Ethan took off after the two immortals.

They were about a hundred feet from the tracks when a

dark shape shot into view on the other side of the river. Ethan scowled.

It was the SUV from the hills. A figure was raising a rifle through the passenger window.

The crack of bullets was almost drowned out by the growing rumble of the approaching freight train. Shots smashed into the ground close to Asgard and Olivia, raising swirls of dirt. Another ripped a tear in the older immortal's left outer thigh. He stepped protectively in front of his niece, his stride unbroken.

Then the train was there, some seven thousand tons of screaming metal and engine on wheels.

Ethan glanced over his shoulder. They had just over half a mile of train left to make their escape. The SUV flashed in and out of view between the freight cars.

Asgard was the first one to reach the tracks. He looked down the train, let go of Olivia's hand, and skidded to a halt. 'Keep running!'

She stumbled past him, turned, and continued sprinting parallel to the charging train.

Asgard rocked tensely on the balls of his feet. He reached up, grabbed the ladder on the porch of a passing grainer car, and jumped on. His feet landed on the platform.

He grasped the side rail tightly and leaned out. 'Olivia!'

The nun turned and raised her hand, her face pale. Asgard gripped her outstretched arm as he came past and lifted her off the ground. He cushioned her body as she slammed into the side of the car and guided her inside the porch. They clung grimly to the ladder and watched as Ethan came abreast of the railway line.

A couple of tank cars zoomed by. Ethan stole a look behind and raised his hand just as a boxcar appeared. His fingers closed on the rung of a side ladder. He swung up, legs dangling in empty space while he sought purchase with his free hand. The wind drag tore at his clothes and the bag on his shoulder. His fingers slipped on the metal bar.

A panicked shout drifted from up ahead at the same time that his grip closed on the rung below. The soles of his boots skimmed the ground next to the tracks. Ethan grunted, grabbed the side rail with his other hand, and hauled himself up. His feet found the bottom rung of the ladder. He closed his eyes and hugged the metal structure for a long moment, his heart pounding inside his chest and his mouth dry. By the time he made his way to the grainer car and the two waiting immortals, the sirens of patrol cars had faded in the distance behind them.

The black SUV was nowhere in sight.

# CHAPTER EIGHT

JONAH KRONDIKE STARED THROUGH THE GLASS CONTAINMENT wall separating his office from the research lab some fifteen feet below.

'Are you absolutely certain it was them?' he said quietly.

'Yes sir,' replied Scoleri on the flatscreen monitor affixed to the wall on his left. 'They fit the profiles.'

An ugly wound marred the middle of the immortal's forehead, a testimony of his recent engagement and death at the hands of an enemy who had eluded them for decades.

Despite the irritation coursing through him, Jonah could not stop himself from smiling.

Mark Scoleri started working for the cause twenty years ago, well after Asgard Godard and Ethan Storm escaped from the army facility in New Mexico. The Crovir Hunter had proven to be one of Jonah's best agents ever since and had been placed in charge of the team of immortals and pureblood immortal-human half-breeds who now worked for Jonah at the facility.

Although he had read Godard and Storm's case files, this was the first time he had engaged in direct combat with either immortal.

Rage at having been bested burned brightly in the Italian's dark eyes. 'We sent men to all the possible stops for the next one hundred miles of that freight train's journey. So far, there's been no sign of the targets.'

'And the police?' said Jonah.

'They're still buying the story we told them: that Godard and Storm were seen leaving the abbey in the middle of the night, after multiple gunshots were fired. The witness is one of our men. He lives close enough locally to justify doing some night-time hunting in those mountains and his credentials are above suspicion. Godard and Storm's descriptions and composite drawings are in the FBI's National Crime Information Center database. They'll have to watch their backs from now on, wherever they go.' Scoleri paused. 'The authorities are treating the nun as a hostage.'

Jonah turned and studied the busy scene in the lab beneath the office. His team was getting ready for the next stage of their experiment.

'Locating and capturing Olivia Ashkarov and Ethan Storm is your number one priority from this moment forth,' he told Scoleri. 'Use as many men as you deem necessary. Our friends in the US Army will be more than happy to provide us with the bodies and firepower you need.'

Scoleri hesitated. 'If I may ask, what's so special about that woman? She seemed pretty ordinary to me.' He grunted. 'Storm I can understand. That bastard's got some unique moves.'

The Crovir Hunter shifted uncomfortably under Jonah's flinty stare.

'Olivia Ashkarov is quite likely one of the most powerful immortals who exists today,' Jonah finally said. 'From the description of your encounter with her, she doesn't yet know the extent of her abilities. Because of the mark she bears, I suspect hers are even more remarkable than her mother's. Had she been in full control of her powers, you and your men would not have walked out of that abbey alive.'

Scoleri's expression sobered.

'Natalia Ashkarov slipped from my grasp when I was days from taking her captive. She found her escape in her final death,' Jonah continued. 'With her gone, her daughter is the only one left in the immortal world who carries their family's formidable bloodline.' He knitted his brow. 'I need that girl. She is the perfect experimental subject for what we're trying to achieve. So is Storm. I don't care what you do to him as long as you leave him a few lives to survive what we'll put him through.'

'And Godard?' said Scoleri.

'You can dispose of him. He is no longer of any use to me.' Jonah smiled thinly. 'And I want proof of his ultimate death. Bring me his ashes.'

Scoleri nodded, a satisfied grin flashing across his face. The video link blinked to black.

Jonah walked over to the drinks cabinet and poured himself a glass of bourbon. He downed it neat and hissed air between his teeth as the liquid scorched a fiery trail down his throat. One thing that had definitely improved over the last eight centuries was the alcohol.

A beep sounded from his desk. He crossed the floor and pressed the answer button on the digital monitor sitting in the middle of the mahogany table.

'Yes?'

One of his scientists spoke through the interface. 'Sir, Subject 505 is ready for Phase Three.'

'Good,' said Jonah. 'And this time, have the dart guns ready. The last test subject made a mess of the place. The clean-up alone put us back a couple of days.' He grunted. 'You should all know by now how the general feels about his precious facility. I can't afford to have him kill any more of you just because you've pissed him off.'

He closed the communication channel while the scientist was still stammering and walked over to the glass wall.

The man who had called him turned to stare up at the window, his face pale. The glass was lined with a privacy film for one-way viewing; the scientist had no way of knowing that Jonah was watching him. He jumped at a sound and turned to watch a couple of guards walk through the main door of the lab, their weapons prepped with a dart syringe containing a powerful narcotic and anesthetic agent.

One of the other scientists approached the terminal and spoke to him. The ashen-faced man nodded slowly and squared his shoulders before joining the group gathered in front of a wide console filled with computer monitors and digital control panels.

Fifteen feet in front of them, on the other side of a secured containment chamber with a thick, reinforced, ballistic-resistant glass window, a colossal figure with dark hair lay strapped to a metal gurney. Bar the army-issue boxer shorts that covered his groin, the man was naked. His eyes were closed and his chest moved slowly and steadily with his breaths. An IV line pumped an infusion into the tube-like vein at his elbow.

Jonah glanced at one of the multiple screens lining the walls of his office. Subject 505's vital statistics looked excellent.

He touched a communication switch at the bottom of the window.

'Begin.'

THE SUN WAS A LOW, HAZY, YELLOW SPHERE IN THE SKY TO the west when Ethan exited San Fernando Valley. The undulating peaks and basins of the Santa Monica Mountains stretched out around him, slopes covered in a tapestry of greens, yellows, and reds dotted with large, traditional, Spanish-style homes and modern, concrete-and-glass constructions.

The engine of the fifteen-year-old, gold-colored Volvo station wagon rattled and creaked beneath the hood as he negotiated several miles of hairpin twists and turns. Asgard sat quietly beside him, his gaze focused blindly on the rolling scenery. Never the most talkative person in the world in the first place, the older immortal had been more taciturn than usual since they left Wyoming. Ethan suspected he knew what lay so heavily on his friend's mind. His eyes moved to the rearview mirror.

Olivia sat glued to the window in the rear seat, her face reflecting curiosity as she drank in the landscape. A mile after they left the Topanga State Park, they crested a slope and caught their first glimpse of the sea. The nun inhaled sharply. Ethan hid a smile.

After their escape from the motel in Lincoln County, the three immortals hid in an empty boxcar on the train for some eighty-odd miles before jumping off on the outskirts of the city of Rock Springs. Three hundred feet south of where they alighted, they came to a chain-link fence surrounding part of a large industrial estate. The parking lots were crowded with the empty cars of employees toiling away in the warehouses and buildings inside the grounds. Ten minutes later, they were in a stolen vehicle headed west on Route 30.

They swapped license plates with cars in Green River and Evanston. By the time they reached Utah Lake and parked outside a small airport serving Springville and Spanish Fork, Ethan was certain the cops and Jonah's men would not find their trail. It didn't take them long to track down the owner of a Piper PA-28 Cherokee light aircraft stored in one of the hangars. Although the man was initially reluctant, a thick wad of hundred-dollar bills convinced him to let Asgard pilot his plane to a private airfield in Los Angeles County.

Considering how wary the older immortal had been of the combustion engine when he came out of the ice in the 1950s, Ethan was surprised at how fascinated he became with flying. Asgard got his pilot's license five years after their escape from the army facility in New Mexico. He used every opportunity to practice his skills and insisted on flying the Cherokee despite the wound on his thigh.

They left the pilot fueling up for his flight back to Utah and hitched a ride to Palmdale, where they bought the second-hand Volvo from a used-car dealership. To minimize the risk that they would be placed by a curious bystander, Asgard and Olivia waited for Ethan at a coffee-shop down the road while he completed the transaction with one of his counterfeit IDs.

The station wagon juddered as it struck a crack in the blacktop. Ethan blinked, his hands tightening on the steering wheel. He saw Asgard glance at him out the corner of his eye.

They had been awake for more than thirty hours. Exhaustion was starting to set in.

Canyons opened around them as the road snaked toward the Pacific shoreline. The houses became scarce, most of them invisible behind tree-shrouded, secured drives and high fences.

The private lane materialized in the middle of a stretch of deserted woodland. Had he not known its exact location, Ethan would have driven past without giving it a second glance. Constructed out of sandstone to mimic the yellow dirt, it started out narrow and blended in perfectly with its surroundings, as the designer had intended. He followed the widening track for a thousand feet and over an artificial rise made of compressed earth to a pair of thick, twenty-foot-tall wooden gates framed by white concrete pillars. Walls topped with barbed wire disappeared between towering trees on either side.

Ethan looked to where hidden pan-and-tilt cameras were mounted atop the barrier and punched a code in the call box on the metal post rising on the left side of the road. A panel slid open on top. A small camera appeared and rotated to scan the interior of the car.

'An unidentified female has been located in the rear of the vehicle,' said a male voice from an invisible speaker a couple of seconds later. 'The facial recognition software cannot place her on any known database, sir.'

Olivia startled and looked around.

'Apply security protocol fifteen, Bernard,' Ethan ordered.

There was a small pause. 'Applying security protocol fifteen, sir. Please supply the password.'

'Perseus,' said Ethan.

'That password is incorrect, sir,' said the invisible Bernard.

Ethan glared at the metal post. 'Did he change it again?'

'Yes, sir.' Bernard cleared his throat. 'Mr. Titus wishes me to inform you that as the major shareholder in the business, he has modified *all* passwords to the default once more.'

Asgard said something rude under his breath.

Ethan's shoulders drooped.

'Howard is standing right next to you, isn't he?'

Bernard hesitated. 'Yes he is, sir.'

'That son of a—'

Ethan became aware of Olivia's gaze on his face and swallowed the rest of the curse.

'The password is H-O-T Rod Forever,' he said in disgust.

'Password accepted. Welcome home, Mr. Storm, Mr. Godard.'

The electromagnetic locks disengaged and the gates swung open on hydraulic pumps to reveal a pristine asphalt road. A line of steel bollards dropped into the ground as the Volvo rolled onto the smooth surface. Seconds later, the gates closed behind them.

'What's a "hot rod?"' said Olivia.

Ethan's foot slipped off the clutch. The engine stuttered. He caught Asgard's warning look, turned the key in the ignition, and changed gears.

'It's an acronym for the guy who owns half this place,' he muttered.

The nun seemingly satisfied with this answer, Ethan followed the access route for a mile as it wound through a wooded gorge. Sycamore and oak trees brushed shoulders with eucalyptus groves on the vertiginous slopes. Low-lying sage scrub and chaparral crowded the gaps between them and revealed the underlying ochre-tinged sedimentary rock that made up the mountains. Shadows moved across the valley as dusk started to fall.

A decorative driveway made from stamped concrete replaced the blacktop. A hundred feet later, they reached the summit of a hill. Olivia gasped.

The land fell away dramatically around them, giving rise to a sweeping vista of a hazy, salt-spray-dusted Pacific Ocean. The setting sun painted the sky and sea with dazzling hues of pink and orange fusing to dark purple. Lights twinkled faintly along the distant Pacific Coast Highway. On the far left, Santa Monica was a bright constellation against the darkening landscape.

A sigh left Ethan's lips. However many times he drove up this road, he never got tired of that view. He could tell from the way Asgard relaxed beside him that the older immortal was also glad to be back home.

The driveway angled around gently to a wide, circular fore-court fronting a stunning mansion that spilled down a series of beautifully landscaped, artificial terraces carved into the side of the mountain.

Set in three hundred and fifty acres of private land, the structure was an ode to modern architecture, with sleek, simple lines, flat roofs, and a clever blend of stone, concrete, wood, metal, and glass. It was also a hive of some of the world's best technologies and host to an extensive security system that incorporated the entire estate and several miles of underground tunnels extending to the ocean and neighboring valleys.

Ethan parked the Volvo opposite a wide marble porch. He removed the duffel bags from the trunk while Asgard secured their weapons. Olivia got out of the car and stayed close to her uncle, her wary gaze inspecting their impressive surroundings.

The front door opened. A tall gray-haired figure in a suit appeared. Soft light streamed around him from the interior of the building.

'Hi Bernard,' said Ethan. He nodded to their solemn-faced butler.

The man dipped his chin.

'Mr. Storm. Mr. Godard. Will you be staying long this time around, gentlemen?'

Ethan glanced at Asgard as they climbed the steps. The older immortal's slight limp had all but disappeared, his latest injury healing at its usual supernatural pace. 'It depends.'

The butler scanned Olivia with the barest flicker of his brown eyes, bowed regally, and took the bags from Ethan. The nun blushed.

They followed Bernard inside an elegant foyer and past several airy openings and glass walls that offered tantalizing glimpses into the rest of the labyrinthine property. Olivia's eyes widened when they reached a floating, spiral staircase spanning three levels of the building. She was still staring at it when Asgard touched her arm and halted her steps before she walked into the back of the butler.

The man had stopped on the edge of an enormous, sunken living area with a south-facing glass wall overlooking the canyon and the ocean beyond. Steel, concrete, and bare stone were the principal building blocks of the multileveled, luxurious room. Cedar floors and textured marble columns added warmth to what would otherwise have been a clinical space, while ingenious lightning showed off splashes of color here and there in the form of canvases and beautiful flower arrangements.

A fire crackled in a large slate hearth to the left. A figure rose from the white, L-shaped suede couch next to it.

'I have instructed Rosa to prepare some light refreshments,' said Bernard.

The butler turned and disappeared through an archway to the right.

Asgard regarded the man by the couch with a frosty air.

'I thought we made it clear that your password was idiotic.'

He headed down the wooden steps to the sunken floor.

Howard Orson Rodney Titus grinned and jammed his hands into the pockets of his designer shorts. A Rolex gleamed on his wrist, the metal glittering against his tanned skin.

'Seriously, you're such a pain in the ass,' Ethan murmured.

His oldest friend rocked back on his heels, unabashed. 'Oh, come on, you guys need to learn to relax! 'Specially you, Asgard. I swear you're living on the edge of a coronary. You should let me hook you up with one of those hot chicks from Santa Monica.' He winked. 'Let off some of that pent up steam, you know what I'm saying?'

'You're pushing your luck,' said Asgard between gritted teeth.

Howard chuckled.

Ethan sighed. The twinkly-eyed, grinning blond man who looked like a preppy Harvard-graduate was in fact a one-hundred-and-fifty-year-old Crovir immortal, master crook, hacker, and insanely savvy entrepreneur.

Ethan had known him for nearly one hundred of those years and was a major shareholder in the ventures that had seen Titus propelled onto the list of the world's twenty richest tech tycoons. The fact that the money Howard used for his first start-up was spoils from decades of a professional thieving partnership with Ethan was not something either Crovir immortal readily advertised.

Asgard was their second-largest investor and the other silent partner in the business besides Ethan, having come on board after the two Crovir immortals helped him retrieve the gold and precious stones he stowed in Europe in the course of his two-hundred-year quest to find Jonah Krondike. Some of the treasure hunts had proven to be challenging, considering the monuments and buildings of historic significance that now stood over Asgard's old hideaways. Digging beneath the Louvre and Vatican City had been sheer torture for Ethan and Howard, with the Bastian noble forbidding the two Crovirs from going after the priceless masterpieces close to hand on pain of death.

These days, the official dealings of their multi-billion-dollar corporation were well above board. Their other private endeavor, and the main focus of their energies for the last forty odd years, wasn't.

Appreciation dawned in Howard's blue eyes. 'And who do we have here?'

He stared at Olivia.

Ethan made the introductions in a tired voice.

'Olivia, this is Howard Titus, our friend and business partner. He's also the one who alerted us to Jonah's mission to hunt you down. Howard, this is Olivia Ashkarov.'

Howard crossed the floor, hand extended toward the nun. She blinked in the face of his mega-watt smile.

There was a silken sound of metal sliding against leather. A blade touched Howard's neck. He froze in his tracks.

'Back off,' growled Asgard. 'That's my niece.'

'And she's a nun, so she's definitely off limits,' Ethan added.

Although alarm was evident on Olivia's face as she studied the impressive arming sword Asgard was holding to Howard's throat, she also looked puzzled. Her expression cleared.

'Oh. I can see why you may have gotten the wrong impression,' she said. 'Although I lived at the abbey, I'm not a nun.'

Ethan gaped. 'Huh?'

Asgard lowered Armistad half an inch. 'What?'

Howard swallowed and rubbed the spot where the Bastian noble's blade had dented his skin.

Footsteps rose from the direction of the foyer. A short woman with glossy black hair and a tray full of canapés stopped at the top of the stairs. Her eyes darted from the sword to Asgard's stormy expression and Howard's contrite appearance.

She gave Bernard a dark look.

'You should have told me Mr. Godard was intending to kill Mr. Titus. I would have prepared less food.'

'My apologies,' murmured Bernard. 'I did not foresee that the situation would deteriorate so rapidly.' He glanced at Olivia. 'That was a terrible oversight considering the presence of the young lady.'

The woman turned and glared at the assembled immortals.

'This had better not be like that incident in 1984. It took me days to get the bloodstains out of the couch.'

'Seriously, you guys are hurting my feelings here,' grumbled Howard.

Ethan barely listened as Rosa, their housekeeper and cook, berated Howard while Bernard looked on with a long-suffering air. His gaze remained locked on Olivia's face.

'Would you care to repeat what you just said?' he asked carefully.

∾

# CHAPTER NINE

'ALTHOUGH I LIVED UNDER THE SAME CANONS AS THE OTHER Benedictine nuns, I remain a postulant to this day. Mother Edwards refused to give me permission to be initiated into the novitiate.'

'A postulant?' said Howard.

Olivia nodded. 'Yes. A postulant is one who wishes to enter a religious order. Once a postulant candidate is admitted into the novitiate, he or she undergoes a period of intense, supervised training prior to being called to take formal vows.'

They were sitting on an open-air, limestone deck next to a beautifully-lit, slate-lined infinity pool that looked out over dark canyons. Carefully-positioned spotlights hidden among the rocks and bushes on the landscaped terraces around the mansion added a warm glow to the evening gloom.

Music reached them faintly from the direction of the kitchen one level above, where Rosa was clearing up after their evening meal. The lively Latin tunes were at odds with the somber mood on the patio.

Ethan did not detect any bitterness in Olivia's expression. Although it was evident that she had wanted to become a fully-fledged Benedictine nun, she seemed to have long come to terms with her mentor's decision to deny her wish.

Howard cocked an eyebrow. 'So technically you could have left that place whenever you wanted to?'

Olivia hesitated. 'Yes. But I never saw the need to leave the abbey. I was happy with my life there.'

'I suspect after your powers became evident, you were pleased at the privacy afforded by such an isolated setting,' Ethan said in a sharper tone than he had intended.

Howard glanced at him, surprise flashing briefly across his face.

Olivia flinched. Her gaze shifted to the invisible ocean. 'You're right. It seemed an appropriate prison for the monster that I had become.'

Guilt stabbed through Ethan. His emotions had been all over the place since he met Olivia Ashkarov. He could not explain why he felt so defensive in her presence. Still, none of this excused his boorish behavior. He leaned forward, lips parting to deliver an apology.

Asgard beat him to it. The Bastian immortal moved from his seat and got down on one knee beside Olivia's chair. He took her hands in his own large ones.

'I am going to say this only once. Beyond that, I will get very angry if you dare repeat those words again. You are not a monster, child. If anything, you are the opposite.' He raised a hand to the back of her head, pulled her forward, and gently kissed her brow. 'You are exceptional. Unique. A gift this world doesn't deserve. In another time and place, you would have been revered as a god, Olivia Ashkarov.' He cupped her cheek. 'And you are a very welcome blessing in my life.'

Tears shimmered on Olivia's eyelashes. She swallowed convulsively, her murmured 'Thank you' barely audible.

Ethan looked away from the intimate tableau and caught Howard's shrewd stare.

'You remind me very much of your mother,' Asgard told Olivia. 'I thought that the first time I saw you, at the abbey.'

Olivia blinked. 'I do?' She hesitated. 'Is that—is that why you looked so shocked?'

'Yes,' Asgard confirmed with a nod. 'Until that point, I didn't know that the Olivia Ash we were trying to rescue was the daughter of Natalia Ashkarov. You are the image of her. People always assumed she was a fragile soul because of the way she looked. But she had an inner core of steel that she drew upon when she needed to.' He grinned. 'It kept your father on his toes.'

'Tell me more.' Olivia wiped her eyes. 'Tell me about them. My mother and my father. And Sara, my aunt.'

The immortal's smile faded. He lowered himself to the deck and looked blindly into the darkness beyond the terrace. Olivia dropped down next to him and hugged her knees to her chest, bare feet peeking from beneath the white, floaty dress Rosa had unearthed from somewhere in the mansion. From Howard's grimace when he had seen her in it, Ethan suspected the item belonged to one of his ex-girlfriends.

'Your father and I met the Ashkarov twins at one of the social events organized by the immortal societies following the end of the war that had blighted our races for millennia,' Asgard began haltingly, after a short silence.

Ethan looked down into his drink. A familiar ache started to swirl through him, like the ribbons of color dancing in his bourbon. Although he had heard the Bastian noble's tale before, it never failed to sadden him and remind him of his own loss at the hands of their enemies.

Howard knocked back his whisky, his expression similarly troubled.

'This is the war you mentioned, back at the motel?' said Olivia.

'Yes,' replied Asgard. 'Your father's name was Kristof

Kovach. He was a Bastian noble and my best friend. He was also an extraordinary swordsman. As Bastian Hunters, we fought in many battles before the first truce was declared in the late 1300s and he saved my life on more than one occasion during that time. Then the plagues came. The Black Death killed more than half the human population in Europe and Asia, with an estimated death toll of around two hundred million souls. The Red Death decimated the immortal races by an equal number.'

His voice grew quiet. 'I lost my mother and many close companions to the illness.' He glanced at Olivia. 'Even your father was not immune, although his affliction was not as serious and he made a full recovery.' He paused. 'But it was the aftereffect of the Red Death that almost brought the immortal races to the brink of extinction. Those who survived the infection discovered they could not bear children. It didn't take long for the two immortal societies to realize that they would cease to exist if their war efforts continued.'

A bitter smile curved Asgard's lips. 'Although factions on both sides had been working toward a solution for peace for centuries, it took the Red Death to force our councils to come to their senses about the futility of a conflict that had gone on for so long that no one could recall the exact reason why it started in the first place.'

Howard rose and poured Asgard another drink. The Bastian noble accepted it gratefully and swallowed half the glass before he continued.

'With a treaty in place, the two races were keen for unwed immortals to choose suitable mates from among their own societies and reproduce. They even implied, quite brazenly at times, that those whose spouses could no longer give them children should choose new partners, for the good of all. To kill two birds with one stone, the First Councils decided to hold functions where Crovir and Bastian nobles could interact civilly with each other for the first time in thousands of years. These events doubled as marriage marts, where immortals could browse for fitting partners, but only from among their own race, since mating between a Crovir and a Bastian was strictly forbidden by one of the immortals' most ancient edicts.'

'That all sounds very...mercenary,' said Olivia.

'I was one of a minority of nobles who had not contracted the Red Death, more by sheer luck than fortitude I must admit.' Asgard's expression grew awkward. 'As such, I became a highly regarded candidate for matrimony.'

'Oh.' Olivia raised her eyebrows. 'You mean, like a prized bull?'

There was a strangled snort. Howard sprayed a mouthful of spirits across the deck and coughed, choked laughter rocking his body. Ethan masked his own grin and slapped his friend on the back. They had never heard this part of Asgard's history before.

Olivia reddened, her eyes moving from the chortling Crovir immortal to Ethan's poker expression. 'I'm sorry.'

Asgard's startled look was replaced by a smile. He chuckled. 'People rarely married for love in those days.' His expression grew sober. 'Despite the fact that your father and I were Hunters, a role few nobles adopted due to its association with a socially inferior status, we became very much "hunted" in those circles. But women wanted me not just because of my disease-free status and my noble origins. As a pureblood immortal, I had become a premium commodity among our races.'

'Pureblood?' Olivia's brow furrowed. 'You said that word at the motel. What does it mean?'

Asgard rocked his glass and watched eddies form in the coppery liquid.

'A pureblood is an immortal whose lineage can be traced all the way back to the progenitors of our races,' he said quietly. 'Purebloods are like royalty in our societies. They were already scarce before the Red Death; after the plague, only a handful remained. My father, Tomas Godard, myself, and my sisters, Catarine and Lily, were four such Bastian immortals, as was Kristof. Although the Ashkarovs lost their extended kin and their patriarch, they were another family of pureblood Bastians who had survived the Red Death.' He glanced at Ethan. 'So were the Knezevics, Ethan's Crovir ancestors.'

Olivia drew a breath in sharply. Her gaze danced across Ethan's stiff face before moving to her uncle. 'My parents were purebloods?'

'Yes. Although Natalia's mother wished for her to marry someone other than your father, someone who had never contracted the Red Death, like me, it was clear to both of us the moment we were introduced that we were ill-suited for one another. However much an offspring derived from our two gifted bloodlines would have been welcomed by our families, there was no way I could be with Natalia, nor she with I.' A wistful smile dawned on Asgard's face. 'Instead, your delicate, blonde mother fell hard and fast for the hulking, red-haired giant who stood by my side. Whereas I lost my heart to the devilish brunette who watched over Natalia.'

Olivia brightened. 'So you *did* marry for love?'

Asgard laughed. 'The four of us did, in the end. And we had many happy years together.' The smile slipped from his face once more. 'Until the day we crossed paths with a Crovir noble by the name of Jonah Krondike.'

His knuckles whitened on the glass and he fell into a meditative silence.

Olivia bit her lip. 'He's the one behind what happened at the abbey?'

Asgard nodded, his expression hardening. 'Jonah Krondike is guilty of some of the most despicable acts ever visited on humankind and immortals alike. Although I haven't gathered enough evidence to present this as fact to the First Councils, I am convinced of his involvement in devastating wars and geno-cides over the last six-hundred-odd years.'

Olivia paled. 'Why? To what aim would someone go to such lengths?'

'To answer that question, I must first tell you of a fable that had its roots in the history of the immortals before it spread to popular human culture,' said Asgard. He turned and looked at her steadily. 'Have you heard of the Elixir of Life?'

She hesitated. 'Yes. It's also known as the Philosopher's Stone, is it not?'

'You are correct. Throughout the history of mankind, many tales have circulated about the origins and properties of the Elixir of Life. And a number of legendary items have been asso-ciated with this mythical entity over the ages.' Asgard frowned. 'I was not one who readily believed in such fanciful stories. As far as I was concerned, they were the figment of people's fevered imagination, even their desperate wish that an article of that nature should exist.' He paused. 'It was not until the day I discovered the existence of a sect by the name of Kronos that I realized there might be some truth behind those accounts after all.'

Olivia looked puzzled. 'Kronos?'

Asgard gazed into the night with hooded eyes. 'In the spring of 1398, when Sara and I were visiting Natalia and Kristof, a group of masked men broke into our castle and killed several of our servants. Natalia had a vision of the event just before it unfolded. By the time we got back, the intruders had disap-peared. We believed it to be a random act of thievery since a number of valuable items went missing from our estate, mostly articles of gold and some of Sara's jewelry. But Natalia remained uneasy for days afterward. We convinced her that it was an isolated incident.'

A muscle jumped in his cheek. 'We were proven wrong a few months later. The same thing happened again, the day after we travelled to Vienna for a meeting at the Bastian First Council. On that occasion, they turned the castle upside down. Natalia was certain they were searching for something. To test the theory that we were being targeted, Kristof and I set a trap. Shortly after that second episode, Sara and I left our home under the pretense of attending a function in the neighboring town. Sara and Natalia stayed with a friend while Kristof and I returned to my castle with our men, under the cover of darkness. The intruders returned to the estate that night. We confronted and eventually overpowered them after a terrible clash. There were a few lives lost among the immortals in our group. All but one of the trespassers were killed.'

Lines creased the immortal's brow. 'They were determined to fight to the death, despite our offer of armistice if they surrendered their weapons. We never got to interrogate the boy we captured. He bit his tongue and drowned in his own blood moments after we seized him.'

Horror flashed across Olivia's face. 'These men were part of this sect?'

'Yes. It was several decades before Kristof and I discovered the name of their group and what their true intentions were.' Asgard's voice turned bitter. 'It was around the time of the attacks that we were introduced to Jonah Krondike. In hindsight, our first encounter was not an accident but a cleverly engineered ploy to help him infiltrate our extended circle of friends. It happened at an event held by the Crovir First Council in the Electorate of Saxony, in what was then the Holy Roman Empire.'

Ice clinked at the bottom of his glass as he absentmindedly tilted it. 'Little was known about the Krondikes at the time and even less so now. They were a wealthy, reclusive noble family who had refused to get involved in the affairs of the Crovir Councils, a rarity among people of their status. Jonah professed to be the only Krondike who survived the Red Death. He became a familiar face at social functions and soon expressed an interest in the history of the noble families. It wasn't long before he was being invited to look at their personal libraries and artifacts.'

The Bastian noble grunted. 'It was only later that we discovered some of those immortals had been the victims of attacks on their persons and properties. In the meantime, Kristof and I were still trying to uncover the identities of the intruders who raided my home. Apart from their weapons, the men had come to the estate empty-handed. But they had a unique marking on their bodies that would eventually help us track down their origins. It also gave me an idea of what it was they had been looking for in the castle.'

'A marking?' Olivia glanced at her right hand. 'You mean, like a birthmark?'

'No,' said Asgard. 'It was a symbol that had been etched into their skin with a pigment. A cross with a rose entwined around it.'

Olivia startled.

Asgard's eyes narrowed. 'You know of it?'

'I'm...not sure. I feel as if I may have seen something similar in one of my nightmares,' she murmured.

Ethan stiffened and exchanged a surprised glance with Howard. Her admission unnerved him, like so many other things about her. Was it coincidence or fate that she had dreamt the very mark that symbolized their enemy?

Asgard observed his niece for a silent moment. 'That doesn't surprise me, considering your abilities.' He turned and gazed into the darkness once more. 'In 1399, while Kristof and I were in Buda investigating a potential lead, Jonah came to my castle unannounced. He claimed he had been traveling in the area and wanted to pay his respects. Although Sara had never taken a liking to the man, she had no reason to refuse him. Jonah asked whether he could look at our family library. Sara grew suspicious and refused, claiming she needed her husband's permission to allow a stranger access to our collection of ancestral manuscripts. Jonah excused himself and left. Natalia arrived at the estate hours later, distraught. She had a presentiment her sister had been in mortal danger. Since nothing sinister actually happened that day, Sara dismissed her fears. Despite my wife's objections, Natalia shared her concerns with us when we returned from our trip.'

Asgard's tone grew leaden. 'To this day, I still blame myself for not trusting Natalia's instincts and for believing Sara instead.' His voice caught in his throat. He took a shuddering breath. 'Not long after that event, Natalia started to have terrible visions of wars that would engulf entire nations in the centuries to come. Many invariably involved shadowy figures bearing the symbol of the cross with the rose. Kristof and I grew more determined to discover the identity of the intruders. Two months later, we unearthed a clue that took us to Pozsony County. We were away for three weeks. It was during that time that Sara was murdered.'

~

# CHAPTER TEN

OLIVIA RECOILED AS IF SHE HAD RECEIVED A PHYSICAL BLOW.

Ethan felt something twist inside his chest at the anguish distorting her features. He clenched his jaw and clamped down on a sudden urge to walk over and wrap his arms around her body to protect her from what was to come.

'Natalia never..."saw" what happened,' said Asgard in a low voice. 'I think the shock of it would have killed her if she had. They were twins after all.' His head drooped. 'Natalia was asleep in her own home at the time of Sara's death. She woke up filled with an unnamed dread about her sister's fate and ordered her men to bring her to our castle. When they got there, the entire estate was ablaze and crows were swarming the place. It was morning by the time the fires died down enough for them to be able to enter the premises. They found evidence of a brutal battle and discovered the burnt bodies of the human servants and men I had left guarding the castle. Scattered among them were the ashes of the immortals in my service. Sara—' His voice trembled. '—Sara's remains were in the library. From the state of the room and the sword by her side, she fought to the bitter end.'

'You told me immortals could survive sixteen deaths,' Olivia said shakily.

Asgard swallowed.

'They can. But there are three ways to permanently dispose of an immortal. Kill them repeatedly until their final death. Tear their bodies into small pieces.' He hesitated. 'And decapitation.'

Olivia raised a trembling hand to her lips.

'From the human corpses Natalia and her men came across, the third method had been employed indiscriminately by the killers,' Asgard continued in a thick voice. 'Kristof and I returned two days later. By then, Natalia had already buried her sister's ashes. It was as I wept before my wife's grave that Natalia told me the news. Sara was with child at the time of her death.'

Ethan's hand bunched into a fist on his knee at the Bastian's tormented words. He could not even begin to imagine what the older immortal had lived through in those moments.

Tears dropped silently into Olivia's lap.

'Sara found out she was expecting shortly after Kristof and I left for Pozsony. She asked Natalia not to send for me. She wanted it to be a surprise upon our return.' Asgard glared at the ground between his feet. 'On that day, Natalia, Kristof, and I promised that we would leave no stone unturned in our quest to uncover who was behind the atrocities that had been committed. Although we never found proof that Jonah Krondike and Kronos slaughtered Sara and the people who had served us, what we discovered over the years and decades that followed convinced us they were the culprits.'

He looked at Olivia. 'Kronos was a group made up of the descendants of pureblood immortal-human offsprings. We never got to the bottom of their exact origins, but we believe Jonah Krondike formed an unholy alliance with them in the middle of the fourteenth century, around the time the Red Death was coming to its natural close.'

Olivia startled.

'A pureblood immortal-human offspring? You mean, like Mother Edwards?'

'The woman who raised you may have been of the same race as the members of Kronos, but she had absolutely nothing in common with that infernal sect,' said Asgard stiffly.

Relief brightened Olivia's face slightly.

'We got our first glimpse of their identity and objectives in the 1400s, in the Kingdom of Bohemia,' said Asgard. 'At the time, we had followed sightings of individuals bearing the mark of the cross and the rose to the town of Klodzko, where a terrible crime had recently been committed. A renowned natural philosopher by the name of Augustus Medevelle and his gifted assistant, Joseph Veceslav, had been found with their throats cut. Medevelle's lifelong mission had been to find a mystical artifact linked with the creation of the Elixir of Life. It was an endeavor that had earned him years of ridicule from his colleagues in the capital and abroad.' He gazed steadily at his niece. 'That artifact was the *Tabula Smaragdina*.'

Olivia gasped.

'The Emerald Tablet?'

Ethan drew a sharp breath. *She knows about the Tablet?*

'Wasn't that one of the Hermetic texts said to be behind the origin of alchemy itself?' she continued.

Asgard regarded his niece with newfound respect.

'You are well-read.'

Her face grew troubled. 'There was a library at the abbey. Most of the books I studied came from Mother Edwards's personal collection though. The first texts she ever gave me to read concerned alchemy and philosophy.' Her eyes darkened. 'I thought it strange at the time, considering the nature of our order. Was she preparing me for—' she waved a hand and indicated the luxurious estate around them, 'for this?'

Asgard hesitated.

'Although I did not know her personally, Margaret Edwards strikes me as having been a singularly astute woman. She knew you would face difficult times in the future.' A melancholic smile curved his lips. 'I think Natalia left her instructions to get you ready for what might come.'

Olivia looked down at her hands.

'But it wasn't enough, was it?' Her voice trembled. 'I could not protect her or the other nuns in the end.'

'I don't think your mother or the abbess expected you to be able to defend yourself against an army of killers, Olivia. You were never trained for physical combat.' Asgard faltered. 'Your talents lie elsewhere.'

His gaze shifted to the shadows beyond the deck once more. 'The Emerald Tablet was one of the objects believed to be behind the *Magnus Opus*, the process used to make the Philosopher's Stone. The other famous relic was the *Mutus Liber*, or The Wordless Book, as it was also known. Although modern historians attribute authorship of the *Mutus Liber* to a Frenchman from the seventeenth century, Kristof and I believed the original text was several millennia old.'

The distant howl of a coyote broke the heavy hush that fell over the patio.

'How—I—this is just so incredible,' Olivia stammered.

'Medevelle and his assistant were on the trail of the Emerald Tablet when they were tortured and killed by Jonah and Kronos,' Asgard continued in a level tone. 'But it seemed they lied to their murderers about their findings and sent them on a fool's errand to Asia. Veceslav proved to have been the more cautious of the two men. After we introduced ourselves to their families and told them of our search for a group of marked individuals we believed to be responsible for the murders, his daughter led us to a field outside the town. Under her directions, we dug up a box her father had interred. In it were copies of the two men's lives' works.' He ran a hand through his hair and let out a tired sigh. 'Fifty years later, Kristof and I unearthed the *Tabula Smaragdina* in North Africa.'

Olivia gaped. 'You *discovered* the Emerald Tablet?'

Asgard dipped his head.

'What did you do with it?' She looked around at the mansion and its grounds, as if expecting to see the relic floating in midair. 'Is it here?'

Ethan masked a smile at the excitement in her voice.

'No,' Asgard replied. 'We knew we couldn't keep the artifact safe while we were still chasing Jonah and Kronos. After much deliberation, we entrusted it for safekeeping to a group of humans in 1478. That fraternity eventually came to be known as the Freemasons.'

Olivia had gone pale. Ethan felt a twinge of sympathy for Asgard's niece. The first time the Bastian noble had related this tale to Howard and him, they had not believed the immortal either. It wasn't until they saw the artifact with their own eyes that they finally grasped the significance of the quest they now found themselves embroiled in.

'And the *Mutus Liber*?' she finally asked.

'We never located it. At least, that's what I believe.'

Olivia's brow furrowed in puzzlement.

'In the middle of the sixteenth century, Natalia convinced us to part ways. She and Kristof would chase after the *Mutus Liber* while I continued to hunt Jonah and Kronos.' Muscles worked in Asgard's throat. 'The last time I saw your parents was in 1595, in Minsk. By then, Kristof and I had disposed of more than a hundred sect members across Europe, Asia, and Africa. Four years later, I tracked Jonah to the Urals. He knew I was closing in on Kronos's primary command post and went into hiding. I evaded the killers he sent after me and found the mountain cabin where he had taken refuge.'

The Bastian noble fell silent.

Olivia studied her uncle with apprehension. 'What happened?'

Despair etched deep lines in Asgard's face. 'I chased Jonah onto a glacier. The shots we exchanged caused an avalanche that cracked the ice. I fell inside a crevasse and was buried in a frozen lake inside the very belly of the mountain.' His voice dropped to a whisper. 'And there I remained until the middle of the last century.'

Olivia gasped, green eyes flaring with shock. 'I'm so sorry.'

She touched Asgard's shoulder.

The Bastian noble grasped her fingers tightly. 'Why, child? It wasn't your fault. You had not even been born yet.'

They sat quietly in a moment of shared grief.

'You said my mother believed Jonah and Kronos had been looking for something when they attacked your castle,' said Olivia. 'Did you find out what it was?'

'Yes, I did. Although Jonah had been correct in assuming the object he sought would be in my possession, he had unwittingly been looking in the wrong place. It was with my sister at the time.'

'Object?'

'The item Jonah and Kronos had been searching for was a gold, sun cross pendant. It was a family heirloom passed down through generations of Godards since time immemorial,' the Bastian noble explained. 'As Tomas's first born child, it was bequeathed to me. But Catarine had always been fascinated with the pendant, so I decided to leave it in her care. When I registered its resemblance to the mark borne by the members of Kronos, I feared my sister would be in danger if the pendant remained with her. I travelled to Prague and took possession of it once more.'

'Where is the pendant now?'

Asgard looked up at the night sky, his expression nostalgic. 'I left it in the care of a Buddhist order in 1415. The group was founded by Guru Rinpoche, the Lotus-Born Second Buddha, in the early part of the ninth century. He had come to know of immortals and created the order to keep our existence a secret from the eyes of humans.' His face darkened. 'It wasn't until I escaped from Jonah's clutches a few decades ago that I discovered Kronos had stolen the pendant from the order in the 1700s. They killed dozens of monks and practically burned their temple to the ground.'

'What was so special about the pendant?'

A frustrated sigh left Asgard's lips. 'I don't know. There was nothing in our family's ancestral manuscripts that attributed any special significance to the object. For all intents and purposes, it was just another heirloom.'

Olivia digested this information in silence. 'So you believe Jonah Krondike wanted to find the Elixir of Life. But why? He is already an immortal.'

'He is. Up to his sixteenth death,' said Asgard.

Olivia's eyes rounded. 'You mean he thought the Elixir would grant him immortality beyond that?'

'It's the only plausible explanation your parents and I came up with during the decades we hunted Jonah and Kronos. We believed their final objective was to conquer both the human and the immortal worlds, hence the conflicts they engendered throughout Europe, Asia, and Africa. If they succeeded in creating chaos and distrust between the empires that existed at the time, it would have presented them with a unique opportunity to seize power. If they became invincible as a result of the Elixir of Life, no one would be able to challenge their supremacy.'

Asgard chuckled mirthlessly. 'It was indirectly thanks to the immortal societies that this never happened. Although they never realized they had been fighting a common enemy for centuries, the Crovirs and the Bastians unknowingly thwarted many of Jonah's and Kronos's attempts to create unrest, thus keeping humankind and the immortal societies from imploding.' His voice faltered. 'But your parents and I always sensed there was something else, something greater to Jonah's plans than achieving true immortality. We just never found out what that other goal was.'

Olivia bit her lip. 'Do you know what happened to my parents?'

Asgard shook his head. 'I don't. We may find answers in the journals left to you by Margaret Edwards.' He gazed at Olivia, his eyes fierce. 'Know this well, child. Your parents would never have forsaken you except to save your life. After Kristof's illness from the Red Death, they never thought they would be able to conceive. Your existence would have been a gift from the gods to them.' He swallowed. 'It must have broken their hearts to part with you.'

She blinked back tears. 'Do you believe they are dead?'

Asgard went still. 'Yes. I would have found them by now if they were still alive.'

Olivia's head dropped forward, her hair a silken curtain that hid her features.

'Thank you,' she said huskily.

The Bastian noble nodded stiffly.

Ethan's admiration for the woman grew another notch. Asgard had been right. Despite her fragile appearance, Olivia Ashkarov possessed great strength of will. A lesser person would have been an incoherent mess in the face of what she had endured in the last day.

She rose to her feet and stepped to the edge of the deck. A breeze ruffled her hair and the folds of her dress while she stood silently gazing out over the dark canyons. Ethan unconsciously held his breath. He had a strange feeling that something dramatic was unfolding before his eyes.

It was almost a minute before she turned and looked at them. 'What does Jonah Krondike want with me?'

Ethan blinked. He barely recognized the woman they had rescued from the abbey. The events of the last twenty-four hours and Asgard's retelling of their shared past seemed to have transformed her into someone else. There was a fresh hardness to her eyes and the rigid lines of her body. Were they seeing the real Olivia for the first time?

'When he dug me out of the ice in the late 1950s,' said Asgard, 'Jonah took me to a secret US Army facility in New Mexico. Over the decade that followed, he conducted countless experiments on the immortals he had captured, including myself.' He grimaced. 'The methods Jonah and his team employed were unnecessarily sadistic. From their setup and the information we have since gleaned, it's evident they had been at it for some time and were targeting immortals of noble and pureblood lineage.'

Olivia jerked in surprise. 'Jonah was the one who rescued you?'

'Rescue is a questionable word,' said Asgard grimly. 'I revived while in transit from the Urals to Perm. I broke almost every bone in my body during my fall on the glacier and my healing had been arrested by the ice. They gave me forty hours to mend before they started cutting into me.'

Olivia blanched. 'How—how did you get out of there?'

'In 1969, Jonah captured the last descendant of the Knezevics.' Asgard glanced at Ethan. 'It was a fortuitous meeting for the both of us. Although I had been planning my foolhardy escape for some time, the assistance of an Elemental accelerated the process greatly.' His eyes grew hooded. 'In hindsight, I doubt either of us would have gotten out of that blasted place alive on our own.'

Ethan felt gratitude flood him once more at the Bastian immortal's words. Meeting Asgard Godard had redefined the course of his existence in ways he could never have predicted. Not only had it provided him with the opportunity for revenge he thought he would never have, it had also given him a friendship that would forever stand the test of time.

For as long as he could remember, the Crovir noble had led a life filled with secrets and lies. Though he had dim recollections of his early childhood, his lasting impressions of that period were of days spent in peace and joy in the city where he had been born. Then came the night everything changed. His only memory of it was of flames and screams, and the frightened sounds from the horses as they rode frantically into the darkness, fleeing an invisible enemy determined to capture them at any cost.

He lost count of the number of times they moved after that, first across Europe and Asia, then to the Americas. His parents never spoke of their past and taught him to blend in with the world of the humans. He was beholden to his older sister, born fifty years before him, for telling him about their origins and the history of the immortal societies. He recalled lying in bed late at night and listening in awe while she spoke of a life he had never known. Of their wonderful ancestral home and the noble company they had kept. Of dazzling balls and exhilarating hunts. Of wonderful voyages to exotic places that others could only dream of. Of their influential position in the hierarchy of the Crovir society, for they had been the last descendants of a proud and venerated family of nobles.

But it seemed that others hungered for the powers of their singular ancestry. Shortly after Ethan turned eighteen, and days from discovering the first of the extraordinary abilities he had inherited from his bloodline, the ones who had chased his family from the only happy home he had ever known finally caught up with them.

He was the only one who escaped the attack. He never saw his parents or sister again.

Ethan had kept a low profile ever since, living under the radar of human and immortal societies alike. He became proficient at changing his identity and moved town whenever he caught a whiff of trouble on his tail. He had been to more cities and countries than he could care to call to mind.

Olivia listened wordlessly while he finished recounting the tale of his past in a wooden voice, her eyes full of sorrow once more.

Her gaze dropped to his hand. 'Can you only control metal?'

Ethan hesitated. 'I can manipulate earth, water, and air to a lesser degree.' He looked at Asgard. 'Your uncle has been training me, but I still can't control fire.'

'Can you show me?' she said after a thoughtful pause.

Ethan hid his surprise at the question. He wavered for a moment, raised his left hand, and concentrated on a polished rock lining a path just beyond the limestone decking.

It trembled slightly before slowly levitating a foot in the air. Olivia drew a sharp breath.

He lowered the rock and focused on a spot above the path. For a moment, nothing happened. Then dirt rose from the ground in a tiny vortex. He made the dust devil dance around Olivia's legs before carefully disposing of the spinning cloud. He moved his attention to the pool.

Ripples broke across the flat surface. A small wave surged through the water and tumbled past the vanishing edge into the trough below.

Olivia's eyes glazed over. 'Oh.'

A quiver suddenly skittered across the inside of Ethan's skull. He froze. Heat filled his veins. He felt power surge through his body and choked on his breath.

A column of water spouted from the middle of the pool and soared twenty feet in the air. The funnel spun rapidly on itself until it resembled a glittering twister. Asgard and Howard jumped to their feet. Ethan heard their alarmed cries dimly through the blood pounding in his ears; he gritted his teeth and tried to lower his arm, fighting for control of his gift. An invisible force kept his hand aimed at the swirling mass.

Asgard grabbed Olivia's shoulder and pulled her back from the edge of the pool. The woman blinked.

The alien sensation inside Ethan's head disappeared. He shuddered and bent over, clutching his hand to his chest while he gasped for air. The pillar of water unravelled and crashed into the pool. The resulting tidal wave washed across the decking and drenched them.

Rapid footsteps sounded from above. Rosa's head appeared over the edge of the metal railing.

'What was that?' she snapped. Her tone turned suspicious. 'And why are you all wet?'

She started for the metal stairs that connected the upper terrace to the swimming pool deck.

Bernard appeared in one of the doorways leading to the patio. There was a gun in his hand. 'Is everything all right?'

Ethan slowly straightened, his eyes never leaving Olivia's face.

'It's you, isn't it?' he said hoarsely.

She paled.

Asgard scowled. 'What do you mean?'

Ethan ran a trembling hand down his face. 'She's the reason that just happened. She...got inside my head somehow.'

Asgard turned to stare at Olivia.

'It was the same, back at the motel.' Ethan faltered. 'And the woods, just after we fled the abbey.' His gaze focused on Olivia once more. 'I have never been able to physically move a living being until last night, but I—somehow, I heard her and felt her fear. I still don't understand what happened next. All I know is that I—'

'You snatched me from the abyss when I started to fall,' Olivia completed in a low whisper.

Howard gave them a puzzled look. 'What are you talking about?'

Asgard stiffened. Understanding dawned in his eyes. He swore.

# CHAPTER ELEVEN

OLIVIA OPENED HER EYES. GOLDEN BEAMS DANCED ACROSS A white ceiling high above her. She bolted upright, her heart hammering inside her chest.

Sunlight filtered through sheer, cream curtains at the end of the room. Beyond them, a wall made of smart glass offered dazzling views of green canyons overlooking the crystal-blue Pacific. Her pulse slowed its wild tempo as she studied the clean lines of the unfamiliar space around her. She was in one of the guest rooms in the mansion. Recollections of the previous day's events filled her mind.

Olivia was surprised she had managed to sleep after the explosive scenes she had witnessed and the extraordinary accounts she had been privy to in the last twenty-four hours. Although she was coming to terms with the fact that her life was now forever changed, she still found it hard to believe that she would never be able to see Mother Edwards or the nuns again, or return to the abbey where she had spent all her life.

She also could not quite grasp that she belonged to a race of supernatural beings whose origins were older than the Bible.

Pulling down the nightshirt Rosa had given her, she rose

from the bed and padded barefoot into the bathroom. It was twice the size of her former bedroom at the abbey and incorporated a walk-in wardrobe and dressing area among its luxurious fittings. She stopped and stared at the racks.

At some point since she arrived at the mansion, they had filled her closet with clothes and footwear. The garments were of a simple yet elegant design and seemed tailor-made for her. She peeked at a label and winced when she recognized an exclusive brand.

She brushed her teeth, showered, and slipped into the clean underwear she found inside a drawer in the wardrobe. She ignored the expensive products arranged on the gleaming dressing table, wrapped a towel modestly around her slender form, and paused undecidedly in front of the clothes racks. She studied the new dresses with pursed lips; they were mostly sleeveless and had low necklines. Her gaze shifted to some jeans.

The denim clung sinfully to her legs when she slipped into them. She shrugged a plain white T-shirt over her head, dried her hair, and put on a pair of canvas shoes.

She stepped outside the room and walked along a gallery with a glass ceiling. She passed a sun deck lined with potted azaleas before reaching the landing with the spiral, steel-and-glass staircase. A delicious smell greeted her at the bottom of the steps. She followed the fragrant aroma to the state-of-the-art kitchen overlooking the infinity pool.

'Good morning,' Rosa said brightly. The woman stood at a chef's range cooker set in an island in the middle of the pale stone floor. She flipped a pancake expertly onto a serving plate and indicated a French press. 'Would you like some coffee?'

Olivia smiled back shyly. 'Hi. Yes, I would love some.'

There was a noise from the terrace. Ethan came up the stairs from the pool deck, opened a sliding door, and walked in.

Olivia stared.

The Crovir immortal was rubbing his hair briskly with a towel. Water clung to his bare arms and chest, the crystal drops highlighting his golden skin and well-defined muscles. Her eyes dropped to the dark swimming shorts hanging low on his hips and his long, toned legs. A slow heat suffused her cheeks.

He stopped in his tracks when he saw her.

Rosa sighed. 'Mr. Storm, how many times have I told you not to traipse in here when you've just been swimming?'

Ethan nodded stiffly at Olivia and strolled to the island. He grabbed a piece of bacon from a plate before walking out of the room.

'Breakfast is in fifteen minutes,' Rosa called out after him. 'Tell Mr. Titus, will you? He's in the bunker.'

Ethan poked his head around the doorway. 'Howard's up?'

Rosa scowled. 'He never went to bed. Bernard said he's been glued to his computers the whole night.'

Ethan frowned and disappeared.

Olivia swallowed. It looked like the Crovir immortal had still not forgiven her.

'Have you seen my uncle?' she asked Rosa.

The cook grimaced. 'He returned in the early hours of the morning.'

Olivia bit her lip.

After Ethan explained what had transpired during the episode at the poolside the previous night, Asgard had stormed off into the darkness beyond the terrace. They'd stared after him for a stunned moment before Olivia made a move to follow in his steps. Howard had stopped her in her tracks.

'He's obviously upset about something,' the Crovir immortal had murmured. 'Let him be. He'll talk to us when he's good and ready.' He had sighed at her expression. 'Don't worry, he knows this land like the back of his hand.'

Ethan had avoided looking at her and headed wordlessly into the house.

Rosa's voice interrupted her dismal musings. 'Hey, are you okay?'

Olivia looked at the steaming drink the woman had placed in front of her.

'Yes,' she murmured.

The cook did not look convinced. Still, she left Olivia alone and returned to her range.

Olivia took the cup and went exploring. Although Howard had promised her a guided tour of the mansion the night before, what had happened on the deck had put a dampener on their plans.

She came across three more lounges, two formal dining rooms, a fully-equipped gym featuring a boxing ring and a fencing area, a heated indoor swimming pool, a sauna, an impressive library with a reading room built into a glass tower, a study, a home-movie theater, a games room, and a cavernous underground garage containing a range of expensive-looking cars, SUVs, and motorcycles. A number of steel doors and lifts guarded by digital security displays appeared in her path. She inspected them curiously before slipping through a pair of sliding doors and onto a patio. She walked past a tennis court and through the terraces and gardens tumbling down the hill-side to an observation deck overlooking a gorge. She shielded her eyes with her hand before studying the mansion at the top of the slope.

Olivia had not fully appreciated the deceptive scale of the building and its grounds the evening before. In the harsh light of day, she saw how the clever design allowed the structure to blend into the landscape. The mansion was also strategically positioned on the crest of the rocky elevation and would prove a tough target to breach for hostile forces. Aside from the safety measures she had already seen, she suspected it was brimming with cameras and security sensors.

Although she was grateful for the hospitality and protection of her hosts, the entire set-up made Olivia uneasy. The three immortals living here were clearly used to danger and primed to do battle at the first sign of a threat. The whole thing spoke of a world as far removed from the one she had known her entire life as the moon was from the Earth.

Olivia turned and gazed out over the canyons. She still could not explain what had happened the previous night. When Ethan related the unsettling feelings he had experienced on the three occasions where he seemed to have lost control of his powers, Olivia had been dumbfounded. There had only been one instance when she had deliberately lowered the barriers she had built over the years to shield her mind from the consciousness of others. It had been during their escape from the motel, when she helped the Elemental destroy the sniper's rifle aimed at them from the other side of the valley.

It was only now that she realized the sin she had committed. So great had her focus been on the perils they faced at the time, she had completely ignored the feelings of the man whose mind she had invaded. Guilt filled Olivia when she recalled the fragments of emotions she had perceived during the precious seconds she had been inside Ethan's head. She had had little regard for his confusion and alarm, and had used him as one would use a weapon. No wonder he was angry with her. She had violated the sacrosanct space that was his consciousness and made him doubt his own sanity.

But what shocked her even more was how easy it had been and how right it had felt.

In all the years she had tried to suppress her curse, Olivia had never fathomed the extent of her abilities. The very thought was anathema to her. Her actions at the motel had been born of fear and desperation. Had she been in a state to consciously analyze what she had been about to do, she would never have attempted it.

That she had breached Ethan's mind as smoothly as she had done was uncanny. It was unlike the episodes at the abbey, where her perception of the nuns' innermost reflections had felt like sneaking into a room and spying on someone's private conversation. With Ethan, she had not been aware of the usual maelstrom of feelings, needs, and expectations that was the constant state of the human awareness. Instead, she had been drawn to the source of his powers, like metal to magnet. She could still see it now, the shimmering, golden tangle of lines deep inside his body that she had touched with her mind. Had he not been so unnerved, she doubted she would have sensed his thoughts.

Olivia shivered despite the heat of the sun. What had transpired with Ethan Storm terrified her almost as much as the incidents at the abbey and the motel.

Footsteps sounded behind her. She turned and saw Bernard coming down the stone steps.

'Mr. Godard wishes to speak to you, miss.'

A flutter of anxiety twisted through Olivia's belly. She followed the man up the slope.

Bernard guided her to a side terrace adjacent to the kitchen and disappeared into the mansion. Olivia ignored the mountain of food laid out on the breakfast table and watched the man standing at the edge of the slate patio.

Asgard was looking out over a wooded valley, hands tucked in his pockets. He had a defeated air about him. He turned when he heard her light steps. An apologetic grimace twisted his lips.

'Hi,' he said huskily.

Relief flooded Olivia. She blinked back tears, stunned by the strength of the feelings coursing through her.

In the short time that she had known this man, he had come to mean the world to her. They were bound by bonds that had been forged in love and blood, over centuries filled with heartache and the desperate need to hunt down the immortal who had wrought havoc in their world.

To Olivia, Asgard Godard was the father she had never had.

Ethan walked out onto the deck. He stopped when he saw them and scowled at Asgard. 'What the hell was with that stunt you pulled last night?'

Asgard eyed the Crovir noble darkly. 'Sit.'

Howard strolled out behind Ethan. His clothes were rumpled and his hair tousled. He yawned, scratched his chest, and rocked to a halt.

'Er, should I leave?' he asked after an awkward pause.

'No,' said Asgard gruffly. 'You should listen to this as well.'

Ethan and Howard pulled out a chair each. Asgard joined them slowly. Olivia took the seat next to her uncle and perched nervously on the edge.

A clatter broke the palpable tension filling the air. Howard paused with his fork in midair, a pancake dangling precariously on the tip.

'What?' he said. 'I'm hungry.'

Ethan muttered something unsavory under his breath and looked at Asgard. 'So, care to tell us what's been bugging you, old man?'

Asgard propped his elbows on the table and scrutinized Ethan over his interlocked hands. 'You said Olivia was in your head?'

Ethan startled. His gaze shifted briefly to Olivia's face. 'Yes.'

'What was it exactly that you heard?' said Asgard.

Olivia stared at her uncle. She sensed anguish behind the coolness in his voice.

'The only time I *heard* anything was in the woods. I sensed her fear. She cried out for someone to help her.' Ethan faltered. 'On the other two occasions, it was just something...alien inside my head. Like a presence. But I knew it was her.'

'How do you know for certain?' said Asgard. He leaned

across the table and pinned Ethan with a sharp-eyed glare. 'Don't think, just answer!'

'Because I recognized the shape of her consciousness,' he blurted out.

Olivia went still. The cadence of her pulse accelerated at the Crovir noble's words.

'It was a brilliant white, tinged with the colors of a rainbow at the edges,' Ethan murmured self-consciously in the face of Asgard's intense look. 'And it was warm, like water heated by the sun.'

A precognitive frisson raised the hairs on Olivia's arms.

Asgard's shoulders drooped. He lowered his forehead to his fists. 'Shit.'

'What?' snapped Ethan.

'Soulmates,' Asgard replied through gritted teeth.

Howard gaped, a half-chewed strip of bacon hanging out of his mouth. 'Huh?'

'The two of you are soulmates,' said Asgard. His eyes shifted from Ethan's puzzled expression to Olivia's blank one. 'Immortals' souls are linked to their destined mates' for eternity. It takes some several lifetimes to find the one they are meant to be with but, when they do, the bond can be instant. It is also absolute.'

Olivia shook her head. 'I—I don't understand.'

Ethan snorted. 'He's saying we're meant to be together. In the *biblical* sense.' He glared at Asgard. 'I don't believe in that bullshit.'

Olivia flushed. She could feel heat radiating off her cheeks in waves.

'Also, I really want to know why you look so pissed, old man,' Ethan added. 'What, you think I'm not good enough for her?'

'No, as a matter of fact, you're not,' Asgard replied bluntly.

Ethan opened and closed his mouth soundlessly.

'The fact that the last descendant of the Ashkarov bloodline will end up with a notorious skirt-chaser brings me nothing but grief.'

A bark of laughter rang across the table.

Ethan gave Howard an icy look. 'Is this amusing to you?'

Howard shook his head, eyes sparkling with mirth. 'Yes. The nun and the playboy. Who would have thought it?'

Olivia hunched her shoulders and wished she could sink right into the floor.

'Whether you believe in it or not makes no difference, Ethan,' said Asgard. 'Sara Ashkarov was my soulmate. There was nothing either of us could have done to stop the wheels of fate turning on the day we met. To not be with her would have been akin to not breathing.' He paused. 'And Natalia Ashkarov was Kristof's intended mate. In the time that they were together, he mentioned that he sometimes sensed Natalia in his thoughts. They were attuned to each other's feelings in a way that even Sara and I weren't.' He narrowed his eyes at Ethan. 'The reason you felt Olivia in your mind the way you did can't be anything else. And I think she augmented your powers.'

Olivia inhaled sharply.

Ethan grunted. 'Augmented my powers? How?'

'You said it yourself. You have never been able to move a living being before you met Olivia. And what happened in the pool last night is also proof of that connection.' Lines creased Asgard's brow. 'I'm still not clear on what took place at the motel.'

'Remote viewing,' Olivia mumbled, her heart pounding against her ribs.

Ethan's head snapped around. 'What?'

Olivia swallowed. 'You know about my visions and night-mares. What I never had time to tell you when we were at the motel was that I can sometimes hear people's thoughts and...

influence their emotions.' She bit her lip. 'And I can somehow see places I've never been to before.'

In the silence that followed, Olivia related her first telepathic experience and the subsequent ones she incurred with the nuns at the abbey. She explained how she had used the techniques Mother Edwards had taught her to protect her mind from others.

'What do you mean by remote viewing?' said Asgard.

Olivia hesitated. 'I used to walk to the ridge above the abbey. From the top you can see Bear Lake on a clear day. About a decade ago, I was in my room when I suddenly wished I were at the lake. The next thing I knew, I *was* there. It felt like a dream. I could see the water as clearly as if I was standing on the shore.' She ran trembling fingers across her forehead. 'There were people around me. I could see them talking but I couldn't hear what they were saying.'

She finally met the eyes of the three immortals, fearful she would see disgust on their faces. She saw only surprise.

'Was that the only time it happened?' said Asgard.

Her uncle looked the most shocked by her revelation.

Olivia shook her head. 'I attempted it again, to see whether that first incident was a fluke. I read an article about an earthquake in China and another one about a mudslide in South America. Both contained pictures of those locations. Within moments of wanting to be there, I was. Both episodes only lasted seconds.' She let out a shaky breath. 'And there are occasions when it didn't work.' She glanced at Ethan. 'Yesterday was the first time in years that I tried to remote view.'

Asgard was silent for the longest time. The color had drained from his face.

'It seems Natalia was right after all,' he finally mumbled.

Olivia shared anxious glances with the two Crovir immortals across the table. 'About what?'

'The last time I met with your mother and father, she told

me of a recurring vision she'd been having,' Asgard related quietly. 'She didn't know when this particular prediction would come true, but she was adamant it would shape the fate of mankind and immortals alike.' He stared at Olivia. 'I had never seen your mother so shaken, not since Sara's death.'

She held her breath. Ethan straightened in his seat.

'Natalia spoke of a group of exceptional beings who would inherit more than just the supernatural gifts of their lineage. She said these immortals' abilities would be like nothing else our world had seen.' Asgard's voice grew hoarse. 'She also foretold that they would face the greatest of challenges together, on the path to fulfilling a destiny that was theirs and theirs alone to claim. And they would be—' he closed his eyes briefly, as if in pain, 'marked in a way that would make them stand out.'

The Bastian noble took Olivia's right hand and gently straightened her fingers until the third eye symbol was exposed to the light.

'You are one of those immortals, Olivia,' he said in a tortured voice. 'No one in the Ashkarov bloodline could do what you can do, not even your mother. She must have known this the moment you were born, when she saw your hand.' His gaze moved to the man staring at him from across the table. 'Ethan is also part of that group. With you at his side, he is finally unleashing his true potential as an Elemental.'

# CHAPTER TWELVE

BLOOD POUNDED INSIDE ETHAN'S HEAD AS HE TRIED TO assimilate what Asgard had just said. In all the years he had known him, he had never once mentioned that he knew something about his birthmark.

'Whoa.' Howard cocked an eyebrow. 'Well, that's not something you hear every day.'

'Do you seriously expect me to believe what you just said?' Ethan asked Asgard coldly after a moment's silence.

A muscle jumped in the Bastian noble's cheek.

'Have I ever lied to you?'

Ethan's hands fisted on the table. He gazed into the immortal's unflinching eyes.

'No.'

'Truly, I wished it wasn't so,' said Asgard in a defeated tone. 'Not just because of the difficult fate that awaits you both, but because I don't want to lose you. Either of you.' He turned to Olivia. 'I have only just found you, child. If something was to happen to you, I don't know what I would—'

He broke off and swallowed heavily. Olivia turned her hand over and gripped his tightly, her green eyes glittering.

Ethan resisted the sudden urge to get up and run as far away from Olivia Ashkarov as he could. That his future was somehow linked to hers scared him like few things ever had. He never wanted to love again, not if it meant losing the ones he cared for. Only two people had managed to breach the walls he had built around his heart in the two centuries since his family was ripped apart, and they were the men seated at the table with him.

Besides, willowy blondes with green eyes were not his type.

He became aware of a stare from his left. Howard was giving him a shrewd look.

'What?' snapped Ethan.

Howard shrugged. 'Nothing.'

'Didn't you say that the union between a Crovir and a Bastian was strictly forbidden by the two races?' said Olivia, her face pale.

Asgard grimaced.

'I did. No one recalls the exact reason for this law. Although many thought it obsolete, the two councils were still adhering to it before I was trapped under the ice. I don't know what their current outlook is on the matter, but I for one do not care about it.' His face darkened. 'I would not let them touch a hair on your head.' He glanced at Ethan. 'Or yours.'

A troubled silence fell across the terrace.

Olivia bit her lip.

'There's something I've been meaning to ask you. What was Jonah Krondike trying to achieve with the experiments he was conducting?'

'We don't know the answer for sure,' said Asgard. 'Ethan and I stole a file from Jonah's room when we escaped the facility in New Mexico. Inside it were lists of immortals he had singled out for capture. We've been using those ever since to try and save as many of his targets as we could.'

'The fact that Krondike's allied himself with part of the US military worries us,' said Howard. 'What they are doing as part of their research flouts every known convention on human rights—or immortal rights, for that matter.' He drummed his fingers on the table, a scowl marring his face. 'We don't know how far up the hierarchy the rot goes in the Department of Defense. My spies and I have only managed to unearth the slimmest of links with the Army Research Lab.'

'Spies?' said Olivia, puzzled.

'Howard's a computer hacker,' Ethan explained. 'A world-class one. He heads a small team of similarly-minded souls. If the DoD ever managed to get into even one of their hard drives, they'd have a heart attack.'

Howard snorted.

'Yeah! As if any of those asshats could.' He grinned at Olivia's expression. 'Relax, cupcake. We're not cyber criminals. It's the only way we've been able to figure out what Krondike and his bastard soldiers have been planning.' He glanced between Asgard and Ethan. 'By the way, the two of you are the prime suspects in last night's murder spree at the abbey. Your pictures are all over the news. Olivia is being treated as your hostage.'

Asgard clenched his teeth.

'You can add Hunters to the selection of people working for Jonah,' said Ethan grimly.

'What?' said Asgard.

'The man you shot in the head in Olivia's room? He was with the sniper targeting us at the motel.'

Asgard's expression darkened. '*Goddamnit!*'

He banged the table with his fist.

Olivia flinched.

'What's a...Hunter?'

'The Order of the Hunters is one of seven sections constituting the First Council of each immortal race,' said Ethan in a hard voice. 'Hunters effectively live to carry out the will of the councils. They are professional soldiers who double as body-guards and assassins for their noble masters.'

'Do these immortal councils know about Jonah Krondike and Kronos?' said Olivia, aghast. 'Do—do they *approve* of what these people are doing?'

Howard scratched his head awkwardly. Ethan avoided meeting Olivia's eyes.

She looked between the three men.

'What is it?'

'I spoke to my father about Jonah and Kronos shortly after Sara's death,' said Asgard stiffly. 'He chose not to believe me. He thought I had lost my mind from grief.'

'Your father?' Olivia knitted her brow. 'I don't understand.'

'Tomas Godard was the Head of the Order of the Hunters at the time of Sara's murder,' said Asgard. 'He was effectively the Head of the Bastian First Council and the leader of our race.'

Olivia gasped.

'You mean he was your *king*?'

Asgard grunted.

'I wouldn't go that far. There was nothing kingly about that stubborn old fool.' He ran a hand through his hair. 'At the time I mentioned the threat Kronos and Jonah Krondike posed to the future of the immortal societies and humans alike, my father refused to talk to the Bastian First Council without any hard evidence. The peace treaty had only been in place for a couple of decades. No one wanted to rock that boat by making unfounded accusations against a prominent noble and ex-enemy. My father and I parted badly after our fight. I vowed I would not speak to him again until I had physical proof of Jonah's culpability.' His shoulders drooped. 'Alas, it was not to be.'

'Tomas Godard was killed during an incident two and a half years ago,' Howard explained at Olivia's anxious look. 'Rumor is the war was going to start again. From the little I gleaned during the moments I managed to breach the Bastian and Crovir security databases, the details of the affair have been hushed-up and are known only to the members of the First Councils.'

'You mean *the* war? The one you told me about back at the motel? The one between the immortals?' Olivia asked her uncle.

Asgard nodded. 'When I started chasing Jonah and Kronos, I cut all ties with my family, more for their protection than anything else. After I woke up from the ice and fled the research facility in New Mexico, I discovered my sisters had long died.' A muscle danced in his jaw. 'Ethan and I were in Asia when my father was murdered. By the time I found out about his death, they had already buried his ashes in Prague.' He faltered. 'I visited his grave last year.'

'Someone high up in one of the immortal societies is helping Jonah Krondike track down Bastians and Crovirs of noble or possible pureblood origin,' said Ethan. 'Although we've rescued dozens of people on Jonah's lists, we were too late to save some. We don't know who to trust in the councils.' He looked around the table. 'The less we have to do with them, the better.'

Howard stirred in his seat. 'Speaking of tracking, I have something to show you. Let's finish up and go to my study.'

They downed the cooling breakfast and headed inside the mansion. Howard stopped in front of a secured lift and tapped a code into the digital display in the wall.

'I thought your office was next to the library,' said Olivia.

Her eyes rounded when he entered his biometric data into the print and retinal scanners that flashed on the screen. The steel doors parted.

'That's my official study.' Howard smiled. 'We're going to the unofficial one.'

They stepped inside the metal cabin and exited it some two hundred feet beneath the mansion.

Olivia stared at the enormous space before them. 'Oh.'

'Welcome to the H-O-T Cave,' said Howard.

Ethan sighed. 'That line does not get any less cheesy.'

'You're just jealous 'cause I came up with it first,' scoffed Howard.

The chamber was two stories deep and had been drilled out of the volcanic granite that made up this part of the Santa Monica Mountains. When they bought the land and designed the foundations for the mansion, Howard decided to create a secure space where they could coordinate their missions away from curious eyes and ears. The bunker could theoretically withstand a nuclear attack and had been modified over the years to serve their needs. Although concrete softened the floors and parts of the walls, he had insisted they leave most of the rock face exposed.

The main floor was dominated by a sunken stage featuring two banks of flat screen computer monitors and a central, round, glass chamber with a digital display table and a three-dimensional laser projector. A passage to the right led to a master suite and a lounge with an open plan kitchen for when the computer genius wanted to bed down in the bunker. An identical corridor to the left connected to an armory and a storage area with a service lift to the mansion's garage.

The curved glass wall up ahead was divided by a floating corridor leading to one of six strategically positioned exits dotted around the cavern, three of which were hidden. Banks of super servers and back up generators were visible on the floor below.

Howard headed down the steps to the workstation on the left and dropped into the large, ergonomic, leather executive chair before it. Keys clattered beneath the immortal's fingers as he started to work a keyboard. They gathered around him.

'Is this what you've been up to the whole night?' Ethan studied the busy screens.

'Uh-huh.' Howard's hands suddenly stilled on the keyboard. He turned and eyed Olivia quizzically. 'By the way, can you hear everyone's thoughts?'

Olivia hesitated. 'It seems I may be able to sense human minds more readily than immortal ones,' she admitted. 'I couldn't read Mother Edwards's either.'

A slow grin brightened Howard's face. 'So, you *definitely* don't know what I'm thinking right now?'

Olivia cocked her head and studied the Crovir immortal with a tiny frown of concentration.

'It rhymes with "boots,"' Howard said helpfully. His gaze dropped by several inches.

She looked down at her T-shirt, flushed, and folded her arms awkwardly across her chest.

Asgard scowled. 'What is *wrong* with you?'

He slapped Howard around the back of the head.

'Ow!' Howard rubbed his scalp gingerly. 'I was just checking.'

'Seriously,' Ethan grumbled. 'I should have killed you when I had the chance.'

Howard chuckled.

Olivia looked between the two Crovirs, her face still red. 'How did the two of you meet?'

'We decided to rob the same bank one night, about a century ago,' said Howard.

'You're *thieves*?' Olivia exclaimed, embarrassment temporarily forgotten.

'We *were* thieves,' said Ethan coolly.

'I remember it like it was yesterday,' Howard began. 'It was winter 1917. Word on the street was a large deposit of cash and gold was gonna be making its way into the vault of the First Chicago Bank. I'd scouted the building for a whole month. Got in from the roof in the end.' He cocked a thumb at Ethan. 'He came through the sewers.'

'I don't do heights,' muttered Ethan.

'We bumped into each other in the ventilation shaft.' Howard grimaced. 'Kinda smelled him before I saw him, really. Anyway, we were having ourselves a nice friendly chat when this bastard broke my nose.'

'You pointed a gun at me,' said Ethan.

'For the last time, the damn thing was empty.' Howard's tone turned sour. 'I won that pistol in a card game with the Sundance Kid. I still can't believe you crushed it to a pulp.' He turned his attention to the computers and resumed typing. 'Suffice to say, I saw the unique opportunity his abilities presented and convinced him to partner up with me. We were doing quite well until he got himself kidnapped by Jonah Krondike.' He frowned at the monitor in front of him. 'Here we go.'

A black command box appeared on the flat screen. He entered a series of complex numbers and letters. The cursor flashed and a new window sprang open.

Ethan scanned the information on display. 'This is from the tracker file you installed in Jonah's spyware?'

'Correct. This was the exact data log when the "capture" mission went live on Olivia two days ago.'

Olivia startled. 'What?'

'In addition to the source that he has in the immortal councils, Jonah has been using a combination of old-fashioned detective work and modern technologies to help him identify individuals of potential interest to use in his experiments,' Howard explained.

'It seems our races have an elevated level of a particular white blood cell called monocytes,' said Ethan. 'They have something to do with our body's ability to heal at an accelerated rate. The more powerful the immortal, such as a pureblood or a strong noble, the higher the level of this white cell. Jonah and the army group he's affiliated with have installed a hidden software in the databases of thousands of hospital labs all over the world to gather that exact data.'

Olivia looked between Howard and the monitor. 'But surely there must be other reasons why these cell counts can be raised, even in humans?'

'I'm glad you asked,' said Howard. 'The answer to that question is yes. What Jonah and his team of scientists recently discovered, however, is a genetic marker that can help identify a pureblood immortal with pinpoint accuracy.'

'A marker?' repeated Olivia.

Howard nodded. 'For every significantly raised monocyte result Jonah got from the information pool they'd been gathering, his team then analyzed the rest of that individual's medical records to see if they could be dealing with an immortal. Ninety-nine percent of the time, they weren't. For the remaining one percent they were suspicious about, they either got their hands on the sample in question or the person themselves to test for this specific genetic signature. Considering the amount of money they invested in this venture, their results have been pretty unspectacular.' He made a face. 'But Krondike must have thought it was worth the expense.'

'Immortals can recover from most injuries and human illnesses,' Ethan explained at Olivia's confused look. 'They would rarely seek medical advice, so the chances of their blood ending up in a lab would be slim at best. They'd have to be comatose or seriously wounded. In the ten years since Jonah's spyware has been in place, they've analyzed a few hundred suspect samples but only confirmed one hit. The man turned out to be a noble who'd been living under the radar of the immortal societies for centuries. He was involved in an accident where he almost lost his leg. He was unconscious when they took him to the hospital.' He paused. 'We got to him an hour before Jonah's soldiers descended on his ranch.'

'Two days ago, the tracking software I installed in Jonah's medical database activated a warning for the second time,' said Howard. 'They'd gotten another hit.'

He looked pointedly at Olivia.

She clutched her chest. 'You mean *me?*'

'Yes,' said Ethan. His tone turned cool once more. 'So, the question is, how did your blood end up in Salt Lake City?'

'I don't know. I haven't—'

Olivia broke off and raised a hand to her lips, horror dawning in her green eyes.

'The outbreak,' she whispered.

The three men shared tense looks.

'What outbreak?' said Asgard.

'Six weeks ago, half the abbey came down with measles,' Olivia explained shakily. 'Someone from the Salt Lake City Health Department and a doctor from the CDC came up and collected swabs and blood samples from everybody. The source was a novice who had transferred in from another state.'

'There's no way you could have known this was going to happen, child,' murmured Asgard in the silence that ensued.

He squeezed her shoulder gently.

'It still doesn't excuse the fact that Mother Edwards and the nuns died because of me,' said Olivia bitterly. She looked down at her hand and hesitated. 'There's something I don't understand. The men who attacked the abbey seemed to recognize my birthmark.'

Asgard froze. 'What?'

'I didn't register it at the time, but the man you shot in my room knew about the symbol,' said Olivia.

Asgard's stunned gaze shifted to Ethan. 'Jonah was also aware of your birthmark. This cannot be a coincidence. Where the devil did he get that information?'

Unease filled Ethan at the Bastian noble's anxious expression. Had the men who attacked his family also known about the symbols? If so, was he also indirectly responsible for the deaths of his parents and sister?

He looked at Olivia then. Anger replaced the guilt filling his heart when he saw the self-reproach darkening her eyes.

*No, none of this is our fault. The one responsible for this madness is Jonah Krondike.*

Ethan clenched his teeth and turned to Howard. 'You said you had something to show us.'

'I've been looking at the log in more detail. There was something odd about it when it came up two days ago. I decided to do some digging.' A mocking smile danced across Howard's lips. 'Turns out this is our lucky day. Someone left a back door open in the operating system. I discovered a hidden digital link and traced it to an address in San Diego.'

A satellite image of the city appeared on the monitor. He zoomed in on a built-up valley to the north and angled the view until a nest of large, white buildings with glittering facades appeared in the middle of an extensive parking lot.

'The company's name is AuGenD,' said Howard. 'Their main area of research is genetics, specifically genomic engineering.' He glanced at them. 'AuGenD invented the test Jonah's been using to identify purebloods. It took my team and I most of the night to infiltrate their network and find the guy who was in charge of the project.' He hesitated. 'I haven't seen such extensive firewalls and encryption software since I broke into the Pentagon.'

A photograph flashed up on a screen to the left. An intelligence file appeared next to it.

'His name is Professor Ian Serle,' Howard continued. 'He's a distinguished visiting lecturer at the University of California, San Diego. The guy's a genius in his field. He's been awarded plenty of top-notch prizes over his career, including a

MacArthur Fellowship and even a nomination for the Nobel Prize in Science.'

Ethan studied the gray-haired man in the picture. Serle's face was heavily lined and a permanent scowl seemed to hover above his deep-set eyes. The creases fanning his thin lips and nose added to his severe expression.

'Divorced. A son who died while serving in the US Armed Forces at age twenty. An estranged daughter living in Japan.' He scanned the rest of the data Howard had gathered on the man. 'There's nothing there that looks suspicious.'

Howard nodded. 'I thought so too until I found his Swiss bank account. It has over fifteen million dollars in credit. I traced the electronic deposits through a series of routers and fake servers to a DoD account in Baltimore.' He grimaced. 'Looks like Serle is definitely in the employ of a branch of the United States government. My spidey sense tells me it's the group working with Krondike. '

Asgard scrutinized the buildings on the live satellite feed. 'You said this company's information system was heavily guarded?'

'Uh-huh,' said Howard. 'I only managed to breach part of it. I suspect they have an equally well-guarded virtual private network.'

He rose from the workstation and strolled inside the glass room in the middle of the stage. They followed him and watched while he worked the digital display table.

The light on the laser projector came on. A three-dimensional structural plan of the AuGenD complex appeared above the table. Howard raised a hand and worked the floating images, his fingers spinning and enlarging various sections.

'I traced the link to this room.'

They studied the space he indicated. It was inside the main building.

'Is that Serle's office?' said Asgard.

'Probably,' said Howard.

'Could they be storing more data locally?' said Ethan.

He recognized the light dawning in Asgard's eyes. The same nervous anticipation was building inside him.

Howard grinned. 'I'd bet money on it.'

# PART TWO: CRUSH

# CHAPTER THIRTEEN

MADELEINE BLACK PULLED UP TO THE SECURITY BARRIER AND rolled down the window of her ten-year-old Toyota Corolla. She showed her ID to the armed guard in the booth and watched impassively while he logged into the security system. The artificial illumination from the computer screen cast a ghostly glow on the man's face and highlighted the lines that furrowed his brow a moment later.

'You're not supposed to be in this evening, Dr. Black.'

Madeleine grimaced. 'Sorry—Hank, isn't it?'

The guard nodded curtly.

'I forgot to warn security admin that I was coming in,' Madeleine continued in a brisk tone. 'Here's the thing, Hank. I have an important meeting on Monday and remembered something I'd missed for the presentation.'

The guard's expression remained cautious.

Madeleine cocked an eyebrow. 'You can check my calendar for next week.'

The guard tapped on the keyboard. Light flickered across his face as another window opened on the screen.

'Seriously, you'll be saving my ass. I'll only be a couple hours, tops.' Madeleine paused. 'You can ring my boss at home if you want to run it past him.'

The guard's frown deepened. He picked up the handset next to him, hesitated, and lowered it slowly onto its cradle.

'Okay,' he grumbled. 'Just make sure you stick to protocol next time.'

She grinned. 'Will do. Thanks, Hank.'

Madeleine knew only too well that her immediate superior, Dr. John Barlowe, was in Vegas for the weekend. He was the lucky recipient of a surprise giveaway she had carefully orchestrated and paid for a month ago. Had the guard rang Barlowe's home, he would have gotten the man's answering service. As for the scientist's cell phone, it was turned off and at the bottom of Madeleine's bag, where it had been since she stole it from Barlowe's jacket earlier that day when she dropped him off at the airport.

The steel barrier rose. Metal bollards dropped ahead of the car. Madeleine drove into the grounds of AuGenD, crossed the empty parking lot, and rolled to a stop in her allocated spot around the side of the main building. Her hands trembled slightly when she slung her bag on her shoulder. She stepped out of the vehicle, looked up at the brightly-lit glass frontage ahead, and took a deep breath.

*Get your act together, Black. You can do this.*

She smoothed the lines from her face, squared her shoulders, and headed inside.

'Hey Kevin,' she said breezily to the night watchman seated behind the curved, marble security desk to the left of the main reception.

The man blinked. 'Oh. Hello, Dr. Black.' He glanced at the computer in front of him. 'I wasn't expecting to see you tonight.'

Madeleine repeated the story she'd given to the guard at the main entrance.

Kevin acknowledged her account with a hesitant nod. 'Well, don't stay back too late, 'kay?'

'I'll be gone before you know it,' said Madeleine.

She headed to a bank of lifts and called one, still feeling the guard's watchful gaze as she got in. She exited the cabin on the fourth floor. Fluorescent strips bathed the corridor ahead of her in a harsh light. She navigated several empty passages, turned a corner, and stopped in front of her lab. She ignored the security cameras observing her every move from both ends of the corridor, swiped her ID badge in the security box in the wall, and punched a code on the keypad. The light turned green on the panel. She walked in the room and closed the door behind her.

It took a few seconds for her to clamp down on the sudden surge of panic flooding her mind. She stared unseeingly at the research facility around her and reminded herself once more why she was doing this. Angry resolve filled her veins and erased all traces of fear from her mind.

Tonight was the culmination of years of hard work in her attempt to solve the mystery that was her mother's murder and the enigma of her own existence.

Madeleine shrugged off her jacket and opened her bag. She removed a second ID card, a flash drive, her phone, and a small flashlight from an internal compartment and slipped them all inside the pockets of her jeans. Next, she checked the Sig Sauer P230 tucked in her rear waistband. The familiar weight of the handgun felt reassuring against her skin when she jammed it back in place.

She logged onto her computer, opened the fake presentation she had put together a couple of days before, and loaded up a software that would deliver typed content at a regular interval over the following hour. To anyone who might later scrutinize her presence in the building, it would look as if she had never left her desk.

Madeleine headed for a workstation at the south end of the

lab, climbed onto the tabletop, and carefully lifted one of the tiles in the dropped ceiling. She pushed it to the side, jumped up, and hooked her forearms over the edge of the square opening. It took but seconds for her to hoist herself into the access space above. She put the tile back in its place, leaving the smallest of gaps to reveal its position from the light shining below.

She would need to know its exact location if she wanted to make a quick exit.

She removed the flashlight from her pocket and switched it on. The beam cut through the musty gloom and danced off pipes, wires, and ductworks. She gripped the torch between her teeth and started to crawl, taking care to keep close to the joists. The last thing she wanted to do was accidentally fall into one of the rooms below.

Forty feet later, she stopped above a ventilation grille and peered into a dimly-lit space below. A sleek, curved, glass-and-metal desk occupied the floor immediately beneath her. It was dominated by a large computer monitor, an ergonomic keyboard, and an external hard drive with an ID card slot.

Madeleine shifted one of the ceiling tiles to the side and lowered herself soundlessly through the opening. She swung her body to and fro and dropped onto the cream carpet next to the desk with the lightest of thuds, knees bent slightly to absorb the shock of her landing.

She was at the computer in a flash and opened up the AuGenD login screen. A fine sheen of sweat coated her forehead as she connected the flash drive to one of the ports at the back of the monitor. One false move and she'd be toast.

AuGenD's online security was second to none. It had cost her several months' salary to get a hacker to design the programs she needed to break through the system's firewall and encryption software from within the company. She loaded up the password finder and was startled to hear it beep barely thirty seconds later. Madeleine raised an eyebrow at the word and numbers that flashed up on the screen.

It seemed Professor Ian Serle was a sentimental man at heart. She had not expected the password to be so simple. He had used his dead son's first name and the date of his funeral.

She opened up the main drive and scrutinized the folders that appeared on the screen. She uploaded another software that would scan for hidden files and was unsurprised when a list populated by eight classified folders appeared under a separate disk after several minutes. They required a further layer of security for access. She clenched her jaw and stared at the secondary external drive sitting on the desk. Her gut instinct had been right.

She took out the other ID card from her pocket, started to insert it in the slot in the hard drive, and hesitated.

The card was an identical copy of the one belonging to Professor Serle's right-hand man and assistant, Dr. Larry Gotenberg. Madeleine had been aware of Gotenberg's interest in her since her first day on the job five years previously. A fortnight ago, she finally took him up on his offer of dinner and drinks. They had gone to the restaurant straight from work. Halfway through the meal, she knocked her wine glass onto his lap. She took his ID from his jacket when he went to the bathroom to clean up and made a duplicate on the digital card copier she had brought in her bag.

Madeleine mentally recited a short prayer, closed her eyes briefly, and slid the pass inside the hard drive slot.

A command prompt sprang open on the screen. She typed in the exact sequence of codes the hacker had taught her and sagged with relief when the prompt disappeared. The classified folders were now accessible. Although she was itching to take a look at their contents to see if they contained any clues about her mother's death, time was not on her side; she had been in Serle's office for just over ten minutes. She selected the folders and copied them to the flash drive. Her heart sank as she watched the bar move ponderously across the download box. The folders contained a lot of data; it would take a few minutes to transfer them across.

She was drumming her fingers beside the computer when a man fell through the ceiling and landed heavily on the floor on the other side of the desk.

'Son of a—' he muttered with a groan.

He crawled onto his knees, winced, and looked up into the barrel of Madeleine's gun.

'Who the hell are you?' she snapped.

Her hands were steady on the weapon while her heart slammed a rapid tempo against her ribs.

The stranger's steel-blue gaze met hers unflinchingly.

She was wondering at his evident lack of apprehension in the face of her loaded pistol when something sharp and cold touched her neck. Madeleine froze. She glanced down and carefully followed the glinting edge of the sword kissing the skin of her throat to a pair of aquamarine eyes that stole her breath away.

'Lower the gun please or my companion will be forced to destroy it,' said the bearded man holding the blade.

His voice sent a shiver down her spine. Madeleine stared, her pulse fluttering with alarm and an entirely unexpected emotion. The man's pupils flared slightly. She licked her suddenly dry lips and saw his eyes drop briefly to her mouth. A hot feeling bloomed low in her belly.

*What in the name of God is going on here?*

She ignored the hammering of her heart, carefully pointed the Sig toward the carpet, and looked past the man's shoulder at the drapes fluttering slightly in the balmy breeze.

*And how the hell did he get in through that window? We're on the fourth floor!*

It was at that moment that a beep sounded from the door.

Before she could make a single move, it opened to reveal Serle and four armed guards. Madeleine recognized Kevin, the watchman, just as she registered the Glock in the professor's hand. She had never seen the other night watchmen.

The men stepped inside the room.

'As luck would have it, I was returning home from visiting a friend when the alarm went off on my phone,' said Serle in a conversational tone. He raised his gun and aimed it squarely at Madeleine's chest while the four guards covered the man rising slowly from the floor and the one holding a sword to her throat. 'It only took me ten minutes to get here.'

Madeleine's stomach lurched. She glanced at the computer. Serle had obviously installed a security program to alert him of any unauthorized access to his hard drives.

*Dammit! I should have anticipated this.*

'And I had such high hopes for you, Madeleine,' Serle continued in the same steady voice. 'Unfortunately, it seems you've inherited your mother's inquisitive nature. Diana was always too curious for her own good.'

Madeleine stiffened. She was out of the chair with her next breath and heard a low hiss of air as the bearded stranger dropped his sword half a second before she decapitated herself on his blade. She glared at Serle. Although her instincts were yelling at her to cool it, years of pent-up fury drowned out the voice of reason.

'What do you know about my mother's death?' she spat out.

The professor smiled faintly and moved to the desk. Madeleine resisted the urge to punch his smug face.

'I guess it was inevitable you would want to find out about your background.' Serle raised a beckoning hand toward her gun. She passed it across reluctantly. 'After all, you age differently than normal humans, don't you, Madeleine?'

She barely noticed the surprised glances the men who had broken into Serle's office cast her way. She stared into the scientist's deep-set eyes and knew without a doubt that he held the answers she had long sought. Her hands fisted by her sides, nails digging so hard into her palms she drew blood.

Kevin reached for the radio clipped to his left shoulder and was about to depress a button when Serle turned and looked at him.

'What are you doing?' said the professor curiously.

'Asking Hank to phone the cops. We need to call this—'

The report of the Sig made Madeleine jump. The bearded stranger grabbed her shoulder and pulled her behind him. The man who had fallen through the ceiling took a step forward, muscles jumping in his jaw.

A crimson patch bloomed on Kevin's uniform, over the left side of his chest. He blinked, looked at the rapidly expanding circle of red, and collapsed to the floor with a puzzled expression. The other guards moved out of the way of his falling body, faces impassive and guns still trained on the two male intruders.

Madeleine's throat and chest tightened. She realized she was holding her breath. Her eyes remained locked on Kevin's face while a silent scream of denial echoed inside her head.

'Make it look like she killed him,' Serle told the three guards Madeleine didn't recognize. He pulled a handkerchief from his pocket, carefully wiped the Sig, and dropped the gun by the dead man's feet. He studied the two men who had broken into his office. 'Now, who are you and what are you doing here?' He aimed his Glock at the guy who had dropped in from the ceiling. 'I would like some answers before I start shooting you in the knees.'

The stranger's expression darkened. 'I don't think we're going to get any more out of this bastard, do you?'

'I agree,' said his bearded companion.

Coldness flooded Madeleine. The guards with Serle looked like killers. The reality of the situation was beginning to sink in; the three of them were not going to make it out of there alive.

Despite this undeniable fact, the demeanor of the intruders remained relaxed. Her fear slowly abated. If they could face death so calmly, then so could she.

A condescending smile curved Serle's thin lips. He cocked an eyebrow at the two men. 'You seriously think you have the upper hand here?'

'You'd be surprised at what we can do,' said the guy with the steel-blue eyes.

# CHAPTER FOURTEEN

Confusion danced across Serle's face a second before he lost all color. 'You are immor—'

It was as far as he got. The Glock in his hand, the weapons in the guards' grips, and her Sig all crumpled into twisted, gray balls. The desk sagged as the metal legs supporting the thick sheet of glass buckled. The computer monitor and the secondary hard drive started to slide across the angled surface.

Madeleine leapt forward and stayed their fall. She noted their crushed edges almost absent-mindedly in the stunned silence that ensued.

'Oops,' muttered Steel Blue.

Madeleine's pulse thrummed rapidly in her ears as she followed his contrite gaze to the distorted sword in the bearded man's grasp.

The latter sighed. 'Just fix it later.'

Time unfroze.

The three guards dropped their mangled guns and charged across the floor. Serle backed hastily out of the room behind them, panic etched sharply in the lines of his face. He turned and ran.

Light glinted on the edge of a wickedly-curved knife as it arced through the air toward Madeleine's face. The fingers of her left hand closed over the flash drive at the same time that the bearded man grabbed the collar of her shirt and yanked her backward. The guard's knife met the twisted remains of his sword with a clang. The computer and the hard drive slid off the edge of the desk and crashed to the floor.

Across the way, Steel Blue delivered a brutal hook punch to another guard's face.

The bearded man dropped his sword, spun on his heels, and jabbed his elbow sharply toward his attacker's throat. The guard deflected the blow with his palm at the last moment.

Madeleine saw the third guard's knife swing up to stab her savior in the ribs. She brought her left leg up and hook-kicked the blade from his hand just as it was crushed by an invisible force into an unrecognizable lump of metal. The guard stumbled backward and gripped his wrist, his expression deadly as his gaze flicked to the man with the steel-blue eyes.

The latter was grinning.

A glimmer of understanding dawned in Madeleine's mind. Steel Blue was the one responsible for the damaged guns, desk, and knife.

*But how?*

There was motion to her left. She bobbed out of the way of the guard's uppercut, delivered a lightning-fast knee thrust to his abdomen, and brought her elbow down sharply at the base of his neck when he doubled over. The man let out a throaty gurgle and fell to the ground.

The bearded man glanced at her, his eyes flaring slightly.

Madeleine flashed a fierce grin his way. She had trained long and hard over the years for the eventuality of this mission; she knew how to defend herself.

The bearded man dropped beneath another guard's swinging foot, punched him in the gut as he came up, grabbed the back of the guy's head, and slammed his face onto the tilted desk. The tempered glass cracked with the force of the blow. Blood spurted from the guard's broken nose and busted lips, his eyes fluttering closed as he lost consciousness.

'Well, I think we're done here, don't you?' Steel Blue said across the way.

He dusted his hands and nudged the still body of the guard at his feet with his boot.

'Indeed.'

The bearded stranger picked up his sword off the floor and slid it with some difficulty into the scabbard strapped to his back.

Steel Blue studied the damaged computer and hard drive. 'Looks like we're not gonna get our hands on Serle's data after all.'

His words surprised Madeleine.

*These guys are also after the information on Serle's private drives?*

Sirens rose in the distance, distracting her. She moved to the window and peered through the drapes. Flashing lights appeared over a rise to the southwest.

Serle must have called the cops after all.

'We've got two minutes, tops,' she said tensely over her shoulder. 'If it's information you're after, I've got some.' She opened her left hand and showed them the flash drive. 'I'll share what I know if you help me get out of here.'

The two men assessed her for a moment before exchanging cautious glances. Steel Blue shrugged.

The bearded stranger hesitated. 'Let's go.'

She looked down at the hand he proffered. Her fingers rose automatically to his.

Heat flashed along her arm when their skin made contact. His hand twitched around hers. Before she could fathom the expression in his stunning eyes, he turned and dragged her toward the door.

Madeleine glanced at the twisted remains of her Sig with a sinking feeling; there was no point retrieving the weapon now. Her gaze moved to the dead guard. Remorse stabbed through her. Although she wasn't the one who had pulled the trigger, she felt responsible for Kevin's death.

They saw no sign of the professor when they exited the office. Steel Blue took the lead and turned left. They made their way along a brightly-lit corridor toward the back of the building and came to a junction.

'This way!'

She indicated the passage to the left and tugged on the bearded man's hand.

'Where does this go?' he said gruffly.

'Service stairs to the basement car park!'

'Sounds good to me,' muttered Steel Blue.

They crossed a series of empty passages, turned a corner, and spied the exit at the end of a narrow hallway. Madeleine half expected to see more guards materialize in their path when they shouldered through the fire door into a dimly-lit concrete stairwell. They raced down the staircase two steps at a time. A cavernous, dark underground space opened up before them beyond the door at the bottom.

'Where's your ride?' said Madeleine.

'Tucked down a side street five hundred feet northwest of here,' said Steel Blue.

A visual map of the area flashed across her mind's inner eye. She scowled. 'Shit! That's a lot of exposed ground to cover!'

She turned and moved rapidly toward a fire exit at the head of a flight of steps to the left. Moonlight greeted them when they emerged into the deserted, south-facing parking lot. They were a third of the way to the chain-link fence that guarded the grounds of AuGenD when a squeal of tires rose from the far right.

There was movement at the edge of her vision. Three black

and white San Diego PD Ford Crown Victoria squad cars skidded into view around the corner of the building.

'Ethan!' barked the bearded man.

'I'm on it!'

Steel Blue staggered to a stop and raised his left hand palm facing out toward the vehicles barreling across the asphalt.

A series of pops echoed across the parking lot. For a second, Madeleine thought the cops had opened fire.

The wheels flew off the cars. Sparks erupted as the vehicles dropped down onto their axles and skidded to a stop in an ear-splitting shriek of grinding metal.

'Whoa!' Steel Blue looked at his hand as if he was seeing it for the first time. 'I could get used to this.'

'Move, boy!' shouted the bearded man.

His grip tightened around Madeleine's hand as they sprinted for the fence line. She had no option but to follow, her mind reeling from what she had witnessed.

*You can worry about that shit later, Black! Just focus on getting your ass out of here first!*

They were at the barrier within seconds. The bearded man pushed through a cut section at the bottom and pulled her after him. Steel Blue was close behind them. Warning shouts sounded in the night. Footsteps pounded the asphalt as the cops gave chase.

They came to a steep incline and scrambled down the dirt slope to the road at the bottom. They headed left and took a sharp right some eighty feet later. A single gunshot shattered the air above their heads as they charged along a tree-lined street. A black Jeep was parked in the shadow of a warehouse halfway down the right-hand curb.

'Give me the keys!' shouted Madeleine as they approached the vehicle at a dead run.

'Why?' said Steel Blue.

'Unless you know this place like the back of your hand, I suggest you let me drive!'

Metal glimmered on her left. Madeleine caught the Jeep keys mid-flight and depressed the button on the fob. The Jeep's lights flashed as the locks disengaged.

Bullets zinged off the asphalt inches from their heels. The bearded man let go of her hand. Madeleine dashed around to the driver's side, yanked the door open, and leapt inside. She started the engine while the two men were still getting in, switched into reverse, and stepped on the gas before the doors slammed shut. The Jeep shot backward along the road.

Up ahead, five San Diego PD officers stumbled to a halt, widened their stance, and raised their guns in double-handed grips. The muzzles of their weapons flashed. The sound of gunfire reached Madeleine above the screaming engine and the rush of blood in her ears.

A couple of bullets glanced off the Jeep's right bumper.

Steel Blue grunted in the rear seat. The policemen dropped their guns as if they'd been stung and took several hasty steps back. Although she couldn't see well enough from the distance, Madeleine guessed the weapons were now useless, distorted lumps of metal.

'That's a neat trick,' she said grimly. 'You're gonna have to teach me that one day.'

'I'm afraid it comes with the blood,' Steel Blue mumbled.

She glanced in the passenger-side mirror, saw what she was looking for, took her foot off the gas, and twisted the steering wheel sharply to the right.

The Jeep lurched around with a sickening screech of burning rubber. The bearded man slammed into the window. There was a thud and a curse from the back seat as Steel Blue was flung against the door.

Madeleine waited until the vehicle almost stopped spinning, changed gears, and floored the accelerator. The Jeep lurched forward. She took a sharp left into the narrow back alley at the end of the street. Moonlight illuminated the deserted landscape populated by chaparral and scattered groves beyond the chain-link fence to their right.

She was formulating an escape route out of the valley when the shrill sound of sirens came from the left. Madeleine glanced between the buildings they were passing and spied a pair of patrol cars racing parallel to them along the main road. One of them veered into a side street and charged toward the Jeep.

A fence appeared at the end of the alley up ahead.

There was motion in the rearview mirror. The patrol car swung in behind the Jeep.

Madeleine stepped on the gas and gripped the steering wheel tightly. 'Hang on!'

The bearded man braced himself against the dashboard and the roof a second before they crashed through the barrier. The fence peeled away from its supporting columns. The Jeep lifted briefly off the ground before juddering back down with a jolt. She navigated around a copse of trees, barreled through some bushes, and burst out onto a patch of open ground.

'You guys better put those seat belts on,' she warned.

'Why?' came the suspicious query from the backseat.

The bearded man had seen what was coming. He glanced at her with an expression that Madeleine chose to interpret as admiration.

'Just do as she says,' he told Steel Blue.

She clipped her own belt across her body, braked gently, dropped gear, and aimed the nose of the Jeep at the edge of the cliff one hundred feet ahead. The second patrol car had joined the first one chasing them. The gap between pursued and pursuers narrowed.

Madeleine's stomach lurched when the ground disappeared beneath the Jeep's wheels. The four-by-four sailed through the air before bouncing onto the angled wall of a concrete culvert.

She felt the vehicle start to slide, corrected the angle of the spinning axles with a flick of her wrist, and let out the breath she had been holding when they bumped onto the base of the tunnel. She veered west and accelerated.

'Where'd you learn to drive like that, Mata Hari?' said Steel Blue.

Before she could phrase a reply, a loud crash sounded behind them. The first patrol car had taken the drop too fast and landed smack down on its front bumper. The vehicle rocked for a moment before tilting over and falling onto its roof.

The driver of the second patrol car proved to be the smarter man. He negotiated the edge of the cliff as carefully as Madeleine had and was soon giving chase once more. She scowled and concentrated on the lay of the land coming up.

The culvert ended some two miles away, on the side of one of the canyons that flanked the hilly valley where AuGenD was situated. At the bottom lay a stream that joined up with the San Diego River and a field of deadly rocks. One hundred feet before the fatal drop, the north side of the tunnel sloped gently back up to the floor of the basin.

Madeleine knew she would have one shot to get it right. She put as much distance between the Jeep and the pursuing patrol car as she could, leaned over the steering wheel, and peered into the gloom.

The finish line appeared all too soon, an insubstantial light-ening of the darkness ahead where moonlight shone across the opposite side of the gorge.

She dropped into third and turned the Jeep toward the north wall. The tires gripped the angled concrete smoothly. The engine screamed under the hood as the vehicle ascended the side of the culvert.

She was starting to think they were going to make it when the front right tire canted and lifted off the ground. The Jeep started to tilt and slide. The man beside her leaned across and steadied the steering wheel slipping through her grip.

'Floor it!' he barked.

Madeleine complied with the command gladly.

They were over the lip of the tunnel a heartbeat later and bounded sharply onto the ground parallel to the culvert.

Brakes squealed at the bottom of the channel to their left. The patrol car had gone into a wild skid and was headed inexorably toward the gully.

She brought the Jeep to a halt in a cloud of dirt. 'Shit.'

Steel Blue moved in the corner of her vision. He pressed his hands against the window and stared at the spinning vehicle below. Lines furrowed his brow.

The patrol car slowed, tires leaving layers of rubber on the concrete.

Madeleine gasped. She glanced at Steel Blue.

*How the hell is he doing that?*

The vehicle looked like it might stop before it reached the cliff edge. Madeleine started to breathe a sigh of relief. It froze in her throat when the back end of the car slipped over the abyss. It started to tilt inexorably.

Just as it was about to drop into the gorge, the front end of the vehicle slammed down onto the concrete, pushed by an invisible force. Sparks flew underneath the carriage as it was dragged forcibly forward.

A grunt escaped Steel Blue's lips. Muscles corded in his neck.

The rear tires of the car rolled up onto solid ground a heartbeat later. It rocked to a stop some five feet from the canyon. The two officers in the front seats sat frozen, eyes wide in ashen faces as they braced themselves against the dashboard.

Steel Blue released a shaky breath and leaned his forehead against the window. His breaths fogged up the glass.

'Let's go, Tarzan,' he murmured.

The bearded man watched his companion silently, his expression enigmatic.

Madeleine swallowed and drove off into the night. It wasn't until the sound of sirens had disappeared behind them and they'd cleared the boundaries of the city that she pulled over in a deserted lay-by off a narrow, backcountry road.

She turned and stared at the two strangers. 'Who *are* you people?'

# CHAPTER FIFTEEN

*Dearest Olivia, if you are reading this, then one of two things has happened. It has either become necessary for me to finally tell you all that I know about who you are and how you ended up at the abbey all those years ago, or the unthinkable has taken place and I have passed from this world. I hope it's the former, although I very much fear it is probably the latter.*

Although she had promised herself she would not cry, Olivia could not help the tears that dropped silently onto the pages of Mother Edwards's diaries.

Asgard and Ethan had given her the volumes they had rescued from the abbey before they left on their mission to infiltrate the facility in San Diego. She sat next to the south-facing glass wall in the sunken living room beyond the foyer, the journals spread out on the floor around her. Moonlight cast a pale glow over the dark canyon and the distant sea to her left. It was gone midnight.

Mother Edwards wrote about how Olivia's parents had appeared on the doorstep of the abbey one winter night in 1913, a sleeping baby girl in tow. Despite their disheveled appearance, it was evident from their words and their bearings that they were of noble birth. Natalia related how she had come to know of Margaret Edwards through another immortal she had met in Florence. In the precious few hours that they spent at the abbey, Natalia and Kristof told the nun their incredible history and the stormy paths their fates had taken. They spoke of Jonah Krondike and Kronos and asked the nun to write down all they had revealed so that their daughter could read their tales in the future.

When Mother Edwards questioned why they trusted her, a complete stranger they had just met, so implicitly with their secrets, Natalia finally broke down and cried. With Kristof holding her in his arms, his own eyes shimmering with unshed tears, the Seer told the nun about the vision she had had of a grown-up Olivia at the abbey. It was at that point that she knew she and her husband would not live to raise their daughter.

'You will give her as much love as I would have, this I am certain of,' Natalia told the nun brokenly.

Olivia's mother had already seen her own death and that of her soulmate. She explained to Mother Edwards that although she had taken steps to influence the course of such events in the past, nature had mostly always taken its course. Before the couple left at dawn, Natalia warned Mother Edwards about the abilities that would manifest themselves when Olivia turned eighteen.

'Tell her not to be afraid of her powers,' Kristof whispered as he cradled the sleeping Olivia in his arms for the final time. He kissed her brow and smiled tremulously when she stirred under his touch. 'Let her know how special she is.'

Mother Edwards had quoted Natalia's final words to her. *"If an immortal with an unusual birthmark of a five-pointed star ever comes to the abbey, you must let Olivia leave with him. She is meant to be with that person."*

Olivia's breath hitched in her throat. She reread the

sentence twice over, unable to believe the evidence of her own eyes. *Had Natalia known about Ethan Storm even then?*

She stared blindly beyond the glass, her mind reeling. Asgard's assertion about Ethan being her soulmate had been correct after all. As the implication of this truth resonated inside her, Olivia flushed. She had never experienced a kiss, let alone touched a man.

She suddenly recalled the immortal's tanned, wet skin that morning when he had come in from his swim. Her mouth went dry and the muscles in her belly clenched. She ignored the pounding of her heart and grabbed the next journal hastily. It took a few seconds for her to see the words swimming before her.

The rest of Mother Edwards's diaries formed a chronicle of her own pureblood immortal-human lineage, her life at the abbey, and notable events concerning her young ward. The nun described her own beginnings in a remote village in south Italy, where she had come to learn about her incredible origins shortly after she entered adulthood. She received the calling to join the Church on her first visit to Rome and took her vows in the years that followed. She stayed in Italy for almost a century, moved to France, and finally settled in North America in the late 1800s. She had been the abbess at the Bear River Mountain order for nearly two decades when Natalia and Kristof turned up on that fateful night.

Olivia froze when she reached the end of the last journal. Taped inside the rear cover was a small envelope. She stared at the yellow, faded paper. Her first name was inscribed on the front in an elegant, flowing script.

She knew without a doubt that she was looking at her mother's handwriting.

She flicked through the previous diaries and noted the faint marks at the back. Mother Edwards had placed the envelope inside every journal, as if fearing the one she was writing at the time would be the final one. Which meant she had wanted Olivia to see the envelope last.

Her fingers trembled as she carefully detached the precious package from its anchor. She ran a finger under the seal without tearing the envelope and lifted the flap. A single folded page lay inside. She slipped it out.

Something fell from within and landed in her lap. It was a silver locket attached to a fine chain. Olivia picked it up and studied the symbol engraved in the middle of the fine filigree on the front. It was identical to the birthmark on her hand. Blood thrummed in her ears when she opened the metal case. Two black and white pictures were pasted inside of the lids.

They depicted the faces of a smiling man and woman.

The photographs blurred. Olivia wiped away fresh tears and studied the pictures with hungry eyes.

Kristof Kovach and Natalia Ashkarov looked happy. And Asgard had been right; Olivia was the image of her mother. She unfolded the sheet of paper and read the dedication written on it.

*With all of our love.*

*Be strong, our precious child.*

*You are not alone.*

A sob escaped Olivia's lips then. She dropped her head against the glass and allowed the tears to fall freely.

*One last time. I will cry one last time. Then no more.*

It was several minutes before she took a deep, shuddering breath to steady herself.

She placed the paper inside the envelope, unfastened the silver cross from around her neck, and slipped on the locket. It settled just above the valley between her breasts, the metal cool against her skin.

Something stirred deep inside of her. The feeling was akin to the one she had experienced back at the abbey, when the assassin's hands were squeezing the life out of her, and more recently still after her uncle's revelations the night before. Olivia now grasped what Asgard Godard and Ethan Storm must have gone through in all the years that they had been trying to thwart Jonah Krondike.

Her fingers curled into fists. Anger filled her core and spilled through her veins. With it came a single-minded resolve. She would do her utmost to help them defeat the immortal who had inflicted so much loss and misery upon their lives.

A sound from the other side of the lounge drew her gaze. Howard came out of a corridor and paused at the rear of the foyer.

'They're back.'

Alarm darted through Olivia at the expression on his face. 'What's wrong?'

She rose from the floor.

'They brought someone with them,' the Crovir immortal replied.

They were halfway up the entrance hall when the front door of the mansion opened.

Asgard walked in. 'Are you certain you've put Armistad back just the way he was?'

Her uncle examined his arming sword with an anxious expression.

'Yes, for the tenth time, I'm *sure!*' Ethan snapped behind him. 'Jesus, you'd think that goddamned sword was your flesh and blood!'

A tall, pretty brunette with pale, blue-gray eyes stepped into view. She was wearing jeans, a T-shirt, and sneakers. She paused near the doorway and looked around.

'Nice pad,' she said guardedly.

'Thanks,' said Howard.

Her head snapped around. She watched him stroll across the foyer.

The Crovir immortal extended a hand. 'Howard Titus.'

The young woman hesitated before shaking it. 'Madeleine Black.'

Howard's cool gaze shifted to Asgard and Ethan. 'What happened?'

~

'DIANA HOLLENBROOKS WAS YOUR MOTHER?'

Asgard stared at Madeleine Black, shock reverberating through him.

It was two o'clock in the morning. They were in the lounge of the bunker. Howard had brewed a fresh pot of coffee and brought a tray with cups to the low table between the chairs.

The woman they had surprised in Ian Serle's office stiffened on the edge of her seat. 'Did you know her?'

Asgard glanced at Ethan. 'Yes. She was one of the scientists who worked in Jonah Krondike's research facility in New Mexico.'

He thought he detected some of Diana Hollenbrooks's features in her daughter's face. He had known the scientist for almost a decade until her sudden disappearance a couple of years before he escaped the army base with Ethan. She had been the kindest person among all of Krondike's subordinates, treating the prisoners with as much dignity as her masters allowed.

Lines creased Madeleine's brow. 'Krondike?'

Asgard studied her for a moment. He sensed her puzzlement was genuine. The fact that Serle had attempted to kill her was also proof that she was not on the enemy's side.

'What do you know of your mother's work?'

Madeleine shrugged. 'She graduated *Magna Cum Laude* from Stanford University and got her post doctorate in Molecular Genetics at Cornell. She was involved in a classified project for the US government in the 1960s. I think she was murdered because of what she knew.'

Silence fell across the room.

'How did your mother die?' said Olivia.

Asgard scanned his niece's face. He could tell something had changed in the way she held herself and spoke. Though still quiet, she was not the self-effacing young woman he had saved from the abbey nearly two days ago. Instead, she seemed... harder, somehow. As if an underlying current of steel now permeated her every movement and word.

'Single gunshot to the head, right between the eyes,' said Madeleine. Her tone was cold and clinical. 'It was a contract kill. Her body was discovered in an underground parking lot in Denver. Cops never found the killer. This was in 1986. I was eighteen at the time and hadn't seen my mother in almost ten years.' She looked from her cup of steaming black coffee to the kitchen. 'Got anything stronger?'

Howard brought a bottle of Scotch across. Madeleine poured a generous amount in her drink, took a sip, grimaced, and set the cup down.

'She left me in the care of the state when I was eight. I woke up one morning and she was gone.' A trace of old bitterness underscored her words for a moment. 'I didn't have any next-of-kin that I knew of and she never told me who my father was. She set up a trust fund in my name, enough money to see me through college and beyond. At the time she abandoned me, I hated her with every fiber of my being.' She swallowed. 'It wasn't until the package arrived that I realized why she did it.'

'Package?' said Howard.

Madeleine nodded. 'A month after I turned eighteen, a man came to see me at the foster home where I was living. I was all packed up and ready for college. The guy was from a law firm in New York. Turns out my mother entrusted them with a sealed envelope the year she disappeared, with instructions to deliver it to me upon her death. Inside it were copies of the work she had been involved in. There was also a note.' Her expression turned bleak. 'It seems she'd accidentally crossed paths with a former associate shortly before she vanished. She left because she didn't want her ex-employer to know about my existence. It was the only way she could think to keep me safe from harm.' She stared blindly at her hands. 'I was going to be majoring in Mechanical Engineering. I changed to Biological Sciences and went on to do post doctorate degrees in Molecular Genetics and Genomics. By that point, I'd long realized that my mother's work centered around some kind of genetic research for the US government. For years I looked desperately for a clue, a link, anything that could point me to something or someone from her past. I eventually found a connection between the papers she had left me and an old research article Ian Serle had published. It bore a striking similarity to some of my mother's data.' She faltered. 'By then, I had also started to wonder why I still looked the same as I did when I was eighteen.'

Asgard realized she was holding back on something. He wondered fleetingly why he could read this woman as if he'd known her for years rather than a handful of hours.

'What is it that you're not telling us?'

Madeleine looked at him for a silent moment, her face haunted. 'How did you know?'

Asgard did not answer.

She took a deep breath. 'You're right. My mother mentioned something else in the note. It was so absurd that I didn't know what to make of it at the time and I still don't.'

Ethan leaned forward. 'What was it?'

'She said that she was the descendant of the offspring of a human and a race of—' Madeleine pursed her lips for a moment, 'of immortals who have walked the Earth since the dawn of mankind.' She paused. A self-deprecating chuckle escaped her. 'Crazy, right? When I realized that I did not age like, well, normal people, I started to wonder whether I was the result of the genetic experiments she had been involved in. I assumed the fanciful tale was just a cover. So I ran some tests.'

'What kind of tests?' said Asgard.

'I analyzed my DNA.'

Asgard exchanged an alarmed look with Ethan and Howard. 'And?' said Ethan.

The woman closed her eyes briefly. 'Turns out I have a bit too much of the good stuff.'

Howard cocked an eyebrow. 'Meaning?'

'I have extra sections of certain chromosomes, the most significant one being chromosome four, which is associated with longevity. The changes are subtle and I didn't pick up on them the first time. It wasn't until I carried out detailed molecular analysis on my samples that I had several sobering *Eureka* moments. In addition to having too much DNA, I also appear to be a mosaic, with a combination of different genetic material within my cells.'

Madeleine rubbed the back of her neck. 'I decided to follow up on Serle and got a job in AuGenD five years ago. It didn't take long to figure out that there was something strange going on at the company. There were plenty of rumors flying about in the scientific community that they had received substantial private contracts from the DoD over the years. Dr. Larry Gotenberg, Serle's assistant, mentioned that the professor had extra layers of security on his computer no one else in the company possessed. Larry was given access to it two months ago. Seems Serle decided to bring him into the fold.'

She propped her elbows on her knees and dropped her chin on her interlocked hands. 'Larry was very ambitious. He worshipped Serle. He'd always shown an interest in me but he got more aggressive about a month ago.' She scowled. 'Now that I think about it, I wonder whether the old bastard put him up to it. I don't know how Serle found out I was Diana Hollenbrooks's daughter. I changed my name to Black when I was eighteen.'

'So you decided to break into Serle's computer to find out what was on it?' said Howard.

Madeleine nodded. 'I copied Larry's ID two weeks ago. Of course, I knew I'd need more than that to access Serle's private drives. Breaking inside AuGenD's computer network is like getting into Fort Knox.'

'More like the Pentagon,' said Howard. He smiled at Madeleine's expression. 'Fort Knox was like stealing milk from a baby. Took me almost two days to crack the Pentagon's codes.'

Madeleine glanced at the glass wall on the right. The edge of one of the computer workstations was just about visible.

'Right,' she drawled. 'Well, I got someone to write some programs to get into the company's systems.'

Howard raised an eyebrow. 'A guy from Milwaukee?'

Madeleine stiffened. 'Atlanta, actually.'

'Ah,' Howard muttered. 'The Prince.'

Madeleine's eyes shrunk to slits. 'How'd you know that?'

'The Prince is part of my extended network of...experts.' Howard grinned. 'Just so you know, there's nothing princely about The Prince. He's a five-foot-four, three-hundred-pound, pasty-faced guy who lives in his mother's basement.' The immortal shrugged. 'Smart and sweet as hell. Made enough money to buy himself ten luxury condos. Still, Mama's home is where he wants to be.'

Madeleine considered this for a moment before removing the flash drive from her jeans. 'I think I managed to download almost everything on Serle's computer and external drive.' Her knuckles whitened on the stick. 'The stuff on here might finally reveal what I am.'

'I doubt that,' said Asgard.

The woman's head snapped up. She glared at him. 'What makes you say that?'

Something shifted inside Asgard's chest. He clenched his teeth and ignored his body's reaction to Diana Hollenbrooks's daughter, feeling somewhat betrayed by his own senses.

'You've seen enough tonight to realize that we are not ordinary humans.' He watched the color drain from Madeleine Black's face. 'Your mother told you the truth. She was the descendant of a pureblood immortal-human offspring, a half-breed who can age at a quarter the rate of an average immortal. And I believe I know who your father was. Among the immortals that Jonah Krondike captured for his experiments was a Bastian noble by the name of Edouard De Castel. Diana Hollenbrooks was in love with him.'

Asgard paused. 'You have his eyes.'

# CHAPTER SIXTEEN

Jonah Krondike ended the call and put the phone back down on the mahogany table.

Ian Serle sounded shaken by what he had seen.

The professor had been working with Krondike since the mid 1980s, after Jonah identified him as someone who could be of significant benefit to his research program. Serle's son had died while serving in the US Armed Forces. In the months that followed, the professor made it bitterly clear among the scientific community and in the acrimonious letters he sent to Congress that he thought much more could have been done to prepare American soldiers for battle. Jonah approached Serle a year after his son's death and convinced him to join his team. After being told exactly what would happen to him if he ever betrayed their trust, the professor was brought into the fold.

It took the man a while to get over the reality of the immortals' existence and that of the half-breed race that had been in Krondike's service since the 1300s. When Jonah executed an immortal in front of him and the man revived, Serle finally accepted the unpalatable truth. Although he was aware of the special abilities possessed by a handful of pureblood immortals, he had never met one until tonight. Seeing Ethan Storm perform at close range had rattled the scientist.

They had known Madeleine Black's true identity ever since she joined AuGenD. Every new member of the company underwent a thorough background check and a medical as part of the hiring process. Their genetic material was tested without their knowledge to see if it matched any of the ones in the comprehensive database that Jonah's team had built over the years.

Madeleine Black's DNA had identified her as the daughter of Diana Hollenbrooks and Edouard De Castel.

Jonah had been aware of Hollenbrooks's interest in the French immortal who had been captured and brought to the research facility in New Mexico in the 1960s, but had not given it much more thought at the time. With Asgard Godard finally in his grasp and the US Army demanding faster results following their investments in the cutting-edge experimental research Jonah's group was conducting, the Crovir noble had more urgent matters to deal with. It wasn't until Hollenbrooks vanished from the military complex days after De Castel's death that he realized the true extent of her involvement with the Bastian immortal. Diana Hollenbrooks had been secretly bribing guards to gain secure, private access to De Castel's cell. Jonah discovered that she even attempted to help the prisoner break free once but never made it outside the complex.

She had been plotting another escape when De Castel died during one of the radiation experiments.

Hollenbrooks reappeared on Jonah's radar briefly in 1976, when she was spotted in a shopping mall in Houston by one of the scientists she had previously worked with. Ten years later, an informant told them Hollenbrooks had been nosing around and gathering evidence on the work Jonah and his rogue US Army had been conducting. The Crovir noble issued an immediate kill order for her.

Although the scientist who spotted Hollenbrooks in 1976

mentioned seeing a dark-haired child with her, Jonah did not make the connection with Madeleine Black until the young woman turned up in AuGenD's employee records and her genetic fingerprint revealed who she was.

Instead of bringing her in for questioning, Jonah asked Serle to keep an eye on the immortal half-breed.

For Madeleine Black's DNA had disclosed more than just her parents' genetic material. As far as he was aware, no one else on Earth possessed her specific genetic profile. She was too unique a specimen to dispose of.

It also quickly became evident that Black had inherited her mother's keen intellect. Diana Hollenbrooks had been a member of Kronos since her birth and one of his best researchers until her sudden disappearance. Jonah was not one to waste valuable resources. To test where Black's loyalties lay and whether she could be a candidate for his research team, Jonah requested that Serle's assistant court her.

Tonight's events had shown all too clearly that Madeleine Black's allegiance was with their enemy. Jonah tapped a finger against his thigh as he pondered a puzzling question.

*How did Godard and Storm end up in AuGenD?*

He mulled the matter over as he made his way to the army base's primary command center. Mark Scoleri stood next to one of the computer terminals spanning the width of the concrete shelter located half a mile beneath the desert. Jonah strolled leisurely to the Crovir Hunter's side.

'Anything yet?'

'The last location we have from the chip on her phone was somewhere north of San Diego. We lost the signal when her battery went dead. It's powered by the device. Once she charges the phone and turns it on, we'll have her. She's disabled her GPS, so she thinks she's safe.'

Scoleri grinned. There was no humor in his smile.

'Good. The second you confirm her location, send in a full

assault team.' Jonah paused. 'The general should be able to get us extra men from the nearest base.'

Scoleri's eyes gleamed. 'We'll get prepped.'

Jonah watched the Crovir Hunter leave the room. Having Black escape with Godard and Storm had turned out to be a blessing in disguise. If everything went as planned, he would have the Elemental and the Seer in his lab by the end of the day.

ETHAN STEPPED OUT ONTO THE TERRACE ADJOINING THE mansion's kitchen. A haze hung over the distant Pacific Ocean to the south. Above it, the sky was a dazzling blue.

Madeleine Black stood at the edge of the patio and stared out over the canyon. Her hands were tucked in the pockets of her jeans and her shoulders drooped. She wore a fresh T-shirt she had borrowed from Olivia's new wardrobe. The garment stretched across her body, a size too small.

A sliver of pity flashed through him; he doubted the woman had slept much. He recalled the horror on her face last night when Asgard had related the reality of the immortals' existence and their influence on human civilizations over several millennia. When the Bastian noble spoke of their own personal histories and described what Jonah Krondike and Kronos had attempted to do in the last seven centuries, including the brutal experiments in New Mexico, Ethan had seen shocked resignation finally dawn in her eyes.

'You believe this Jonah guy had something to do with my mother's murder?' she said in the frozen silence that fell across the bunker.

'We know how Jonah works,' said Asgard. 'He might as well have pulled the trigger himself.'

A muscle jumped in Madeleine Black's cheek. She stared at the floor. 'I need some time to process this.'

Howard had shown the woman to one of the guest suites before heading back to the bunker's lift.

'You need to get some rest,' Ethan told him curtly.

'I'll catch some sleep down there.' Howard shrugged. 'Might as well get working on that flash drive.'

A noise brought Ethan back to the present. He looked over his shoulder and saw Olivia walk out into the sunlight. She slowed when she spotted him, her expression somewhat wary.

'Hi,' she murmured.

He bobbed his head in acknowledgement. Asgard was a few seconds behind his niece.

Ethan's gaze shifted to Olivia once more. There was something...different about her. He had noticed it since their return last night and sensed Asgard's awareness of the change. She had shown them the locket she had found in the abbess's diaries before she retired for the evening. Asgard had studied the faces of his dead friends for the longest time, a melancholic smile hovering on his lips.

Madeleine Black turned at the sound of their steps. Instead of looking tired and dejected, Ethan saw unwavering determination in her eyes and the rigid lines of her jaw. Admiration darted through him. This woman was a survivor through and through.

'We need to see what's on that flash drive,' she said stiffly.

Before any of the immortals could utter a response, Howard strolled out of the house, a laptop in hand.

'Put the coffee on,' he told Ethan. 'This shit changes everything.'

Asgard frowned. 'What is it?'

Ethan headed inside the mansion and came out a short time later with cups and a steaming pot of freshly-brewed coffee. Rosa and Bernard had gone shopping for the morning.

'What'd I miss?' Ethan said.

Asgard sighed. 'Not much. Howard is basking in his own genius.'

Howard grunted from where he sat at the table. 'I'd like to see you have a go at this stuff, Ice Man.'

Madeleine was scowling. 'So, let me get this straight—what you're saying is that the files were protected by additional layers of security and you accidentally fried a third of the data while you were trying to decode it?'

Howard shrugged. 'Look at it this way. If *you'd* attempted it, you would have lost everything.'

Madeleine swore and ran her fingers through her hair. 'What the hell did I go through all that trouble for?'

'Don't feel so sorry for yourself,' said Howard magnanimously. 'I backed them up first.'

Ethan could practically hear Madeleine Black's patience tick toward an explosive meltdown.

'You know, you could have started with that in the first place,' she said between gritted teeth.

'You're an ass, Howard,' said Asgard.

A giggle broke the tense silence.

Olivia pursed her lips and muttered a quiet, 'Sorry.'

'Ah, a woman after my own heart.' Howard sighed. 'If I didn't know for a fact that your uncle would stab me repeatedly in the heart with that damn sword of his, I'd make a serious play for you. Besides, it figures that the one woman I might be remotely interested in in almost a hundred years is already promised to my best friend.' He grimaced. 'I might as well have the word "wingman" tattooed on my forehead.'

Olivia blushed.

Ethan's gut twisted with a sudden, hot feeling. Shock resonated through him when he realized it was jealousy. *What the hell?*

Madeleine raised an eyebrow, her gaze shifting between Olivia and Ethan. 'Oh. You two are an item?'

'No.'

Ethan had to bite back the words *not yet* before they left his lips.

'They're soulmates,' said Asgard.

The Bastian immortal was giving him an inscrutable look.

Madeleine wrinkled her nose. 'What's that, some kind of cryptic immortal destiny stuff?'

'You're not far off,' said Asgard.

He explained about immortal soulmates and the irrefutable bonds that existed between them. 'However much someone might want to deny that fact, in the end, fate will always win out.'

Ethan sensed the Bastian immortal had directed the last statement at him. He shifted uncomfortably.

Madeleine observed Asgard for a silent beat. 'These soulmates, you're only meant to have the one?'

'Yes.'

'Hmm,' she muttered. 'Interesting.'

'We done with the maudlin crap?' said Howard.

Asgard grunted. Ethan shrugged.

'Before we start, I should let you know that you've made the NCIC and Interpol's lists of wanted criminals,' Howard told the two men. He brought up the agencies' websites. 'Not only are you the prime suspects in the massacre at the abbey, you're also suspected of killing the guard at AuGenD. Madeleine will undoubtedly join your ranks before nightfall.' He glanced at the Seer. 'Krondike hasn't been able to pin anything on Olivia, so she's still being treated as a hostage. For now.'

Ethan frowned at the composite drawings featured on the wanted pages. Asgard's face had gone stormy. They had expected nothing less of Jonah Krondike.

Madeleine sighed. 'Guess I can kiss my career goodbye, huh?'

'You can always go back to mechanical engineering,' said

Howard. 'Or you could work for one of the research facilities run by immortals. There are many of them.' He smiled at her expression. 'You're gonna have plenty of time on your hands if we survive this.'

'Right,' she drawled.

Howard tilted the computer screen so they could all see. 'The flash drive contained eight folders. I need to retrieve copies of the last four from the secure server before I can analyze them further. What I found in the others was too significant for me not to share.'

Ethan tensed.

'The first three folders contain research files, each pertaining to a particular scientific field. There's one about accelerated physical development, another one about nanotechnology, and the third concerns behavior modification. The fourth folder has lists of names and what looks like a hell of a lot of personal medical data.'

He tapped on a couple of keys and ran his fingers lightly over the trackpad. Several windows popped open.

'What does this mean?' said Olivia.

'Hell if I know,' snorted Howard. 'But it all sounds like some pretty serious stuff. Whatever this is, it must have something to do with what Jonah Krondike is trying to achieve.'

Madeleine indicated the laptop. 'May I?'

'Knock yourself out,' said Howard. He pushed away from the computer.

Madeleine pulled a chair over and hunched over the keyboard. Overlapping windows filled the monitor. She scanned the information that came up, her fingers moving rapidly over the trackpad.

It was several minutes before she stopped and took a deep breath.

Ethan didn't like the look on her face. 'Well?'

Over the hour that followed, the scientist gave them a summary of the information in Serle's secured drives.

'Accelerated physical development speaks for itself. The practice of using drugs and hormones to increase muscle bulk, lean body mass, and enhance performance has been around for decades. An adult male athlete's baseline strength has been said to increase by as much as twenty percent following anabolic steroid use. Much of the information on here comprises established papers published in academic journals across the world over a period of fifty years.'

Asgard placed a hand on the back of her chair and leaned on the table. 'You said "much of the information." What's in the rest of the folder?'

'Like Howard said, some serious shit,' Madeleine replied bluntly. She glanced at the Bastian noble's fingers close to the computer. 'There's a bunch of research data about drugs I haven't heard of. Their composition is like nothing I've seen before, although a lot of heavy organic chemistry seems to have been involved in their synthesis. And it looks like most went to Phase One clinical trials, despite the significant adverse effects noted in the animal experiments.'

'You mean they've tested the drugs on humans?' said Olivia. She squared her shoulders at the surprised looks that came her way. 'I read a lot.'

'You're correct,' said Madeleine with a nod.

'What were the side effects?' said Ethan.

'Pretty much everything you might expect from overuse of a potent anabolic steroid. A range of neuropsychiatric and physiological symptoms that would have the FDA shaking in its boots. We're talking anything from frank psychosis and severe depression to heart attacks and strokes. If the data is to be believed, they had a seventy percent failure rate in the majority of their studies.'

'By failure you mean—?' ventured Howard.

Madeleine's eyes gleamed with a cold light. 'Death.'

Asgard went still. 'Who were the subjects?'

'They don't specify that information. The men and women who underwent these experiments were identified by a number.'

'When's the most recent data from?' said Ethan.

'About six years ago. They seemed to have identified the precursor of a promising new drug they were going to try out on the next batch of—subjects.'

A buzzard shrieked high above them in the ensuing hush.

'Go through the other folders,' Asgard instructed.

Madeleine brought up the next window.

'The one on behavioral engineering shows small cohort studies and Phase One style clinical trials using a combination of new drugs and programs involving brutal physical and psychological regimes. Again the initial failure rates were sky-high, with mass suicides and excessive aggression that resulted in the project leaders…terminating the affected subjects.'

Horror dawned on Olivia's face. 'You mean they *killed* them?'

Madeleine dipped her chin. 'But of everything I've read here so far, the things that terrify me the most are in the nanotechnology files.'

The four immortals shared anxious glances.

'The information indicates that they have not only made amazing advancements with nanodevices and nanoparticles, but also in the field of bionanotechnology.'

'Bionano what?' said Ethan.

'Bionanotechnology. It's basically the merging of biotechnology and nanotechnology. If the data is to be believed, then they've achieved the ultimate goal in cellular engineering.'

They stared at her blankly.

'They've been working with DNA nanotechnology. That means tinkering with genetic material at a biomolecular or nano level.' Madeleine sighed. 'They can change the genetic composition of whole cell lines.'

A yawning, dark pit opened up in Ethan's stomach at her words. He stared at Asgard and saw the same dread reflected in the Bastian's eyes.

'The immortals,' breathed Ethan.

Madeleine gazed at them in confusion. The color drained from her face a second later. 'Oh God.'

# CHAPTER SEVENTEEN

'What?' said Howard, his eyes darting from one shocked expression to another.

'If they believe the immortals' abilities of increased strength, advanced fighting skills, healing, and surviving death itself lies in their DNA, then they could introduce this genetic material in others,' said Ethan.

'And if your and Olivia's powers could be imitated by copying your genes into someone else's body, then it would explain why Jonah is so keen to get his hands on you,' Asgard added in a dark tone. He scowled. 'I still don't understand why Jonah tortured and killed so many immortals though. He's a sadistic bastard, but there's always a motive behind his actions.'

Madeleine turned to the laptop and started working the keyboard once more. Lines furrowed her brow. 'Genetic expression and proteonomics.'

Howard blinked. 'Huh?'

'Think of lab experiments on animals. At the extreme end of research, mankind has subjected what he considers to be lesser creatures to what amounts to torture. Vivisection, deliberate infection, poisoning, electrocution, isolation, food and water deprivation. I think a significant component of Jonah Krondike's experiments involved analyzing what happened to immortals under...stressful conditions, at a biochemical level.' Madeleine indicated the screen. 'Most of these new drugs could have been derived from proteins and other chemicals extracted from the subjects' bloodstreams and organs.'

The scientist closed her eyes and inhaled deeply. When she opened them once more, Ethan glimpsed fear in their depths.

'The content of each of these folders has horrifying implications on their own. In combination, they may mean something worse. We need to take a look at the other folders on your server.'

She studied Howard bleakly.

'What about the fourth one, with the lists and medical data?' said the Crovir immortal. 'What do you make—?'

A trilling noise interrupted him. He removed his cell from his pocket, glanced at the screen, and took the call. 'Hey Bernard. You and Rosa almost—?'

Ethan's pulse jumped as he watched Howard's expression change.

The Crovir immortal pulled the laptop across, jammed the phone between his ear and his shoulder, and started typing rapidly while he listened.

'Okay. You know what to do,' he said tersely. 'Be safe.'

He disconnected, jumped to his feet, and grabbed the computer. 'Bernard just spotted a dozen army vehicles barreling their way toward our location. They'll be at the main gates in five minutes.'

They were halfway to the patio doors when an alarm sounded on Howard's laptop. He tapped a key. A digital map of the estate filled the screen. Security sensors flashed red on the southeast perimeter.

'They've entered our air space,' he said grimly.

The sound of rotors drew their eyes to the sky.

Two Apache helicopters rose out of the next canyon and headed straight for them. Flashes erupted from the automatic machine guns mounted under the fuselage of the aircrafts. Rounds pelted the patio.

They turned and ran, Ethan's fingers closing on Olivia's hand just as they dashed inside the kitchen.

Madeleine stopped in the doorway and whirled around to face the approaching helicopters. '*Hey, some of us are mortal, assholes!*'

'Will you get in here!' roared Asgard.

He grabbed her around the waist and stormed into the mansion. Bullets peppered the spot where she had stood and chipped the marble floor several feet inside the house.

Howard paused at the central island and tapped a couple of keys on the laptop. Blast-resistant steel shutters started to drop down the windows and doors of the property, their electronic whir lost in the sound of gunfire from the helicopters. The light began to fade.

'That should buy us some time!'

He closed the computer and followed them as they raced for the bunker's lift. Muffled explosions sounded somewhere above when they entered the steel cabin. The doors started to close.

'Wait!' said Asgard.

He stabbed the open button on the control panel with his finger and slipped out through the widening gap.

'Where the hell are you going?' Howard shouted after his disappearing figure. The Crovir's gaze shifted to Ethan. 'Is he kidding me?'

Running footsteps rose from the corridor a moment later. Asgard skidded into view and jumped inside the cabin. The doors closed and the lift started its descent.

The Bastian noble tossed Ethan the sheathed twin blades and body harness before strapping his arming sword to his back and securing the holster holding his revolvers. 'How soon until they breach the building?'

'Depends how much firepower they brought with them,' said Howard. He was working the laptop frantically. 'I'm pretty sure those are Hydra rockets we're hearing. And I wouldn't be surprised if those helicopters had Hellfire missiles.' Another alarm beeped on the screen. He stared at the flashing sensors around the estate. 'Shit! These guys are everywhere!'

'How did they find us?' said Olivia.

Her fingers twitched against Ethan's palm. He looked down and was surprised to see that he was still holding her hand.

Howard scowled. 'I don't—'

A deafening boom drowned out the rest of his words. Violent tremors rocked the lift.

A feeling of sudden weightlessness filled Ethan. He stared into Asgard's startled face.

'We're dropping too fast!' yelled Howard.

Ethan released Olivia's hand and pressed his palms against the closest wall. It took but a heartbeat for him to map out the structure of the cabin. He clenched his teeth and channelled his powers into the metal. An ear-splitting screech erupted from outside. A grunt left his throat.

The lift juddered and slowed. It reached the bottom of the shaft with the faintest of jolts.

'Whoa,' muttered Howard.

The doors slid open. Another explosion echoed somewhere above, startling them.

'Move!' said Asgard.

Red lights pulsed against the walls of the bunker as they ran out into the dimly-lit cave.

'In there!' shouted Howard.

He indicated the glass chamber in the middle of the sunken stage.

'Hang on!' Ethan veered left and ran toward the armory.

He was inputting his biometric data into the security display on the door when Asgard reached his side.

They moved methodically around the room, jamming guns, magazines, and grenades in a pair of rucksacks. As they exited the chamber, a faint whine reached Ethan's ears. He pushed his bag into Asgard's hands and headed for the storage area.

The service elevator stood on the opposite side of the room. His heart slammed against his ribs as he watched the number change on the digital indicator above the doors.

He turned and sprinted toward the Bastian noble. 'They're here!'

Olivia and Madeleine were already in the glass room, the latter holding Howard's laptop in her hands.

They jumped down the steps and bolted toward them. Ethan staggered to a halt in the doorway.

'*Howard!*'

The Crovir immortal was bent over a computer station, his fingers moving frenetically over the keyboard. A ping sounded in the distance. Ethan turned.

Figures in army uniforms rushed toward the platform from the direction of the service elevator. They opened fire as they came, the muzzles of their machine guns flaring repeatedly in the gloom. Howard cursed and charged toward the glass chamber. A bullet slammed into his left shoulder when he was three feet from the threshold. He stumbled and started to fall.

Ethan lunged forward, grabbed his arm, and yanked him inside just as Asgard punched a button on the control panel. The doors slid closed.

Faint thuds rose around them as shots pelted the glass exterior.

Madeleine stared at the men who had surrounded the chamber, her fingers white on the laptop. 'It's bulletproof?'

'Uh-huh,' said Howard.

He was already working the digital display table. Olivia tore a strip off the bottom of her shirt and tied it around his shoulder.

He winced. 'Thanks.'

A three-dimensional plan of the mansion flashed in front of them. Madeleine was gaping at it when a muffled boom made her jump.

One of the soldiers had lobbed a grenade at the doors.

'It's also blast proof, dumbasses,' said Howard, glancing at the men on the other side of the glass wall. He shrunk the floating laser image with his fingers and scowled at the handful of flashing amber dots a few miles beyond the perimeter of the estate. 'I don't know how these bastards did it, but they found most of our escape routes out of here.' He closed the projection and shut down the display table. 'Let's go!'

'Go?' said Madeleine. She looked around, bewildered. 'Where?'

Howard took the laptop off her, grabbed a digital satellite phone from a concealed drawer, and moved to the left of the table. Asgard and Ethan herded the two women toward him.

A four-foot section of the metal floor started to sink beneath them. Madeleine stared at the steel walls of the secret lift rising around their legs.

Howard grinned and waved at the soldiers. 'Goodbye!'

He stabbed his middle finger at the ceiling just as they disappeared from view. Thumps resonated above their heads when they exited the cabin one floor below. The soldiers were firing at the curved glass wall that overlooked the lower level.

'This way!' said Howard.

They followed him down a row of towering computer servers to a steel door set deep in the rock face in the south wall of the cave. A distant blast brought a scattering of dust down around them as he punched a code into the security display.

The door led to a tunnel lit by ambient security lights. Cool, dry air washed over them when they went through. Howard came through last and secured the opening behind them. Twenty feet inside the passage, he stopped and removed the satellite phone from his pocket.

Madeleine looked at his hands. 'Where's the laptop?'

'In the bunker.'

He chewed his lower lip and stared at the phone's display, his thumb hovering over the touch screen.

'What are you doing?' said Madeleine.

Howard hesitated.

'Press the button,' ordered Asgard.

Ethan studied the tortured expression on his friend's face, took the device off him, tapped the command key, and handed the phone back.

Tremors from a violent detonation shook the ground and walls around them.

'What just happened?' said Madeleine as they hurried along the sloping tunnel.

She glanced at Howard over her shoulder.

'We just killed the servers,' said Ethan.

Madeleine paled. 'The data.'

'It's safe.' Howard's expression was grim. 'I transferred everything to the backup servers.'

'The mansion?' said Asgard.

'We've got five minutes until she blows.'

Olivia slowed and stared at them. 'What do you mean?'

'We rigged the whole place with explosives in case something like this ever happened,' said Ethan.

He exchanged dark looks with Asgard and Howard. Although they had made plans to cover all eventualities, none of them had ever thought it would come to this. Their enemy had won the upper hand once more.

Faint rumbles travelled through the ground a short while later.

Olivia flinched. Ethan glanced at her and knew she was thinking of the abbess's diaries, now forever lost to the inferno that raged where the mansion once stood.

The explosions continued for almost a minute.

They came to a curve in the tunnel. The ground leveled out. A mile and a half later, a steel door lit by a green security light appeared in the distance.

'Wait,' said Howard when they were ten feet from the exit.

They stopped while he checked something on the satellite phone.

He froze a couple of seconds later. 'Shit.'

Ethan stiffened. 'What?'

He showed them the display. 'This is one of two tunnels whose location they hadn't found. There are six external security sensors in a fifty-foot radius of that door. Five of them have been triggered.'

Ethan's stomach lurched as he studied the flashing dots on the screen.

'How the devil did they find this place?' said Asgard.

'I don't kn—'

The color suddenly drained from Howard's face. His stunned gaze moved to Madeleine.

'Do you have a cell phone?'

'Yes, but I disabled the GPS yesterday, when I went to AuGenD.' Madeleine removed the device from the back pocket of her jeans. 'The battery was dead. I found a charger in the kitchen this morning.'

'May I?' said Howard.

Madeleine shrugged. 'Sure. But I don't see how it's going to—'

Howard tucked his satellite phone in his pocket, took the cell off her, and smashed it against the wall.

'Hey!' Madeleine scowled. 'What the—?'

Howard pried off the broken rear cover. He studied the

internal workings under one of the security lights and carefully tipped out a small object the size of a grain of rice.

'What is that?' said Asgard guardedly.

'It's an active RFID chip.' Howard scowled. 'A radio frequency identification chip.'

He dropped the microchip and ground it into the floor with his heel.

Madeleine gazed at Howard in wide-eyed horror. 'You mean it's been transmitting a signal, giving away our location?'

'Yes,' said the Crovir immortal bitterly. 'It's ultra high frequency, detectable below ground. Likely powered by the battery, which is why they didn't come for us last night.'

'Oh God, I'm so sorry—'

Madeleine pressed her hands over her mouth.

'You weren't to know,' said Ethan curtly.

Olivia laid a hand gently on Madeleine's arm.

Asgard stared at the steel door. 'They know we're here?'

Howard nodded. 'And that's the only exit out of this tunnel.'

The Bastian noble stood still for a moment before taking his rucksack off his shoulder. He handed Madeleine a Sig Sauer P250 and an FN90 assault rifle.

'Do you know how to use this?'

She took the ammunitions pouch he gave her, looped the rifle's sling over her head, and tested its weight in her hands. 'Show me.'

Howard tucked two Glock19s in his waistband, grabbed a submachine gun from Ethan's bag, and clipped a magazine belt around his hips.

Ethan loaded a pair of Colt semi-automatic pistols and placed them into the small of his back. 'You gonna be okay with that shoulder?'

'Yeah.' Howard grimaced. 'I have no intention of becoming those bastards' lab rat.'

Ethan looked at Olivia. 'Do you want a—?'

'No,' she said with a firm shake of her head.

She tore her gaze from the bagful of weapons.

Ethan studied the resolve in her eyes. 'Stay behind me.'

She dipped her chin.

'They'll come at us hard and fast.' Asgard had swapped his twin long-barreled Colt revolvers for an MP5. 'Keep low.'

Madeleine and Howard nodded.

Asgard glanced at Ethan. 'You know what to do.'

Ethan clenched his jaw. He would only use a physical weapon as a last resort.

They took up position behind the door while Asgard entered a code in the security display. The screen beeped. The exit unlocked with a faint pneumatic hiss. Warm air rushed in through the narrow gap at the doorjamb.

The first rounds slammed into the steel panel a second later. Asgard steadied it with his foot, poked his head an inch around the edge, and scanned the exterior surroundings. A bullet streaked past his temple and struck the wall of the tunnel. He pulled back sharply.

'Twenty men, seven to the right, five to the left, and eight dead ahead!' he shouted above the clatter of machine guns. 'They're about fifteen feet away!'

Ethan took a shallow breath and stared at the door.

'And this time, mind our weapons,' Asgard added with a grunt.

Heat flowed through Ethan's chest. He felt his Elemental powers rise, stronger and more intense than they had ever been, ever since that first time he sensed Olivia in his mind. The alarm that had initially accompanied his experience of this upsurge had faded with the incidents at AuGenD. He was now more confident about his ability to control the unearthly force coursing through his veins. He focused.

The gunfire outside suddenly slowed. It stopped a moment later amidst alarmed shouts.

Asgard yanked the door open and stepped out into a wooded clearing. He dropped to one knee, steadied the butt of the machine gun against his shoulder, and fired rapidly at the group of men who stood staring in horror at their crushed weapons on the other side of the glade.

Howard and Madeleine fanned out next to him and shot at the soldiers diving behind the trees to the east and west.

Ethan hunkered down behind Asgard and felt Olivia move at his back. He looked around the clearing and disabled the handguns the soldiers were pulling from their tactical vests. To his surprise, he discovered he didn't have to lift his hands to turn the weapons into unrecognizable lumps of metal.

A round object thudded on the ground four feet from Asgard. The Bastian noble stiffened.

Ethan narrowed his eyes at the grenade.

It rose and retraced its arc through the air toward a gaping soldier, detonating among the trees and driving several men to the forest floor.

'You *seriously* have to teach me that trick!' yelled Madeleine.

'There's more of them coming!' warned Howard.

Figures rushed between the trees amidst the growing roar of engines. Two army Jeeps came plowing through the undergrowth from the south and braked to a halt some twenty feet from the clearing. The gunfire redoubled.

Ethan was working on destroying the soldiers' weapons when he felt a sudden prick in his neck. He raised a hand and stared at the small metal object he removed from his skin.

It was a miniature dart.

Puzzlement turned to horror as the soporific effect of a powerful sedative started to kick in. Ethan turned and spotted the immortal Asgard had shot in Olivia's room at the abbey. The man's eyes gleamed in triumph behind the tranquilizer rifle resting against his shoulder.

Ethan's legs started to go weak. He swayed and crumpled to his knees.

Olivia gasped behind him. '*No!*'

The sound tore through his mind, raw and filled with outrage. A wave of intense pressure drove him down at the same time that pain exploded behind his eyes, choking his breath. His limbs grew heavy, the drug working its way through his bloodstream. He thudded face-first in the dirt.

It took every ounce of his fading strength to fight the physical force battering him and raise his head. What he saw defied comprehension.

Branches bowed and creaked in the trees and underbrush, leaves rustling and drifting away wildly in a raging wind that seemed to blow outward from the middle of the clearing, lifting clouds of dirt and debris off the ground.

The soldiers who had attacked them were on the ground, hands clamped to their heads and faces twisted in agony while the invisible storm buffeted them. Several of the men were throwing up. Some were unconscious. The immortal who had shot Ethan with the tranquilizer dart cowered against a tree, blood trickling from his nose, his mouth a rictus of pain.

Asgard was on his knees, knuckles white and teeth clenched while his hands gripped his temples. A crimson trail flowed out of his right ear. Madeleine and Howard lay a few feet away, their weapons discarded while they fought the same invisible energy threatening to crush their bodies.

And in the middle of it all stood Olivia Ashkarov.

Her hands were curled into fists at her sides, nails biting into skin. Her face was an icy mask of rage and her eyes blazed, dark green and unfocused.

It was at that moment that Ethan glimpsed the terrifying extent of the powers of the one destined to be his soulmate. As his awareness started to fade, he glimpsed movement out the corner of his eye.

Asgard had crawled to his feet and was stumbling toward his niece.

'Olivia!' he shouted hoarsely.

The last thing the Elemental saw was the Bastian noble wrapping the frozen Seer in his arms.

# CHAPTER EIGHTEEN

GENERAL WILLIAM FITZPATRICK GUNNERSON STARED AT THE scenes of devastation being broadcast on the news channel. A male reporter's voice overlaid the dramatic images relayed live from a media helicopter.

'So far, local authorities have refused to issue a statement as to the nature of the explosions that rocked this normally quiet neighborhood several miles south of Topanga State Park at around ten-thirty this morning. The Los Angeles County and Ventura County Fire Departments have been battling the blaze that started on an isolated estate located on several hundred acres of privately-owned land since lunchtime today. The property is believed to be the home of reclusive tech billionaire Howard Titus, CEO of STAEGH Corp. An anonymous source has revealed a possible link to the suspected terrorist activities that took place in the Bear River Mountains three days ago, where fifty-nine Benedictine nuns were brutally murdered. The same source also suggested a connection to the more recent break-in that resulted in the murder of a guard at a biotech company in San Diego last night. With a dry winter behind us and a summer that promises to be scorching, small brushfires have already spread to neighboring canyons and are being brought under control by local fire fighters working with the Mountains Recreation and Conservation Authority.'

Jonah pressed the mute button on the remote.

'This source, I take it it's one of our people?' said Gunnerson, his voice low and passionless.

Jonah studied the man standing in the middle of his office, deep inside the military base where the research facility was located.

With a headful of closely-cropped gray hair and battle-hardened brown eyes, Gunnerson cut a commanding figure. Born into a family with an impressive pedigree of soldiers who had served God and country ever since the first Gunnerson fought for the Confederate states in the American Civil War, he had been in the army his entire life. After graduating valedictorian at West Point, the boy who wanted to follow in his great-great-grandfather's footsteps went on to an illustrious military career that eventually earned him the Medal of Honor and a Distinguished Service Cross for his actions in the Vietnam War.

Now a four-star general in the United States Special Operations Command, he was the current leader of the US Army group working with Jonah.

In the years that he had known him, Jonah had come to recognize Gunnerson's many moods and tics. It amused the immortal that no one in the DoD knew the general's true nature. To the public and the federal drones who worked with him in Washington, Gunnerson was a highly-decorated soldier and a man of honor, dedicated to the service of his country. To those with a more intimate association with the general, he was an extreme narcissist and a closet sadist. Very few people had ever dared openly defy the man. The handful who tried to hold him to account for his illegal, covert practices had either ended up the victims of fatal accidents or deliberate character assassinations.

Gunnerson's current body language and tone indicated extreme rage. The last time Jonah recalled seeing him in this state, the man had killed two of his scientists. It had been a sobering experience for Jonah's team and an unwelcome headache for the immortal, who had had to find suitable replacements for the dead men.

The Crovir noble suppressed an impatient sigh. The only reason he had tolerated his unholy alliance with humans for so long was because he needed their resources, now more than ever.

After Asgard Godard's zealous attempts to destroy Kronos in the middle of the last millennium, it had taken Jonah several hundred years to grow his army of faithful followers to the size he would need to achieve his long-term goals. On the cusp of the first big tactical move that would have heralded the beginning of the end game, his troops had been decimated by the joint efforts of the two immortal societies a few years ago. The death of Alberto Cavaleti, his closest associate and one of the longest-serving members of Kronos, had dealt a doubly-heavy blow to Jonah's scheme.

He knew full well that Gunnerson and his cronies in the DoD considered him an employee rather than an equal partner in their ongoing venture. As far as they were concerned, they were exploiting his knowledge of the immortal races to further their own dark gains. They had no notion of his final objective and all that he had done over the course of the last eight centuries to achieve it. By the time the truth finally dawned on them, it would be too late for the US government and the human race.

'Yes,' Jonah said. 'The source is ours.'

'This is a mess, Krondike,' said Gunnerson.

'The two immortals we are trying to capture are among the most powerful beings alive today, General. I never said this was going to be easy.'

Gunnerson watched him broodingly.

'You had better take care of this. I do not want a whiff of scandal following me back to Washington.'

Jonah could not have cared less about Gunnerson's long-held political aspirations. He leaned nonchalantly against his mahogany desk and thought of the loaded gun lying in the drawer next to his leg. He resisted the urge to take it out and shoot the man scowling at him from across the room.

The Crovir noble could not wait until the day when humans would be put firmly back on the evolutionary ladder where they belonged, subservient to the higher race that was destined to rule the Earth. The Axis alliance's defeat by the Allied forces during the Second World War had been a source of great frustration to him, halting the promising experiments he had been conducting in Nazi Germany under the pretense of helping the Third Reich fulfill their power-mad Führer's Master Race aspirations. A bitter taste filled his mouth at the thought of how often the immortal societies had unknowingly thwarted his plans over the years.

*Once we are in power, they will also have to learn their place in the new world order.*

'My men will make sure not to leave any trace of your involvement in this matter, *General*,' Jonah drawled.

He observed the aggravated expression that flashed in the man's eyes and held back a grin. He knew the soldier struggled to be barely civil to him at times. Like many of the senior army officials associated with the project, it galled Gunnerson that he had to show some measure of respect to the immortal who had made all their plans possible.

The man moved to the glass wall overlooking the lab below.

'You said you had some results to show me?'

'Indeed. Follow me.'

They headed out of the office and through the corridors of the research facility to a room two stories high and a third the size of a football field. An observation platform protected by reinforced glass ran along the upper level of the underground chamber. Several scientists stood on the deck, tablet computers in hand while they studied the figures on the floor below.

The general froze beside Jonah when he registered what he was seeing.

'Are those—?'

'Yes. Subject 505 successfully underwent Phase Three two days ago. We brought Subjects 506 and 507 out of stasis twelve hours later. This is Phase Four.'

The glass muffled the sounds of the dramatic action taking place on the training field, where three gigantic figures engaged a group of twenty-five soldiers in close, unarmed combat. Jonah glanced at the timer on the wall and smiled. Four minutes into the practice test and more than half of the troop lay on the ground, incapacitated or unconscious. Technicians occasionally ran out into the middle of the fray and dragged the injured men to the safe zone running around the perimeter of the battle ground, where the medics tended to their wounds.

A team of armed soldiers watched on from the secured doors at either end, tranquilizer rifles and stun batons at the ready in case the test subjects became unmanageable.

'Bar the expected level of aggressiveness and ruthless focus we bioengineered into them, these three have so far shown no signs of the psychotic behavior demonstrated in the previous batch,' said Jonah.

Gunnerson walked up to the wall and laid a hand on the glass. His face filled with wonder and his eyes gleamed with a fanatic light as he stared at the evidence of their long-sought success.

'They are—'

The general stopped, visibly moved beyond words.

'Yes,' muttered Jonah. 'They are all that we had hoped for.'

For once, he shared the man's excitement. They were in the

concluding stages of an experiment that had taken the immortal and the US government decades and millions of dollars to conduct. Despite their many false starts and failures and the deaths of hundreds of test subjects, including almost every immortal he had ever captured, the Crovir noble had known this day would come. His secret experimentation on Boyko Dragov, the pureblood immortal-human half-breed protégé and right-hand man of Alberto Cavaleti, had proven that years ago.

'How many soldiers did you enroll in this group?' said Gunnerson.

'Twenty five,' said Jonah.

Gunnerson glanced at him. 'And you're waking all of them up?'

'Yes. We've brought in more staff to speed things up. The remaining subjects should be entering Phase Three in the next forty-eight hours.'

'Hmm. That's good,' grunted Gunnerson. Despite his reluctance to appreciate the immortal's achievement, it was evident the general was more than satisfied with their progress. 'How soon until you start on the next batch?'

'I am delaying that for the time being.'

Gunnerson turned and looked at him as if he had grown another head.

'Why? We've finally succeeded, goddamnit!' The man's cheeks flushed with anger. 'I want at least two hundred men ready by the end of the year.'

Jonah shrugged. 'You can get down on your knees and beg me, Gunnerson. It won't make a difference. I almost have the Elemental and the Seer within my grasp. I want to see how much more we can achieve with their DNA.'

Gunnerson faltered at these words. His gaze shifted to the three giants now standing silently amidst the sea of fallen opponents they had successfully defeated.

'Do you really think we can improve on them?'

'Yes,' said Jonah in a hard voice. 'What happened to our men when they engaged those two immortals this morning is proof of that. I am not planning to stop our experiments until I get my hands on them and exploit the full extent of their powers.'

GOLDEN LIGHT STABBED THROUGH ETHAN'S EYELIDS, ROUSING him. He stirred and blinked.

A familiar, ornate Tiffany lamp glowed on a bedside table some twenty inches from his nose. He pushed up on an elbow and groaned at the throbbing pain in his head.

The noise woke the woman sleeping in the chair next to the bed. Ethan's hand stilled on his temple.

Olivia straightened, her fingers gripping the armrests. A tortured expression filled her face.

'I'm sorry,' she whispered.

Ethan sat up and rubbed his face. 'Why?'

She lowered her gaze and bit her lip.

'For what...what happened outside the tunnel.'

'Considering we appear to be at the safe house and not in Krondike's lab, you have nothing to apologize for,' he said gruffly. 'You saved us.'

'But I—'

The bedroom door opened and Howard walked in with a tray. He stopped when he saw them. A bandage peeked out from under the neckline of his T-shirt.

'Ah, the prodigal son returns,' he said. 'Had a nice nap?'

Ethan grunted and glanced around the room.

'What happened?'

Howard put the tray down on the bedside table.

'Well, after your girlfriend almost killed us, we hotfooted it out of the canyon while Jonah's men were still lying around the place trying to unscramble their brains.'

Olivia's shoulders drooped.

'Hey, I'm not saying what you did was necessarily a bad thing,' said Howard. 'It's just...none of us were expecting it. It'd be nice to get a warning next time.'

'She didn't know she was capable of doing that,' said Ethan.

Olivia startled. 'How did you—?'

'You would have mentioned it.' Ethan was astonished to find himself smiling slightly. 'Besides, you forget—we appear to have...a connection.'

She held his gaze while color slowly flooded her cheeks.

'Should I leave?' said Howard.

He cocked an eyebrow, an amused light dancing in his eyes.

Ethan sighed. 'How did we get here?'

'We took the SUV we'd stashed in the cave a few miles from the estate and hired a private helicopter in LA. We got here a couple of hours ago. You slept like a baby the whole way through.'

Ethan glanced at the tray. 'Is that soup?'

'Uh-huh.'

'What am I, five?'

He pushed the covers off his legs and rose from the bed. Cramps shot through his calves, remnant effects of the tranquilizer. His knees almost gave out beneath him. Olivia grabbed his shoulders and steadied him. Ethan froze.

Her touch burned him through the cotton T-shirt he wore. A light, citrusy scent wafted off her skin and hair, filling his head. Heat seeped down his arms and spread across his body, wildfire singing along his veins. This was different from the way he felt when he wielded his powers. For one thing, manipulating objects didn't make the muscles of his belly clench with desire.

Howard groaned.

'Seriously, stop that. I feel like I'm watching something indecent.'

Ethan blinked. Olivia's face was only a couple of inches away, her green eyes wide with surprise and a degree of apprehension. He'd unconsciously leaned in to kiss her.

*Oh shit.*

He straightened stiffly, appalled at his own body's betrayal. Dragging his gaze from the glistening lips so close to his, he turned to Howard.

'Madeleine and Asgard?'

'They're downstairs getting dinner ready.'

A few minutes later, they strolled into a beautiful country kitchen. Towering glass windows took up the left wall of the room. A deck was visible in the soft glow of external nightlights. Beyond it, moonlight bathed a sun-bleached wooden jetty and coated the crest of the surf crashing gently onto a sandy beach. A motorboat bobbed in the water next to the dock.

The safe house was situated on the shores of a lake just over an hour and a half's drive northeast of Sacramento. Set on secluded private land in the middle of a thick conifer forest, the luxurious two-story, wood and stone chalet afforded them the safety and privacy they needed for a bolt-hole.

Madeleine was leaning against the marble-topped island in the middle of the room.

'Wow. I've never seen anyone hunt, pluck, and cook a pheasant in under an hour before. I'm impressed.'

She bit into an apple. Asgard placed a tray of basted meat back in the oven. He looked pointedly from her to the boiling pan on the cooking range next to him.

'Oh. Right.'

She joined him and stirred the contents of the pot.

'Somehow, this picture of domestic bliss pisses me off as

well,' muttered Howard. 'I'm starting to feel like the ugly duckling no one wants to hook up with.'

Madeleine turned and eyed him coolly. 'Did you ever consider it's because of that smart mouth of yours?' She ignored the scowling Bastian noble next to her and looked at Ethan. 'I see Metal Boy is up.'

Ethan exhaled loudly. 'I do have a name you know.'

Madeleine shrugged. 'It's my way of coping with all the reality-defying, supernatural stuff I've seen in the last twenty-four hours.' She indicated Olivia with a tilt of her chin. 'Psychic Girl was quite worried about you.'

A strained silence followed.

'Do you always say the first thing that comes to your mind?' said Asgard.

'Life's too short to beat around the bush.' Madeleine paused and grimaced. 'Hmm. I can't quite use that expression in present company, can I?'

A stifled chuckle rang out across the kitchen.

All eyes shifted to Olivia.

'Sorry,' she mumbled, abashed.

Madeleine smiled. 'I like your girlfriend's sense of humor, Metal Boy.'

Ethan's protest died in his throat. He had already admitted to the connection that existed between him and the willowy blonde standing a foot away. There was not much point denying it further.

'By the way, what happened to the cook and the butler?' said Madeleine.

'They're lying low at another safe house,' said Asgard curtly. 'If they lose contact with us for more than five days, they'll assume other identities and terminate all association with us.'

Madeleine grimaced. 'That's...rough.'

Asgard's eyes grew hooded. 'It's the way immortals live their lives.'

It wasn't until they'd finished the meal that Ethan got to ask the question he had been yearning to voice since he woke up.

'What exactly happened back at the tunnel?'

They were in a lounge overlooking the dark lake. A fire popped and crackled in the stone hearth at the head of the room. This close to the Sierra Nevada Mountains, the nights were chilly.

Howard finished dropping ice in the drinks he had poured from the mini bar and handed him a tumbler. Ethan accepted the glass gratefully and downed a mouthful of the amber liquid. The whisky scorched a fiery trail down his throat.

'Psychokinesis,' said Asgard. He returned Ethan's stare with a steady gaze. 'I believe what we were subjected to this morning was a physical manifestation of Olivia's psychic abilities.'

Ethan digested this incredible statement with a frown. He thought back to their first encounter with Asgard's niece. 'That must be what we experienced the night we met her.'

'What?' said Olivia.

'When you ran from the Jeep and escaped into the woods, before you fell from the gorge.' Ethan studied the shock reflected in her green gaze. 'Asgard and I felt some kind of... pressure wave coming from you.'

'You were upset at the time,' Asgard told Olivia gently. 'That must have been the trigger this morning as well. It was an automatic response to what happened to Ethan.'

Ethan blinked. *I'm the reason she did that?*

'You were under attack,' said Asgard steadily. 'Olivia's body responded to that challenge the only way it could, by unleashing her powers. That's how strong the connection already is between the two of you.'

Ethan swallowed. That statement terrified him almost as much as Asgard's initial confession yesterday morning that he and Olivia Ashkarov were predestined to be together.

'That's some pretty heavy stuff,' said Madeleine.

'Was my mother able to do what I did this morning?' said Olivia after a short silence.

Asgard hesitated. 'No.'

Olivia looked into the glass she was holding. She raised it to her lips, swallowed the entire contents, and started to cough.

'Whoa, steady there, girl,' said Howard. 'Whisky that good needs to be sipped, not drank like water. 'Specially when it's a sixty-year-old malt.' His brow furrowed as he studied her flushed face. 'Was that your first drink?'

Olivia finally caught her breath. 'Yes.'

Howard cocked an eyebrow. 'Want another one?'

Asgard gave him a disapproving look.

'Relax, granddad.' Howard took Olivia's glass for a refill. 'It's not everyday someone finds out they can potentially kill with their mind.'

Olivia inhaled sharply. 'Is that what you think happened? Did I—did I kill some of those men back there?'

'I think you got very close,' Ethan said quietly in the awkward silence that followed. 'If Asgard hadn't stopped you, that could have been a real possibility.'

She stared at him, her face pale.

'It's evident you can influence each other's powers,' said Asgard. He observed the two of them with a thoughtful expression. 'You need to develop and control that ability.'

'How?' said Ethan.

'By training together,' said the Bastian noble.

# CHAPTER NINETEEN

'THIS IS IT. THIS IS THE LAST OF THE FOLDERS I RETRIEVED from the backup system.'

Asgard stared at the computer screen. 'How fast can you analyze them?'

Howard ran a hand through his hair. 'I had a hell of a lot more hardware to play with at the mansion,' he said mournfully. 'The only way we're going to be able to extract this data is if I ask my network for help.' He sighed. 'I don't want to put those guys' lives in danger. Most of them are human.'

Sunlight streamed through the tall windows on the left and danced on the green waters of the lake some forty feet away.

They were in the study on the lower floor of the chalet. Stacked in the stone cellar beneath the wooden floorboards was a scaled-down version of the servers Howard had installed in their main home.

Two days had passed since they escaped the attack at the mansion. A glitch in the system during the transfer meant it had taken Howard almost twice as long to recover the files from the backup servers.

'We may not have any other option,' said Madeleine in a hard voice.

Asgard glanced at her. He was acutely conscious of his growing awareness of the enigmatic woman who had stormed into their lives a mere sixty hours ago. The feeling disconcerted him like few things had in his long immortal existence. Although he was reluctant to put names to the complex emotions coursing through him when he was in her presence, there was no denying the fact that physical attraction featured among them. That made him feel guilty and angry.

*I found and lost my soulmate. So what the devil is this?*

Oblivious to the storm brewing inside him, Madeleine spoke once more.

'I understand your reluctance,' she told Howard. 'From what you said before though, your associates are used to playing along the fine line of the law. I guess the question you need to ask yourself is this—do you trust them to do the job well and to keep their findings a secret?'

The Crovir immortal was silent for some time. 'You're right.'

Over the hours that followed, he separated the contents of the folders and forwarded coded sections to twelve hackers around the world.

'It's done,' he said somberly when he hit "send" on the final email.

'How long until we hear back from them?' said Asgard.

Howard shrugged. 'Twelve to twenty-four hours. I'll be decoding the largest section of data.'

'Can we take a look at the folder with all the names and medical records?' said Madeleine.

Howard pulled up the information. A noise outside drew his gaze to a window overlooking the forest.

His expression turned troubled. 'Are those two okay out there?'

'Yes,' said Asgard. 'There's nothing any of us can do about that particular matter. They have to work this out between themselves.'

'AGAIN,' SAID ETHAN.

A layer of sweat beaded his forehead. Olivia raised her fingers to his face, lines furrowing her brow as she concentrated. After the last two days of intense training, the Crovir noble knew what to expect.

Power surged through his chest. He kept his eyes locked on the towering evergreens to the north of the clearing, inhaled deeply, and lifted his left hand.

The trees creaked and bowed away from him. The earth shifted at the base of several trunks, roots lifting from the ground. Birds flew from tall branches, dark bodies rising against the sky and agitated trills echoing across the forest.

Ethan's fingers twitched as he manipulated the energy flowing from his body, dropping mental resistors in its path. The trees slowly returned to their upright position, trunks groaning in protest. He released the breath he had been holding and lowered his hand.

*Asgard was right. We needed to do this.*

He swallowed and indicated a large rock formation to the left. 'Let's try those.'

Olivia looked uncertain. 'Are you sure?'

'Yes.'

This time, Ethan kept his hand at his side and directed the incredible, unearthly force blossoming in his heart with his mind only.

For a moment, nothing happened. Then, dust shifted in tiny whirlwinds at the base of the boulders. They levitated slowly in the air. Olivia gasped.

The rocks rose four feet before dropping back down with a resounding crash.

'How much weight was that?' whispered Olivia.

'A hell of a lot more than those trees,' said Ethan, panting slightly. *And three times as much as the cop's car from the other day.*

What was happening simultaneously scared and electrified him. He sensed they had barely touched upon what they could achieve together. And if he was correct in his assumptions, then the effects of their combined powers would be out of this world.

Olivia dropped her hand from his face. An acute sense of loss shot through Ethan. He blinked.

Silence filled the space between them. It was gradually replaced by the awareness that had plagued him since he awoke at the lake house.

Judging from the look on Olivia's face and the way she stiffened, she also felt the undercurrent of tension that had been growing between them over the last two days. She bit her lip.

Ethan's gaze dropped to her mouth, his pulse now racing for an entirely different reason. He ignored the small warning voice at the back of his mind and took a step toward her. She retreated. He held her gaze and moved forward once more, his entire being filled with the intense need to touch her. This time, Olivia stood her ground, her eyes darkening to a stormy green. She tilted her head and stared at him.

The desire in the depths of her pupils was his undoing. Ethan groaned and lifted a hand to the back of her head. His lips met hers a heartbeat later.

The world around them disappeared as heat poured through his body from the point of contact. It grew in ferocity, a tidal wildfire of need that singed his skin and made the muscles of his abdomen clench. His other arm locked around her waist and he crushed her against him, tongue parting her lips and delving inside her mouth to taste the essence of her. Olivia trembled.

Ethan froze, sensing her sudden fear in the way she tensed. It took all his willpower to release her and step away. They gazed at each other, chests heaving while they struggled to regain some measure of control over their ragged breathing. Olivia raised tremulous fingers to her red lips.

Ethan stifled a groan. 'Stop that.'

She blinked. 'Stop what?'

'The way you're looking at me.'

Olivia went still. 'How am I looking at you?'

Ethan closed his eyes briefly. *Oh sweet Lord, have mercy! She's not even aware she's doing it.*

'The same hungry way I'm looking at *you*,' he said between gritted teeth. 'Like I want to strip you down, push you to the ground, and take you, right here, right now.'

She gasped and took a hasty step back, color filling her face.

It was then that several earth-shattering truths struck Ethan.

*She grew up in an abbey. Which means she's never been with a man. That was probably her first kiss.*

Instead of terrifying him, the realization that he would be her first...everything made desire sing along his veins once more. He ran a hand down his face and did his best to control his raging libido.

'Let's go back,' he said more tersely than he intended.

Olivia nodded shakily. She turned and practically scampered toward the lake house. The sight would have drawn an amused smile from him had his gaze not dropped to her slim waist and hips. He bit back another groan.

∼

'So what you're saying is that all of these men served in the US Armed Forces at one time or another in the last forty years?'

Asgard stared at the names filling the monitor.

'Uh-huh,' said Howard. 'Funny thing is, most of them are classed as either killed or missing in action. Which kind of makes you wonder.'

'Wonder what?' said Asgard.

'Your immortal friend is saying that we're looking at medical data on these men months after the dates when they supposedly died or disappeared,' said Madeleine quietly.

Unease darted through Asgard. He straightened.

'It's clear these guys were enrolled in some kind of secret government experiment,' Madeleine continued. 'If you put that fact together with the information we know from the other folders, then the pieces of the puzzle come together to make a pretty terrifying picture.'

Howard and Asgard looked at her.

'Serle and Krondike must be involved in some kind of super soldier program,' she said in a hard voice. 'That's the only logical explanation for everything we've read so far.'

A strained silence descended on the study.

'Shit,' Howard muttered dully.

Asgard's chest tightened in trepidation. *Is that Jonah's true objective? To create a race of powerful humans using the genetic material and other chemicals he has gleaned from his research on immortals?*

Something didn't add up though—and it was a big something. *What were the last six hundred years about? And why the devil was he looking for the Elixir of Life and the sun cross pendant?*

They were missing pieces of the puzzle; he was certain of it.

'Now what?' Howard ran a hand through his hair. 'Even if the other coded folders contain data that confirm our suspicions, it doesn't tell us where Krondike is or how far along this crazy scheme he and his team may have gotten. What do we do with this information? Go to the US government?' His tone turned bitter. 'For all we know, this goes all the way to the top.

The president himself could have given the go-ahead for this project.' He looked at Asgard. 'I don't think we have any option but to involve the immortal societies. This is too big for—'

'No!' said Asgard.

Madeleine stared at them. 'What are you talking about?'

Howard gave Madeleine a brief account of their relationships with the councils who ruled over the immortal races—or the lack thereof. Asgard had not elaborated on the topic when he told her about the Crovirs and the Bastians a few nights ago.

Madeleine cocked an eyebrow at Asgard. 'Wait, so you're some kind of...*prince*?'

Asgard grunted noncommittally.

'I wouldn't go that far. He behaves like a wounded bear most of the time.' Howard studied Asgard with an exasperated air. 'So, what would you have us do?'

The Bastian noble studied the names on the screen. 'Let's see what we can find out about these men.'

The study door opened behind them and Ethan walked in.

Asgard turned to him. 'How did it go?'

'Better than I thought it would,' Ethan said gruffly.

Asgard looked past his shoulder. 'Where's Olivia?'

Ethan stopped in his tracks and rubbed the back of his neck. 'She's, er, in her room.'

Howard narrowed his eyes. 'Your ears are red.' He studied his best friend for a silent beat. 'Did something happen?'

'What do you mean?' said Ethan, his tone defensive.

A slow grin parted Howard's lips. 'You *dog*, you kissed her, didn't you?'

Ethan flushed. Madeleine sighed and shook her head at Howard.

'What?' he said with a shrug.

'You're such a child,' she murmured.

Ethan avoided Asgard's gaze. 'What have you got?'

IT WAS EVENING BY THE TIME THEY FOUND THEIR NEXT LEAD.

'This is from a short article in the Carson City News dated three years ago. It's an interview with the widow of one of the dead soldiers on our list,' said Madeleine.

She had printed off the feature. They gathered around the table while she read out the piece.

'"Gillian Hofstadter, widow of US Army Lieutenant Mason Hofstadter, 3rd Battalion, 75th Ranger Regiment, claims that her husband did not in fact die in action during the ongoing Operation Enduring Freedom in Afghanistan in December 2009, as proclaimed by the United States government. She maintains that he made contact with her a month after his official funeral service. Although she has not heard from him since, Gillian Hofstadter has put in a request with the Department of Defense to find out the exact circumstances of her husband's death and to have his remains exhumed for a postmortem and DNA analysis. A DoD spokeswoman declined to comment on whether any such investigation was currently in progress and whether they had acquiesced to Mrs Hofstadter's demands. The spokeswoman stated that their thoughts were with the grieving family of Lieutenant Hofstadter and those of all army personnel who had perished in the service of their country."'

There was an inset photograph in the middle of the article depicting a young couple with their arms wrapped around each other. The man was wearing his army service uniform and the woman a beautiful summer dress and a proud smile.

'Says here she left Fort Benning after her husband's death and came to Carson City to be with her family. She was teaching history at Carson High at the time of the interview,' Madeleine added quietly.

Howard wheeled his chair over to his computer and tapped on the keyboard.

'There's a Gillian Hofstadter registered at an address in Carson City,' he said shortly. He showed them the house on a satellite map. 'Picture on her driving license matches that of the woman in the article.'

Madeleine stared at the monitor. 'Is that the Nevada DMV database?'

'Uh-huh.' Howard looked at Asgard and Ethan. 'Her place is only two-and-a-half hours drive from here.'

'What are you saying?' said Olivia.

'He's suggesting we go visit the widow Hofstadter,' said Ethan.

Olivia had joined them in the study a couple of hours ago. From the way she maintained a subtle distance from him, Ethan gathered that she had not quite recovered from the shock of her first kiss. This only made him want to kiss her more.

Howard rubbed the back of his neck. 'I've mined all known sources of US military personnel records and found nothing that we didn't already know about these missing men. This is the only clue we've come up with in the last six hours.'

'He's right,' said Asgard. 'We should talk to this woman.'

Ethan glanced at his watch and pushed away from the table. 'If we leave now, we should be there by—'

'Not you,' interrupted Asgard.

Ethan gave him a puzzled look.

'You should stay and practice some more,' said Asgard.

His gaze shifted between Ethan and Olivia.

'I think we're done for the day,' said Ethan stiffly. *Besides, if we continue what we were doing earlier, we're going to be practicing more than just using our powers.*

Asgard looked at Madeleine. 'Still, I believe the woman we're going to see will respond better to a female touch.'

Madeleine pointed at her chest. 'Who, *me?*'

'He has a point,' said Howard.

Madeleine held Asgard's gaze.

'Okay,' she said with a curt nod.

They left an hour later in one of the two four-by-fours Howard kept in the garage at the lake house.

Ethan stood on the porch and watched the vehicle's tail lights disappear between the trees. He turned to see Olivia in the doorway. 'Shall we?'

She squared her shoulders and nodded.

OLIVIA WOKE UP WITH A PARCHED THROAT. SHE BLINKED AT the dark ceiling before reaching for the switch on the bedside lamp. Soft light flooded the room. She picked up the empty glass on the side table and padded barefoot into the bathroom.

She filled the glass at the sink, swallowed a few gulps of water, and was wiping her mouth with the back of her hand when she saw her reflection in the mirror. The sea-green eyes staring back at her were filled with an oddly sensuous light. Olivia froze. The memory of the devastating kiss from earlier flashed through her mind and brought with it a shocking and unwanted realization.

The hunger that had filled her soul when Ethan Storm touched her still hummed somewhere deep inside her body, a need that ached to be quelled. The feeling was like none she had ever experienced before and it scared her half to death.

She recalled the incident from a few hours ago, when they had practiced using their powers in tandem once more. This time, the Crovir noble had wanted to know just how far his presence influenced her abilities and had had her remote-view several locations from pictures he pulled up on the internet.

Finding herself on top of the Empire State Building had startled Olivia, as had her unscheduled mental trip to the summit of Mount Fuji, an isolated monastery in Tibet, and the middle of a Bolivian jungle. The ease with which her mind had translocated to those places had been even more surprising, as had the length of time she had maintained the spatial connection.

When Ethan asked her to try and read his and Howard's minds, Olivia balked at the request.

'It's part of who you are,' he said with a scowl. 'Don't you want to know—?'

'No,' Olivia interrupted vehemently. 'That's one thing I won't do.'

He'd stared at her, fists clenched at his sides.

'You never know—it might be fun,' Howard told Olivia in the strained silence. He raised his hands at Ethan's glare. 'Hey, I'm only trying to lighten the mood.'

Ethan let out an exasperated sigh and stared at the fireplace. 'Well, I guess we'll never find out just how far your—'

The flames leapt in the hearth, yellow light flaring across the dimly-lit lounge.

Ethan startled and took a step back. 'What the—?'

The fire roared high up the chimney and spat out sparks. Bright specks landed on the floorboards and started to smoke. Howard jumped up from the couch and stamped them out.

Ethan looked at Olivia, his eyes wide with shock. 'Are you doing this?'

'I—I don't know,' she stammered, her heart in her mouth.

His gaze shifted to the fire. A focused frown furrowed his brow. He flexed his fingers.

The light faded as the flames gradually returned to their normal flicker.

Ethan blinked.

'Wow,' muttered Howard. 'So you *can* do fire.'

Olivia shuddered when she recollected the expression that had flashed on Ethan's face. He had looked both awed and angry, as if she had once more invaded the sanctity of his mind without his permission. She refilled the glass and headed back toward the bed.

The vision came suddenly when she was halfway across the floor.

# CHAPTER TWENTY

*FIRES RAGED ACROSS A DESERT LANDSCAPE, THE FLAMES BUFFETED by a violent wind. The deformed shapes of army vehicles were visible in the midst of the blaze, their twisted shells black with soot. Sparks erupted from undercarriages as several were forcibly pushed across the ground. Screams punctuated the explosions echoing in the distance.*

*Brightness suddenly flared on the horizon, an eerie, blindingly-beautiful white cloud that mushroomed silently from the ground and rose rapidly toward the pale blue sky, dampening all sound.*

*A shadow appeared in her field of vision. A man grabbed her shoulder and shouted something. His blood-stained features blurred. Olivia blinked.*

*Ethan's face swam into focus. He stared at her with a desperate expression before taking her head in his hand. His lips landed on hers a heartbeat later.*

A cry escaped her when the vision ended, the image shattering into a million pieces. Olivia returned to the present with a jolt and found herself crushed against a warm, naked chest. She stiffened.

'Sshhh,' soothed Ethan. 'It's okay. You're all right.'

He stroked her hair gently, one arm wrapped around her slender frame while the other cradled her head to his shoulder.

The glass was on the floor by their feet, water spilled across the floorboards.

Olivia's heart thundered against her breastbone, the sound so loud that she wondered whether the man holding her could hear its frantic beat. Her breathing gradually slowed as the aftereffects of the vision faded. It was almost a minute before she raised her head and stepped awkwardly out of his embrace.

Ethan's arms fell to his sides. He indicated the glass. 'I heard a noise.'

Olivia swallowed, her voice stuck somewhere in her throat.

'Do you want to talk about it?' said Ethan, his tone full of concern.

*No. I want you out of this room!*

Olivia stared at the half-naked man standing before her, her heart pounding.

His legs were clad in cotton pajama bottoms that hung low on his hips and did nothing to hide the solid strength of his limbs. Corded muscles stretched his honey-colored skin from his wide shoulders all the way down to his lower abdomen. Her gaze followed the fine line of dark blond hair arrowing down from his navel and disappearing under his waistband.

'Like what you see?'

Olivia's head snapped up. Ethan was watching her with an amused expression.

She flushed, mortified by her brazen behavior. She had practically stripped him with her eyes—not that he was leaving much to the imagination.

He reached across the space separating them and fingered the sleeve of her cotton nightdress. 'I gotta admit, I'm not normally a fan of this kind of nightwear. On you, it looks downright sinful.'

Air froze in her lungs. His eyes had darkened to a molten,

navy blue. His fingertips scorched her skin where they touched her.

He watched her carefully, like a hunter would its prey.

'This...whatever it is...' He waved a hand between the two of them. 'It's going to happen.'

Olivia's mouth went dry as his meaning sank in.

A rueful smile curved his lips at her expression. 'You know, I was angry when Asgard told me we were meant to be together. Angry and...well, terrified.'

Ethan's gaze grew hooded. It was a while before he spoke again. 'After losing my family, I promised myself I would never again care for another person as deeply as I had them. Love, and all its complications, was not something I ever wanted for myself.'

Olivia kept deathly still, afraid to break the spell between them. This man, this powerful immortal predestined to be her soulmate, was confessing something she sensed he had never before divulged to a living soul. This realization both humbled and frightened her.

'I'm still scared of this connection between us,' Ethan continued in a low voice. 'But I'm not going to run away from it anymore.'

Olivia drew a shuddering breath. His admission seemed to be sealing something between them, an invisible contract she had yet to acknowledge.

Ethan raised a hand and cupped her chin. His eyes focused on her mouth. She shivered when he rubbed the pad of his thumb across the plump flesh of her lower lip.

'I want this. I want you.' He paused, his hot gaze rising to meet hers. 'How about you?'

Heat ignited from where he touched her and slowly filled her veins. Olivia closed her eyes and felt the hunger sleeping deep inside rise to the fore once more.

'Yes,' she breathed.

He took three steps to the door, closed it, and returned to take her in his arms. His mouth met hers with a desperation that matched her own need.

This time, she parted her lips of her own accord.

~

ETHAN STIFLED A GROAN AS HE SPEARED HIS FINGERS through Olivia's hair, holding her head in place while he learned the shape of her mouth.

He had been awake when he heard the dull thud coming from down the corridor. When he entered Olivia's room and saw her by the bed, a glass rolling at her feet while she stood frozen in a psychic daze, the need to protect her had him automatically reaching for her.

The desire that slowly filled her face after she awoke from the vision had stopped him in his tracks and sent his blood churning with lust. It had also drawn a stilted admission from the depths of his soul; never in his immortal lives had he been as honest and as vulnerable in front of a woman as he had in that moment. Her reaction to his words and her breathless acquiescence to his question undid the last restraints of his self-control.

He reached for the hem of her nightdress and pulled it over her head, their lips breaking contact for a couple of torturous seconds. He ran his hands from her wrists all the way down her arms, his thumbs skimming the sides of her cotton-covered breasts before curving into the elastic band at her hips and pulling her against him. She tensed and drew back slightly at the intimate contact, a trace of alarm dampening the passion in her eyes.

'It's okay,' Ethan murmured, his heart slamming against his ribs. 'I won't do anything you don't want me to.'

He wondered shakily how he was going to keep this promise

when all he wanted to do was push her down on the bed and take her.

Her next words were his undoing. Her fingers curled around his nape and she rose on the tips of her toes to bring her lips to his. 'Don't stop.'

He deepened the kiss and peeled off the rest of her clothing. When her hands dropped to the waistband of his pajamas, he covered them with his own and rested his forehead against hers, his breathing ragged.

Her teeth flashed in the golden light bathing the room.

*The little imp!*

Olivia gasped when he lifted her in his arms and kneeled on the bed. Ethan laid her down and crouched above her, his gaze skimming the length of her body. He stilled, his breath catching in his throat.

He had never seen anything so beautiful in his life as the woman who lay beneath him, her face flushed with desire, the silver locket with the third eye gleaming against her fair skin. He ran a finger down her cheek to her chin, tilted her head, and angled her mouth for his kiss.

A shiver danced along her limbs as she watched him strip. He returned to the bed and gently lowered his body onto hers, his weight pressing her into the mattress. She trembled beneath him. Ethan closed his eyes for a moment, struggling for control. Her hands found his chest. He shuddered and opened his eyes to fathomless green depths. Her fingers flittered across his skin, at first timid then growing bolder in her exploration, her gaze locked heatedly on his. She stroked his shoulders and arms before gliding down his spine and around his hips.

That was when he felt the flutter in his mind.

Ethan froze, heart filling with wonderment as the sensation increased, bringing with it nuances of brightly-colored emotions. He knew this feeling.

'Is that you?' he whispered.

Olivia's eyes flared. 'You can—'

'—feel you.'

They stared at each other for a breathless moment, stunned by this new, intimate bond. Ethan dipped his head and kissed her neck, eager to test his theory.

She let out a breathy moan and tilted her head back into the pillow, exposing her skin to his lips. Color bloomed behind his eyelids, gold tinged with red. He felt her pleasure and almost lost it there and then.

The next hours were the most humbling of the immortal's entire existence.

He held himself back for as long as he could, afraid to hurt her. It wasn't until Olivia wrapped her legs around his waist and sank her teeth in his shoulder, eyes blazing a brilliant jade and passion sending streaks of red streaming across his conscious-ness, that he finally took her. She stiffened for a moment, pupils widening. Ethan kept still, his lips meeting hers in a heated kiss while he waited for her pain to fade. A visceral hunger threat-ened to consume him when she arched her hips against his. He gritted his teeth, curved one hand around her thigh, and gave in to his need.

When she shattered beneath him, her breathless cries echoing in his ears and the brightness of her feelings flooding his mind with a searing white light, he shattered as well, his body shuddering above hers.

It seemed but a moment before desire clawed at his insides once more. He lowered his head to take her mouth, his lips hard and desperate. From the way Olivia gripped his hips with her thighs and clawed desperately at his back, she was just as eager to resume their carnal dance.

It wasn't until their sated gasps filled the room some time later and he lay with his head against her breast, her heart thrumming rapidly against his cheek and her fingers curled in his sweat-slicked hair, that Ethan realized something momentous.

All that he had ever experienced before, with the dozens of women who had graced his bed during the decades of his existence—that had been sex. *This* was making love.

～

MADELEINE DRUMMED HER FINGERS AGAINST HER THIGH AND stared at the motorway ahead.

An accident just south of Lake Tahoe had delayed them by an hour. She glanced at the clock on the dashboard. It was nearly ten o'clock.

They were still some forty minutes from Carson City.

'Will you relax?' said the man beside her.

Their eyes met briefly. Asgard turned his head and focused on the road once more, one hand resting loosely on the steering wheel.

She found herself staring at his fingers. They were long and elegant, the nails short and blunt.

*Hmm. I wonder how they would feel against my—Whoa! Where the hell did that come from?*

Asgard glanced at her. 'Hey, are you okay?'

*Does he look like that when he's about to—?*

Madeleine bit her lip, opened her window, and fanned herself. The torrid image that had just flashed before her inner vision had her face burning.

'Seriously, do you want me to pull over?' said Asgard.

Madeleine felt the SUV slow.

'No!' she said more harshly than she had intended. 'I'm— I'm all right. I'm just feeling a bit...hot.'

She swallowed convulsively and kept her eyes directed at the rolling, dark landscape outside the window.

There was no denying it any more. She wanted Asgard Godard and she wanted him badly. The intensity of her desire for the immortal shocked her to the core, especially considering it had only been a few days since their first meeting. Sure, she hadn't been in a relationship for some time but she had dated plenty of attractive men over the years. This need was something else, something she had never experienced before. She was going to have to put some distance between them if she didn't want to rip his clothes off and have her wicked way with him.

Besides, she was only just getting used to all that had happened since she broke into AuGenD and discovered the reality of the immortals' existence.

Madeleine heaved a sigh of relief when they finally turned onto the residential street where Gillian Hofstadter lived. Asgard pulled over at the curb halfway down the road and switched off the engine.

The house opposite was a one-story, shingle-roofed building with a pale-blue stucco and brick exterior. It sat in the middle of a row of similar properties, a gravel path dividing the lawn at the front. Lights were visible between the gaps in the drawn curtains at the windows.

They stepped out of the SUV and strolled up the footpath, Asgard scanning their surroundings with hooded eyes. He had left his sword in the vehicle.

The front door opened before they reached it. Gillian Hofstadter appeared in the doorway. She was wearing jeans, a long-sleeved plaid shirt, and a tired expression.

'I didn't think you were going to make it.' She glanced up and down the street before pulling the door open. 'Come on in.'

'Sorry, we were delayed by an accident,' said Madeleine with an apologetic grimace.

Guilt flashed through her at the deception they were about

to play out on the widow. Before they left the lake house, she had called the woman from the secure line in Howard's study to arrange their meeting. They decided they would pretend to be private investigators working on behalf of another soldier's family, their objective to uncover a potential conspiracy to conceal the true facts behind the disappearance of a number of army personnel over the last ten years.

'May I see your ID?' said Mason Hofstadter's widow once they were seated in her lounge.

'Sure.'

Madeleine took their fake Utah detective licenses and handed them to the woman. It had taken Howard a scarily short amount of time to make the IDs.

She scrutinized the cards for several seconds before handing them back with a rueful smile. 'Sorry, it's just habit, I guess.'

'That's okay,' said Asgard.

An uncomfortable silence fell across the room.

Their host cleared her throat. 'You said you wanted to ask some questions about my husband?'

'Yes,' said Madeleine. She leaned forward in the armchair. 'What happened three years ago?'

The schoolteacher's hands twitched on her lap. She took a deep breath and composed herself for a moment before she started to talk.

'As you probably know, Mason was part of the 75th Ranger Regiment. This meant he was a member of one of the best and most well-trained special ops forces in the world.' Gillian Hofstadter looked at them steadily, her gaze unflinching. 'I say this without pride or arrogance. It's simply a fact.'

Her hand rose to the silver crucifix at the base of her throat, her fingers fiddling unconsciously with the metal. 'It wasn't Mason's first time in Afghanistan. He'd been there on at least ten prior occasions on reconnaissance and combat missions.

When he told me he was going back in September 2009, I didn't think anything of it.' A bitter smile twisted her lips. 'Well, other than the usual fear and anxiety that any soldier's wife experiences when her husband goes into battle.' She paused, a muscle jumping in her jawline. 'I was at work when the call came. I remember the headmaster coming to the door of the class I was teaching and just standing there with this look on his face. I knew right away that Mason was dead. Two soldiers turned up ten minutes later to deliver the official news of his death.'

'Did the army give you any information about what happened?' said Asgard.

The schoolteacher shook her head. 'No. It was a covert mission, so they couldn't release any details of the events that led to his death. All they told me was that he was killed alongside three soldiers from another battalion, during an ambush by the enemy. His body was flown to Fort Benning two days later, on Christmas Eve. He had a military funeral the next day.' She swallowed. 'I moved to Carson City the week after.'

'Did you see the body?' asked Madeleine gently.

The woman shook her head. 'It was a closed-casket ceremony, as many of these funerals are.' Her voice trembled slightly. 'I was told his body had been...ripped apart by an explosion.'

Madeleine shared a troubled glance with Asgard. 'I'm sorry we had to ask you to relive that painful memory, Mrs. Hofstadter.'

The widow wiped a tear from the corner of her eye. 'It's all right. If this helps you find out what happened to all those soldiers, including Mason, then I can relive those moments a thousand times more.'

Madeleine waited a beat before voicing the question they had come to Carson City to ask. 'You said in the interview you gave to the newspaper a few years ago that you thought you heard from your husband shortly after his death?'

Gillian Hofstadter's gaze dropped to Madeleine's left hand briefly. 'Are you married?'

Madeleine startled. 'Er, no.'

The schoolteacher's expression softened. 'Have you ever been in love?'

Madeleine hesitated before shaking her head, acutely conscious of the immortal sitting a few feet from her. 'Not really.'

'Oh.' Surprise flashed across Gillian Hofstadter's face. She recovered and clasped her hands in her lap. 'Then you'll have to trust me when I tell you that there's no way you wouldn't recognize the voice of the man you loved, even in your dying moments.' She looked at Asgard then. 'Your partner appears to understand what I'm talking about.'

Madeleine's breath caught in her throat at the sad light darkening the immortal's beautiful eyes.

'Exactly four weeks after Mason's funeral, I received a phone call late at night,' the schoolteacher continued in a hard voice. 'It wasn't the greatest connection, but I knew it was Mason straight away. He spoke for only a couple of minutes.' She frowned at her hands. 'He told me he'd been enlisted in some kind of secret government program and that the army had faked his death as part of the enrollment. From the way he spoke, I think he regretted his decision.' She looked up then, her face pale. 'He sounded scared, like he was being forced into something he didn't want to do.' Her gaze switched from Madeleine to Asgard and back again. 'In all the years I had been with Mason, I had never known him be afraid of anything.' She closed her eyes briefly. 'He told me he loved me and that he was sorry. The call ended after that.'

'You told the army about this?' said Asgard in the stilted silence that followed.

'Yes. I had a friend who works at the phone company trace the call first.' The schoolteacher scowled. 'It was a good thing I did. Once I informed Mason's superiors at Fort Benning of the incident, details of that call disappeared from my phone records.'

Madeleine knitted her brow. If what the widow said was true, then the US Army was engaging in activities that breached the fundamental rights of its serving soldiers. And, so far, she had no reason to doubt the woman sitting across the room from her. Gillian Hofstadter looked to be in full possession of her faculties and did not seem the type to come up with fanciful tales.

'Was that when you asked the army to exhume your husband's body?' she said quietly.

'It was my last resort,' said the widow. Anger underscored her words. 'After weeks and months of getting nowhere with the guys at Fort Benning, I went to the DoD. They were just as unforthcoming with information. My requests in the last three years seem to have become mired in a maze of bureaucratic tape that has no end. My lawyers say they've never seen anything like it.'

She faltered then. Madeleine narrowed her eyes at the nervous look that darted across Gillian Hofstadter's face.

Asgard straightened in his chair. 'What is it?'

'David, one of my lawyers, was involved in a near-fatal crash last year,' said the schoolteacher in a subdued voice. 'Although we have no evidence to prove our suspicions, the firm he works for believed it was a deliberate act of sabotage—and I agree. The truck that drove into David belonged to a private transport company that has contracts with the DoD.' She rubbed her forehead with trembling fingers. 'My husband's case files were in the rental car at the time. David had flown to Washington to have a meeting with the Attorney General. The paramedics dragged him out of the wreckage minutes before the vehicle blew up.'

Madeleine bunched her hands before relaxing them slowly. She glanced at Asgard and saw her anger reflected in his brooding gaze. She had no doubt Jonah Krondike and his army friends were behind the incident Gillian Hofstadter had just recounted. It sounded like the kind of thing they'd do.

'Where did you trace the phone call to?' said Asgard.

# CHAPTER TWENTY-ONE

OLIVIA STIRRED AND BLINKED.

A man's naked chest appeared before her in the soft daylight washing through the windows of the bedroom. She tensed and looked up into a sultry blue gaze.

'Hey,' Ethan said softly.

Olivia registered the intimate way she was curled up against him and felt his ribcage move with his breathing. The sensations electrified her and brought back sensuous memories of the previous night.

'Hi,' she whispered.

'How do you feel?'

His hand moved on her back, fingers fluttering across her skin. Olivia stretched her legs against his to test the soreness of her muscles and heard him inhale sharply. Heat flooded her face when she saw the desire in his eyes.

She had not known she was capable of such passion until she'd laid her fingers on her soulmate's body. The hunger that had swamped her consciousness when Ethan touched her almost doubled when she reciprocated in turn. The feel of his hot skin and flesh against hers, the rasp of his breath catching in his throat as she explored his body with her hands, the feverish light in his eyes when he kissed her, the low sounds he made as he moved above her...all had ignited her senses and burned away her fears.

Although the tumultuous events of the last few days had brought about a sea of change inside her, she sensed one more difference this morning. For the first time in her life, she felt... complete, as if a missing part of her she hadn't even been aware existed had returned to her.

She stared at the man responsible for this latest, earth-shattering transformation and replied to his anxious question the only way she could. She rose up on an elbow, curled a hand around his nape, angled her head, and kissed him.

Her lips twitched in a smile at the groan that rumbled through him. Ethan wrapped one arm around her and flipped her onto her back, his other hand reaching down to grasp her thigh while his tongue parted her mouth to deepen the kiss. She gasped at the feel of his body pressing her into the mattress and clutched desperately at his head.

They froze when a knock sounded at the door.

'We're having a council of war,' said Howard through the wood. 'Make yourselves decent and come on down.'

Ethan pulled his lips from hers and dropped his face against the side of her neck.

'Dammit.'

Olivia shivered at the feel of his breath on her skin.

Ethan looked up. His eyes darkened when he saw her face.

'One day, I'm going to lock us away and we're going to do this for hours on end.'

She blushed at the explicit images that flashed across her mind.

Ethan grinned. Her pulse stuttered at the dazzling brilliance of his smile. He dropped a swift kiss on her lips, rolled, and scooted out of the bed. Olivia propped herself on her elbows and watched him pull his pajama bottoms back on. The sight of hard muscles bunching under his naked skin made hunger stir in the pit of her stomach. She bit her lip.

Ethan gave her a smoldering look that told her he knew exactly what she was thinking.

'See you downstairs.'

He strolled out of the bedroom. Olivia dropped back on the pillow and covered her face with her hands. Her heart already ached at his absence. A memory darted through her mind. She hadn't told him about her latest vision. She took a deep breath, pushed the covers back, and walked into the bathroom.

Asgard, Madeleine, and Howard were talking quietly at the breakfast table when she walked into the kitchen ten minutes later.

Olivia slowed, feeling suddenly flustered.

'Hello,' she said hesitantly.

'Hi,' Asgard replied in an awkward voice.

Howard grinned and raised his cup at her, blue eyes twinkling mischievously.

'Sleep well?'

Madeleine nudged the Crovir immortal sharply in the side with her elbow.

'Ignore him,' she said in a disgusted tone as he swore and grabbed a towel to dab at his spilled coffee. She looked at Asgard. 'And what's wrong with you?'

'Well, she *is* my niece,' Asgard muttered into his coffee.

'So?' said Madeleine. 'This is not the dark ages. And judging from what you've told me about this immortal soulmate business, I suspect you weren't exactly a saint when you were courting your wife.'

Asgard choked on his drink and scowled at Madeleine. She stared back, undaunted.

Olivia's gaze switched from her uncle to the woman beside

him. A precognitive flutter danced across her consciousness. She suppressed a smile.

A warm hand landed on the small of her back and curved around her waist.

"Morning,' said Ethan breezily. He dropped a kiss on Olivia's head and strolled to the coffee machine. 'So, what happened in Carson City?'

∼

ETHAN FROWNED. 'SIERRA VISTA?'

A satellite map of Arizona occupied the computer screen on the desk in the study. Howard zoomed in on a built-up area some seventy-odd miles southeast of Tucson.

'Uh-huh,' said Madeleine with a nod. 'Gillian Hofstadter traced the call her husband made to her in January 2010 to a public phone booth in that city.'

'And you believe her?' said Ethan, still skeptical.

Madeleine glanced at Asgard. 'We both do. She's as sane as they come and everything she's done to date to try and uncover the truth behind her husband's disappearance shows intelligence and focus. She's not the type to delude herself into believing something that didn't happen.'

'Besides, Sierra Vista makes for an interesting location,' said Asgard.

Ethan raised an eyebrow. 'It does?'

Howard smiled. 'Yep.'

He tapped on the keyboard. The satellite map panned out to the left. About one mile northwest of the city and a similar distance south of an airport was a sprawling complex covering thousands of acres of desert land.

'What's that?' said Ethan.

'That, my friend, is your next lead,' drawled Howard. 'Fort Huachuca.'

Olivia straightened up from where she leaned against the table. 'A military base?'

'Yes,' said Howard. 'The place has been there in one form or another since the US calvary was still fighting the Apaches. It's served as a command center, a training ground, and a proving ground for a range of army service branches in the last sixty years. The US Army Intelligence Center and the Network Enterprise Technology Command are among the groups currently located on the site.'

'It's also home to a large medical center,' said Madeleine. 'My guess is Mason Hofstadter was taken to that place as part of some sort of initial screening and assessment for the research program. The range of dates for the medical data we have on him matches what his wife gave for the phone call.'

'Before you ask, no, they don't appear to have any virtual databases that can be mined from here,' Howard added. 'Anything they have must be in physical format.'

Ethan stared at the compound on the screen before looking at Asgard. 'Are you saying what I think you're saying?'

The Bastian noble dipped his chin. 'We're breaking in there.'

JONAH KRONDIKE STUDIED THE THREE TEST SUBJECTS through the glass containment wall separating the observation station from the subterranean firing range below. Spent cartridges littered the ground at the men's feet. A range of semi-automatic handguns and boxes full of magazines occupied the tables between them. They finished reloading the weapons in their hands, raised their arms, and fired rapidly at the distant targets, their movements perfectly synchronized and their expressions focused.

'Perfect scores again,' murmured the sergeant standing next to Jonah.

The immortal looked at the timer on the wall. The soldiers had been on the range for ten minutes and had gone through more than three times as many targets.

A phone buzzed in the background. One of the technicians answered it.

'Sir?' he called out to Jonah a moment later. 'It's Agent Scoleri on the line.'

Jonah strode to the console and took the receiver.

'What is it?'

'I have some news that's going to make your day,' said the Crovir immortal without preamble.

Jonah stiffened, thoughts about the test subjects' superb performance on the firing range vanishing from his mind. 'You found them?'

'Not quite,' drawled Scoleri. 'We discovered a piece of undamaged hardware from their bunker. Our techs have managed to access some of the data on it. They've identified some of Howard Titus's accomplices in the hacker world. We're dumping tracers on their connections in case our targets get in touch.'

'Good. Have a full team ready to deploy at a moment's notice. This time, I don't want them to know you're coming until you're looking them in the eye.'

MADELEINE CLOSED THE DOOR AND STRODE ACROSS THE study, two steaming coffee cups in hand. 'How are you doing?'

Howard looked up distractedly from the computer screen, blond hair sticking out at odd angles from his head where he'd ran his fingers repeatedly through it. Madeleine hid a smile.

Despite the fact that the man seated at the computer had

more than a century on her, she had started to feel like his wiser, older sister. She was still surprised at the easy camaraderie that had developed between her and the immortals she now found herself associated with.

Having been alone for most of her adult life, it felt strange to think that she might finally belong somewhere.

'Not too bad. I got the files from the others about three hours ago.'

He accepted the drink she proffered with a grateful smile and turned back to the computer, worry lines furrowing his brow once more.

Although Howard adopted a casual attitude and indulged in lighthearted banter, Madeleine knew the loss of his estate in the Santa Monica Mountains still weighed heavily on his mind. Her gaze switched to the screen. Her hand froze with the cup halfway to her lips.

'What the—?'

She put her coffee down on the desk, grabbed a chair, and wheeled herself next to the Crovir immortal.

'That bad, huh?' said Howard at her expression. 'I kinda thought this stuff looked shit scary.'

Madeleine reached across and scrolled down the monitor. 'Is this everything from the coded data you were working on?'

'Almost. I've got a couple dozen megabytes left to go.'

Madeleine sat back and waited impatiently while Howard decoded the rest of the files, trying not to dwell on the awful truth they seemed to imply. He paused a minute later and looked at her pointedly.

'What?' she snapped.

His gaze shifted to her bouncing knee.

'That's not helping.'

'Oh. Sorry.' She forced herself to relax and reached for the cooling coffee. 'Any news on the guys?'

Howard dipped his chin curtly. 'They landed in Tucson

about an hour and a half ago. They should be inside the fort by now.'

Anxiety darted through Madeleine.

It had been six hours since Asgard and Ethan left the safe house to go to Sierra Vista. They had taken a private jet from Sacramento and Asgard had flown the plane across to Arizona. The obvious wealth displayed by the immortals hardly surprised her. After all, they had been around for some time.

When she asked Howard about it, he explained that though the US government had seized STAEGH Corp's assets and the personal accounts of its CEO and main shareholders, the three men had stashed away enough money and gold in private offshore accounts and bank vaults to last them several more lifetimes.

'What about your employees?' said Madeleine.

'We had a back-up plan in place with our firm's lawyers,' the Crovir immortal replied. 'In case something like this ever happened, they would all receive a significant redundancy package and letters of recommendation for their next employer.' He grinned. 'Oh and the offer to come and work for us again if we were to rise from the ashes. Our employees are quite... unconventional in that sense.'

Madeleine rolled her eyes. 'What, as in they love defying authority and living dangerously?'

Howard chuckled. 'Why, yes. That's what made the company so successful in the first place. We only use the best.'

The study door opened, jolting Madeleine back to the present. Olivia walked in with a plate of sandwiches.

Howard grabbed one and chomped down hungrily, crumbs flying everywhere while he continued to type with one hand. 'Thanks.'

'I feel like giving him a bib,' Madeleine muttered.

Olivia smiled and sat on the edge of the desk. Twenty

minutes later, Howard's hands finally stopped moving on the keyboard.

'Well?' said Madeleine.

He blew out a sigh and pushed back from the table. 'I've put all the decoded files together in a continuous stream. It'll probably make more sense if you read it.'

Madeleine wheeled herself across to the computer and navigated to the start of the document. She scrolled down slowly and felt fear form a cold weight in the pit of her stomach with every slide of her fingers. It was several minutes before she spoke.

'Like I suspected, the ultimate goal of Jonah Krondike and the army group he's working with appears to be the creation of a new race of super soldiers. Various governments have tried to do just that in the past and all have failed, including our own CIA's Project MKUltra, which ran from the 1950s to the 1970s. The background to the data in these folders appears to stem as far back as the Second World War, with a lot of the original research carried out in German concentration camps.'

Howard's face darkened. 'You mean, Krondike was working for the Nazis?'

Madeleine nodded curtly. 'Though I think he was more interested in the scientific advancements they could procure than the politics of war. The period where Asgard was a prisoner of Krondike appears to be when they made the first big leap in their research.'

'That's when they obtained access to his DNA,' said Olivia, a trace of anger audible in her voice.

'Yes,' Madeleine said. 'And the DNA of all the immortals they captured subsequently.'

She clenched her jaw at the thought of the father she had never known. Somewhere within the complex fields of data she was staring at were the blood, sweat, and tears he had shed during his years of capture. A slow rage ignited deep in her belly.

The need to avenge both her parents stoked the flames higher and dampened her trepidation. 'Their biggest break-through came about six years ago.'

'Wasn't that around the time the data in the other folders stopped?' said Howard.

'Yes. That's when they obtained all the ingredients necessary to start their next experiment.' Madeleine scowled at the monitor. 'Jonah Krondike's human enhancement program is made up of four broad phases. Phase One consists of preparing the test subjects with a rigorous regime of physical and mental training, before using performance-enhancing drugs and chemicals derived from their research on the immortals to accelerate their physical development. It also includes the use of specific techniques and medications to modify their behavior. This alteration of their physiological systems continues into Phase Two.'

She paused, fingers clenching on the trackpad at the enormity of what was laid out on the screen.

'Madeleine?' Olivia said anxiously.

'It's okay. This is just so—' Madeleine took a deep breath. 'Phase Two places the subjects in a prolonged coma during which their DNA is manipulated. This is when Jonah's scientists use bionanotechnology to bind immortal genetic material into the dormant subjects' own chromosomes. It's by far the longest phase of the program. In that time, the subjects' muscles and brains are constantly stimulated by electrical signals and their bodies filled with drugs to augment the processes started in Phase One.'

'Jesus,' Howard murmured. 'This is sounding more and more like a Frankenstein freak show.'

'You're not far off,' said Madeleine darkly. 'Phase Three is the tricky part. From their results, it seems this is the period where they had to...terminate many of their subjects.'

'What happens in Phase Three?' said Olivia.

'They wake them up,' said Madeleine. 'It seems most of the subjects showed extreme aggression and psychosis. There's mention here of research staff being injured by several subjects going on a rampage before they were taken down by security.' She furrowed her brow. 'The final phase consists of battle-condition training and testing of those subjects who made it through Phase Three without being killed.'

Silence fell across the study.

'Has anyone made it to Phase Four?' said Olivia.

Madeleine shook her head. 'I don't know. The stuff on here is a few months old. It looks like Serle hasn't input the latest information into the database yet.' She hesitated. 'Looking at the timeline of the experiments, they should be awakening a batch of twenty-five subjects about now.'

'Damn!' Howard ran a hand through his tousled hair. 'This is bad. We've got to—' He broke off and stiffened in his seat. 'Olivia?'

Madeleine looked around.

Olivia was standing rigidly next to the desk, her face pale and her gaze lost somewhere in the scenery outside the window overlooking the lake.

Despite never having seen one before, Madeleine knew she was witnessing one of the immortal's psychic episodes. 'What is it?'

Olivia didn't seem to hear her. 'Something...something is...' She snapped out of her stupor and looked at them in wide-eyed horror. 'They're here!'

Madeleine shot out of the chair, heart slamming against her ribs as she looked wildly through the windows.

'Who's here—?' said Howard with a puzzled expression.

The sound of helicopter rotors rose from the direction of the lake.

'Shit!'

He bolted to his feet and hit a couple of keys on the computer.

They were almost out of the room when glass shattered behind them. Smoke bombs and flash grenades sailed through the broken windows and clattered onto the floorboards.

## CHAPTER TWENTY-TWO

THE DOOR BLOCKED OUT THE LIGHT AND MOST OF THE explosive sounds from the bombs.

'The weapons bag!' Howard shouted as they raced down the corridor toward the rear of the chalet.

Madeleine snatched the backpack from under the console table in the lobby. 'Got it!'

She grabbed the Sig Sauer, jammed a couple of magazines in her waistband, and threw the bag at Howard.

He caught it, removed a submachine gun, and looped an ammunition belt holding magazines and grenades around his shoulder. 'We need to get to the boat!'

Fear had taken an icy grip of his heart. They were heavily outnumbered and the chances of them making it out there alive without Ethan and Asgard were slim at best. Despair made acid churn in his stomach.

*You can't give up!*

Howard glanced at the women with him and saw angry determination overcome the panic on their faces. He gritted his teeth.

*If they want us, they're gonna have to come and get us!*

Gunfire erupted outside the front of the property. Bullets thunked into the walls of the chalet and punched through glass. White fumes billowed down the passage behind them as more smoke bombs were lobbed inside. The detonations of flash grenades followed close behind.

They dashed across the kitchen and barged through the French doors opening onto the rear deck. Howard spotted movement out the corner of his eye, pulled Olivia behind him, and fired at the masked soldiers coming around the side of the building. The reports of the Sig Sauer echoed the shots from the submachine gun as Madeleine opened fire on the soldiers coming the other way.

'Get ready to move!' he said.

He yanked two grenades from the belt, launched the first one at the men in front of him, and threw the second toward the opposite end of the deck.

They jumped off just as the bombs exploded and raced for the jetty. Dirt and gravel puffed up around them as bullets peppered the ground in their wake. They leapt onto the wooden boards and sprinted toward the boat. Halfway down the pier, Madeleine cried out and stumbled.

Olivia lurched to a halt and whirled around. '*Madeleine!*'

Red bloomed on Madeleine's left flank where a bullet had struck her. She winced, clamped a hand over the wound, and half-ran, half-limped toward them.

'Keep going!' Howard ordered.

He tossed the backpack at Olivia, dropped to one knee, and opened fire on the soldiers chasing after them.

Olivia shouldered the bag, wrapped an arm around Madeleine, and helped her to the boat. The vessel rocked in the water when they jumped in.

'Key's in the ignition!' Howard shouted over his shoulder.

The roar of the motorboat engine rose above the sound of

gunfire. The Sig Sauer's bullets whizzed past him and struck one of the soldiers.

'*Howard!*' Madeleine yelled.

'Go!' he screamed.

Howard heard her curse. The boat started to accelerate, rotors spinning through the water. He rose and ran backward, the submachine gun shuddering in his hands as he continued his assault on the men charging across the beach. Wood chips erupted ahead of his legs where shots splintered the weathered boards. He turned and bolted toward the end of the pier.

The boat was five feet from the dock when he jumped. Heat flared on his left thigh as he soared over the water.

He hit the aft deck, collapsed to his knees, and rolled. A harsh grunt escaped him when he struck the starboard side. Olivia stumbled across the boat, dropped to her knees, and clamped a hand over the bullet wound on his leg. Howard ignored the fiery pain lancing through his flesh, sat up, and brought the submachine gun up above her head to shoot at the soldiers who stood firing at them from the jetty and the shoreline.

Madeleine reloaded the Sig, pushed the throttle all the way forward, and twisted around. A grim expression darkened her pale face as she raised her arm at their attackers and pulled the trigger repeatedly.

Shots scored the water and thudded into the stern of the vessel.

'*Get down!*' Howard shouted at Madeleine.

He covered Olivia's head with his arm and pulled her next to him as he flattened himself to the floor of the boat, pulse racing and stomach twisting with horror at what he had just seen.

The deadly whistle of the rocket-propelled grenade reached his ears a moment before the boat suddenly turned. He glanced toward the controls in time to see Madeleine let go of the wheel and throw herself to the deck. The missile whooshed past the port hull and struck the surface of the lake some thirty feet away. The detonation brought a cold shower of water on their heads and caused the vessel to lurch violently to the side. The engines screamed, propellers churning empty air for a breathless moment. The boat rocked back down with a loud thud and splash, and started to accelerate again.

Howard cautiously lifted his head and looked around, amazed they were still in one piece. 'Nice move.'

Madeleine smiled weakly, rose to her knees, and grabbed the Sig where it lay on the deck. The relentless gunfire continued from the direction of the lake house. With the boat now just under half a mile from shore, the bullets fell harmlessly into the water.

Howard tensed. The soldier who'd fired the RPG was loading another one into his shoulder-held launcher.

Madeleine blanched. 'Shit! There's three of them!'

Howard's mouth went dry when he saw two more dark-clad figures raise their launchers. He tightened his hold on the submachine gun. 'We're not out of range of those yet!'

That was when Olivia shifted beside him. She knelt on the deck, raised a hand, and laid her palm against the side of his face.

Alarm flashed through Howard when he registered the steadfast light in her blazing eyes. 'What are you doing?'

'This is the only way I can think to protect you.'

A different kind of fear gripped Howard. He swallowed. Olivia raised her other hand toward Madeleine. The scientist hesitated before moving closer. The boat rolled and skipped across the water as it hit a countercurrent, causing her to stumble slightly.

Olivia touched Madeleine's face gently when she came within reach.

'Are you sure about this?' said Madeleine.

'No.' Olivia's expression hardened. 'Get ready.'

She closed her eyes.

The clatter of the distant gunfire faded as a heavy weight wrapped around Howard's head. He clenched his jaw and steeled himself for the excruciating pain that was to follow. One second passed. Then two and three. He blinked and stared at Madeleine, seeing his own shock reflected on her face.

Bar a mild sense of pressure and the complete absence of sound, he could feel little else.

The same could not be said of the soldiers on the shore.

Howard watched, mesmerized, as they dropped their weapons and fell to the ground, bodies writhing in agony and mouths open on screams that never reached his ears. The two rocket-propelled grenades that had been launched veered to either side of the boat before hurtling harmlessly across the lake, their trajectories modified by an invisible wave. The stretch of water between the boat and the beach had similarly flattened under the unseen psychokinetic force emanating from the vessel. The tops of the trees edging the lake bowed backward into the forest, branches shuddering and leaves shaking in the silent storm.

A fine sheet of sweat broke out on Olivia's forehead. Her fingers trembled on his skin.

Awe filled Howard at the sheer, ungodly power of the woman touching him. On the other side of Olivia, Madeleine gaped at the shoreline, her gaze wide and unblinking.

There was movement in the sky to the left. Howard turned his head with some difficulty and saw a helicopter rise above the treetops on the far side of the lake.

SCOLERI GLARED AT THE DISTANT BOAT. THE ROTORS WHINED.

The helicopter rocked slightly, buffeted by the edge of the psychic pressure wave.

'Maintain a safe distance!' he barked at the pilot. He twisted in his seat and stared at the man lying on the floor of the main cabin. 'Have you got her?'

'Yes,' said the sniper.

His hands were steady on the rifle and his eye glued to his scope.

'Take the shot,' Scoleri ordered.

THE BULLET STRUCK OLIVIA IN THE CHEST. SHE GASPED AND blinked, shock flaring through her a second before pain erupted at the site of the entry point.

'*No!*' screamed Madeleine.

Howard caught Olivia as she fell. He laid her on the deck, his face ashen with fear. Madeleine leaned over her and pressed a hand on the wound in her ribcage, tears welling in her pale eyes.

Olivia coughed and choked. The metallic taste of blood flooded the back of her mouth. A black circle started to encroach upon the edge of her vision. The roar of her racing heart filled her ears.

'Ethan,' she rasped, staring blindly past Howard and Madeleine at the blue sky.

Consciousness faded and darkness filled her world.

# PART THREE: BURN

# CHAPTER TWENTY-THREE

THE SOLDIER AT THE SECURITY CHECKPOINT SCRUTINIZED their IDs.

'Major Reed, Captain Davies,' he acknowledged with a curt nod before handing the cards back. 'What is the purpose of your visit to Fort Huachuca today?'

Ethan took the counterfeit badges Howard had hastily made that morning and rested an elbow casually on the edge of the sedan's window. 'We have a meeting with the commander of your medical center. It was a last-minute arrangement.' He glanced at the computer visible in the booth behind the soldier. 'Check your schedule.'

Asgard sat silently beside Ethan, his expression appropriately aloof behind his black aviator glasses. He'd had a haircut before they left the chalet.

The flight to Tucson had been uneventful. They'd hired the rental at the airport and swapped the number plates for the fake ones they'd brought with them. Anyone checking the vehicle registration would find its owner to be one Captain Arnold Davies, from Fort Irwin, California. As far as Ethan was concerned, the real Major Reed was also currently a resident there. They'd come by the army uniforms at one of the surplus stores in the city.

The soldier returned shortly, an apologetic grimace on his face. 'I'm sorry about that, Captain. Looks like the official visitors' list was updated in the last couple of hours. I have you scheduled for a meet with the Commander at 15:00. Just follow the road to the right and take a left at the roundabout. You can't miss it.'

Ethan thanked the man, closed the window, and stepped on the gas. Only then did he release a small sigh of relief. Howard had promised he'd have them on the visitors' list by the time they landed in Tucson. Asgard removed the aviator glasses, dropped them in the glove compartment, and extracted two handguns. Armistad was in the trunk of the car, as were Ethan's swords.

Cool air poured through the vents as they drove across the yellow, barren desert. Buildings appeared up ahead and to the right, the structures shimmering faintly in the summer heat. The tail end of the Huachuca Mountains rose against the cloudless sky on the horizon.

The medical center was an L-shaped, ochre-colored, three-story complex located at the south end of the base. They followed the service road to the back, parked opposite an exit door, and walked around to the front entrance. One of Howard's associates had managed to pull up the floor plans of the building while they were flying out of Sacramento. Howard forwarded the file to the satellite phone he'd given Ethan.

'Your best bet is the storage rooms in the basement,' Howard said when he called them. 'The medical data we looked at was several years old. If the base was indeed where these soldiers were initially assessed, I doubt the information we're seeking is in active case files.'

Two soldiers came out of the glass front doors as they approached them. The men stopped talking, dipped their chins respectfully when they saw Ethan and Asgard's uniforms, and walked by, their chatter resuming once more.

Ethan kept his gaze focused straight ahead as they walked into the cool, bright lobby and passed the information desk. They headed down a busy corridor, turned left at a junction, and pushed through a door halfway down the passage. It opened onto a staircase. A nurse was strolling down the steps from the floor above. Asgard smiled and held the door open for her.

She blushed, murmured a hasty 'Thank you,' and walked out into the first-story corridor.

'Wow,' said Ethan as the door closed behind her. He stared at Asgard. 'I think that's the first time I've seen you try to charm someone.'

'Shut up,' said Asgard.

They walked down the stairs and came to a service door at the bottom. Ethan tried the handle; it was locked. He touched the metal plate, heard a soft click, and opened the entrance.

Bare concrete replaced linoleum on the other side. Harsh light from fluorescent strips showed exposed pipes and cables running along the ceiling and the tops of the cinder-block walls. A faint rumble rose above the hiss of steam from the ductworks as they approached an intersection.

The vibration travelled through the soles of Ethan's boots. 'Incinerator?'

'Yeah,' murmured Asgard. 'And generators.'

They turned the corner and bumped into someone.

'Whoa there, big fella!' said the man Asgard had collided with.

The stranger staggered back a step. He looked to be in his fifties and was wearing grease-streaked overalls. A tag inscribed with the name "Jim Hernandez" was pinned over his heart.

His brow furrowed when he registered their uniforms. 'What are you—?'

'You the caretaker?' said Ethan.

The man straightened. 'Why, yes. What I want to—'

'Sorry about this,' said Asgard.

He punched the guy in the face.

Jim Hernandez went down like a brick. They carried him to a janitor's closet, wrapped a couple of cable ties around his wrists and ankles, covered his mouth with the duct tape they found inside a tool box, and locked him inside.

They found the first storage room at the end of the corridor.

Ethan manipulated the lock open and flicked the light switches on the wall. 'Oh boy.'

Rows of shelves stacked with brown boxes stretched out before them. They filled the entire floorspace and rose all the way to the ceiling.

Asgard walked to the closest one and touched the side of a carton. 'At least they're labeled. Let's start with December 2009.'

It took half an hour for them to realize that the information they were after was not there. They hadn't found any evidence of army research experiments having been carried out at Fort Huachuca either.

Ethan's heart sank. 'There's another storage room on the other side of the basement.'

They made their way to the second chamber and found a similar layout to the first room. They found the right section and started to go through the boxes on the shelves.

'There are several cartons missing from here,' said Asgard some time later.

Ethan turned from the row he was inspecting and joined the Bastian noble. He frowned when he saw the boxes Asgard was staring at. The numbers on the labels did not follow the expected sequence they'd observed so far and showed at least four missing containers.

*Could this be it?*

Asgard ran his hand through his hair and let out a frustrated sigh. 'Looks like there's nothing here after all. Damn! What a waste of a trip.'

'There might be a receipt or a transfer slip,' said Ethan.

He grabbed the end box. Asgard lifted the other one reluctantly.

They found a piece of paper at the bottom of the second carton.

'"Containers 111641-111644 transferred to Building 4489, US Army Facility Yuma Proving Ground,"' Ethan read out.

Excitement flared through him. It died in the next moment as he reread the address. He looked at Asgard and saw the same anxiety dawn in the immortal's eyes. They had both heard of the Yuma base. It was one of the largest army installations in the world.

They put the boxes back, left the room, and exited the hospital through the fire door at the end of the basement. No one stopped them as they strolled to the sedan. Ten minutes later, they were headed north on State Route 90 back up to Tucson. Asgard waited until they hit the interstate highway before ringing the hospital.

'There's a man locked up in the janitor's closet in your basement,' he said curtly and disconnected.

Ethan frowned at the road. They were passing through the west end of the city of Benson. A scattering of one-story buildings dotted the desert plains to the right.

'Yuma is big,' he said grimly. He glanced at Asgard. 'Too big for just the two of us to handle.'

A guarded expression dawned on the Bastian noble's face. 'What are you saying?'

Ethan's grip tightened on the steering wheel. 'I'm saying we need help, Asgard. I know you don't want to hear this, but I think it's time for us to—'

The pain came from nowhere, stabbing through his chest and causing him to lose his breath. Ethan doubled over, tears flooding his eyes. His world went white and a dull ringing filled his ears.

He felt the sedan lurch across the asphalt and heard Asgard's muted curse. Unseen hands snatched the steering wheel from his grip. Horns blared in the background, the sounds muffled. Gravel rattled under the carriage and the sedan came to an abrupt stop. The belt dug into Ethan's chest as he jerked forward and slammed back into the seat. He heard Asgard shout his name.

Sound and sight returned in a dizzying rush. Ethan gazed dazedly at the traffic speeding past his window. Asgard had pulled over in a lay-by.

The Bastian noble grabbed his shoulders and shook him. 'Hey, stay with me!'

Ethan blinked and rested his forehead against the steering wheel. His heart thundered inside his chest like he'd run a marathon and his breaths came in hard, fast pants. Underscoring the frantic beats was a searing ache that made him want to weep.

'It's Olivia,' he mumbled in a choked voice.

Asgard froze beside him.

Ethan turned his head and stared at the immortal, a single tear escaping his eye and rolling down his cheek. 'Something's happened to her.'

# CHAPTER TWENTY-FOUR

ETHAN STOOD IN THE DOORWAY TO OLIVIA'S ROOM AND stared at the bed where they had made love less than twelve hours ago. White down and debris littered the floor and the sheets. Moonlight streamed through the broken windows and showed the bullet holes in the walls and ceiling. He turned with a heavy heart and headed downstairs.

The safe house was a scene of devastation. From the empty shells on the ground and the blast damage outside, it seemed the enemy's attempt to take the place had been met with fierce resistance. They'd found blood on the rear deck and the beach. There was also a large collection of bloody footprints inside the boat.

Ethan found Asgard standing on the terrace. He was staring at the vessel sitting lopsidedly on its keel halfway up the beach, where it looked to have been dragged. His hands were fisted at his sides.

'That's where they shot her?'

Ethan hesitated. 'Yes.' A strange numbness had replaced the agony filling his soul. The only time he recalled experiencing such a crippling feeling was the day he lost his family, all those years ago. 'Jonah must have taken them to Yuma.'

Asgard remained silent.

'You know what you have to do,' said Ethan after a while.

This time, Asgard turned and looked at him, a muscle jumping in his cheek.

'We need to at least try,' Ethan added, an edge of steel coating his words. 'Irrespective of my powers and your abilities as a Hunter, the two of us can't take on an entire army base.'

He handed the satellite phone to Asgard.

The Bastian noble stared at it as if it were a snake. He closed his eyes for a moment. When he opened them again, Ethan saw bitter resignation in their depths. He took the phone and dialed a number.

Ethan waited quietly, tension coursing through his limbs. It was half a minute before the call was answered.

'This is Asgard Godard. I need to speak to Victor Dvorsky.'

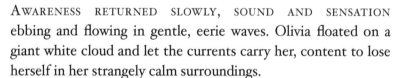

AWARENESS RETURNED SLOWLY, SOUND AND SENSATION ebbing and flowing in gentle, eerie waves. Olivia floated on a giant white cloud and let the currents carry her, content to lose herself in her strangely calm surroundings.

The pain struck without warning, a hammer driving straight into the middle of her chest. She cried out, eyes slamming open, her vision blurring with tears. Her voice sounded shockingly weak to her ears.

A white ceiling appeared overhead. Olivia squinted at the bright lights shining down on her.

Ice formed in her veins when she registered the equipment beside the bed she lay on. A monitor beeped steadily to the right, its colorful screen showing her vitals. The high-pitched tone speeded up slightly as her heart rate increased. Next to it was a bag of clear fluid hanging from a metal stand. She followed the plastic tubing leading from the bottom of the pump to the intravenous line in the crook of her right elbow. A rack holding several infusion syringes hung on the other side of the bed, the various lines connecting to another intravenous access in her left elbow. An invisible machine hummed behind her head, the steady throb sending faint vibrations through the firm surface beneath her. She felt the prick of needles in her scalp.

She moved to sit up and found she couldn't. Her breaths came in rapid pants and the pain in her chest returned ten-fold at the effort it took to merely lift her head off the bed. She curled her fingers into fists and felt something dig into her skin. Her gaze traveled down the length of the gurney to the thick leather straps binding her wrists and ankles. She made out the shape of a dressing on her chest, underneath the plain hospital gown covering her body.

An alarm went off as her pulse rocketed, panic squeezing air out of her lungs. She squirmed and kicked feebly against the restraints.

'Now, now, there's no need for that. The straps are there to keep you safe,' boomed a loud voice, startling her. 'Besides, you wouldn't want to re-open your wound. You just had major surgery to get that bullet out. You were lucky. Our sniper missed your heart by an inch.'

Olivia's frantic gaze skimmed past the speakers at the edges of the ceiling to the glass window opposite the end of the bed. Her mouth went dry at the sight that met her eyes.

There was a laboratory beyond her prison. At least a dozen staff in white coats milled about the vast space, working computers and banks of complex machines. Armed soldiers stood near a pair of steel doors set in a distant breeze-block wall.

A female scientist glanced at her briefly before talking to

her colleague. They chatted animatedly about something on the screen before them.

Olivia found her gaze drawn to a man who stood watching her silently from the other side of the partition. He was tall and of solid build, with ice-blue eyes, dark hair peppered with gray, and a beard. She stiffened.

Although she had never seen a picture of Jonah Krondike, she knew she was looking at the immortal who had destroyed her and Ethan's families. He raised his hand and examined a small metal object lying in his palm.

Anger blossomed inside her when she recognized the locket that had been bequeathed to her by her parents.

He laid the casing on a table and strolled closer to the wall. 'It's remarkable how much like your mother you look.'

Trepidation fluttered through her. She scanned the room behind him, searching for Madeleine and Howard.

'If you're looking for your friends, they're not here,' said Krondike.

Olivia tried not to show her relief. Krondike's words implied that her companions were still alive. Her thoughts flitted briefly to Ethan and her uncle.

*Do they know what happened at the chalet? Are they there, right now, wondering where we are?*

Grief almost overcame her then. She squeezed her eyes shut for a moment. *I have to be strong. They will come for us!*

She flexed her fingers and reached deep inside her mind. Her gaze returned to the immortal on the other side of the glass. 'What do you want?'

'It's quite simple, really,' said Krondike. A faint smile curved his lips. 'I desire your powers.'

Another alarm sounded inside the room. Olivia heard a rising buzz from the machine behind her at the same time that electronic whirrs echoed from the syringe pumps connected to her arms. The numbers on the displays increased rapidly.

Several of the scientists gathered excitedly around a bank of computers behind Krondike.

'Ah.' The immortal's gaze never left hers. 'I see you're attempting to use your psychokinetic ability.' His smile turned snake-like.

Olivia's puzzlement lasted only seconds before agonizing pain ripped through her head and shot down her spine. She arched against the mattress, eyes wide-open and a scream leaving her throat. The pain came again, stronger than before, a river of fire that flooded her mind and body, burning all coherent thought in its path. Every muscle in her body tensed as she jackknifed helplessly off the bed once more, unable to control the reflexes governing her spine. She heard a low crack as her jaw locked in spasm.

Krondike's voice reached her dimly through the loud ringing in her ears. 'That's right, little girl. Your powers won't work. Not with the drugs we're pumping into your body and the machine attached to your head.' His tone was chilly, unfeeling. 'You'll be pleased to know that the chemicals we're injecting you with are used by the military and various intelligence agencies when they want to extract information from their most valuable assets. The side-effects tend to be...unpleasant.' He paused. 'The device currently delivering electric shocks to your body is a special treat of mine. I had it made just for you.'

Olivia tasted blood on her tongue; she'd bitten the inside of her cheek. The pain became a constant, pulsing presence behind her eyes. Waves of black swam across her vision. Numbness bloomed along her limbs as her senses shut down in protest. She gritted her teeth and tried to focus on controlling her clenched muscles.

She might as well have tried to touch the moon. The shadows clouding her eyes intensified. This time, Olivia welcomed the darkness that folded her in its arms.

ETHAN'S NAILS DUG INTO HIS PALMS UNTIL HE DREW BLOOD.

Asgard glanced at him. 'What's wrong?'

The Crovir noble kept his gaze focused on the sky. 'Nothing.'

The paralyzing headache that had gripped him for the last five minutes finally started to ease. He blinked and inhaled shakily.

Ethan saw no point in worrying Asgard further. He knew the feelings he was experiencing belonged to Olivia. He tried not to dwell on the suffering their enemy was inflicting on the woman who now meant the whole world to him. To do so would mean losing his mind.

A light breeze blew across the tarmac and ruffled his hair and clothes, bringing a whiff of diesel.

They'd parked the Jeep at the end of a row of private hangars occupying the northwest sector of the Sacramento Executive Airport. It had been seventeen hours since Asgard had rang the most powerful immortal in Bastian society to ask for help.

A white dot appeared on the horizon, a speck among the larger bodies trailing the skies on their way in and out of Sacramento International to the north. It grew rapidly in size and took the shape of a sleek, twin-jet aircraft. Sunlight sparkled on the wings beneath the engines as it angled toward the runway.

Ethan felt Asgard stiffen beside him. To his surprise, he saw the Bastian noble look away from the private jet landing on the tarmac. He followed his gaze to the roofline of the closest building. A couple of dark shapes were visible where none had been present before. Ethan caught the glint of sniper rifles. He frowned and looked around.

Two SUVs with blacked-out windows had appeared behind

them. He spotted two more snipers lying in a field some three hundred feet to the left.

'They're good,' he said quietly.

Asgard remained silent, his expression flinty.

The aircraft taxied along the runway before turning and heading their way. It rolled to a stop a short distance from where they stood. Ethan examined the elegant contours of the plane and recognized the model as a Gulfstream G450. It was an aircraft Asgard had been itching to fly for some time.

The whine of the jet's engines died down and was replaced by an expectant hush. The cabin door opened. Steps unfolded to the ground with a faint electronic whirr.

A man stepped out of the aircraft. He was over six feet tall and sported a slender build beneath his dark suit. The wind stirred his red hair and outlined the bulge of the gun holster beneath his arm. Pale gray eyes inspected the area carefully before coming to rest on Ethan and Asgard. The man turned and spoke to someone inside the plane.

A second figure appeared beside him. This man was almost as tall as the first. Silver streaked his black hair and beard, giving him a distinguished look. His suit was of a finer cut and looked three times as expensive as his companion's. Dark eyes narrowed under thick eyebrows when he saw Asgard. He walked briskly down the steps and strode across the tarmac toward them, anger evident in the rigid lines of his body. Ethan tensed.

ASGARD'S HEART TWISTED WITH A WAVE OF BITTERSWEET emotions as he watched his oldest rival stop a couple of feet away.

Standing before him was the only immortal he had ever

envied in his entire existence. The one who had taken his place in his own father's heart all those centuries ago.

'Hello, Victor.'

Victor Dvorsky snarled, drew his arm back, and punched him in the face. *'You bastard!'*

Asgard rocked back on his heels and heard a series of familiar metallic noises above the ringing in his ears.

The Bastian Hunters who'd had them in their sights stared at the twisted remains of their weapons with stunned expressions. A tire came off one of the SUVs and thudded onto the asphalt. The vehicle creaked and sagged lopsidedly on its axle.

The red-haired immortal at Victor's side pulled out his crumpled gun from under his jacket. 'What the hell—?'

Asgard turned to Ethan and blinked at the rage flushing the Crovir's face. The younger man stood braced for battle, his hands curled into fists at his sides.

The Elemental had been pushed to his limits by the events of the last day and was more than ready to snap. Asgard could hardly blame him. He'd felt close to breaking point once or twice himself in the last twenty hours, not just at losing Olivia and Howard to their enemy, but also a certain brunette with blue-gray eyes.

He laid a gentle hand on Ethan's shoulder. 'It's okay, boy. They won't hurt us.'

The Crovir twitched at his touch. He blinked as if coming out of a daze and looked at the damaged weapon in the red-haired immortal's hand. 'Did I do that?'

Asgard nodded. Victor stared in dull incomprehension.

'Hey, boss,' said the red-haired immortal. 'I don't know whether this explains the crazy shit that just happened, but that guy has a birthmark on his hand.'

His gaze was riveted to the pentagram on Ethan's skin. Victor followed the man's gaze. Color drained from his face.

'Dear God,' he whispered after a frozen moment. He scrutinized Ethan, eyes searching his features for only he knew what. 'You're one of them!'

Olivia didn't know how much time elapsed before she regained consciousness. When she came to, her gown was still damp with sweat and shivers racked her aching limbs. The pain in her chest was tolerable compared to the agony she had just suffered.

She licked her dry lips and looked toward the end of the room.

Jonah Krondike stood watching her from the same spot where she had last seen him. He was smiling faintly.

Her breath caught in her throat when she saw the figures beside him.

Madeleine and Howard sat in a pair of wheelchairs. Their wrists were strapped to the metal armrests and they were each flanked by two soldiers. Their faces, what was visible of them from where they rested with their chins against their chests, looked blood-streaked. Howard raised his head and watched her from a puffy left eye. His right one was heavily bruised and swollen shut. He tried to smile through his split lips.

Tears welled up in Olivia's eyes.

A third man stood next to Madeleine. It was the immortal who had tried to kill her at the abbey and who more recently had captured them at the lake. The skin over his knuckles was raw and bloodied.

She knew instantly that he was the one responsible for the state of her two friends. Anger surged through her.

Krondike's smile widened. He gave a signal to the other immortal. The latter grinned and punched Madeleine in the gut, his movement lightning fast. The woman jerked in the chair. A spray of blood escaped her lips.

Howard cursed and struggled against his restraints. A soldier struck him at the base of the neck with the butt of his rifle. He sagged and shook his head dazedly.

Bile burned Olivia's throat. She masked her fear and despair, and glared at Jonah Krondike. 'Why are you doing this?'

'What, this?' Krondike glanced at the bloodied figures next to him. He shrugged. 'I'm just trying to make a point.'

He looked at the immortal next to Madeleine once more. The latter yanked on Madeleine's hair until her chin tilted toward the ceiling and slapped her with the full force of his body behind the blow.

A snarl of rage escaped Olivia as she watched the woman's neck snap sideways.

'*Stop it!*' she yelled as the man lifted his hand once more.

Krondike raised a finger. The other man froze.

'You don't want us to hurt your friends?' said the older immortal.

For the first time in her life, Olivia felt hate fill her heart. She had wanted revenge for her parents' death and retribution for the destruction this man had wreaked in the lives of the people she had come to love. She had known anger in the days that had come to pass since the violent act that had wrenched her from the first home she had ever known, and she had experienced ice-cold fury when their enemy had dared attack the man she loved. But she had never before experienced such intense, visceral loathing for another living being. It scorched her soul and made her blood boil with unfathomable rage. She made a promise to herself there and then.

Before this ordeal was over, she would kill Jonah Krondike.

'Answer me, little girl,' Krondike said silkily.

Olivia clenched her fists and tried to curb the violent emotions swirling through her. She would play this man's game for now and let him think that he had won.

'Yes.'

'Then all you have to do is cooperate,' said Krondike. 'As long as you obey my commands, I will see to it that no further harm comes to these two.' He indicated Madeleine and Howard. 'But if you dare defy me again, I will execute them before your very eyes. Understood?'

*God help me, if it's the last thing I do, I will wipe your existence from this world!*

'I said, *is that understood?*' Krondike barked.

The man who had hit Madeleine pulled her head back farther. Olivia saw the scientist bite her swollen lip.

'Yes,' she whispered, dropping back on the bed.

# CHAPTER TWENTY-FIVE

VICTOR DVORSKY, THE HEAD OF THE BASTIAN FIRST Council and leader of the Bastian race, glared at Asgard. 'You're an asshole, you know that, right?'

Asgard scowled. 'I've been called worse things by better people.'

Ethan sat in the executive chair across the aisle and observed the bristling men curiously.

'Wow. The legendary Asgard Godard, huh?' muttered the red-haired immortal beside him.

His name, Ethan had learned, was Anatole Vassili.

Ethan raised an eyebrow. 'Legendary?'

Anatole grimaced. 'Well, the story goes that old man Godard was grooming his son to be the next leader of the Order of Bastian Hunters and, by default, the *de facto* ruler of the Bastian race. That was until the heir to the Godard dynasty decided to pull a vanishing act. His disappearance became the stuff of myth over the centuries that followed, particularly when rumors of possible sightings across the continents started circulating. Victor's father, Roman Dvorsky, took over Tomas

Godard's role after the latter abdicated his position in the sixteenth century.'

Victor directed a cold stare at the red-haired immortal. 'What are you still doing here?'

'I'm your bodyguard, boss,' Anatole replied in a hurt tone. 'I'm meant to be at your side.'

'Isn't there something you could be doing?' said Victor. 'Somewhere else?'

Anatole scratched his head and looked around the interior of the jet. 'Well, no, actually.' His pale eyes glinted with a mischievous light as he looked at the three immortals. 'Besides, this looks too good to miss.'

A resigned expression washed across Victor's face. He sighed.

In that moment, Ethan decided that he would trust Victor Dvorsky. That the leader of the Bastians could tolerate such lip from one of his subordinates indicated the immortal was not the narcissistic, power-hungry dictator the Crovir had thought he might be. Perhaps he could be reasoned with. It was also evident from the way Victor Dvorsky's men acted around him that they would gladly lay down their lives for their ruler, and not just because they served him.

'You know very well my father considered you his son more than he ever did me,' Asgard said bitterly.

Surprise darted through Ethan. This was news to him.

'Fathers and sons will always have their differences,' Victor retorted. 'I've had plenty with mine over the years. Besides, you were as stubborn as the old guy.' His knuckles whitened on the table that stood between them, grief and anger warring on his face. 'Do you know how much Tomas wept when he thought you were dead? The last sighting we had of you was in 1582! He had already lost Catarine by then!'

Remorse flashed in Asgard's eyes. 'I...didn't know about Catarine.'

An old hurt made the Bastian leader look haggard. 'Tomas and I were there on the day she died,' he murmured after a short silence. 'We were too late though. Both she and Balthazar had already perished in the most brutal of fashions.' He closed his eyes for a moment, as if unable to bear his recollections. 'The only silver lining to the whole ghastly affair was that we managed to save Lucas.'

'Lucas?' Asgard repeated, puzzled.

A sour smile twisted Victor's lips. 'Yes, Lucas. Catarine's son.'

Asgard paled. 'What?' He opened and closed his mouth a couple of times before stammering, 'I—I have a nephew?'

'Not just a nephew,' said Victor. 'You have a niece as well. Lily had a daughter before she passed. Her name is Anna.'

Asgard sagged in the chair.

A wave of sympathy coursed through Ethan. He had rarely seen the Bastian look so shocked.

'Hey, don't forgot the other guys, boss,' said Anatole quietly.

Asgard stared dazedly between the two men. 'What other guys?'

Victor sighed. 'There are a couple of other immortals out there who have a...distant relationship with you, of sorts.' A frustrated sound escaped him. 'God, if I had known you were alive, I would have dragged you from whatever hole you were hiding in and brought you home myself! All the heartache and misery Tomas and Lucas lived through could perhaps have been avoided.'

'That would have been a difficult task to accomplish,' Asgard said in a haunted voice.

'Why?' barked Victor.

'Because I was trapped in ice for nearly four centuries.'

Victor went deathly still.

'Is that why you haven't aged?' he said after a while.

Asgard nodded.

Victor rested his elbows on the armrests of his chair and steepled his fingers under his chin.

'Start at the beginning,' he said coldly. 'And this time, leave nothing out.'

~

MADELEINE BLINKED AND OPENED HER EYES. AIR HISSED through her lips at the pain that lanced across her face. It was followed by a low groan as she began to feel the rest of her injuries one by one.

'You okay?'

She looked toward the source of the voice.

Howard sat against the wall opposite her. His hands were shackled to an iron ring above his head. He looked like hell.

*No wonder I didn't recognize his voice*, Madeleine thought weakly. She saw the blood coating her own clothes and hid a grimace. *You probably don't look so hot yourself, Black.*

'How long was I out?'

Howard dropped his head against the stone wall. 'A couple of hours. They checked our bullet wounds before they brought us back here.' His voice turned wry. 'Guess they wouldn't want either of us to die from an infection now, would they? After all, we appear to have become useful bargaining chips in Krondike's insane game.'

Madeleine became conscious of the throbbing in her flank. She squirmed on the hard floor. Metal jingled above her. She carefully turned her head and looked around the gloomy cell. It looked to have been carved out of solid rock. Sorrow filled her as she studied the dark corners.

*Is this the kind of place my father was tortured and killed in?*

Despair twisted her stomach with her next thought.

*Was this how Asgard lived for ten years, chained to a wall like an animal?*

'Hey, don't give up,' Howard said sharply from across the way.

Madeleine closed her eyes for a moment. 'What makes you think I'm giving up?'

'Well, you're looking kind of maudlin.' Howard made a face. 'I gotta warn you, I don't do crying women.' He paused. 'Not unless they're crying in pleasure, obviously.'

Madeleine stared. 'Really? Right here, right now? You're making *sex jokes?*'

'Well, it sure beats sitting here thinking, "Oh God, oh God, we're going to die."'

She sobered at the cold reality of his words.

'Howard?' she said after a while.

'Yeah?'

'I'm glad you're here with me.'

'Yeah.'

Madeleine bit her lip. 'Just in case we don't make it out of here, I'm also glad I met you.'

Her confession was greeted by a suspicious hush. She squinted into the shadows. 'Are you crying?'

'No!' came his choked denial. 'Besides, we *will* make it out of here.'

'You think?'

'Yeah.' Howard hesitated. 'I think the two of you will anyway.'

'What do you mean?'

He exhaled loudly. 'You see, as the two love interests, you and Olivia are bound to survive. Me? Not so sure. I'm the lovable sidekick and best friend to one of the heroes. I could easily end up with a bullet in my skull.'

Madeleine decided to ignore his "love interest" comment.

'You're an immortal,' she said dryly.

Howard grunted. 'Well, yeah, but I've got a limited number of lives, remember?'

'Have you ever died?' she asked after a while.

He was quiet for some time. 'It was before I met Ethan.' He shifted against the wall. 'What can I say, I was a cocky eighteen-year-old.'

'Howard?'

'Yeah?'

'You're still cocky.'

'I resent that.'

A comfortable silence stretched out between them.

Madeleine finally asked the question that was troubling her. 'You felt it, didn't you?'

He didn't reply right away. 'What do you mean?'

'That fleeting thought that didn't belong to us.' Madeleine scrutinized Howard. 'Olivia's thought.'

He watched her mutely.

'It must be because she connected with us somehow, when she protected us at the lake,' Madeleine added. 'She said she could get into other people's minds, didn't she?'

'Yes, but not immortals. And not yours either.'

'She's different now,' said Madeleine insistently. 'Asgard said so himself. That Ethan and Olivia augmented each other's powers by virtue of their bond as soulmates. You've seen with your own eyes how Ethan's abilities have grown. The same surely applies to Olivia.' She bit her lip. 'Which means she could project *her* thoughts into someone else's head. I think that's what she did unconsciously in that lab.'

He was unable to hide his unease this time. 'What are you saying?'

'I'm saying that if you sensed what I sensed from her, then you know she's putting herself at risk by fighting Krondike on her own.' Madeleine paused. 'I hope she doesn't do something stupid.'

'Well, let's hope Ethan and Asgard get here before that happens,' muttered Howard.

Madeleine gazed blindly at the floor. 'Do you really think they can save us?'

'They have to. The alternative is too horrible to consider.'

Madeleine pulled a face and winced when her bruised muscles protested. 'You mean our deaths?'

'No,' Howard said in a hard voice. 'The stakes are much higher than that.'

VICTOR DVORSKY STUDIED THE IMMORTAL SITTING ACROSS from him. 'That's quite some story.' He concealed his alarm behind a neutral tone. 'I have heard of the Krondikes. They were a very old family of nobles. Again, I presumed their blood-line had died out centuries ago.'

Asgard Godard grunted. 'It's the truth. Jonah Krondike is still alive.' A muscle jumped in his cheek. 'My father also refused to believe me when I told him of my original suspicions. If he had, maybe things would have turned out—differently.'

Asgard had spent the last hour and a half recounting one of the most incredible tales Victor had ever heard. As the former Head of the Bastian Counter-Terrorism Section and the current Head of the Order of Bastian Hunters, he had heard plenty of those in his immortal lives. If what Asgard said was true, and Victor had no real reason to discount his words despite the sibling rivalry that had existed between them, then the immortal societies were very likely about to face their greatest challenge yet. He pushed his apprehension aside for a moment and scrutinized the Crovir immortal across the aisle.

'You are the first-born son of Jakob and Irena Knezevic?'

Ethan Storm dipped his chin, his eyes steady.

Victor's gaze dropped to the Crovir's hand. 'I had heard a little of the Knezevics' abilities but had never seen them for myself. We thought the last of their bloodline had perished.' He hesitated. 'From your earlier demonstration, I presume you can manipulate metal?'

Ethan shared a cautious glance with Asgard. The latter shrugged.

'Among other things,' the younger immortal admitted grudgingly. 'I can influence water, earth, air, and fire as well.'

Victor felt his mouth go dry. *Wait till I tell Dimitri.*

Asgard startled in the opposite seat. 'You can do fire?'

'Uh-huh.'

'Since when?'

'Since, well, a couple of nights ago,' Ethan mumbled.

'Why didn't you tell me?' said Asgard accusingly.

'We were otherwise occupied, remember?' snapped Ethan.

A chuckle broke the tense moment. Anatole was grinning.

Asgard scowled at the red-haired immortal. 'What are you laughing at?'

'This is great!' Anatole started counting on his fingers. 'We've got the guy and his lady wife who can't die, the guy who can heal and gift life, the scary chick who could beat all our asses combined, and now these two. Elemental Boy and Psychic Girl.' His grin widened. 'It's a regular superhero squad!'

Victor ran a hand through his hair. 'Is everything a joke to you?'

Anatole's smile faded. 'Well, no. Rats aren't. I don't like rats.'

'What does he mean?' said Asgard. He was staring at Victor, his face ashen. 'Do you know other immortals with supernatural abilities?' He glanced at Ethan. 'Is that what you meant earlier when you said he was one of "them?"' He leaned across the table and grabbed Victor's arm. 'Tell me!'

Victor looked at him, surprised by the strength of emotion in his voice. 'Why?'

Grief burned brightly in Asgard's gaze. 'Because the last time I saw Natalia Ashkarov alive, she told me of a recurrent vision she'd had in the months leading to our meeting. It was about a group of immortals who would possess incredible powers, the likes of which our races had never seen. Some of them wouldn't have been born at the time she made the prediction.'

Shock resonated through Victor. 'Natalia said that?'

Asgard nodded, his expression numb. His grip relaxed on Victor's sleeve. 'Yes. They were among the last words she spoke to me. She also said that these immortals would bear marks that would identify them as the special beings that they were.' He looked at him beseechingly. 'Do you know the identity of those other immortals, Victor?'

Victor stared at him for some time.

'Yes,' he finally admitted. 'As does Dimitri Reznak.'

Asgard inhaled sharply. 'Dimitri? That old fox?'

Victor sighed. 'He's a few years younger than you. If anyone should be called an old fox, it would be you.'

'Who's Dimitri Reznak?' said Ethan.

'He's the Head of the Crovir Immortal History and Culture Section, and a member of their First Council,' said Victor, his gaze locked on Asgard's face. 'He's also my closest friend of more than six centuries and the one partly responsible for thwarting Kronos's plans to destabilize the world a few years ago.'

Asgard tensed. 'What?'

In the hour that followed, Victor retold the events of the winter when the Catholic Church was almost toppled by Kronos, the sect of pureblood immortal-human half-breeds whose history they'd discovered was intimately linked with that of the immortal races.

'Kronos stole a pair of tombs and a stone box containing ancient scriptures from a cave in the Eastern Desert Mountains, in Egypt. Dimitri spent centuries looking for the location of that burial site. His life-long obsession has always been to discover the truth behind the origins of the immortal races and he was certain the cave contained the answers he sought. Kronos was after the tombs for entirely different reasons. Their first goal was to destroy the Catholic Church by revealing the existence of immortals and casting doubt on the texts that make up the Bible and thus, the identity of Jesus Christ himself. Their second aim was to try and achieve true immortality by using the contents of the tombs to make the Philosopher's Stone.'

Asgard ran a hand through his hair. 'So Kristof, Natalia, and I were right all along,' he muttered.

Victor nodded curtly. 'Kronos stole an important artifact, a sun cross pendant, from a Buddhist sect founded by Guru Rinpoche, the Lotus-Born Second Buddha. It was a seal for one of the tombs and had apparently been left in their care by an immortal in—'

'—1415,' breathed Asgard.

Victor drew in a breath sharply. 'That immortal was *you*?'

Asgard nodded shakily. 'That pendant was passed down generations of my family. Kristof and I also discovered another element said to have been crucial to making the Philosopher's Stone, namely the Emerald Tablet. We entrusted it to the Freemasons in the latter half of the fifteenth century.' He hesitated. 'We never uncovered the whereabouts of the *Mutus Liber*.'

Victor's heart thudded against his ribs. The enormity of what was unfolding was not lost on him. *Fate sure moves in mysterious, twisted ways.*

'Alexa King, Dimitri's goddaughter, took the Emerald Tablet from the Freemasons. It was later stolen from Dimitri's estate in Sumava and was subsequently recovered in the Ural Mountains, when Alexa defeated Kronos. As for the *Mutus Liber*, Kronos discovered it in an abbey in Breggia, in 1989.'

Asgard opened and closed his mouth soundlessly.

'What was inside the tombs, the ones Kronos stole in Egypt?' said Ethan.

Victor looked at him steadily. 'The remains of Crovir and Bastian, the first immortals. Their embalmed hearts were found inside a second cave located beneath the first one.'

Asgard's eyes widened further.

'Come again?' said Ethan dully.

'Crovir and Bastian are not just the names of our two races. They were men born in the thirty-eight century BC. They were brothers, actually.'

'Brothers?' Asgard repeated.

Victor dipped his chin. 'Crovir and Bastian's father was a man called Romerus. From the Sumerian scriptures Dimitri found in Egypt and the ones he subsequently recovered from Kronos, it seems Romerus was a direct descendant of Adam and Eve.'

Asgard shared a dazed glance with Ethan.

'Crovir and Bastian had three sons and three daughters each, ' Victor continued. 'It was their children who gave rise to our races. Not only that, it seems some of those siblings were truly special indeed.' He hesitated. 'Lucas and Anna are the pureblood descendants of Tobias and Baruch, the first-born sons of Crovir and Bastian. As such, they possess the gift of true immortality and will survive their seventeenth deaths. Lucas did just that three years ago, during the incident that cost your father his life and almost led to a second war between the immortal races. He bears an alpha and omega birthmark on his chest.'

Stunned silence fell across the cabin.

'Catarine's son survived his seventeenth death?' Asgard said hoarsely. 'And he is one of the marked ones?'

'Yes,' said Victor. 'Although Dimitri was involved in stopping Kronos from achieving their goals that same year, it was his goddaughter, Alexa, who defeated the man we believed to be their leader, a pureblood immortal-human half-breed called Alberto Cavaleti. Alexa is the descendant of Mila, Crovir's third daughter. It was Mila who killed Crovir and Bastian during the very first immortal war over four millennia ago, a war triggered by the original immortals' cruel reign over the empire they ruled. Mila was the greatest warrior in the kingdom and forged the very first three-spear weapon. Alexa bears the mark of a trishula on the back of her neck and is quite likely the strongest and most physically deadly immortal alive today.'

Asgard rubbed his face with trembling fingers. 'And the last immortal? You said there was another one. A man who can heal and...gift life?'

'His name is Conrad Greene. He's a semi-retired senior intelligence operative working for the Bastian First Council and was one of the best generals I ever had when I was in charge of the Bastian Corps. He's the pureblood descendant of Rafael, Bastian's second-born son and the greatest healer who ever lived in those times. Conrad bears an Aesculapian snake birthmark around his left forearm. Rafael used those very snakes in many of his healing rituals and was said to keep them as pets.' Victor studied the two shocked immortals guardedly. 'Conrad can do much more than Rafael though. Two years ago, he gifted one of his seventeen souls to the US president, after the latter was fatally wounded by a sniper.'

A deathly hush greeted the end of his narrative.

'Dimitri discovered old cities in the complex of caves beneath the Ural Mountains where he chased Kronos to,' Victor added. 'He believed they were the birthplace of the sect.'

'The cabin where I tracked Jonah must not have been far from there,' said Asgard with a dumbfounded expression. 'So you're saying the sun cross pendant was a seal for one of the original immortals' tombs? The one who gave rise to our race, Bastian?'

Victor shook his head. 'Not Bastian. The Godards' seal was

for the tomb of Crovir. Anna has the second seal, passed down to her by her Crovir father. Hers should open Bastian's tomb.'

'What?'

'Whoever made those seals gave each one to the other brother's family.' Victor smiled humorlessly. 'We think this was a deliberate move and a clever one at that. Maybe they knew that war would eventually break out between the brothers' descendants. This could have been their way of ensuring the lineage of the original immortals would never dare commit the unthinkable and attempt to do anything to their ancestors' remains.' He faltered. 'It might even have been the Seer of that time.'

'There's one thing I don't get,' said Ethan in the silence that ensued. 'Okay, so there're many things I'm not getting,' he confessed reluctantly. 'Don't crows come for our bodies upon our final death?' He looked between Victor and Asgard. 'So how the hell did these guys, these original immortals' bodies and hearts survive?'

'That is a puzzle indeed, and one that Dimitri and I have been unable to solve,' said Victor. 'We believed Kronos intended to use the hearts in combination with the *Mutus Liber* and the Emerald Tablet to create the Philosopher's Stone and try to achieve true immortality, beyond the seventeenth death. But—'

'But?' said Asgard.

'Dimitri always suspected Alberto Cavaleti was working with somebody else,' Victor said quietly. 'From what you've told us, that someone was Jonah Krondike.'

Asgard gazed blindly at the table. 'I agree. Kristof, Natalia, and I also hypothesized that Jonah and Kronos wanted to achieve true immortality. But there was something else, some other twist to his plan we felt we were missing.' Lines furrowed his brow. 'It may have something to do with his work with the US Army and the experiments he carried out on me and the other immortals he captured in the mid 1900s.' An urgent light blazed in his eyes as he gazed at Victor. 'There are a few things I had yet to mention. From the data we stole in San Diego a few days ago, Madeleine thought Jonah was involved in a research program to create super soldiers. We interviewed the widow of a ranger who was said to have died in Afghanistan but who had apparently been recruited into the study in 2009. He phoned his wife a month after his alleged death. She traced the call to Sierra Vista, in Arizona. That's where Ethan and I were yesterday. We went to Fort Huachuca to see if we could find any trace of whether he had ever been there and, if so, where he was taken to afterward.'

The trepidation that had been simmering in Victor's mind since Asgard Godard revealed the extraordinary story behind his disappearance all those centuries ago intensified.

He leaned forward. 'And?'

'They went to Yuma, Victor.' Asgard's voice had gone deadly. 'As in the Yuma Proving Ground.'

Silence fell inside the aircraft.

'Shit,' muttered Anatole.

# CHAPTER TWENTY-SIX

PRESIDENT JAMES WESTWOOD PLACED HIS HANDS ON THE Oval Office desk and leaned toward his computer's video camera. 'What?'

Victor watched him steadily. 'I said that it looks as if a rogue branch of the US Army has been assisting an immortal by the name of Jonah Krondike in an illegal research program aimed at creating super soldiers. From the evidence I've heard in the last few hours, it appears this state of affairs has been in play since the middle of the last century. Possibly longer, James.'

The brown eyes staring at them from the other end of the video conference grew stormy.

Ethan swallowed his surprise. He knew that a handful of the human world's leaders had been made aware of the existence of the supernatural beings who walked among them. He just hadn't expected Victor Dvorsky to be on first-name basis with the most influential one of them all.

'And you trust this source?' said Westwood.

His gaze shifted briefly to the man opposite Victor.

The Bastian leader looked at Asgard. 'Yes.' He hesitated.

'Asgard Godard is, technically speaking, a contender for my current role.'

Westwood raised an eyebrow.

Ethan watched Asgard carefully. A few years after he had gotten to know the Bastian, he had asked him what he would do if he was ever given the opportunity to take over the role that should rightfully have been his.

'Yeah, as if I need *that* headache,' Asgard muttered presently. 'Trust me, the last thing I want is to assume the mantle of leadership.'

Ethan hid a smile. Asgard had just given President Westwood and Victor Dvorsky the same answer he'd given the Crovir back then.

Victor scowled. 'You're right. With your people skills, we'd be at war with the entire world within a month.'

A sullen hush descended inside the cabin as the two immortals glared at each other.

'Are you sure you guys are friends?' said Westwood.

'I wouldn't go that far,' Asgard grumbled.

Westwood tapped a finger on the desk. 'I'll talk to the Secretary of Defense and the Joint Chiefs.' He hesitated. 'I'd be surprised if Bill knows anything about this, Victor. Some of the guys in the DoD, on the other hand, can be laws unto themselves. I'll get in touch when I know something.' He was about to end the call when he seemed to think of something. 'How's Greene?'

Victor's face relaxed slightly. 'He's on a mission in Chile.'

Westwood gave him a look of disbelief. 'Really? How the hell did you manage that?'

'I sent Hartwell there first,' said Victor. 'Then I called him and said she was in trouble.'

Westwood straightened. 'Was she?'

'Of course not,' Victor replied. 'Besides, it's kind of my pre-wedding gift to them.'

Westwood made a face. 'So you're saying Greene and Hartwell would like nothing else but to be charging through a jungle killing bad guys, rather than lying on a beach somewhere?'

'All the action makes for great sex, Pres,' said Anatole cheerfully.

This earned the bodyguard a battery of wooden stares from the president and the two nobles sitting across the table from each other. Ethan could only gape, aghast at the immortal's familiar tone with the leader of the free world. There had to be some history between them he was missing.

'I mean, think about it,' the red-haired immortal continued unabashed. 'Intense life-and-death situations. All that adrenaline pumping through their veins. I bet they're making out like bunnies.'

'I thought I had lost the ability to be surprised at the stuff that comes out of your mouth,' said Victor dully. 'I stand corrected.'

Anatole grinned. 'Why, thanks boss.'

Westwood shook his head and sighed. 'Tell Greene I say hi.'

The view of the Oval Office blinked out to black.

Asgard gave Victor an inscrutable look. 'You appear to be on friendly terms with him.'

Victor shrugged. 'He owes us his life.' The scowl returned to his face as he watched the man opposite him. 'Why did you not come to us earlier with this information? From what you've told me, Jonah Krondike and Kronos appear to have been behind many of the wars the immortal societies have fought for more than half a millennium.' Anger hardened his voice. 'Was it pride that stopped you, Asgard? If so, then you're a bigger fool than I gave you credit for.'

'We didn't know who to trust,' said Asgard.

Victor seemed unconvinced.

'The only way Jonah Krondike got his hands on so many

immortals for his experiments was because someone in the societies was helping him,' said Ethan. 'Hell, there may be more than one person giving him assistance.'

The Bastian leader froze.

'After all that time trapped under a mountain and a decade spent in Jonah's clutches, I wasn't going to waltz into the Bastian headquarters seeking help from people who may very well have been my enemies,' Asgard added vehemently.

A muscle jumped in Victor's jawline. 'I know we've had our differences over the years, but you should've known me well enough to realize I could've been trusted.'

'Could you?' Asgard's tone turned sour. 'My own father refused to believe me, Victor. And who can tell how you could have changed over the years? The heart of a man can go from the purest white to the darkest, most rotten black in the space of one lifetime. Who knows how evil the heart of an immortal can grow in several hundred years?'

Pain flickered in Victor's eyes.

'You are the son of the man whom I loved as much as my own father,' he finally said in a low voice. 'You are the brother of the woman whom I treasured more than life itself.' He closed his eyes briefly. 'And you are the uncle to the immortal whom I consider my godson.' He paused. 'You can trust me, Asgard. I am not your enemy.'

Asgard's face flushed with emotion. He watched the Bastian leader for silent seconds before swallowing and nodding. Ethan felt some of his trepidation dissipate.

Victor sighed. 'Anatole, if you don't wipe that asinine grin off your face, I'll wipe it off myself.'

Anatole's smile slipped from his lips. 'Geez, boss, you're such a buzzkill.'

~

Westwood got back to them two hours later. Unease trickled through Asgard when he saw the look darkening the president's face.

'What's wrong, James?' said Victor cautiously.

'I've just had a meeting with the National Security Council,' said Westwood. 'The Chairman of the Joint Chiefs is finding the prospect of a rogue US Army branch working to create an army of super soldiers hard to swallow. He wants concrete proof before he goes barging into the DoD to accuse his staff of treason.' He paused. 'I didn't mention the immortal aspect of our problem, obviously.'

'What proof we had was destroyed by Jonah Krondike and the soldiers in his employ,' said Asgard. 'Howard Titus no doubt has backup of the data somewhere but, without him, we can't access it.' He glared at Westwood. 'Our friends are in the hands of one of the most dangerous immortals on this planet. Aside from the super soldiers he's intending to create, if Krondike succeeds in harnessing Olivia Ashkarov's powers, then God save your army and every other military force in the world.'

'Let's hope it doesn't come to that, then,' snapped Westwood. He looked at Victor. 'I've convinced the Security Council that we should send some men to investigate.' He sighed. 'The timing of this couldn't be worse, Victor. There's a huge international training exercise taking place in Yuma right now. It involves most of our NATO Allies, with some three thousand military personnel on the ground as of today and more joining them tomorrow. I can't terminate the operation without incurring some serious questions from our foreign friends.'

'What are you saying, James?' said Victor.

Asgard glanced at the immortal, sensing the question was redundant.

'I'm saying you've got two hundred and fifty men, Victor. Unofficially, of course. They're all special ops and are among the best-trained soldiers on the planet. They'll assist you inside

Yuma.' Westwood smiled faintly. 'The personnel at the proving ground will be told your movements are part of an unscheduled exercise. With all the action taking place there, they might not notice your presence anyway.' His expression hardened. 'Find me the culprits, Victor. I guarantee you I will have them prosecuted with the full force of our laws.'

'Thanks, James,' Victor murmured. 'Your assistance in this matter is all I could ask for.'

'There's no need to thank me, Victor,' said Westwood gruffly. 'What's happening concerns all of us.' His gaze flitted to Asgard. 'Like your friend said, if this immortal and the humans aligned with him achieve their goals, then we're all going to be in deep shit.' He faltered. 'Just promise me one thing. Try not to—'

'I'll keep innocent human casualties to a minimum, James,' Victor cut in. 'You have my word.'

'Keep me informed of any significant developments,' said Westwood. 'I'll send you details of your contact.'

He ended the call.

'He came through,' Asgard said quietly.

Surprise echoed through him at what had just transpired.

Victor's lips curved in a smile. 'Westwood is a good man.'

'Still, two hundred and fifty soldiers isn't going to cut it,' said Ethan. He rose and strode agitatedly up and down the aisle. 'How many can you mobilize?'

'A couple of thousand if I had a few days,' said Victor. 'From your account though, time appears to be of the essence. I can have five hundred Hunters here in the next eight hours.'

Asgard exchanged an anxious glance with Ethan. 'Kronos may have been disbanded by your actions a few years ago, Victor, but I suspect Jonah has many immortals and half-breeds working with him and alongside the rogue army group's soldiers. What about the Crovirs?'

'Vlašic hasn't gotten back to me yet,' said Victor. 'He wants to discuss this matter with his councils before he considers whether to offer us his assistance.'

Ivan Mihael Vlašic was the current Head of the Order of the Crovir Hunters and the leader of the Crovir race. Asgard knew little of the family. Vlašic had come to power shortly after the deaths of Tomas Godard and Agatha Vellacrus, the previous ruler of the Crovirs.

'Will he deliver?' said Asgard.

'I don't know,' said Victor. 'Vlašic is an enigma. He's the youngest head the Crovir First Council has ever had.' He shrugged. 'He's the youngest head *any* council has ever had.' His eyes grew thoughtful. 'He's an accomplished politician, that's for sure. And he plays his cards close to his chest.'

'It doesn't sound like you're particularly fond of him,' said Ethan.

'I don't have to like him,' said Victor in a neutral voice. 'I just have to be able to work with him.'

'We can't waste any more time,' said Ethan in a strained voice. 'We need to move and we need to do it now.'

Victor dipped his chin. 'I agree. I know of at least one Crovir noble who'll help us.'

He was on the phone again a moment later. Static buzzed through the speakers when the call finally connected. They could see little on the screen.

'Dimitri, are you there?'

There was movement and rustling on the line. 'Hang on a minute,' said a male voice gruffly.

A muffled curse came through seconds later. It was followed by scuffling sounds and silence.

Victor frowned. 'Dimitri?'

'What?' snapped the voice.

A face shrouded in dim light appeared on the computer screen. It belonged to a man with thick-set features, a broad nose, and a square jaw.

'Where the hell are you?' said Victor. 'I can barely see you.'

'I'm in a cave, in China.'

Victor pursed his lips. 'Are you treasure hunting again?'

Dimitri glared at the camera on his phone. 'I do not treasure hunt! I'm here on official Crovir business.'

Victor raised an eyebrow. 'Really? What official Crovir business is that?'

Dimitri hesitated. 'Well, if you must know, I'm looking for certain...cultural artifacts.'

Victor rolled his eyes. 'So I was right. You're treasure hunting.'

'What do you want, Victor?' Dimitri said coldly.

'Look who turned up.' Victor angled the laptop slightly.

Asgard stared at Dimitri face on. He hadn't seen the Crovir noble in over six hundred years. The man appeared as irritated as the last time he'd seen him.

'Hi, Dimitri.'

The Crovir noble studied him with a puzzled expression. His eyes cleared. '*Asgard?!*'

'Yeah,' muttered Victor. He turned the device back toward him.

'What the hell is going on? I thought he was long dead!' Dimitri scowled. 'And why does that bastard look no older than the last time I saw him?'

'Trust me, that should be the least of your concerns right now,' said Victor.

He spent the next fifteen minutes apprising Dimitri of the situation.

The Crovir's face grew more and more somber as he listened. 'I can be there in nineteen hours,' he said curtly at the end of Victor's account. 'I'll contact our other friends in the councils. We should be able to get you a few hundred men by the morning.'

A SERIES OF ELECTRONIC BEEPS ROUSED OLIVIA FROM A LIGHT slumber. She blinked and looked around in time to see the steel door to her prison open. A black-clad figure strolled across the pale linoleum floor and came to a stop beside the bed.

It was the immortal from the abbey. She now knew his name.

Scoleri watched her silently. 'Not much to look at up close, are you?' he said finally. 'Jonah claims you're the most powerful immortal in the world.' He smiled faintly. 'I gotta admit, you pulled some neat tricks back in Santa Monica and at that lake house. But *the* most powerful?' His eyes grew curiously intense and he looked down her body and back up to her face. 'I seriously doubt that. I could snap your neck with my hands.'

Olivia masked a shudder of distaste and studied the ceiling, a wave of tiredness washing over her.

Jonah's scientists had spent the last day poking and prodding her. They'd taken blood samples, performed various scans, and injected her with more drugs. Although some of the chemicals had had unpleasant side-effects, none had given her the same level of pain that Jonah Krondike had inflicted on her when she first came to. She had no doubt the Crovir noble would use the machine attached to her head again. It was still there, humming faintly in the background, its pointy grips firmly embedded under her skin.

Alarm spiked through her when Scoleri raised a hand and trailed a finger down her bare arm. She stared at him and stiffened at the look on his face.

'What are you doing?'

She gazed frantically at the chamber beyond the glass window. There were only a handful of scientists in the lab. Olivia could only presume this meant the hour was late. She had lost track of time, down in this hellhole.

One of the men outside met her panicked stare briefly. He lowered his head and walked out of her range of vision.

Scoleri followed her line of sight. He looked back at her, a malicious smile on his lips. 'Oh, don't worry about them. They'll do as they're told, if they know what's good for them.' He leaned down and suddenly took hold of her chin, his grip cruel. 'Why, I could climb on this bed and rape you, and they wouldn't lift a finger to help you.'

Fear flooded Olivia at his words at the same time she registered the chilling intent in his eyes. '*No!*'

She struggled against the straps binding her to the gurney. Scoleri chuckled, his gaze heated. He kissed her then, his tongue invading her lips with bruising force.

Olivia gagged and tried to close her mouth. Scoleri's grip tightened on her jaw, locking it open. Revulsion brought acid to the back of her throat. Her skin crawled when he ran a hand down her body. He twisted the hem of the gown at her knees and yanked it up to her thighs. Goosebumps broke out across her exposed skin. She stared into the immortal's eyes as he took her mouth roughly and knew that he would carry out his threat, if only to prove that he could physically dominate her.

The thought of a man other than her soulmate touching her intimately filled her heart with ice. Olivia froze, a whimper of despair escaping her. Tears flooded her eyes.

Scoleri's fingers dug into her skin, his lust growing in the face of her terror.

*Stop.*

The word blazed through Olivia's consciousness, shattering her fears and bringing with it a wave of heat from deep inside her heart. She gasped at the alien sensation.

Scoleri's mouth stilled on hers. He pulled back slightly and scanned her face, puzzled. 'What are you—?'

Alarms tore through the room. The immortal straightened

and stared at the monitors above her. His eyes darkened. An ugly expression distorted his features.

Olivia was aware of a commotion in the outer chamber as the scientists rushed toward a computer station.

Scoleri glared at her. 'Really? You want to play that game?'

He raised a hand and slapped her forcefully across the face.

Stars burst in front of her eyes and her neck twisted violently to the side. The metallic taste of blood oozed across her tongue. Olivia bit her lip, turned her head, and glared at the immortal. Her psychic powers surged.

Scoleri reached behind her and flicked a switch.

Fire burst inside her head. Olivia screamed as the powerful electric current coursed down her body. Her toes curled on the bed, her spine arching off the mattress, every single muscle contracting violently. The straps dug into her wrists and her ankles, cutting her circulation. Her fingers clawed helplessly at the mattress as she struggled to catch her breath.

She thought she heard shouts coming through the speakers in the ceiling. Scoleri ignored them, his hateful gaze focused on her face. He pressed a button on the machine attached to her head.

Olivia's eyes rolled back in her skull as even stronger shocks shot across the metal needles in her scalp. Her body bowed farther off the gurney. Sight and sound faded. A hazy light filled her consciousness. Her blood thundered in her ears, her pulse impossibly fast. An eternity passed, stretching her agony into forever.

Her heart missed one beat. Then two. Then three. It galloped wildly for a moment, fluttered, and finally slowed to an irregular shudder.

The last thump flooded her mind with dazzling brilliance.

# CHAPTER TWENTY-SEVEN

'Sir, I'm afraid to inform you that Building 4489 does not exist.'

'What?' said Ethan.

Major Steve Reynolds was the man in charge of the Rangers they'd met up with at the Los Alamitos Army Airfield in California and the ones who would be joining them from another US Army base. He shrugged muscular shoulders and looked at Ethan steadily.

'We've scoured all available data on the existing structures in the Yuma Proving Ground. Considering we're talking of a facility larger than Rhode Island, that's plenty of buildings,' drawled the soldier. 'There is no record of any construction having ever had that number assigned to it.'

Ethan leaned over the narrow camp table in the back of the C-17 Globemaster III transport aircraft taking them to Yuma. A topographic map of the proving ground was stretched out across the surface.

'We saw a piece of paper at Fort Huachuca that said otherwise, major,' said Asgard.

Reynolds's eyes narrowed slightly. 'I have been informed by

my direct superiors that I am to trust you implicitly, sir. I would appreciate the same courtesy. Believe me when I say that we can't find that building. Either it never existed or there's more going on here than meets the eye. Considering the nature of this mission, I can safely assume it's the latter. I've been told we're searching for a secret research lab where illegal experiments are been carried out on civilians and soldiers alike, correct?'

'Yes,' said Asgard.

As far as Ethan was aware, the major didn't know the "civilian" subjects were immortals.

'The proving ground covers more than thirteen hundred square miles of mountainous terrain and desert plains,' said Reynolds. 'Without knowing the approximate location of this facility, this will be like hunting for the proverbial needle in a haystack. Especially if it's below ground, like you suspect it might be.'

Ethan exchanged an anxious glance with Asgard.

It was past four in the morning. They'd lifted off from the airbase fifty minutes ago and were still two hours out from their target destination.

*We have to figure out where to start looking before we rendezvous with the rest of the Rangers and the immortals at Yuma. We're just going to waste time otherwise.*

'Are there any medical facilities in the proving ground?'

'There's a health clinic in the JFK Warfare Center. It's in the neighborhood where the resident staff is based,' said Reynolds. 'It's too small to host anything on the scale you're thinking of.'

Asgard placed his hands on the table and scrutinized the chart. 'Run us through exactly what's on the site.'

'Although the base employs a few thousand civilians, there are less than two hundred military support personnel who live and work on site. The main administration buildings and housing quarters for the staff are located here, just southeast of

the Laguna Dam and to the east of the Colorado River.'
Reynolds pointed out an area to the left of the map. 'The
proving ground itself is a U-shaped area framing the Kofa
National Wildlife Refuge, to which it also has limited access.
The west arm of the U is the Cibola Region, with the KOFA
Region on the east and the Laguna Region forming the
south bend.'

Ethan followed the major's finger as it moved across the
paper. 'KOFA?'

'King of Arizona', said the Ranger. 'It's the name of an old
gold mine in King Valley. The KOFA region represents the
KOFA Range, the DoD's main artillery testing ground. It offers
a forty-six-mile firing area and is used to evaluate anything from
mortars to tanks. There's also a Mine and Countermine Test
and Training Complex, as well as a Smart Weapon Testing
Range to the east.'

'What of the other areas?' said Asgard.

'Cibola is the site of the Cibola Range. It features live fire
and ammunition ranges, mounted and unmounted navigation
courses, and long-range artillery and missile testing facilities.
The most important use for Cibola, however, is advanced avia-
tion testing. With an unrestricted airspace pretty much equiva-
lent to the size of the proving ground itself, they've done
everything there from trialling out new planes and helicopters
to airdrops and UAV testing. Even NASA uses the site to check
the chute systems for its space capsules.' Reynolds tapped the
south end of the map. 'The smallest of the regions, the Laguna
Test Center, contains the Laguna Army Airfield and the Castle
Dome Heliport, both of which feature their own research and
testing facilities. It also has extensive courses for vehicle testing
and combat training, an ammunition holding area, drop zones,
meteorological stations, instrument sites, firing ranges, and two
aerostat sites.'

Ethan's pulse drummed rapidly. The complex geography of

the proving ground aside, there was far too much territory to cover in the time that they had. Westwood had promised them the soldiers and unreserved access to the site for one day only.

'The place we're looking for will be isolated.' His gaze moved to Asgard briefly. 'The...man we know to be in charge of this project won't want it near curious eyes and ears, so we can pretty much rule out the area to the south.'

Reynolds raised his eyebrows. 'You've met him?'

'Yes,' said Asgard. 'We were his prisoners for some time.'

The Ranger straightened. 'Where was that?'

'His previous research facility was a former army base in the San Andres Mountains, in New Mexico,' said Ethan distractedly. An uneasy feeling was seeping through his chest. His stomach started to churn. 'It's abandoned now.'

He blinked as a shiver ran down his spine.

Asgard stared at him. 'Are you okay?'

'You don't look so good,' grunted Reynolds.

Ethan swallowed and waved a hand dismissively.

'I'm fine,' he said, ignoring the icy sensation crawling inside his skull. 'I was gonna say that the middle of a missile firing range doesn't seem like the kind of location he'd—'

ASGARD HEARD ETHAN GASP A SECOND BEFORE HE COLLAPSED. He lunged and caught the younger immortal as he started to fall.

Alarm tore through him when he registered the Elemental's deathly-pale face. He lowered him swiftly to the floor of the aircraft.

Ethan's eyes snapped wide open. He stared blindly at the ceiling, a muffled cry passing his lips. His jaw clenched shut and he arched off the floor, his whole body tensing violently. Twitches coursed along his limbs.

Fear knotted Asgard's gut. 'Ethan!'

Reynolds turned toward the rear of the plane and shouted, '*Medic!*' before moving around the table toward them. 'Is he having a seizure?'

'I don't think so,' Asgard mumbled. 'He's never—'

Footsteps approached at a run. A couple of soldiers appeared in the light bathing the table.

'Step away, sir,' one of them ordered briskly. She lowered herself next to Ethan and touched the immortal's wrist. '*Jesus!*'

She yanked her arm away sharply and gaped at the convulsing man.

'What is it, Staff Sergeant?' barked Reynolds.

'He's burning up, sir!'

Asgard stared at the soldier's red fingertips. He grabbed Ethan's face in his hands. Incandescent heat radiated from the unresponsive immortal's skin. He gritted his teeth against the scorching pain and gazed desperately into the younger man's unseeing eyes.

'*Ethan!*'

It felt like a lifetime before the Elemental finally blinked. His body went limp and his gaze focused on Asgard's face. The expression in the blue depths broke the Bastian noble's heart.

'Oh God,' Ethan whispered weakly. 'Olivia.'

His eyelids fluttered closed.

JONAH GLARED AT SCOLERI. 'WHAT WERE YOU TRYING to do?'

The Crovir Hunter looked at him moodily. 'I was trying to break her. That's what you wanted, wasn't it?'

'Yes,' hissed Jonah. 'But I didn't want you to fry her brains until she died!'

He studied a video display on the wall. It showed a figure lying still inside the containment room in the main research lab.

Olivia Ashkarov had suffered a cardiac arrest during the forceful electrocution administered by Scoleri. Despite the scientists' attempts to revive her, they had been unable to bring her back. They would have to wait for her to reawaken of her own accord.

'How long will it take until she comes around?' the Crovir Hunter muttered.

'You know as well as I do that that depends on the immortal,' snapped Jonah. 'It might be half an hour, it might take half a day, who knows. It's probably her first death as well, so it could be even longer.' He stared irritably at the Hunter. 'Have you discovered Storm and Godard's whereabouts yet?'

'No. We're still searching for them.'

'I want you to stay away from Ashkarov from now on, understood?' Jonah said sharply.

Scoleri hesitated before nodding reluctantly. He turned and headed toward the door.

'Of course, once we've finished harnessing her abilities, you may do with her as you wish,' Jonah added dismissively.

He looked at the other screen on the wall. It showed Subject 505, the first super soldier who'd made it through Phase Three.

'In the end we won't need any of them.' Jonah furrowed his brow. 'The immortals or the humans. The army we will build will crush any military force in the world, including the immortals who defy us.'

Scoleri exited the room with a cold smile.

~

WHERE IS THIS? OLIVIA BLINKED. WHERE AM I?

She looked at the hospital gown covering her frame. It was the one she had been wearing in the lab.

Her last memories returned in a flash of distorted images and sounds. She inhaled sharply and raised trembling fingers to her lips.

*Did I die?*

She lowered her hand to her chest. Her eyes grew round. She couldn't feel her heart beating.

*I'm dead.*

Instead of panic, Olivia felt only a strange sense of peace. After all, she was in a place where no one could hurt her.

Beneath her bare feet lay an insubstantial whiteness. It puffed up slightly when she shifted her weight, as if it were a cloud or fog. She twisted on her heels and scanned the limitless white horizon surrounding her. She was alone.

*What do I do now?*

The answer came in the form of a breeze. It blew up suddenly, ruffling her hair and making the gown flutter against her legs. The whiteness in front of her billowed in tortuous waves and parted to expose ivory sand.

The wind came again, stronger than before. This time, it whispered her name. Olivia stiffened and looked around wildly.

There was no one there.

The clouds were dissipating, revealing more sand. She took a step forward, then another. The ground moved beneath her feet, warm grains rolling across her bare toes. She looked up and followed the wind as it danced through the air and raised faint dust devils ahead.

The landscape changed, becoming more desert-like with each passing step. Rolling dunes appeared in the distance. The sky overhead changed from white to the palest blue. The ground gradually rose, as if she were approaching a hill. She started to climb.

An eternity passed before she reached the summit of a cliff.

The sight that met her eyes at the top made her gasp and sag to her knees.

It was the scene from her nightmare, the one she had on the day the abbey was attacked.

The battlefield spread out from the base of the hill all the way to the silent army standing on the other side of a blood-soaked expanse. A fortress burned in the distance, flames leaping from the rooftops of buildings and reaching orange fingers toward the sky. A cloud of smoke stained the air above the glowing citadel.

And there, a dozen feet in front of her, standing in a line on the crest of the elevation and facing the battleground, were eleven figures in gilded chain mail and armor.

Olivia stared fearfully at the slender shape in the middle.

The woman's long, fair hair was piled up securely in a knot at the back of her head. Tendrils had escaped the golden mass and shivered slightly in the wind. She held a sword in her right hand, the hilt abnormally large in her slim fingers. Blood gleamed on the edges of the weapon and stained the handles of the sheathed daggers on the outsides of her thighs.

Olivia scanned the other silhouettes, her eyes absorbing details of their fierce profiles. There were five men and five women beside the blonde with the bloody sword. Shock resonated through her when she saw the silhouette of one of the men. Movement captured her gaze. She looked around in time to see the central figure turn to face her. Olivia froze.

She was looking at herself.

The woman stared. A small smile curved her lips. She walked toward her, sword in hand and leather boots carving fresh steps in the sand.

Now that she could see her clearly, Olivia detected subtle differences from her own features. The stranger's lips were fuller, her forehead broader, her nose straighter. And she carried herself with more confidence than Olivia had ever felt in her entire existence.

She pushed off the ground and rose shakily to her feet just as the stranger stopped before her.

They were the same height.

Olivia stared into green eyes a similar shade to hers. 'Who are you?'

'I am you,' replied the stranger.

Olivia blinked. An echo underscored the woman's words, as if many voices had spoken. She glanced sideways. The other figures in the line had changed. There were now only nine of them. They turned to face her.

Olivia took a step back, shock flaring through her.

They were all fair-haired women with eyes that ranged from emerald to jade. And they all looked like they could be sisters.

Her knees went weak when she recognized the person at the end of the row on the right. '*Mother?*'

Natalia Ashkarov watched her silently, her eyes brimming with love.

Olivia gazed at her for the longest time before focusing on the woman in the chain mail armor. 'I—I don't understand.'

'This is a memory.' The stranger indicated the battleground behind her. 'A memory passed down my bloodline to every Seer who came after me. *My* memory.'

Olivia studied the blackened sky and the bloodied corpses beneath it. 'This is the past?'

The figure nodded. 'Yes. It is a past. And a beginning. One of many in this long forgotten era.'

'The beginning of what?' said Olivia.

A shadow crossed the stranger's face. Her eyes dimmed. 'The beginning of a war.'

Olivia straightened. '*The* immortal war?'

The stranger looked at her steadily. 'In a sense.'

Olivia watched her silently. 'You said...that you were me. What did you mean?'

'A piece of me lives inside you.' Sadness tinged the stranger's voice. 'As do a piece of my brothers, sisters, and cousins inside the ones who inherited their bloodlines and the marks.'

She reached down, took Olivia's right hand, and turned it over. The third eye symbol seemed to glow against the skin of her palm.

Images and feelings flooded Olivia at the woman's touch. They sped across her inner vision, a myriad of faces, places, and feelings from a past that stretched across several centuries and lifetimes. At times magically euphoric and at times heart-wrenchingly sad, they brought a sharp pain to her chest and tears to her eyes.

*These are her memories and thoughts. The memories of the first Seer.*

'Navia,' she whispered.

The stranger smiled and dipped her chin in acknowledgment. 'Yes. That is my name. And now, I fear you must return, Seer.'

Olivia blinked. 'Return? Return where?'

'To the present,' said Navia.

'I—' Olivia bit her lip. 'But I died.'

Navia shrugged. 'It happens to the best of us. More importantly, that is why you are here, now.'

'What?'

Navia raised a hand to Olivia's chest, her eyes burning with an intense light. 'It is only in this death that you can claim your true powers. *Our* powers. The power of ten.'

Olivia felt a jolt deep inside her body. Her heart thumped once.

The other Seers came toward her and laid their hands over Navia's, where it lay on her chest. The last one to touch her was her mother.

'Be strong, child,' said Natalia. She caressed Olivia's cheek and gazed deep into her eyes, her expression as fierce as the rest of the Seers. '*Believe in yourself.*'

Heat exploded inside Olivia.

~

SOMETHING BEEPED IN THE SILENT LAB.

Dr. Barry Riese opened his eyes and blinked at the computer in front of him. The lines and numbers on the screen remained unchanged. Heart rate zero. Blood pressure zero. Respiratory rate zero. Even the electroencephalogram was as flat as a pancake.

Patient 451 remained as dead as she had been for the last two hours.

He glanced at the bank of analyzers next to the terminal. They whirred and buzzed, the only sounds in the room beside the faint hum from the computers. *Must have been one of them.*

He wiped drool from the corner of his mouth and pushed himself up, wincing at the kink in his neck. He'd fallen asleep at his desk.

A snore rose from his right. He turned and saw his night-shift lab companion, eminent Harvard neurochemist Dr. Fraser Dunn, dozing in a chair, head propped against the backrest and mouth wide open.

Barry squinted at the digital clock on the wall. It was almost six in the morning. They had another two hours to go before the dayshift started. He stood and headed for the coffee machine in a corner of the lab.

They would normally have kept themselves busy analyzing and testing samples from the experimental subject in the containment room throughout the night, as they had done on so many other shifts in the last ten years. But Mark Scoleri changed all that when he went in there and started fooling around with the woman.

Barry had seen the waif-like blonde look at him in panic when Scoleri started touching her. He'd avoided her gaze and strolled to one of the machines on the other side of the lab. He was being paid handsomely for the job he was doing at the research facility and didn't want to jeopardize what could end up being a lofty retirement nest egg. Besides, he had seen worse — much worse—in the time he had been working for his employers. And he knew the penalty for betraying them. He didn't want to end up as another body in the incinerator.

'Fraser, you want some coffee?' he called out over his shoulder.

He glanced at the steel doors on the far side of the room. The soldiers normally stationed at the lab had been dismissed for the rest of the shift.

'No point guarding a dead body,' Scoleri said before he left. 'Just call them when she comes to.'

Barry sighed. He wished he'd been assigned to the other research level, where the remaining super soldiers had been awakened and were undergoing baseline testing. Although he'd been scared the first time he'd seen the brutes up close, he had to admit it was more exciting than watching a corpse.

'Hey, Fraser?' he said in a louder voice.

His reply was another snore. His hand stilled on the coffee pot. *Was that another beep?*

He turned and stared toward the monitor at his desk. Cold fingers brushed against his mind. His grip loosened on the handle.

The pot crashed to the floor, spilling hot coffee across the white linoleum.

# CHAPTER TWENTY-EIGHT

DUNN SNORTED AND STARTLED IN HIS CHAIR. 'HUH?' HE blinked and looked around dazedly before wiping his mouth with the back of his hand. 'Did I fall asleep?'

Barry's heart slammed wildly against his ribs. A few hot drops of coffee had scalded his shin. He was barely aware of the sting, his gaze riveted to the strong, steady vitals on the monitor at the terminal where he'd been sitting a moment ago. He looked to the figure behind the containment wall and felt his mouth go dry.

The icy sensation inside his head increased as an alien presence infiltrated his consciousness.

Dunn turned and followed his line of sight. *'Jesus!'*

The neurochemist jumped to his feet and staggered back toward Barry. Glass crunched beneath his shoes. He skidded on the wet floor and fell on his ass.

Patient 451 was sitting up in the bed. She stared at them calmly, her expression cold and oddly curious. Her skin seemed to glow from within, filling her face with a terrible light. But that wasn't what made Barry's bladder clench in terror.

The medical equipment inside the chamber had lifted off

the floor and was spinning violently in the air above the gurney. The leather straps that had bound the patient's limbs to the gurney fluttered uselessly from the metal frames, caught in the same silent, gravity-defying twister.

The woman reached up and pulled out the electrodes in her scalp. She opened her hand and studied the wires for a moment before releasing them. They shot out of her grasp and joined the maelstrom near the ceiling.

Barry whimpered when her gaze shifted to him and Dunn once more. Intense pain gripped his skull. He cried out and clutched his head. Dunn curled over and threw up.

The glass containment window trembled a second before it exploded. The lights went out.

Barry threw his arms up as he was lifted off his feet by a powerful force. He smashed into the back wall of the lab and heard a couple of ribs crack.

Shards flew across the room and sliced the backs of his hands and arms as he slid to the ground. Emergency lights flickered above him. The red flash of an alarm punctuated the dim glow.

He sat there for a stunned moment before searching the gloom for Dunn. Another whimper left his lips.

The neurochemist had not been as lucky. He'd struck one of the analyzers with the back of his head; blood oozed from the depression in his skull and pooled on the floor where he had come to rest, his unseeing eyes fixed on the ceiling.

The pressure inside Barry's head doubled, bringing a scream to his throat. It came out a choked grunt as whatever unholy force at work inside the room squeezed the remaining air from his lungs. Panic gripped him when he heard glass pop and break on the other side of the chamber. He kicked weakly at the floor and tried to push himself up.

Patient 451 came around a workstation. She headed slowly toward him, her steps steady.

The broken, glittering fragments on the floor should have cut into the soles of her feet. Instead, they moved from her, scattering across the linoleum as if brushed by a wind.

Something drew the woman's gaze. She slowed and stopped by a table.

Through the agony searing his senses, Barry saw her lift a silver necklace with a locket from the surface. It was the one she had been wearing when she arrived at the lab. She locked it around her neck and drew closer.

When she stopped in front of him and cocked her head to the side, her green eyes glinting with a chilling expression, Barry knew he'd be lucky if he got to enjoy even a single cent of the cash he'd been putting away.

His vision collapsed in a flow of vivid, flickering images. It was as if someone had reached inside his mind and pressed a rewind button. He saw the interior of the lab, the passages outside, and the entire area of Level Five, where the main research facilities were located. The stark pictures were followed by the vast command center and escape tunnel on Level Six. Nausea twisted his stomach when the motion sped up, the snapshots blurring as if the person in control of his memories had grown impatient.

The rest of the half-a-mile-deep, billion-dollar subterranean complex under the Sonoran Desert flashed before his eyes.

The training ranges, prison cells, weapons rooms, and ammunition holdings on Level Four; the research labs and cave holding the dormant soldiers on Level Three; the secured chambers of the first subjects to successfully undergo Phase Three; the staff quarters and alternative command and communication hub on Level Two; the immense hangar on Level One, carved out of the mountain itself and holding millions of dollars worth of military equipment and weapons; the artificial lakes, air ducts, and cooling towers that constituted the life force of the entire base; the underground power plants two miles south that fed the facility; the open-roofed cave with the helipads; the tunnels leading to the entrances and exits in the neighboring valleys.

All of it played across the inside of Barry's head like a film.

*Shit. I should never have taken this job.*

It was the last thought he had before his consciousness vanished in a searing light.

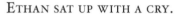

ETHAN SAT UP WITH A CRY.

His heart thundered inside his chest and his breaths came in short, sharp pants, tunneling his vision to a tight, dark circle. Tremors shook his limbs. He became aware of his clothes clinging clammily to his body and heard a distant shouting. He blinked. The roar in his ears faded and the dark veil across his eyes cleared in time for him to see Asgard.

The Bastian noble slapped him hard across the face. 'Hey, snap out of it!'

Ethan hissed air through his teeth. '*Goddamnit!* I really wish you'd stop doing that!'

Asgard leaned in and peered at him. 'Oh. You're back.'

Ethan looked past the immortal's shoulder. He was on a stretcher inside the dimly-lit cargo hold of the Globemaster. From the dozens of eyes trained on him, he guessed he'd been the center of attention for a while.

'What happened?'

He could feel his racing pulse and ragged breathing start to settle.

'That's what we should be asking you.' A figure appeared out of the gloom. 'You've been out of it for two hours,' said Reynolds.

A soldier appeared next to him. She squatted by the stretcher and started examining Ethan.

'There's no need for that.' He drew back and tried to push her away. 'I'm all right.'

The woman ignored him and shone a light in his eyes. 'I doubt that, sir. Your heart rate's been close to one-sixty for the last half-hour and you're, pardon the language, sweating like a hog in the Sahara.'

Ethan grudgingly allowed her to complete her assessment. She sat back on her heels a moment later and observed him with a curious expression.

'Staff Sergeant?' said Reynolds.

'He's fine, sir. Don't know how, but all his vitals are normal.'

'Is he fit to participate in the mission?' said Reynolds.

The staff sergeant opened her mouth to reply.

'If you think you're stopping me, you've got another thing coming,' snapped Ethan.

He rose from the stretcher and rubbed the back of his neck before walking a few steps under Reynolds's watchful gaze. He could feel strength returning to his limbs. In fact, he was starting to feel amazing.

'How far are we from Yuma?'

'We land in five minutes,' said Reynolds curtly.

Ethan turned to Asgard and finally answered the unspoken question in the Bastian noble's face. 'Yes, she did. But she's back.'

Reynolds gave them a puzzled look.

Asgard closed his eyes briefly at the confirmation of Olivia's death. The inflection in Ethan's tone registered belatedly.

He stiffened. 'And?'

'She's...stronger. Much stronger than before.'

Even if he had a hundred years, Ethan couldn't explain the feelings being transmitted across his mental bond with Olivia. All he knew was that he had never before experienced the power he could feel pulsing through their connection. His soul-mate was...different. And his own abilities had grown once more, resonating with her newfound strength. He felt it in the way his birthmark tingled.

'The facility.' He looked at the major. 'I know where it is. We need access to satellites.'

Ethan watched the soldier head toward the bank of computers at the front of the plane. He gritted his teeth and projected his thought to the woman he loved. *Hang on. I'm coming for you.*

A thrill shot through him when he heard her faint reply.

*I'm waiting.*

JONAH OBSERVED THE CHAOTIC SCENES ON THE SECURITY feeds from the cameras inside the main research level. On the one hand, what he was seeing sent a trace of fear through him, the first he'd experienced since the day Asgard Godard chased him on the glacier in the Urals. On the other, it thrilled him like little else had in the last few hundred years.

Olivia Ashkarov's death appeared to have unlocked the full potential of her extrasensory and psychokinetic powers. And the effects were all too devastatingly clear to see.

He'd been on Level Two when the alarms started going off and had joined Scoleri in the secondary command center there. The room was a hive of activity as Scoleri barked orders at his men and the human soldiers attempting to secure the lower floors of the facility.

'I want her captured at any cost,' said Jonah. 'Use every ounce of tranquilizer in the base if you have to. And get snipers in position. I doubt anyone is going to be able to get to her at close range.'

Olivia moved down a corridor lined with flashing crimson lights. The scorching hotness inside her chest had abated to a tolerable warmth. She could feel the unearthly energy thrumming through the golden lines surrounding her heart, each representing a piece of her soul. Beneath it was the electric force that was the power of the other Seers, the spark that had ignited her own abilities beyond anything she had ever experienced.

Figures with guns materialized in her path, men and women who sought to stop her.

They dropped away as quickly as they appeared, powerless to resist the psychic pressure that blasted through their heads. Weapons fell uselessly to the ground and bullets went astray in the face of the psychokinetic waves emanating from her body.

Olivia marveled as how much easier it now was to get inside their heads. And not just theirs—she could feel other minds out there. The minds of half-breeds and immortals. Although she couldn't overpower their consciousness as she could the humans, she could still hurt them.

She came across several training ranges and armories as she negotiated the fourth level of the complex. Muted explosions followed in her wake as she disabled the machines and crushed the contents of the arsenals, like she had done the labs and control room below. She'd discovered she could tap into some of Ethan's elemental powers since she'd awoken from her first death. She couldn't manipulate things as well as her soulmate could but she was able to cause enough destruction to incapacitate their enemy.

More soldiers turned up to challenge her. She delved inside their heads before switching off their minds, brushing them aside as easily as she would flies. Among the thoughts she accessed, Olivia searched for the location of the person she wanted to find the most.

Jonah Krondike.

'MADELEINE?'

'Yeah?'

'Can you hear that?' said Howard.

Madeleine shifted on the floor and winced. The iron manacles around her wrists were digging into her skin where her arms dangled above her head. The wall behind her had taken on a physical presence determined to etch its every line and groove into her back. Even her butt had gone numb.

She was surprised either of them had managed to get even an hour's sleep.

'Hear what?'

'That rumbling.'

Madeleine hesitated. 'Well, I didn't want to say anything, but your stomach's been making noises for a while now.'

'I don't mean that,' snapped Howard. 'You really can't hear it? It feels like—'

The ground trembled slightly.

'—an earthquake,' he finished quietly.

They stared at each other. Madeleine swallowed as the tremors intensified. Their gazes swung to the cell door.

'How far underground are we?' said Howard.

'Your guess is as good as mine,' muttered Madeleine. 'They didn't exactly give us a grand tour when they brought us here.' She paused. 'Why?'

'Quakes are more destructive beneath the Earth's surface,' he replied stiffly. Bangs suddenly rose in the distance. 'And unless it's the Fourth of July, I'm pretty sure those were gunshots. Get ready. Something's happ—'

They both jumped when the door exploded off its hinges and struck the opposite wall of the cell. The quake intensified, bringing dust down from the ceiling of their prison. A slight pressure gripped Madeleine's skull as she stared at the distorted metal panel sliding to the floor. She drew in a sharp breath; she knew this feeling. She heard a voice inside her head and looked toward the doorway.

*Madeleine.*

A figure stood there. Madeleine froze, fear sending a shiver racing down her spine.

It was Olivia.

The immortal's slim figure was covered with a plain hospital gown and her feet were bare. There was a strange glow to her face, as if her skin were filled with an inner light. Her eyes glowed a brilliant jade.

Olivia looked between the two prisoners. 'Are you okay?'

Madeleine nodded shakily. Metal groaned above her. The weight around her wrists disappeared, the manacles clattering noisily against the wall. A corresponding rattle sounded from across the cell as Howard's shackles broke under an invisible force. She saw her own wonder and dread reflected in his gaze.

*In some ways, this feels like that time back at the mansion, when she unleashed that psychic storm. And the thing she did at the lake house, where she shielded us from the harmful effects of her powers. But...something's different.*

For one thing, the energy she sensed from the Seer felt electric and incredibly powerful.

'Come,' said Olivia.

They rose and followed her cautiously out of the cell. Madeleine wondered whether Howard felt as helpless to resist the Seer's command as she did.

*I will not hurt you. I have to maintain this level of control to get us out of here.*

Madeleine startled at the words that streamed inside her head. She opened her mouth to voice a question but was cut off by Howard.

'You can get inside my mind?' said the Crovir immortal in a stunned voice.

'Yes,' said Olivia.

Bodies littered the end of the corridor. The soldiers looked to be unconscious, their breathing so shallow Madeleine first thought them dead.

*I've suppressed their consciousness. I will only kill if I have no option.*

Olivia's words sounded strangely detached inside Madeleine's head. She stared at the immortal's back, awestruck at the supernatural forces she was witnessing once more.

'What happened to you?' said Howard in a low voice.

Olivia glanced at them. 'I died.'

'LET ME GET THIS STRAIGHT,' SAID REYNOLDS. 'YOU'RE telling me the location of the complex was revealed to you through a psychic connection with one of the prisoners we're meant to be rescuing?'

Although the major's tone remained even, the expression in his eyes told Ethan he was not buying his story. It also indicated a short fuse was burning toward a fiery end somewhere.

They were standing in the shadow of the Globemaster, on the tarmac of the Laguna Army Airfield. The Rangers were offloading their equipment from the plane's cargo hold. Although the sun had just risen above the horizon, the chilliness of the desert night was already dissipating. And it seemed they weren't the only ones who were up. Distant gunfire and explosions carried from the battle ranges to the north and east, where the training exercises were already in full flow.

A Lockheed C-5 Galaxy bringing the rest of the Rangers and several all-terrain vehicles touched down on the runway to the right, its super-sized tires squealing. Another two Globemasters, a couple of C-130 Super Hercules, and an Airbus A400M were lining up to land behind it.

Reynolds's gaze shifted briefly to the military aircrafts in the sky. As far as Ethan had gathered, the major had been told a foreign contingent would be joining them on their mission. The Ranger did not look thrilled by the lack of details on the troops who would be working alongside the soldiers under his command.

'Look, with all due respect, I am not taking my men and women out into the desert on a wild goose chase just because you think you're hearing voices inside your head,' said Reynolds stiffly. 'I don't care if—'

'Satellite pictures coming through, Major.'

Reynolds turned to the intelligence officer manning a field laptop a few feet away. 'That was fast.'

The sergeant hesitated. 'We had a little help from our friends, sir.'

He glanced at Ethan and Asgard.

Reynolds scrutinized the immortals. 'You guys have surveillance satellites in our skies?'

Ethan shrugged. Asgard remained silent. They didn't know the exact details of the Bastian councils' capabilities, but judging from what they'd seen so far, it was pretty extensive; it was best if they pretended to be in the know.

A real-time image of the proving ground appeared on the computer screen.

Ethan's pulse sped up. 'Pan out to the east.'

Reynolds gave him a guarded look while the sergeant complied with his instruction. The immortal ignored the major and focused on the desert landscape unfurling on the monitor. A range of mountains came into view, a mass of jagged summits interspersed with tortuous, shadowy canyons. An immense flat plain stretching at least ten miles across emerged beyond them.

Ethan went still when he spotted the black peaks on the far side of the lowland.

'There, stop!' he barked.

The sergeant froze the screen.

'Where is that?' said Ethan tensely.

'That's part of the KOFA Region,' said Reynolds. 'It's not far from the Smart Weapon Testing facilities.'

'I mean that range two miles east.'

'There's nothing there. It's just part of the Kofa Mountains.'

'Trust me, there's something there,' said Ethan in a hard voice.

'I've been on this proving ground on more than a hundred training exercises,' said Reynolds. 'There's—'

'Sir, there are more images coming through,' said the sergeant. He tapped on the keyboard and opened another window.

A series of shots filled the screen. They stared at them for confused seconds.

Ethan inhaled sharply when he grasped what they were looking at.

'What the—?' Reynolds muttered, his face losing some of its color.

The sergeant gaped, his wide-eyed gaze fixed on the pictures.

A cell rang, startling them.

Asgard took the satellite phone out of his tactical vest and answered the call. 'Victor?' The Bastian noble paused, a frown darkening his face. 'Yeah, we're looking at it.'

The new multispectral satellite imagery that had been sent through to the intelligence officer's laptop showed a massive, circular underground structure extending thousands of feet beneath one of the mountains Ethan had identified. It was connected to the surrounding valleys by a network of tunnels, some of them as much as a mile long.

'Fuck me,' muttered the sergeant.

Reynolds cocked an eyebrow.

'Sorry, major,' said the soldier. 'But that place is bigger than

Raven Rock.' He enlarged the central pictures. 'It seems to have six levels, the lowest being half a mile beneath the surface of the desert. The top one appears to have been blasted out of the mountain itself.' He studied the screen. 'Whole structure's shaped like an inverted, broad-based cone, sir.' He scrolled down. 'Looks like they've even got their own power plants south of the main complex. And a heliport inside some kind of giant pit.'

Asgard disconnected and held the phone tightly in his grip. 'That area is under the control of a special branch of the army inside the United States Special Operations Command and the DoD. It's a top secret R&D site. The man in charge is a General William Gunnerson.'

$\sim$

# CHAPTER TWENTY-NINE

JONAH GOT THE CALL AT 06:29.

'Get out. They're coming for you,' said the man at the other end of the line.

Terse voices punctuated the alarm echoing across the command center around Jonah. They'd just lost Level Four.

The Crovir noble turned away from the clamor and clutched the cell to his ear. 'What do you mean?'

'Godard contacted Dvorsky last night. The Bastian First Council got in touch with us shortly after. The Crovir First Council just agreed to assist the Bastians and the US Army. It seems Victor didn't reveal all he knew until now.' The man hesitated. 'I'm sorry, we didn't have any other choice.'

Jonah frowned. 'I understand.'

'Godard and Storm discovered your approximate whereabouts yesterday. They're in Yuma right now, with troops of Rangers and several hundred immortals.'

Sweat broke out on Jonah's forehead. He looked at the camera feeds filling the west wall of the control hub and focused on the row at the top. They showed the desert landscape outside the base and the access tunnels. Scoleri had already increased security at the main entry and exit points.

'How did they find out about this place?' hissed Jonah.

'I don't know. Victor didn't reveal that part of the puzzle to the council. I'm sending some of my own operatives among the Crovir Hunters joining the assault teams.'

Jonah clenched his teeth. 'I'll be out of here by then.'

'Good. And they know about Gunnerson. US Army Counterintelligence is closing in on his location in Washington as we speak.'

Anger flooded Jonah at his accomplice's words. 'He knows too much. Terminate him.'

'I ordered the hit five minutes ago.'

THE CONTAINMENT DOOR CRASHED OPEN, THE THICK STEEL panel bouncing off the wall inside. Olivia stepped through the doorway and disappeared into the gloom beyond. Howard walked in behind her, Madeleine in his wake.

The Crovir immortal stopped and blinked. 'What is this place?'

As his vision adjusted to the shadows, he made out a gigantic cave below the steel walkway they stood on. The far side was at least four hundred feet away. Dim spotlights dotted the high ceiling and the rock walls rising around them.

His gaze focused on the space beneath their feet. Rows of bullet-shaped, metal structures lined the floor of the chamber as far as the eye could see. Each of the capsules was connected to an array of complex equipment and monitors. Emergency lights throbbed behind glass windows set in the distant walls and showed the empty labs beyond.

Olivia turned and headed for a metal staircase on the right.

Howard glanced at Madeleine. She shrugged. They followed her.

They were on the lower floor seconds later. The Seer crossed over to the nearest row of metal structures, her bare feet silent on the smooth concrete. She stopped in front of one and wiped at the curved surface. An aperture appeared beneath her hand. Howard stiffened.

It was a small window.

'Are these what I think they are?' said Madeleine.

Howard turned and saw the scientist on the other side of the aisle. She was looking inside one of the capsules, her face pale.

'Yes,' said Olivia. 'They are suspension pods.'

Howard's mouth went dry. He stepped over to where the Seer stood and followed her steady gaze.

A monstrous figure floated in a murky liquid inside the tank. He was naked but for some gray trunks covering his groin. An endotracheal tube rose from his mouth and connected to a mechanical ventilator on the outside. Lines and wires dotted his body. He looked to be asleep.

Dread filled Howard as he looked at one of the monitors on the side of the pod. Waves pulsed steadily across the screen, indicating normal vitals. The label at the top said "Subject 550."

'This is Phase Two, isn't it?'

'Yes.'

Olivia turned and made for the middle of the cave. Madeleine and Howard followed slowly, their anxious gazes lost on the tanks stretching out around them.

The Crovir immortal felt a sudden flicker of pressure inside his head. The hairs on his arms rose at the spike in the Seer's psychokinetic powers.

'What are you doing?' said Madeleine.

Olivia closed her eyes. 'I'm stopping the process.'

~

'THAT BITCH!' SCOLERI GLARED AT THE SECURITY FEEDS FROM the cave on Level Three. The computers monitoring the status of the experimental subjects showed their tanks going offline one after the other. 'Is she disabling the pods?'

'Yes,' said one of the technicians. 'Basic life support is still working though. She hasn't killed them.'

Scoleri chewed his lip. Jonah had already left the command center. 'Where are the snipers?'

'They're in the ventilation system above the cave. It's about the only place where they can get long-range sight on the target down there.'

'Good,' said Scoleri.

A nervous voice called out from the other side of the room. 'Sir, we're detecting an unknown convoy heading our way.'

Scoleri's gaze swung to the security feeds showing the outside of the facility. He could see no sign of their enemies yet. 'Part of the training exercises?'

'No. We have a schedule of the activities taking place across the proving ground. The vehicles and helicopters coming toward us don't appear to be part of the program.'

Scoleri scanned the camera displays. 'Mobilize our troops to defend our access points. Use every possible means to delay them. I want to secure Olivia Ashkarov before they get here.' A savage smile curved his lips. 'And release the super soldiers from their holding chambers. Let's see what they can do on a real battlefield.'

~

THE LEAD SNIPER STARED THROUGH THE SCOPE OF HIS RIFLE. The target's neck came into focus three hundred and fifty feet beneath the dome of the cave.

'Sniper Two, what's your position?' he murmured in his microphone.

'I'm in the north ventilation shaft. In position and target acquired.'

'Sniper Three?'

'In position in the west ventilation shaft. Target acquired.'

'Sniper Four?'

'East ventilation shaft. Target acquired.'

The lead sniper moved his finger to the trigger. 'Fire at will.'

HOWARD HEARD SOMETHING CLANG ON A NEARBY TANK. A small object skittered across the aisle ten feet away.

Further clangs and thuds echoed across the cave as more objects struck the suspension pods and the ground around them.

'What the hell are those?' barked Madeleine, looking up.

Howard followed her gaze and saw tiny silver arrows raining down from the ceiling.

'Shit! Those are tranquilizer darts!'

He moved toward Olivia.

Lines marred the Seer's brow as she concentrated on disabling the suspension pods. Although the psychokinetic force she was exerting had shifted the projectiles from their trajectories, the reach of the pressure field protecting them had shrunk since she started directing her focus on the tanks.

'Olivia! Watch out!' he shouted.

The Seer blinked.

A dart twisted through the air and found her neck. Two more sank into her arm and leg.

ONE THOUSAND FEET ABOVE THE SONORAN DESERT, ETHAN felt a stutter in the link with his soulmate.

The Black Hawk helicopter was still twenty miles from the target site.

'Ethan?'

The Crovir noble met Asgard's anxious stare across the cabin.

'Hurry.' The Elemental gritted his teeth. 'We need to hurry!'

THE DRUGS SEEPED INTO HER VEINS AND BROUGHT A WAVE OF lethargy crashing down on her body. Olivia shook her head and staggered sideways. Arms caught her as she started to fall.

MADELEINE PEERED ABOVE THE TOP OF THE TANK. BULLETS pinged off the metal, raising sparks close to her head. She ducked behind the structure.

The snipers had switched to live ammunition.

They had pulled Olivia under the cover of one of the suspension pods. Howard crouched over the Seer and felt her pulse; he had removed the darts from her neck and limbs.

A fine sheen of sweat coated Olivia's brow. She moaned and shifted agitatedly on the floor, eyes fluttering rapidly beneath her lids.

From the scattered thoughts fleeting through Madeleine's head, it was obvious the immortal was trying to fight the effects of the chemicals coursing through her bloodstream. She peeled one of Olivia's eyelids back and registered the pinpoint pupil in a sea of green.

'I really wish we had some guns,' said Howard bitterly. Another volley of shots scored the floor next to the tank. 'I should have taken a couple from the soldiers we came across before.'

Madeleine stared at the room on the other side of the row of tanks in front of them. A wild scheme was taking shape in her mind.

'Shit,' Howard muttered.

Madeleine looked at him. 'What?'

'I think I just saw a soldier poke his head around that containment door.'

She followed Howard's worried gaze to the steel walkway in the distance. A couple of black-clad figures slipped through the opening.

Ice filled her veins. It was time to see whether her crazy-ass plan could work.

'Stay with her!' she ordered the Crovir immortal.

Madeleine whirled around, grabbed a freestanding cart next to the tank, and used it as a shield to scuttle across the aisle. Howard yelled something behind her. His words were lost in a loud crash as the medical equipment on the trolley fell on the floor.

Shots slammed into the top shelf of the cart and peppered the ground around its legs.

Madeleine clenched her teeth and kept moving toward the line of suspension pods. She reached it seconds later, let go of the cart, and slipped beneath the cover of a tank. She rolled to the other side and scrambled to her knees.

The lab she had her eyes on was now only fifteen feet away. Glass cabinets were fixed to the wall on the far side of the room. Their shelves were filled with boxes and vials of drugs. She was only interested in one of the standing units.

Madeleine poked her head from under the protective curve of the tank. Bullets whined through the air and struck the floor five feet away.

*Hmm. So they haven't got a perfect line of sight on my position.* She studied the spot where the shots had landed. *But they will once I get close to that wall.*

She looked over her shoulder.

Howard was gaping at her with a "What-the-hell-are-you-doing?" expression from the other side of the aisle, Olivia cradled in his arms.

Madeleine squinted into the gloom to the right. She could see movement some two hundred feet away.

Her gaze alighted on the bottom of the cart she'd abandoned. A large syringe pump had survived its impromptu trip across the cave; it lay on its side on the lower shelf. She slipped under the pod, grabbed it, and crawled back to face the lab again. She hefted the device in her hands and studied the glass window, her heart pounding in her chest.

*You'd better be moving at the speed of light when this hits, Black.*

Madeleine squatted on her heels and took a deep breath. She leapt to her feet, lifted the pump above her head, and hurled it at the window in front of her in one quick motion. She was running before it crashed through the glass. Bullets whizzed around her. The alarm tearing through the lab became audible as the pane started to shatter.

Madeleine winced. *This is gonna hurt like a bitch!*

She jumped and twisted sideways, smashing shoulder-first into the window. What remained of the glass exploded into glittering fragments beneath the impact of her body. Madeleine curled up protectively as she sailed into the room beyond, shards slicing across the exposed skin of her hands and arms. Her hip glanced off the edge of a countertop, sending numbing pain shooting down her leg. She landed hard on the floor and skidded toward the cabinets on the opposite side of the room, the alarm painting the walls around her with pulsing red light.

A gasp escaped her lips. She threw her arms out, spun onto her back, and brought her legs up, grinding her teeth at the throbbing pain in her left hip and flank. Her feet collided with the metal base of one of the cabinets, halting her deadly slide and sending shock waves up her spine. The unit shuddered above her. Madeleine swallowed and stared at the glass wall, blood roaring in her ears.

*Bingo!*

She'd stopped in front of the cabinet with the word "Resus" stamped over it in red.

She rose to her knees, yanked the door open, and scanned the contents of the shelves. She registered the names on the vials on the top one before focusing on the stack of pre-filled syringes beneath them. She grabbed several, jammed them inside the pockets of her pants, and twisted around to stare at the shadowy space beyond the broken window. Sporadic gunfire echoed across the cave as the snipers continued their assault on the area where Howard sheltered with Olivia.

Madeleine glanced at the door at the back of the lab. *There's no way we'll be able to get her out through here. I'm gonna have to do this where she is.*

She bit her lip. *But how the hell do I get back out there without being shot to pieces?*

She studied the interior of the room. Her frantic gaze landed on a couple of fire extinguishers and an axe by the door. She snatched them from the wall, placed them on the counter beneath the window, and climbed on top. She peered out into the cave.

More soldiers were pouring through the door on the upper walkway to the right. The first men were about twenty seconds from where Howard crouched with Olivia.

*This had better work.*

Madeleine wedged the first fire extinguisher against the windowsill with one foot and raised the axe in both hands. Her thought went briefly to a certain Bastian immortal with blue-green eyes. She scowled.

*Dammit, I should have ravished that grumpy bastard when I had the chance!*

She brought the blade down sharply on the head of the fire extinguisher. It parted with the body of the canister with a violent pop and disappeared in the direction of the cave, white fumes jetting out at high pressure in its wake. She kicked it out of the window and went to work on the second canister.

A thick cloud formed outside the lab when Madeleine rolled the red cylinder out onto the ground. She slipped under the cover of the smoke.

Shots rained down around her as she darted to where the closest tank should be. The hulking shape of the pod materialized out of the mist. She ducked under it, rolled out into the aisle on the other side, and scrambled to her feet.

Shadowy shapes appeared some thirty feet up the row as she lunged toward where Howard hunched, his arms wrapped protectively around Olivia.

A bullet punched through the flesh of her right calf. Madeleine cried out and started to fall.

Howard reached out, grabbed her arm, and yanked her into the cover of the suspension pod, his face grim. She ignored the burning pain in her leg, removed two of the syringes from her pocket, and crawled across to Olivia.

The soldiers were mere seconds away.

'What are you—?' Howard started.

Madeleine yanked the caps off the needles with her teeth, said a short prayer, and jabbed the syringes straight into Olivia's chest.

A FRESH WAVE OF HEAT EXPLODED INSIDE OLIVIA AS THE NEW drugs shot through the chambers of her heart. One jolted the golden lines of her souls while the other raced through her accelerating bloodstream, erasing the effects of the potent chemicals dampening her consciousness. Her powers erupted from their sedative prison and burned away the last vestiges of the tranquilizers.

She opened her eyes in time to see a soldier point a pistol at Madeleine's head.

∿

HOWARD BLINKED. ONE SECOND HE WAS STARING INTO THE barrel of a gun. In the next, the men crowding around them had gone flying across the cave. They slammed into the nearby tanks and walls and slid to the ground, unconscious.

Olivia sat up beside him.

Howard swallowed at the pulsing energy radiating from the immortal. He could hear a faint hum from the tanks beside them as the metal vibrated to the tune of the psychokinetic field.

'You're back,' he said weakly.

Olivia acknowledged his words with a dip of her chin and rose to her feet.

'Thank you,' she told Madeleine in a hard voice.

Madeline nodded shakily.

Olivia stepped out into the middle of the aisle and turned to face the wave of men charging across the floor toward them. More soldiers appeared in the doorway above the steel walkway.

The Seer narrowed her eyes.

Howard looked at the syringes in Madeleine's white-knuckled grip. 'What was in those?'

Madeleine winced and pressed a hand against the fresh wound on her leg. 'An antidote for the tranquilizers and adrenaline. They always had them around the labs at AuGenD when they did these kinds of experiments.'

Howard tore a piece off the bottom of his shirt and tied it around her bleeding calf. Movement above caught his eyes. He looked up in time to see a man with a rifle fall from a collapsing air duct. The soldier screamed, his arms and legs pinwheeling wildly through empty space. Three more followed, the metal shafts they lay in giving away violently beneath them. Their bodies thudded to the ground seconds later.

Howard's gaze shifted to Olivia's enraged face.

*Oh boy. They've gone and pissed her off now. I almost feel sorry for them. Almost.*

# CHAPTER THIRTY

THEY LANDED IN A SHALLOW VALLEY AMIDST THE FOOTHILLS of the Kofa Mountains, forty miles northeast of the Laguna Army Airfield.

Ethan and Asgard jumped to the desert ground with Reynolds and a group of Rangers. More soldiers poured out of the second Black Hawk helicopter. Immortal Hunters in tactical gear piled out of the other two aircrafts, a Bastian team leader at their head.

'The entrance we're headed for is half a mile over that rise!' shouted the Rangers' intelligence officer. He indicated a hill to the east. 'The latest thermal pictures show a large concentration of bodies near it. They know we're here, sir!'

Apprehension flitted through Ethan.

The major voiced the question in his mind. 'How did they figure out we were coming? We didn't know where we were going ourselves until twenty-five minutes ago!'

'We are aware of at least one traitor among the foreign councils assisting us,' said Asgard in clipped tones. He met Ethan's eyes briefly. 'He or she must have warned Jonah.'

Ethan clenched his teeth. *It must be the Crovir Council. Victor only just confirmed the details of our plans with them.*

'Jonah?' Reynolds repeated.

Asgard dipped his head curtly. 'Although Gunnerson is listed as being in charge of this facility, the...man who's really running the show goes by the name of Jonah Krondike.'

Reynolds gave him a shrewd look. 'From what you said before, you seem to know this guy well.'

A muscle twitched in Asgard's jawline. 'Let's just say he's an old enemy.'

'The rest of our convoy won't be here for another fifteen minutes.' Reynolds glanced at the helicopters flying past overhead, on their way to the other tunnels they'd spotted on the multispectral images. 'I want all the exits covered before we make our move. Let's look at that map again.'

Ethan turned from the group and headed some twenty feet to the south. He could feel the violent power pulsing through his link with Olivia. She was angry. And he feared if he didn't get to her soon, she would be consumed by her rage. The consequences, he suspected, would be beyond devastating. He studied the dirt and sand beneath his boots for some time before walking back to the Rangers and the immortals.

'They know we're here so we've lost the element of surprise,' he told Reynolds. 'What if we could regain it?'

The major straightened. 'What do you mean?'

Ethan indicated the spot where he had stood a moment ago. 'There's a ventilation duct over there that leads straight inside the facility.'

Reynolds looked at the intelligence officer. 'Is that true?'

The soldier frowned at the image on the laptop. 'It's difficult to tell, sir.' He pursed his lips and magnified the picture. 'Hmm.'

'What is it, sergeant?' snapped Reynolds.

'Well, there *is* a faint line on here that could be a passage,' the man murmured dubiously.

Reynolds's suspicious gaze swung to Ethan. 'How the hell could you know something like that?'

Ethan masked his growing impatience behind a steady stare. 'Same way I told you where the facility was.'

Reynolds's expression grew troubled. He ran a hand through his hair. 'How far down?'

'Twenty feet,' said Ethan.

Reynolds turned to his men. 'Dig some holes for explosives. Let's—'

'I've got something faster and more discreet than C4,' said Ethan. He caught Asgard's stare and shrugged. 'Well, it's not as if we were going to be able to hide it from them forever.'

He twisted on his heels and took several steps toward the area where he had detected the structure under the desert floor.

'Hide what forever? What is he talking about?' said Reynolds behind him.

'Major?' said Asgard.

'Yeah?'

'Did your superiors tell you anything unusual about this mission?'

The major hesitated. 'Unusual how?'

Ethan focused his powers. The pentagram on his left hand started to tingle.

'So they *did* tell you something?' said Asgard quietly.

Reynolds blew out a frustrated sigh. 'If you *must* know, they mentioned a cockamamie story about some supernatural shit we might see. We weren't to breathe a word of it to anyone, on pain of being court-martialed and never seeing the light of day again for the rest of our miserable lives.'

'Ah.' The Bastian team leader sounded relieved. 'That's great. We can just get on with it then. It was going to be a pain in the ass to keep up the subterfuge when we're working so closely with humans.'

'What subterfuge?' Reynolds sounded like he was close to popping that fuse again. 'What do you mean, *humans*?' There was a twang of metal. 'And where on God's earth did that sword come from? I thought that was a rifle on your back!'

'His name is Armistad,' said Asgard coolly.

'I don't care if it's called Mittens! That thing belongs in a museum!'

Further metallic noises followed.

'You've *all* got swords?' barked Reynolds.

'I'm afraid it's part of our gear,' said the Bastian team leader calmly.

The ground started to tremble. Sand and pebbles danced across the surface of the desert. Uneasy murmurs broke out among the soldiers.

'Major?' said Asgard. 'Tell your men to keep their fingers off their triggers.'

'They always have their fingers off the trigger,' Reynolds replied stiffly. The tremors intensified. 'What's going on?'

'You're about to witness some of that supernatural phenomenon your superiors warned you about,' said Asgard. 'So do me a favor, will you? Tell them to keep their fingers *off* those triggers. We wouldn't want anyone to get hit by friendly fire.'

Reynolds grudgingly gave the command to his men.

Heat blossomed inside Ethan's chest. He directed the formidable elemental energy throbbing through his blood at the ground before him.

A five-foot fracture tore through the desert. It widened rapidly, sending spidery arms across the land. Giant chunks of rock and dirt rose across a twelve-foot area. They drifted silently in the air before crashing down a short distance away, making the ground shudder once more.

Ethan exhaled slowly and walked to the edge of the

crevasse. Metal screamed as he peeled the roof off the ventilation shaft below. Sunlight streamed inside the dark channel.

'We'll have to climb down.'

Reynolds stared at him, his mouth opening and closing soundlessly. The rest of the soldiers gaped. Most had tightened their grips on their automatic weapons. The immortals seemed duly impressed.

Ethan checked his guns and unsheathed his blades. 'Shall we?'

~

Madeleine limped along the passage, Howard's arm wrapped firmly around her waist. They were on Level Two of the facility.

Olivia walked ahead of them, her steps steady. She had placed the rest of the suspension pods they'd found in the cave on basic life support mode before destroying the other research labs on that floor.

Madeleine's gaze roamed the deserted rooms and passages around them. This level was larger than the ones they'd ascended through and seemed to contain the staff's living quarters. More soldiers rushed into their path and quickly collapsed under Olivia's psychic influence. Some tried to use tranquilizer shots again, but none of the darts came within striking distance of the Seer.

*Even if they did, I know how to reverse the effects now,* she thought.

Howard lifted a couple of MP5s off the unconscious soldiers and passed one to her. Madeleine looped the strap around her neck and gripped the weapon firmly.

~

Scoleri glared at the image of Olivia Ashkarov advancing ruthlessly through the upper level of the base. She was almost at the command center.

'Where are the super soldiers?' he barked.

'They've been deployed on Level One and at the exits, sir.'

'Get three of them down here,' said Scoleri. 'We need to stop that woman!'

He checked his weapons, grabbed a couple of magazine belts from an ammunition cabinet, and slid his sword into the harness at his back. He was about to storm out of the room when one of the men at the control terminals called out to him.

'Sir, we appear to have a breach in one of the ventilation shafts! Pressure's dropped right off the charts.'

Scoleri twisted on his heels and walked to the workstation. 'Where?'

'It's one of the air ducts to the west.' The soldier indicated a pipe on the map depicting the facility's ventilation system. 'We detected four helicopters in that area twelve minutes ago.'

Sweat pooled on Ethan's face and trickled down his back as he ran in a half-crouch along the gloomy conduit, the flashlight attached to his tactical vest illuminating the path before him. Asgard and the rest of the men followed in his wake, their boots raising faint vibrations on the metal floor and their breathing echoing against the narrow walls.

The tunnel forked up ahead. Ethan slowed to a stop and scrutinized the two passages.

Asgard turned to the Rangers' intelligence officer. 'Which way?'

'The one to the right goes straight to the second level. This one should take us to the top floor.'

The sergeant indicated the channel on the left.

'I'm detecting a hell of a lot of heavy equipment and weapons up there,' said Ethan.

'Let's split up,' said Reynolds.

'Agreed,' muttered the Bastian team leader.

Asgard looked at Ethan. 'Your powers would serve us best on the upper level.'

Ethan hesitated. Although his every instinct was telling him to go to the second floor, he knew the Bastian noble was right. He nodded reluctantly and watched the immortal step inside the tunnel to the right.

'Asgard?'

The immortal paused and looked over his shoulder.

'Olivia is on Level Two,' Ethan said quietly. 'Howard and Madeleine are with her.'

Asgard's eyes flared in the gloom. He dipped his chin jerkily.

Ethan watched him disappear with half the Rangers and the immortals. He turned and headed up the passage on the left with Reynolds and the remaining men.

They had traveled some two hundred feet when a detonation suddenly shook the walls of the ventilation shaft. Ethan froze.

A dim light appeared up ahead. The floor trembled as it grew rapidly in brightness.

His mouth went dry. Incandescent flames filled the passage and raced toward them in a deadly roar.

'Get down!' he barked.

The men around him dropped to the ground, Reynolds cursing colorfully.

Ethan moved to the front of the group, sheathed his swords, and focused his powers on the approaching wall of fire, his heart pounding erratically against his ribs.

*Let's see how much stronger I've become.*

The blaze shrieked as it collided with the wave of energy he projected. The fire started to slow, flames bucking and stuttering. Ethan clenched his teeth and raised his hands in front of him. The inferno came to a shuddering halt some ten feet from where he stood, crackling and spitting angrily against the elemental force opposing it. Heat licked his skin and brought a layer of perspiration to his brow. He curled his fingers and concentrated on manipulating the mass of burning energy before him.

The fire retreated, slowly at first, then accelerating as rapidly as it had stormed their way. Shadows filled the tunnel once more as the flames disappeared with a low rumble.

Ethan swallowed, somewhat stunned by what he had just accomplished. He lowered his arms, filled with a sense of urgency once more.

'Let's go!' he told the men behind him. 'And don't touch the walls.'

Reynolds glanced at the glowing sections of metal as he started after him. 'Did you just stop that fire?'

Ethan did not reply. He could see another light in the distance. This time, it wasn't the flames from an explosion. He accelerated.

OLIVIA COCKED HER HEAD TO THE SIDE. HER SOULMATE WAS drawing closer. She could feel it in her heart. Fierce joy coursed through her, dimming some of the rage that had filled her soul since she'd awakened. She studied the room she stood in and crushed the remaining camera monitors and computer terminals lining its walls and floor. The men and women who had been working at them already lay unconscious, guns lying uselessly by their still bodies.

Many of the soldiers and civilians had been immortals and half-breeds. Despite Howard and Madeleine's help, the effort it took to physically knock them all out had sapped some of her strength. She found herself slightly out of breath as she wielded her newfound powers.

Steel doors bounced noisily against the walls behind her. Olivia turned as three colossal figures stepped inside the command center she had just destroyed.

Howard paled as he stared at the men. 'Shit. Looks like some of the test subjects made it out of Phase Three after all.'

Madeleine clenched her jaw.

Olivia assessed the super soldiers with a frown. They were twice the size of an average man, their powerful bodies bulging with overdeveloped muscles and their frames augmented by drugs and genetic manipulation. Their faces looked bullish, the flesh bloated as a result of the experiments they'd undergone.

Although their physical presence was a cause for alarm in itself, the thing that worried her the most was their minds. They were different from the ones she'd encountered inside the base so far. Neither human nor immortal, and not quite like the half-breeds she had sensed either. Their chemistry was all wrong. And they weren't responding to her psychic will.

Anxiety flashed through her when she registered their thoughts. They were focused on one thing and one thing only: to accomplish their mission, at all costs.

'Oh God,' Madeleine mumbled.

Her gaze was locked on one of the soldiers.

Olivia studied the dark-haired giant on the left and heard the words in Madeleine's mind. 'Do you know him?' She paused. 'His name is Mason Hofstadter?'

'Yes,' Madeleine replied shakily. 'I'm pretty sure that's the husband of Gillian Hofstadter, the woman Asgard and I visited in Carson City.'

Olivia felt the faintest flicker then. The soldier had had a sliver of a reaction to his wife's name. It disappeared in the next moment.

'You will come with us,' Hofstadter stated in a deep voice.

He raised the automatic weapon in his hands. It looked like a toy in his grip.

'I don't think so.' Howard leveled the MP5 and fired at the soldiers.

At such close range, most of the bullets thudded into their bodies. They didn't move so much as an inch.

'You're kidding me,' Howard whispered. 'They're wearing body armor?'

'No. It's not just body armor.' Madeleine stared at the blood oozing out of several wounds on the men's bodies. 'I don't think they're capable of feeling pain.'

Olivia shivered at her words.

Hofstadter depressed the trigger on his weapon. She flinched as the shots bounced off the psychokinetic bubble emanating from her body.

The three soldiers followed the bullets' deviated trajectories with their eyes. They laid down their weapons and started across the room.

*They're fast learners.*

She was shocked they could even move in the face of the pressure wave she was projecting. She fisted her hands and drew on her powers.

The men stopped. They leaned forward, as if facing a gale. One of them lifted his foot and took a step forward. His boot landed heavily on the floor.

The gap between the super soldiers and the place where she stood narrowed. Alarm darted through Olivia. She took one step back.

*God, help me stop these men!*

She became aware of a mass of different thoughts approaching the command center, a mix of humans, immortals, and half-breeds. One group appeared to be fighting the other. Her breath caught in her throat when she recognized one of the many streams of consciousness.

'Asgard,' Olivia whispered.

ASGARD PUNCHED A SOLDIER IN THE JAW, DUCKED BENEATH A swinging blade, and drove his elbow into his assailant's stomach. The man grunted then gasped as the arming sword penetrated his chest with a single thrust. The Bastian noble pulled the blade out of the falling body, stabbed another enemy soldier in the gut, and slashed a deep cut into a third's neck. He glanced at the battleground around him, where Rangers and immortals engaged the adversary in close combat.

They'd heard a faint detonation just before they reached the end of the ventilation shaft that had brought them to the second floor of the facility. Asgard had no time to give any thought to Ethan and the men with him when he saw the wave of enemy soldiers and immortal agents who stood waiting for them.

Two men rushed him. Asgard dropped beneath a dagger, jabbed a knee in the first man's groin as he came up, and drove the hilt of his sword into the other's jaw.

The Bastian team leader punched someone in the face next to him and reverse-kicked another soldier in the head. 'We're close to the command center!'

Asgard saw the sign he indicated above a corridor to the left. He turned and fought his way toward the passage, stabbing and striking the soldiers in his path with renewed resolve. Olivia was there. He knew it somehow.

A doorway appeared up ahead. He knocked out the last man in his path and stormed across the threshold a moment later.

Asgard reeled back at the wave of pressure that washed across his skull. He recognized his niece's psychic energy. Unlike what he'd experienced when they'd escaped from the mansion though, he could feel no pain. It appeared she had gained a new level of control over her abilities.

He rocked to a halt, his gaze moving from the destruction around him to the unconscious bodies littering the floor and the six people still on their feet.

Olivia seemed both frail and incredibly powerful where she stood in the middle of the room, her expression determined.

The three figures she faced were nearly twice as tall as she and three times as wide. The fabric of their uniforms strained against their muscular torsos and limbs. Their hands were the size of shovels and their necks as broad as an average man's thigh.

Alarm knotted Asgard's stomach. *Super soldiers.*

The men's faces were curiously blank as they stared at the Seer. One of them took a slow step forward, his body tilted slightly as if pushing against an invisible wall.

Lines furrowed Olivia's brow.

A computer monitor sailed past her and smashed into the super soldier's chest. The man's eyes moved briefly to the woman behind Olivia.

Madeleine yanked a printer free from its wires. She favored her right leg, raised the device above her head, and threw it with a grunt. A crimson patch widened on her left flank.

The soldier batted the machine away like a fly.

# CHAPTER THIRTY-ONE

Anger flooded Asgard when he registered the bruises and blood streaking Madeleine's face. Mixed with it were intense relief that she was alive and a flood of other emotions he did not want to name.

Howard looked similarly beat-up next to her. He grabbed a computer from the workstation next to him and hurled it at one of the other soldiers. It struck the man with a thud before smashing to the ground. The giant continued his advance unhindered and crushed the remains of the device under his foot.

Asgard raised his arming sword and bolted in the direction of the closest figure. Olivia's alarmed gaze moved to him. He heard a panicked *Stop!* in his thoughts.

The soldier turned and ducked just as the immortal reached him, his movements stunningly fast for his size. A hammer-like fist swung up toward Asgard. The Bastian noble flung himself backward. The blow glanced off his right shoulder and sent numbing pain down his arm. He landed on his back, his sword striking the ground with a clatter. A shadow swooped above him.

He gasped and rolled out of the way of the soldier's boot. It landed on the ground with a solid thud inches from his head.

A group of Rangers and immortals dashed inside the command center behind him.

Asgard jumped to his feet and gripped his sword with both hands. 'Be careful. These men are—'

'*Watch out!*' Howard yelled from the other side of the room.

One of the super soldiers grabbed two automatic weapons from the floor with a lightning-quick move and swung them at the men by the door. Asgard dove for the floor and steeled himself for the shots that were to come, his heart slamming against his ribs.

Olivia raised one hand in the air just as the giant depressed the triggers.

The bullets swerved upward and thudded into the ceiling, raising a cloud of plaster dust. The guns crumpled in the super soldier's hands, crushed by the same unseen force that had thwarted the course of the projectiles.

Shock echoed through Asgard. *She can manipulate metal?*

*Yes,* said Olivia inside his head. *I can access some of Ethan's powers.*

Asgard looked into his niece's eyes and saw the staggering truth reflected in their blazing depths.

The super soldier studied the ruined weapons in his hands. He dropped them and turned toward Olivia, his face still impassive.

'What the hell's going on?' The Bastian team leader stared, open-mouthed. 'Did that—that girl just stop those bullets?'

'That "girl" is my niece,' said Asgard. 'And those aren't normal soldiers.'

'You don't say,' muttered one of the Rangers. 'This supernatural shit is piling up mighty fast. I feel like I'm in the world's worst nightmare right now.'

'It's not over yet,' said Asgard grimly.

Ethan blocked two strikes to his head, crushed the swords swinging toward him, and delivered a series of rapid punches and kicks to his attackers.

Reynolds stood his ground a short distance from him, his face a focused mask as he fought several dark-clad men.

They'd exited the ventilation shaft onto a steel walkway above an immense cave carved out of the mountain rock. Four access tunnels were visible at the corners, along with vast store-rooms holding hardware and ammunition. Rows of military vehicles and crates dotted the two hundred thousand square feet of concrete floor space. It was also currently full of enemy soldiers and agents.

Ethan hook-kicked a man to the ground and glanced around. With half their forces still en route to the site and the other half engaged in a fierce confrontation at the main entrances and exits to the facility, the Rangers and the immortals were heavily outnumbered.

Sporadic gunfire punctuated the sounds of the battle. Although he had destroyed as many of the enemy's weapons as he could, more kept appearing as their adversaries drew upon their extensive cache of arms.

*And that's the least of our problems.*

Ethan looked anxiously across the cavern to where a group of Rangers and immortals fought twelve colossal figures. Despite their superior strength and fighting skills, even the Bastians were no match for the super soldiers. The Crovir noble gritted his teeth as he watched four Rangers and two immortals go flying to the ground. He drew on his powers and started toward them, casting aside the men who stood in his path with a wave of elemental energy.

A familiar figure stepped in front of Ethan moments before he reached the giants. It was the dark-haired immortal from the abbey. Ethan now knew his name from his mental connection with Olivia.

Scoleri grinned. 'I was hoping I'd see you.'

A grunt sounded behind Ethan. Reynolds sailed past him and struck the hood of a nearby Humvee with a sickening thud. The Ranger lay stunned for a moment before rolling onto his side and shaking his head dazedly.

Ethan was halfway to the vehicle when he caught a flash of metal out the corner of his eyes. He leaned sharply back at the waist and saw Scoleri's sword skim past his face. The weapon crumpled before it completed its deadly arc.

Scoleri straightened and stared at his twisted blade. 'I thought you might do something like that.' His gaze met Ethan's, his dark eyes glinting with a malevolent light. 'I don't think you'll be able to do anything about him, though.'

Ethan realized his mistake too late. He heard Reynolds utter a choked warning. A crushing force gripped his head and lifted him off his feet. Pain exploded behind his eyes.

❧

SWEAT BEADED OLIVIA'S FOREHEAD AS SHE BACKED UP against the wall and faced the super soldiers in the command center. She swayed slightly, her breathing heavy and fast as she continued her mental assault on the barriers protecting their psyches.

Asgard and the soldiers with him fought desperately to stop the giants' progress. They might as well have been trying to move the ocean's tides.

Olivia watched as the Rangers and Bastian Hunters who had come to Asgard and Ethan's aid fell under the enemies' powerful blows. Most rose repeatedly, their bloodied faces full of grim determination. She knew from reading her uncle's thoughts that even more men were converging on their location in the Arizona desert, soldiers dispatched by the US president and the leaders of the immortal races.

Desperation choked her throat. *It's too late! They won't make it in time to stop Jonah Krondike.*

Asgard lifted Armistad to defend her once more, his arms trembling. A gasp left her lips when a super soldier knocked him clear across the room. The immortal struck the far wall with a loud thud and slid to the floor.

*Stand down!*

If Asgard heard her plea, he gave no indication of it. He crawled to his feet and leaned unsteadily on the hilt of his sword, blood dripping from a fresh wound on his head and eyes blazing with iron resolve.

A sudden burst of pain shot across her mental link with Ethan, startling her. Olivia blinked.

It was at that point that the super soldier called Mason Hofstadter finally reached her. A shadow fell across her face as he slowly raised a hand against the psychokinetic wave she projected.

Olivia heard Asgard shout her name a second before the giant closed his fingers around her head. She registered the intent in the man's expression and tasted blood as she bit her lip.

*No! It can't end like this. Not after everything we've been through. Not after all the pain and heartache Asgard and my parents have had to endure. Not after Ethan and Madeleine's losses.*

Mother Edwards's face swam before her vision. *And not after her death and that of all the nuns at the abbey!*

As the super soldier started to squeeze her skull, Olivia closed her eyes and centered on the shimmering lay lines of her soul, despair echoing in every beat of her racing pulse.

*Please. Give me strength.*

The golden threads throbbed just as excruciating pain enveloped her head. They expanded and multiplied with her next heartbeat, enveloping the very core of her being with a blinding light. The hairs rose on her arms. Her skin tingled, struck by a thousand sparks. Olivia gasped as unearthly energy bloomed inside her chest and shot along her veins, filling her body with fire. Her birthmark blazed.

She lifted her hands and placed them on the super soldier's temples. He rocked back on his heels as she blasted through the walls of his mental resistance, pulverizing them to nothingness. And deep inside the vicious prison created by Jonah Krondike's ruthless experiments, Olivia discovered the remains of the very human and tortured mind of Mason Hofstadter.

Ethan leaned against an armored truck and wiped fresh blood from his mouth.

The giant on the ground crawled to his knees before climbing to his feet.

'You gotta be kidding me!' Reynolds's chest heaved with effort. 'What the hell are these guys made of?'

Despite his fractured ribs, the major had found a metal pipe from somewhere and was holding it in a white-knuckled grip. The makeshift weapon had already acquired several dents from contact with enemy soldiers.

The immortal next to them winced and hopped on his unbroken leg. 'Yeah. You would have thought being hit with a flying Humvee would have stopped anyone.'

Ethan watched the giant grimly, his own breaths coming in short, sharp pants. The vehicle he'd used to free himself from the deadly attack lay on its roof some twenty feet away.

Of the Rangers and immortals who had stormed the upper level, fewer than half remained on their feet. They stood with Ethan and Reynolds, their injured comrades in their midst.

The other super soldiers were making their way across the

floor toward them. Ethan focused on a row of Jeeps and dragged three of them across the floor into the figures.

Metal screamed and crumpled. The giants slowed for a moment before pushing the vehicles aside.

A loud rumble tore through the air. Ethan looked to the right.

A gap appeared in the lower south face of the cave. It grew as two sets of thick concrete walls parted to reveal a shallow, rocky incline. Beyond it lay sunlit desert.

'Did we see that on the satellite pictures?' said Reynolds quietly.

Ethan shook his head. 'I don't think so. It would have looked like part of the wall anyway.'

Reynolds scowled. 'They're going to get away!'

Engines rumbled into life around them as the men who had survived the assault on their base started filing inside the army vehicles.

Blood pounded in Ethan's ears. With the current training exercises taking place in the proving ground, it would be impossible to find the enemy soldiers if they reached the other troops deployed on the site.

A Jeep squealed to a stop next to Scoleri. He opened the door, placed a foot inside, and turned to Ethan.

'Once these men are done with you, they're going to bring us your girlfriend. And Storm?' The immortal's grin turned malicious. 'She tasted nice. I'm going to enjoy making her scream under me once Jonah's finished with her.'

Rage dropped a red mist across Ethan's vision. He moved toward Scoleri.

JONAH RELOADED HIS AUTOMATIC WEAPON AND AIMED AT THE figures on the other side of the cave. Shots echoed around him as the men Scoleri had sent to ensure his safe escape exchanged gunfire with their enemy. Bullets glanced off the two Sikorsky helicopters parked fifty feet away and the Black Hawks that had brought the Rangers and the Bastian Hunters to the heliport.

Fury thrummed through the Crovir noble. He had not expected Asgard Godard and Victor Dvorsky to move so fast, nor for the US government to have agreed to come to their aid so decisively.

*I have to get out of here. There's too much at stake.*

He turned to one of the immortals next to him. 'Get Scoleri to send backup!'

The man nodded and spoke into the microphone pinned to his collar.

A FIST THE SIZE OF A FOOTBALL SLAMMED INTO ETHAN'S flank. His ribs cracked. Air left his lungs in a shocked wheeze. He sailed across the room and slammed into a crate, blood spraying from his lips. As he fell to his knees and tried to draw a breath past the spasm of shock locking his throat, Ethan saw a shadow swoop across the floor toward him.

The super soldier's foot connected with his arm with the force of a hammer. Numbness bloomed down the limb as the bone shattered. Black spots swam across his vision.

The floor around him was littered with the bodies of fallen Rangers and Bastian Hunters. Reynolds and the last immortals who had fought the super soldiers lay a few feet away, injured and unconscious. Scoleri's vehicle had disappeared in the yellow wilderness beyond the concrete doors. The trucks and Jeeps carrying the rest of his men were shrinking shapes on the desert plain.

A warning shout reached him dimly. Ethan recognized Asgard's voice. Hope rose inside him, bringing with it a fresh surge of strength. He raised his left hand and blocked the super soldier's blow with a burst of elemental energy.

The giant's fist stopped in mid air, inches from his head. The figure grunted and took a step forward, his face impassive. Two more super soldiers joined him.

It was at that point that Ethan felt Olivia's rage flood his mind.

'*YOU WILL NOT TOUCH HIM!*' she roared.

Chaos erupted around him.

INCANDESCENT FURY FILLED OLIVIA WHEN SHE SAW THE super soldiers standing above her soulmate.

Psychokinetic energy surged from her and washed across the cave, crushing everything in its path. The floor shook beneath her feet. Explosions went off as the fuel tanks of vehicles and crates of ammunition detonated.

The super soldiers stumbled, pushed by the invisible wave that surged toward them. They fell and rolled across the ground before coming to a stop near the concrete doors. Some gripped the edges to prevent themselves from being propelled outside.

Olivia headed toward where they lay, her body trembling with uncontrolled anger. Debris shifted before her, forced aside by pulses of sheer mental pressure.

She stopped in front of the giants and reached inside their heads, tearing the obstacles she found until she located the surviving threads of their human minds. She flexed her fingers and snuffed out their consciousness as she had all the other humans who had crossed her path.

The super soldiers collapsed.

Olivia walked past their still bodies and stepped out into the sunlight. Her gaze locked onto the vehicles racing across the desert toward distant hills. She sensed streams of consciousness belonging to the enemy and some of the Rangers and immortals who had attempted to stop them in a large space beneath the mass of rock.

It was the heliport she had seen in the scientist's mind when she'd awoken in the lab.

A fresh tide of rage rose through her when she came across Scoleri's thoughts. Next to his where those of the man she had been searching for.

Outrage clashed with apprehension inside Jonah Krondike's mind.

Olivia reached inside her soulmate where he lay on the concrete floor of the cave and focused on the elemental powers pulsing in the golden lines around his heart.

'Burn!' she growled.

HEAT SEARED ETHAN'S CHEST. HE STIFFENED, HIS EYES flaring blindly in shock. Power swamped his body, stronger than anything he had ever experienced.

He arched his back and cried out as his elemental abilities exploded.

THE AIR SHIMMERED IN FRONT OF OLIVIA. FLAMES BURST into existence with a thunderous boom twenty feet from where she stood. They expanded rapidly to form a vast wall of fire.

The blaze rippled and roiled as it raced across the desert, growing exponentially in size and burning all in its path.

Asgard grunted, his arms trembling with effort as he tried to push off the shaking ground.

Madeleine and Howard lay a short distance away, bodies flattened to the concrete floor by the psychokinetic energy whirling around them, debris flying above their heads. Madeleine grimaced and stretched out a hand toward Asgard. He reached across the floor and curled his fingers around hers.

Most of the Rangers had fainted at the incredible pressure beating down on them. Only the immortals remained conscious, some just barely so.

Although he couldn't feel any pain, Asgard was nonetheless aware of Olivia's emotions. Her anger vibrated through his mind, a crimson sea of undiluted wrath intent on the destruction of the ones she held responsible for ruining the lives of all those she had come to love, and all those she had lost.

He lifted his head a couple of inches, only to freeze when he finally saw what lay beyond the doors of the cave.

Asgard could only stare in awe at the devastation raining down on their enemies.

The tires of the vehicles at the rear of the convoy lifted off the desert floor seconds before the flames reached them, rising on the tide of violent pressure. The fuel tanks detonated, killing most of the men inside. Those who survived the explosions perished in the fiery storm that swept across the plains, their screams carrying in the hot wind.

The destructive wave rolled across the wasteland, smashing through the remaining trucks and Jeeps, kinetic energy driving the burning wreckage across the blackened ground.

A shape rose in the sky above the hills, contours shimmering in the blistering air. Rotors glinted in the sunlight.

Olivia zeroed in on the helicopter and the immortals inside. *You will not get away!*

She drew on Ethan's powers and struck the aircraft with a burst of elemental energy. It shuddered and rocked wildly before righting itself, continuing its passage across the desert and taking with it the man who had brought so much pain into her life.

Olivia's gaze dropped to an area ahead of the aircraft's path. Despite the fact that she had only seen the facility in the scientist's memories, she was able to remote-locate to the power plants underneath the desert.

ETHAN ROLLED ONTO HIS SIDE, HIS HEART THUNDERING inside his chest. Olivia's rage swept through his body and mind, a physical presence that threatened to consume his very being. He focused on the burning ball of energy inside his chest, tapped into his powers, and rose to his knees.

Sweat mixed with blood dripped from his face and struck the floor beneath him. He climbed unsteadily to his feet and turned toward the concrete doors.

Ethan had but a moment to grasp the destruction his soulmate had wreaked before incandescent light bloomed on the horizon, nearly blinding him. He squinted and raised a hand to cover his face.

Through the gaps between his fingers, he saw the gigantic explosion mushroom from the desert, a searing cloud that engulfed a helicopter in the sky above it. He knew instantly from Olivia's thoughts that Krondike and Scoleri were inside the aircraft.

The intense blast from the power plants leveled the rest of the enemy vehicles and gusted across the land in an expanding circle that annihilated everything before it.

Movement to the right drew Ethan's gaze. Alarm stabbed through him when he recognized the helicopters and army trucks bringing more Rangers and immortals to the enemy base.

*Olivia!*

The Seer remained deaf to his warning, her fury unabated.

Ethan stared at the inferno about to engulf the men coming to their aid, his mouth dry with fear.

'Stop her!' Asgard shouted behind him.

Ethan gritted his teeth and moved toward his soulmate.

OLIVIA FROZE AS THE SCENES UNFOLDING BEFORE HER EYES resonated with a memory deep inside her.

*I have...seen this before.*

A man stepped in front of her, blocking the sight of the violent conflagration that filled the earth and the sky. He grabbed her shoulder with his good arm and shouted something. She stared blankly at his blurry, blood-stained face. It belonged to someone she knew.

The man stepped closer. Olivia blinked when she finally recognized the face of her soulmate.

Desperation burned in Ethan's eyes. He curled a hand around her head and kissed her.

A warm glow filled her soul from where he touched her. The emotions he projected with his lips washed through her and smothered the rage that burned inside her heart.

Olivia gasped. The reality of all that had happened and all that was still unfolding imprinted on her straight from Ethan's thoughts.

*Help me*, he whispered inside her mind.

She nodded shakily. He took her hand in his and turned to face the raging inferno in the distance. Olivia closed her eyes and fully linked her mind with his as they focused their combined powers on the destructive forces she had brought into existence and which now threatened to ravage their allies.

Seconds before it reached the helicopters banking sharply in the sky and the vehicles skidding across the desert, the incandescent storm shuddered and stopped in the face of a wall of pure psychokinetic and elemental power.

She felt Ethan concentrate on squashing the angry, boiling flames raging against the invisible bubble they had projected around the blaze and lent him all of her strength, augmenting his ability even more. They remote-located to the power plants beneath the desert and extinguished the source of the massive explosion before sucking all the air out of the dome with their combined energies, removing the final fuel that fed the fire.

Eerie silence blossomed across the desert when the blaze finally abated.

ASGARD BLINKED. THE GROUND HAD STOPPED MOVING. Debris crashed around him and brought an uncanny stillness in its wake. The force driving him to the floor had disappeared. He staggered to his feet, Armistad clasped in his hand.

Ethan and Olivia were on their knees on the shallow incline outside the cave. Their arms were wrapped tightly around each other, their bodies trembling. Tears streamed down his niece's cheeks.

Asgard limped toward them.

'I'm so—' said Olivia.

'Don't!' Ethan pulled away and gripped her face in his hands. He stared fiercely into her eyes. 'Don't, Olivia. Without you, we'd be dead. You saved us. You saved *all* of us.'

She turned and looked at Asgard as he approached, green eyes full of remorse.

'Ethan is right, Olivia.' He stopped before them as they rose to their feet and brushed a finger against her cheek. 'Natalia and Kristof would be proud of you.' He looked out to the desert and the burning wreck of the helicopter in the distance, still reeling from all that had come to pass. 'You avenged them.'

Murmurs broke out behind them. The Rangers and immortals were sitting up and staring at the destruction inside the cave and the ruined landscape beyond with dazed expressions.

Crows appeared in the sky above the twisted remains of the army Jeeps and trucks that littered the blackened wasteland. The helicopters and vehicles bringing reinforcements stormed toward the mountains.

Madeleine and Howard walked out into the sunlight. Anxiety washed through Asgard when he saw the blood soaking her shirt and trouser leg.

'You shouldn't be walking,' said Asgard. He turned and took several steps toward her.

Madeleine hobbled to a stop in front of him, her expression strangely determined. 'Never mind that.'

She reached up, grabbed his head with both hands, and pulled him toward her.

Asgard had but a second to grasp her intent before her lips landed on his. He froze, shock resonating through him. It was followed by a wave of heat and need that rocked his soul. He groaned, dropped Armistad, and hauled her up against him, unable to fight his feelings for her any longer.

Whatever this connection was, he was as powerless to resist it as the one he had had with the only other woman he ever loved, all those centuries ago.

Madeleine responded to his fierce kiss with a moan, curled one thigh around his leg, and gripped his shoulders with biting strength.

'Sheesh, get a room,' Howard muttered.

Asgard blinked and slowly released the soft mouth beneath

his, suddenly conscious of a set of avid stares. Madeleine's cheeks were flushed and her eyes gleamed brightly, their depths full of the same hunger he felt thrumming through him.

'Once these wounds heal, we're gonna have sex,' she stated. 'And it's gonna be hot.'

Asgard swallowed convulsively.

Ethan chuckled. Olivia smiled.

'You hussy,' Howard said with a grin.

Reynolds limped out of the cave and stared at the scorched desert stretching out to the distant hills. 'What the hell happened?'

# EPILOGUE

**May 2013. Sumava National Park, Bohemian Forest. Czech Republic.**

OLIVIA STARED AT THE HAUNTINGLY-BEAUTIFUL LANDSCAPE outside the window of the SUV.

An hour had passed since they left the airport where Asgard landed their private jet in South Bohemia.

Madeleine and Ethan sat next to her on the rear seat of the vehicle. Her soulmate's gaze was also lost in the scenery, his fingers resting loosely around hers. The injuries he had suffered at the hands of the super soldiers had already healed. Olivia flexed her fingertips against his and felt them twitch in response. He looked at her then, his blue eyes warm, a loving smile curving his lips despite the anxiety that resonated through them both.

Three weeks had passed since the incidents at Yuma. In that time, the US government had reinstated all of STAEGH Corp's frozen assets and ordered a detailed inquiry into the activities of the US Army group that had supplied physical assistance as well as substantial financial aid to Jonah Krondike over a period spanning more than half a century. Despite the destruction of the command centers inside the base at Olivia's hands, the investigators had managed to salvage the contents of some of the hard drives they had discovered below the Sonoran Desert.

Howard supplied them with backups of the files Madeleine had copied from Ian Serle's computer at AuGenD. As for the professor, he was apprehended a couple of weeks after the events in Arizona, when he attempted to cross the border into Mexico.

William Gunnerson, the four-star general behind the rogue army faction, would never get to reveal all he knew of the secret projects he had overseen, nor be brought to justice. He was discovered with a bullet in his head the day after Asgard and Ethan stormed the research facility.

The remains of Mark Scoleri and Jonah Krondike were never identified from the ashes scattered across the scorched desert.

The US government also took over the care and rehabilitation of the subjects in the super soldier program, with the assistance of a group of Bastian scientists. From the initial reports on the men who had been taken out of the suspension pods and the super soldiers who made it out of Phase Three, it seemed the physical changes they had undergone secondary to their genetic manipulation would likely be irreversible. Only time would tell what the long-term psychological effects of the drugs that had been used on them were going to be.

It took twelve hours for the super soldiers whose consciousness Olivia suppressed to come around again. As for the other humans, it was a couple of days before they awakened. Madeleine called Gillian Hofstadter one week later and told her about her husband's whereabouts.

In the aftermath of the dreadful day when she and her soulmate had decimated a good portion of the KOFA Range, Olivia met Victor Dvorsky and Dimitri Reznak, the immortal nobles who had come to Asgard and Ethan's aid. She liked them straight away.

Victor and Dimitri not only revealed the incredible stories of the other immortals who formed part of the group of special beings Natalia Ashkarov had told Asgard Godard about several centuries ago, but also the astounding truth behind the origins of the immortal races.

The two men were the reason why they were here in Europe today, on their way to see some very important people.

Asgard sat in the front passenger seat and spoke quietly with the red-haired driver who had picked them up from the airport, a jovial Bastian called Anatole Vassili. From their conversation, it appeared Anatole knew the immortals they were going to meet quite well.

They had travelled through miles of lush fields hedged by low hills before heading into the mountains rising against the skyline to the west. The roads grew more winding as they climbed through the foothills of the soaring peaks and the fields gave way to towering spruce and pine forests. Shortly after signs for the Sumava National Park started to appear, Anatole turned onto a private forest track. The woods thickened around them, sunlight stabbing the shadows filling the spaces between the trees in thin streams.

He finally slowed before a set of imposing, black wrought-iron gates. They opened ponderously to reveal a wide, stone-lined driveway.

The trees crowding either side started to thin out after a few hundred feet. Olivia drew a sharp breath when they parted seconds later to reveal an immense park surrounded by forest.

Stunning gardens dotted with fountains, ponds, and arbors stretched out around them all the way to the distant trees. Anatole headed up the drive toward the magnificent chateau in the middle of the plot. The building's cream limestone walls and red mansard roof became more evident as they drew closer. Tall, leaded windows fronted its facade and smoke spouted from several chimneys.

Asgard grunted. 'He's got nice digs.'

Anatole grinned. 'Is it true you're older than him?'

Asgard made a face and nodded reluctantly.

They pulled up in a courtyard framed by the two wings of the chateau. Thick oak doors stood beneath the portico at the head of a split-level terrace. One of them opened as they climbed out of the vehicle. Their host appeared on the threshold.

'I'll bring your luggage to your rooms,' said Anatole.

He gave Olivia an encouraging smile before driving off.

Dimitri strolled down the steps. 'It's good to see you again.'

He kissed Olivia and Madeleine on the cheeks and shook the men's hands.

'Is Victor here?' said Asgard.

'Yes. He arrived last night, with Lucas and his family. The others should have landed at the airport just after you.'

He led them inside a beautiful marble foyer dominated by a grand staircase. A middle-aged woman with silver-blonde hair and blue eyes appeared on the other side of the lobby. The smell of baked goods drifted from her clothes as she approached.

'Mr. Reznak, you do realize that I'm the housekeeper, don't you?' she admonished the Crovir noble gently.

Dimitri grimaced. 'Sorry, Marie. I thought you probably had your hands busy with the kids.'

The woman smiled. 'They are the most well-behaved children any parent could wish for.' Her eyes sparkled. 'But they do like their sweets.'

Dimitri introduced them to his housekeeper.

Marie Fawkes gave them a friendly smile and murmured, 'I shall bring refreshments,' before disappearing down a hallway.

Olivia tensed as Dimitri led them through the chateau. Ethan squeezed her hand.

'Stop worrying,' he whispered.

'What if—what if they don't like us?' she stammered.

'Then I'll pin them down with some elemental energy while you get into their heads and convince them otherwise.'

Olivia chuckled nervously.

They entered an elegant reception room with triple aspect views over the park and the courtyard a moment later. Olivia paused. Her gaze travelled over the opulent furnishings and expensive paintings dotting the large space before landing on the three figures seated on a cream brocade sofa to the right.

Victor Dvorsky rose and crossed the floor to greet them. 'Glad you could make it.'

Olivia locked eyes with the handsome couple who got up behind him.

The man was as tall as Ethan and built along leaner lines. His eyes were a different shade of blue from her soulmate's and projected a quiet yet powerful presence. The woman next to him was nearly as tall, with olive-green eyes framed by thick chestnut curls.

Olivia's mouth went dry. She recognized their features. Ethan glanced at her, likely sensing her surprise across their mental bond.

Asgard went deathly still.

'This is Lucas Soul, Catarine's son,' Victor told the silent Bastian noble in a grave voice. 'And this is Anna Soul, Lily's daughter.'

Asgard's face slowly flushed as he stared at the couple.

'Hi,' said Lucas Soul. His eyes darkened with emotion as he walked toward Asgard. 'It's good to meet you.'

Asgard swallowed.

Anna came across and hugged him tightly.

'Hello, uncle,' she said in a choked voice.

Asgard blinked and returned her embrace just as fiercely. A long moment passed before he stood back and scanned their faces hungrily.

'You—you have your mother's eyes,' he told Lucas huskily, touching his shoulder. He looked at Anna and raised a hand to her hair. 'And you have your mother's complexion.'

The couple smiled tremulously.

Victor studied Olivia. 'You're looking more rested than the last time I saw you.' He pressed his lips to her cheek, before turning and kissing Madeleine. 'As are you.'

Madeleine grinned and linked arms with Asgard. 'Why, thank you. This big guy's been taking care of me.'

Asgard opened and closed his mouth soundlessly. Victor glanced from Madeleine to Asgard's reddening ears, his eyes sparkling in interest.

'I'm Madeleine by the way,' Madeleine told a bemused Lucas and Anna Soul. 'I'm a spring chicken compared to you, so it'd be damn weird if you started calling me aunt.'

Dimitri snorted.

The sounds of large paws and tiny feet striking wooden floorboards rose from the hall outside the doors. A golden retriever skidded into view, the remains of a cake in his jaws. He darted past them and disappeared behind a chair, bushy tail spinning.

Two small figures dashed inside the room in his wake.

A precognitive flutter darted through Olivia as she gazed upon a little girl with chocolate-colored hair and blue eyes, and a boy with dark hair and green eyes. They both shared the same exquisite bone structure and looked to be about two years old.

'Bad doggie, Bob!' the little girl admonished. She waved a finger at the chair where, if the noises were anything to go by, the golden retriever was inhaling the cake. 'That was *not* for you!'

Olivia startled. The girl's speech was crystal clear and far more advanced than she would have expected for a child her age.

The boy went still. He tapped the girl's shoulder, his green gaze locked on the immortals standing beside Victor. 'Lily, look.'

The girl stared. Her eyes grew round.

Olivia felt warm fingers brush her consciousness just before the child bolted across the floor, her brother in tow.

The little girl collided with Asgard's leg and hugged it tightly. 'Grandpa Asgard!'

The Bastian noble rocked on his heels as the little boy latched onto his other leg. He stared open-mouthed at the two children clinging to his limbs.

'Grandpa?' Madeleine repeated.

'Our children, Tomas and Lily,' said Lucas.

He took Anna's hand and shared a warm glance with her.

The children launched themselves at Olivia and Ethan and took turns hugging their legs. 'Uncle Ethan! Aunt Olivia!'

'Er, hi,' Ethan said hesitantly to the two bright faces studying him.

The children's grins widened.

Tomas walked over to Asgard. 'Pick me up, Grandpa Asgard.'

Asgard complied, his expression still stunned.

It was then that Olivia felt another presence in her mind.

*I've been waiting to meet you!* said a small voice excitedly. Lily Soul beamed at her and raised her arms commandingly.

Olivia hesitated before hoisting the little girl into her arms. Her heart thudded wildly in her chest as she looked deep into sparkling blue eyes. 'Is that you?'

Lily nodded, a grin dimpling her cheeks. She touched Olivia's face with plump fingers.

The Seer inhaled sharply at the power she felt thrumming through the physical contact. She looked over at Tomas, shock sending her pulse racing even faster. He reached across from Asgard's hold and laid his hand gently against her other cheek.

Olivia blinked. 'Oh.'

Tears formed in her eyes at the blindingly-beautiful energy pouring into her from the two children.

Ethan stiffened. 'Olivia?'

'What is it?' said Asgard anxiously.

Olivia studied Lily and Tomas Soul with wide-eyed wonderment. 'They have the same powers as us.' She looked at Ethan and projected her feelings to him. 'And more.'

'What?' said Anna.

She exchanged a startled look with Lucas. Victor and Dimitri shared a similarly-shocked glance.

Olivia raised her eyebrow at Lily. *They don't know?*

Lily shook her head, a mischievous light dancing in her eyes. *It's a surprise.*

A wave of contentment flooded Olivia then and washed away the apprehension that had plagued her ever since they started out on this trip. This was where they belonged. Here, with these children.

She smiled at Lily. 'That's cheating, you know.'

Lily giggled.

'Is she...talking to you?' Asgard said hoarsely.

Olivia's smile widened.

'Yes,' she said to the stunned immortals.

Before any of them could voice the questions bubbling from their lips, a noise drew their gazes to the windows looking out toward the front of the chateau. A pair of black SUVs appeared at the end of the driveway and raced toward the castle, engines gunning. They swerved around the fountains and ponds and tried to cut each other off as they careened down the drive, sending arcs of gravel flying in the air behind them.

Dimitri sighed. 'Every single time.'

The SUVs screamed into the courtyard and screeched to a stop in front of the portico, one a couple of seconds ahead of the other.

A woman with short black hair climbed out of the first vehicle. A blond man stumbled from the passenger seat, covered his mouth, and heaved.

A dark-haired couple and a German Shepherd got out of the second SUV. The woman was shaking her head with an expression not dissimilar to Dimitri's. The dog trotted over to the blond man and pawed at his back while he bent over some rose bushes.

They climbed the steps to the portico, the dark-haired man gesticulating animatedly to the woman from the first SUV. The blond man lagged behind them with the dog. Voices rose from the hall seconds later.

'Admit it, King! That was cheating!' growled a male voice.

The dark-haired man from the second SUV stopped in the doorway of the reception room. His gray-blue eyes narrowed as he stared down the corridor at someone.

Olivia registered the snake tattoo wrapped around his left forearm.

*No, that's not a tattoo. That's a birthmark.*

Her gaze flicked back up to his face. Recognition flared through her once more.

'I'll admit no such thing, Greene,' said a female voice.

The woman with the short black hair came into view. Her eyes were the color of silver and her features shockingly attractive. She faced the man with a casual pose that nonetheless projected a simmering, deadly intent.

Olivia froze. She knew this woman's features as well.

The man with the snake birthmark scowled. 'You threw

metal spikes on the goddamn road!'

The woman shrugged. 'So? Those SUVs have run-flat tires. You weren't in any danger.'

'Face it, Conrad, you lost this race.' The other dark-haired woman appeared with the German Shepherd in tow. She patted the man on the back. 'Besides, I think Zachary's barfing in Dimitri's downstairs closet.' Her hazel eyes gleamed as she glanced at the woman with the black hair. 'I suspect Alexa's in trouble.'

The latter looked uneasily in the direction of the foyer. 'Really? He's throwing up?'

Lily jumped out of Olivia's arms and ran across to her. 'Auntie Alexa!'

The woman's silver eyes softened when she turned and saw the girl. 'Hello, sweetheart.' She caught Lily as the little girl leapt toward her and kissed her forehead.

Lily waved at the German Shepherd. 'Hello, Rocky.'

The dog sat down and grinned, his tail blurring as it swept the floor.

Tomas slipped out of Asgard's arms and barreled into the dark-haired man's leg. 'Uncle Conrad!'

The man smiled and ruffled his hair. 'How're you doing, kid?'

'Uncle Conrad, Bob stole one of the cakes we made with Marie,' Tomas stated in a solemn voice.

The golden retriever poked his head around the chair and pricked his ears at the sound of his name. He whined, licked the cream around his chops, and disappeared from view. The German Shepherd rose and scampered toward the chair.

The man lifted the boy in his arms. 'Did he now?'

'Yes.' Tomas bobbed his head energetically. 'And look. Grandpa Asgard is here, with Uncle Ethan and Aunt Olivia.' He pointed to where they stood. 'And that's Madeleine.'

The man and women in the doorway straightened, their

eyes carefully assessing the four strangers in their midst.

Footsteps sounded behind them. The gorgeous blond from the SUV trotted into view and laid a hand on the shoulder of the woman with the silver eyes.

'Seriously, babe,' he groaned. 'Not everything has to be a competition.'

Remorse flashed across the woman's face. 'I'm sorry.' She raised an eyebrow, stepped closer, and trailed a finger down his chest. 'I'll make it up to you.'

The blond brightened, ice-blue eyes darkening to indigo.

'You're talking about sex, aren't you?' the man with the snake birthmark said dully.

Tomas pulled a face. 'Eeew!'

Lily giggled.

MILD TENSION COURSED THROUGH ETHAN AS HE STUDIED THE immortals gathered around the room.

Despite his reassurances to Olivia, he had been just as nervous to meet the distant cousins whose existence they had only discovered three weeks ago.

Ethan gazed at Alexa King, the woman with the short dark hair and silver eyes who bore a trishula birthmark on her neck. According to Dimitri, it was King's enhanced fighting skills, combat intuition, and weapon proficiency that made her the perfect immortal warrior, unbeaten by any other in all of immortal society. She had only ever suffered one death and that was to protect the man who sat beside her, her genius husband Zachary Jackson, a Harvard professor reputed to be the most intelligent human alive today. Even though she sat in a relaxed pose next to her soulmate, Ethan could feel the dangerous vibes she emitted. As for Jackson, he was now more than human, having received a blood transfusion from Lucas Soul when he was on his deathbed three years ago, after being nearly fatally wounded by Alberto Cavaleti. He had acquired some of the healing abilities of immortals as well as delayed ageing as a result.

Conrad Greene, the immortal healer with the Aesculapian snake birthmark on his left arm, sat in the next chair. His fiancee, Laura Hartwell, perched on the armrest and watched Ethan with a shrewd expression. She was a special Bastian operative who worked closely with Victor; along with Greene, she had played a crucial role in averting the deadly international plot that involved the assassination of President Westwood two years ago.

And then, there were Lucas and Anna Soul, the most incredible immortals of them all.

Dimitri finished explaining the startling findings he had made when he compared their genetic material with those of Crovir and Bastian, the brothers who had given rise to the two races of immortals.

'Because their parents were pureblood immortals directly descended from the two brothers, Lucas and Anna's genetic composition is unique among the immortals.'

'That's fascinating,' murmured Madeleine.

Dimitri smiled faintly. 'I believe your genetic makeup is pretty unique itself.'

Anna straightened, her green eyes full of curiosity as she glanced between Madeleine and Dimitri. 'Oh. Is it?'

Madeleine explained the findings of the tests she had carried out on her own DNA a few decades ago.

'A mosaic of an immortal and a half-breed?' Anna repeated in a surprised voice.

Madeline dipped her chin. 'Yes. I...got my hands on some of the earlier research Jonah Krondike carried out in the 1960s and 70s. It seemed he did a lot of radiation experiments at the time, with my father as one of the subjects.'

'I'm sorry,' Anna said quietly in the somber hush that fell across the room.

Madeleine smiled. 'It's okay. It's in the past.'

Asgard squeezed her hand gently. She glanced at him, her eyes glimmering.

Dimitri turned to Olivia and Ethan. 'From the information in the scriptures, we gathered the two of you are of the line of—'

'Navia, the third daughter of Bastian, and Jared, the second son of Crovir,' Olivia breathed.

Ethan startled at the emotions he could feel coursing through his soulmate. They were of deep-seated reverence mixed with a trace of trepidation.

Shock flared across Dimitri's face.

Victor narrowed his eyes at Olivia. 'How do you know that?'

Olivia took a deep breath. 'Because I was there, during the war when Crovir and Bastian died. Mentally, at least.'

She told them then of the nightmare that had plagued her for almost a hundred years, the one where she stood in the middle of a row of eleven, powerful, armor-clad warriors who faced an immense army across a blood-soaked battlefield.

Ethan felt the hair rise at the back of his neck when his soulmate explained what had also transpired in those hours when she had died. She had never spoken of it to him before.

'You mean—those were memories?' he stammered at the end of her narrative.

Olivia threaded her fingers with his. 'Yes. They were the memories of Navia, the first Seer.'

'So, you're saying the battle you dreamt of and the one where you...found yourself after your first death, really happened?' said Conrad quietly.

'You were there,' said Olivia.

The immortals around the room startled and glanced at each other uneasily.

'What do you mean?' said Anna.

'I recognize your faces.' Olivia looked at the immortals who bore the birthmarks. 'You do not just carry the genes of the ones who gave birth to your specific bloodlines. You bear a remarkable resemblance to them.' She turned to Ethan and touched his cheek gently. 'As do you.'

Ethan swallowed when he read the undeniable truth in her eyes.

Olivia's glittering gaze shifted to the two children who dozed in their parents' arms. 'I think I understand now.'

Lucas stiffened. 'What?'

Anna sat frozen next to him, her expression just as tense.

'You know they're special, don't you?' Olivia said quietly.

'Yes,' said Alexa in a hard voice.

Conrad leaned forward in his seat, his posture strained.

OLIVIA GAZED AT ALL THE INCREDIBLE PEOPLE WHO WERE ready to rise and defend the two figures who slept innocently in their parents' arms.

'But do you know why?' she asked, her hands shaking at the enormity of the truth she had grasped from her psychic connection with Lily and Tomas Soul.

Lucas and Anna exchanged guarded glances.

'We are aware that they're developing at a faster rate than normal children, human or immortal,' said Anna, her arms curling protectively around Tomas.

'And their minds are different,' murmured Lucas. He touched Lily's face with a gentle finger. 'They're not just smart; they possess intuitive intelligence.'

Victor watched Olivia solemnly. 'Tell us what you know.'

Olivia closed her eyes briefly. When she opened them again,

she found herself the focus of a battery of intense stares. 'Lily and Tomas possess all our powers.'

Anna glanced at the boy in her arms. 'What do you mean?'

'They can do everything we can, although their individual strengths will vary.' Olivia saw the meaning behind her words sink in on the stunned faces around her. 'They can survive their seventeenth death and every death that comes afterward.' She paused and smiled shakily. 'Although I sense death will never dare cross their path.' She looked at Conrad. 'They will be able to heal and gift life.' Her gaze switched to Alexa. 'They are going to be the most powerful warriors this world has ever seen.' She stared into Ethan's shocked eyes. 'They will be able to manipulate all the elements.' She inhaled deeply. 'And their psionic abilities will be beyond anything I could ever hope to achieve.'

Silence descended on the room.

'That's—' Dimitri trailed off, his face pale.

'Is this a result of their genetics?' said Lucas.

His arms tightened around Lily.

Olivia hesitated before shaking her head. 'No.'

'What do you mean?' murmured Asgard.

Olivia looked at her uncle. 'I mean there is more to this than just bloodlines. The—the only way I can explain it is that they appear to be touched by some higher power. As all of us are, to an extent.'

Dimitri straightened then and stared blindly into space.

'Divine beings,' he said hoarsely.

His words resonated inside Olivia. 'Yes.'

'The Lotus-Born Buddha,' murmured Zachary.

Alexa frowned at her husband. 'What?'

'Dimitri told us this before, remember? About Guru Rinpoche's theory that immortals were ultimately descended from the gods themselves,' said the Harvard professor quietly.

'I never truly believed the abbot when he told me that,'

muttered Dimitri.

'Neither did I,' said Victor dully.

A hesitant voice broke the deep hush. 'You know, this doesn't sound like some kind of random process to me,' said Madeleine.

'What do you mean?' said Asgard.

'Look at you,' said Madeleine. Her gaze danced across their faces. 'Look at where you all started and where you've all ended up. You were born worlds apart from each other and are linked in ways that defy logic, and yet, here you all are. Despite the harsh hand fate dealt each and every one of you, you've overcome your troubles and have been brought together, right here, right in this very moment in time.'

'You're saying there are higher forces at work here?' said Reznak.

Madeleine shrugged. 'Can you blame me for not believing otherwise after everything I've heard and seen?'

Asgard hesitated. 'Natalia told me that the immortals who would bear the birthmarks, and possess abilities than none in our races have ever had, would go on to face even greater challenges together. She also said that they had a destiny to fulfill—one that none other than they could achieve.'

They all stared at the sleeping figures in Lucas and Anna Soul's arms. Olivia sensed a fundamental shift inside her soul as her entire world realigned itself around these two extraordinarily precious children. She felt the same change resonate inside Ethan and everyone else in that room.

*Our fate is linked with theirs. And not just ours.*

*The fate of the entire world rests on their shoulders.*

## THE END

# THANK YOU

Thank you for reading LEGACY.

I would be really grateful if you could consider leaving a review on Amazon, Goodreads, or other platforms where you buy your books. Reviews are vital for authors and all reviews, even a couple of short sentences, can help readers decide whether to pick up one of my books.

## WANT FREE BOOKS AND EXCLUSIVE EXTRAS?

Join my reader list today for free books, exclusive bonus content, new release alerts, giveaways, and more.

Go to the link below to find out more.

www.ADStarrling.com/free-download-offer

# ACKNOWLEDGMENTS

To my editors Liam Carnahan and Sara Litchfield. As always, you get me.

To my assistant Kate Tilton. Thanks for doing such a great job with "Legacy" and for your ceaseless support.

To the real Major Steve Reynolds. Thanks for agreeing to feature in the book. Sorry about the broken ribs. At least I didn't shoot you.

## FACTS AND FICTIONS

Now, for one of my favorite parts of writing my books. Here are the facts and fictions behind the story.

### San Andres Mountains Army Facility

The San Andres Mountains army facility in New Mexico where Asgard Godard is held prisoner from 1959 to 1969 is pure fiction. I chose these mountains for their isolated position and based the fictional army base on the Cheyenne Mountain Complex in Colorado, which is home to elements of NORAD (North American Aerospace Defense Command) and other U.S. government agencies. The Cheyenne Mountain Complex was the site of the famous Stargate Command in the TV series **Stargate**.

### Progeria

Progeria is factual. It is an extremely rare and progressive genetic condition that causes children to age rapidly and prematurely. It is caused by a mutation in the *LMNA* gene on chromosome 1, which results in the production of the wrong form of a structural protein called lamin A/C; this protein is responsible for holding the cell's nucleus together. Progeria is not an inheritable disease and remains incurable. Most of those affected die in their teens or twenties as a result of cardiac disease and stroke.

The disease that Olivia Ashkarov believes she has, the opposite of Progeria, does not exist. There are a handful of people in the world with delayed ageing but no cause has been found for their condition. One hypothetical name suggested for the state of delayed ageing is Anageria.

Interestingly, the secret to longevity may very well lie on chromosome 4. Researchers have found extra genes on this chromosome in families with a history of living 90 years and longer. This is why I gave Madeleine Black extra sections of chromosome 4 and it forms the underlying scientific explanation for why the offsprings of pureblood immortals and humans possess the gift of longevity.

### Sorrento Valley, San Diego

Sorrento Valley in San Diego is near the top of the list of where the most innovative research in genetics and biotechnology is being carried out in the U.S. today. AuGenD, the company where Madeleine Black works, is fictitious. The work AuGenD is an anagram of "unaged" and mimics *augendae*, the latin word for "enhance". It signifies Jonah Krondike's ultimate goal of extending life and his work with the U.S. Army on an advanced human enhancement program aimed at soldiers.

### Super Soldiers

The concepts of super soldiers and human enhancement are not new ones and have been immortalized in science fiction books, films, and computer games since the middle of the 20th century, with the best example of all being Marvel Comics' Captain America. Yet, many technological and scientific advancements of recent times originated in fiction. The most visually vivid example for me remains the tablet-like devices used in the Star Trek TV series in the 1970s and our current generation of mobile devices.

Unsurprisingly, governments have been working on human enhancement for military purposes for quite some time, from the clandestine human experimentations that took place in the U.S., Germany, Japan, and Russia during World War II, to the 1950s Project MKUltra, the CIA's most publicized secret program aimed at controlling human behavior.

In fiction, drugs, eugenics, genetic engineering, cybernetic implants, extreme training regimens, and brainwashing are the methods of choice for enhancing humans and producing super soldiers.

In real science, human enhancement is already happening with advances in human genetic engineering, nanotechnology, biotechnology, information technology, neural implants, cybernetics, and brain-computer interfaces coming together to overcome the current limitation of the human body.

In **Legacy**, I used a combination of performance enhancing drugs, physical and mental training regimes, and bionanotechnology techniques that allowed the recombination of immortal DNA with human DNA for Jonah Krondike's work on a human enhancement program for the U.S. military.

### Fort Huachaca

Fort Huachaca does exist and is home to the U.S. Army Intelligence Center and the U.S. Army Network Enterprise Technology Command, among other divisions of the U.S. military.

### 75th Ranger Regiment

The 75th Ranger Regiment is an elite special ops force working under the U.S. Army Special Operations Command. As such, Rangers are among the best-trained men and women in the world. With a history going back more than two hundred years, Rangers have one of the most rigorous training programs of any military force and have a singularly high mission success rate on the battlefield.

## Yuma Proving Ground

The Yuma Proving Ground does exist. It is one of the largest military installations in the world and covers an area of almost 1400 square miles, included its own protected air space. It serves as a developmental and desert environment testing facility for weapon systems and munitions for the U.S. military, as well providing a desert-like training environment for the U.S. Armed Forces and its NATO allies. The facility has been used extensively to test anything and everything from battle tanks to long-range artillery, from UAVs to attack helicopters, and from aerostats to NASA space capsule chute systems.

The Yuma Proving Ground secret underground research facility in *Legacy* is fictional and is based on the Raven Rock Mountain Complex near Camp David.

**And that's it for the science and technology lesson folks! Want to check out more Extras? Then visit my website at www.adstarrling.com**

## ABOUT THE AUTHOR

AD Starrling's bestselling supernatural thriller series **Seventeen** combines action, suspense, and a dose of fantasy to make each book an explosive, adrenaline-fueled ride. If you prefer your action hot and your heroes sexy and strong-willed, then check out her military thriller series Division Eight.

When she's not busy writing, AD can be found looking up exciting international locations and cool science and technology to put in her books, eating Thai food, being tortured by her back therapists, drooling over gadgets, working part-time as a doctor on a Neonatal Intensive Care unit somewhere in the UK, reading manga, and watching action and sci-fi flicks. She has occasionally been accused of committing art with a charcoal stick and some drawing paper.

Find out more about AD on her website

www.adstarrling.com where you can sign up for her awesome newsletter, get exclusive freebies, and never miss her latest release. You'll also have a chance to see sneak previews of her work, participate in exclusive giveaways, and hear about special promotional offers first.

Here are some other places where you can connect with her:

www.adstarrling.com
Email: ads@adstarrling.com

# ALSO BY A. D. STARRLING

### Hunted (A Seventeen Series Novel) Book One

'My name is Lucas Soul. Today, I died again. This is my fifteenth death in the last four hundred and fifty years. And I'm determined that it will be the last.'

*National Indie Excellence Awards Winner Fantasy 2013*

*National Indie Excellence Awards Finalist Adventure 2013*

*Next Generation Indie Book Awards Finalist Action-Adventure 2013*

*Hollywood Book Festival 2013 Honorable Mention General Fiction*

### Warrior (A Seventeen Series Novel) Book Two

The perfect Immortal warrior. A set of stolen, priceless artifacts. An ancient sect determined to bring about the downfall of human civilization.

*Next Generation Indie Book Awards Winner Action-Adventure 2014*

*Shelf Unbound Competition for Best Independently Published Book Finalist 2014*

### Empire (A Seventeen Series Novel) Book Three

An Immortal healer. An ancient empire reborn. A chain of cataclysmic events that threatens to change the fate of the world.

*Next Generation Indie Book Awards Finalist General Fiction 2015*

### Legacy (A Seventeen Series Novel) Book Four

The Hunter who should have been king. The Elemental who fears love. The Seer who is yet to embrace her powers.

Three immortals whose fates are entwined with that of the oldest and most formidable enemy the world has ever faced.

## Origins (A Seventeen Series Novel) Book Five

The gifts bestowed by One not of this world, to the Man who had lived longer than most.

The Empire ruled by a King who would swallow the world in his madness.

The Warrior who chose to rise against her own kind in order to defeat him.

Discover the extraordinary beginnings of the Immortals and the unforgettable story of the Princess who would become a Legend.

## Destiny (A Seventeen Series Novel) Book Six

An enemy they never anticipated.

A brutal attack that tears them apart.

A chain of immutable events that will forever alter the future.

Discover the destiny that was always theirs to claim.

## The Seventeen Collection 1: Books 1-3

Boxset featuring Hunted, Warrior, and Empire.

## The Seventeen Collection 2: Books 4-6

Boxset featuring Legacy, Origins, and Destiny.

## The Seventeen Complete Collection: Books 1-6

Boxset featuring Hunted, Warrior, Empire, Legacy, Origins, and Destiny.

## First Death (A Seventeen Series Short Story) #1

Discover where it all started...

### Dancing Blades (A Seventeen Series Short Story) #2

Join Lucas Soul on his quest to become a warrior.

### The Meeting (A Seventeen Series Short Story) #3

Discover the origins of the incredible friendship between the protagonists of Hunted.

### The Warrior Monk (A Seventeen Series Short Story) #4

Experience Warrior from the eyes of one of the most beloved characters in Seventeen.

### The Hunger (A Seventeen Series Short Story) #5

Discover the origin of the love story behind Empire.

### The Bank Job (A Seventeen Series Short Story) #6

Join two of the protagonists from Legacy on their very first adventure.

### The Seventeen Series Short Story Collection 1 (#1-3)

Boxset featuring First Death, Dancing Blades, and The Meeting.

### The Seventeen Series Short Story Collection 2 (#4-6)

Boxset featuring The Warrior Monk, The Hunger, and The Bank Job.

### The Seventeen Series Ultimate Short Story Collection

Boxset featuring First Death, Dancing Blades, The Meeting, The Warrior Monk, The Hunger, and The Bank Job.

### Mission:Black (A Division Eight Thriller)

A broken agent. A once in a lifetime chance. A new mission that threatens to destroy her again.

### Mission: Armor (A Division Eight Thriller)

A man tortured by his past. A woman determined to save him. A deadly assignment that threatens to rip them apart.

### Mission:Anaconda (A Division Eight Thriller)

It should have been a simple mission. They should have been in and out in a day. Except it wasn't. And they didn't.

### Void (A Sci-fi Horror Short Story)

2065. Humans start terraforming Mars.

2070. The Mars Baker2 outpost is established on the Acidalia Planitia.

2084. The first colonist goes missing.

### The Other Side of the Wall (A Short Horror Story)

Have you ever seen flashes of darkness where there should only be light? Ever seen shadows skitter past out of the corner of your eyes and looked, only to find nothing there?

### AUDIOBOOKS

Hunted (A Seventeen Series Novel) Book One

Warrior (A Seventeen Series Novel) Book Two

Empire (A Seventeen Seres Novel) Book Three

First Death (A Seventeen Series Short Story) #1

Dancing Blades (A Seventeen Series Short Story) #2

The Meeting (A Seventeen Series Short Story) #3

The Warrior Monk (A Seventeen Series Short Story) #4

# MISSION:BLACK EXTRACT

**Chapter One**

**June 2014. Gulf of Aden, Arabian Sea.**

The man standing outside the communications room of the cargo ship yawned and stretched out the kinks in his neck. He adjusted the sling of his AK-47 rifle before leaning against the steel compartment door behind him. It wasn't long before his chin started to droop and his breathing grew slow and deep.

Twelve feet away, in an adjacent passageway, Rachel Carter crouched against a bulkhead. She ignored the cold metal at her back and the vibrations traveling through her boots from the engine room several decks below, her gaze focused on the miniature mirror on a stick she held in her left hand. Through it, she could see the snoozing guard outside the communications room.

She stole a glance at her watch before slipping the mirror inside her tactical gear. Adrenaline surged through her veins. She gripped her Sig Pro tightly in both hands, her muscles tensing in anticipation of the upcoming battle. Right on cue, a male voice started a countdown in the wireless receiver in her ear.

'All stations, this is Alpha One. On my mark in three, two, *one!*'

Rachel twisted, dropped to one knee, and squeezed the trigger twice. A distant explosion shook the bowels of the ship at the same time the bullets left the suppressor at the end of her gun and slammed into the guard's chest and head. He jerked and slid down the door, his grip relaxing on his weapon.

Rachel was up and running before the dead man hit the deck. She grabbed the AK-47, slung it around her neck, and dragged the guard's body down the passage. She was back at the communications room in seconds. She rapped the door twice with her knuckles and stood to the side of the doorjamb.

The sound of gunfire rose from the direction of the galley and the main deck. Alarmed shouts followed in the distance.

Rachel rose on the balls of her feet. By now, the men inside the communications room would know the ship was under attack.

The door opened without warning. An automatic rifle burst into life and a spray of bullets ripped through the doorway. The shots slammed harmlessly into the opposite bulkhead.

Rachel yanked the pull ring on a stun grenade and lobbed it through the opening. She turned, dropped on her heels, pressed her hands over her ears, and closed her eyes tightly. The flash from the subsonic deflagration registered as a bright light through her eyelids, the accompanying bang of the grenade throbbing through her bones.

Footsteps sounded on her left just as she rose to her feet. Two men turned the corner of the passage. They stopped, shock registering on their faces at the sight of a tall, blonde woman in the midst of the battlefield. That brief hesitation cost them their lives.

By the time they started to raise their assault rifles, Rachel had cut them down with the AK-47. She strode inside the communications room and stopped a few steps past the doorway.

The chamber was fifteen by twelve feet. A bank of tables crowded the bulkhead to the left. Sitting atop them were the merchant ship's radio and satellite communication hardware, its lifeline to the outside world. Two men lay groaning on the floor ahead of her.

The hairs rose on the back of Rachel's neck.

Satellite infra-red images over the last twenty-four hours had shown three guards permanently stationed inside the ship's communications room and a fourth posted outside.

Instinct had her dropping to the ground. There was movement out of the corner of her eye. The AK-47 slipped from around her neck and clattered across the floor as she hit the deck. She rolled onto her back and saw a blade swoop across the space where she had been a second ago. She narrowed her eyes.

One thing satellite images didn't tell you was the size of your opponents.

At six foot three and over two hundred and fifty pounds, the third guard was a virtual colossus. Though the flash grenade had incapacitated his companions, it seemed to have had little effect on him.

He charged toward her.

*Shit, too close!*

Rachel flipped onto her feet, swooped at the waist, and brought her right leg up in a roundhouse kick. Her boot made contact with the man's left ribcage. An 'Oof!' left his lips. He slowed a fraction.

She whipped her Kbar knife out in time to block his blade. Her earpiece buzzed to life.

'Alpha Two, this is Alpha One. What's your status, over?'

*Busy trying not to get myself killed!*

Rachel jumped back to avoid the knife heading toward her heart. Rage darkened her opponent's face as she continued to evade him, her movements nimble in their deadly dance. He roared and attacked with savage, wild swings of his blade.

She smiled. *That's right, big guy, get angry all you want.*

'Alpha Two, this is Alpha One. I repeat, what's your status?'

Had she not been trying to dodge her opponent's attempt to disembowel her, Rachel would have sighed at the undercurrent of tension in her team leader's voice. She glanced to the right. The fight had brought her next to the communications equipment.

*Time to finish this.*

She stepped up against the closest table just as the large man barreled toward her, jumped in the air, and drove her left knee into his chest. He grunted and toppled backward. She went down with him, her thighs straddling his upper body. They landed hard on the deck.

He brought his arms up, his knife arcing toward her face while his other hand reached for her throat. She blocked his blade and gritted her teeth as his fingers closed around her windpipe. Instinct would have had her trying to free herself from his grip. She ignored it, switched her Kbar to her free hand, leaned into his hold, and slashed her knife across his neck in a clean movement.

The man's eyes widened as arterial blood started pouring from the gash in his flesh. He dropped his blade and clutched helplessly at the scarlet flow with both hands, a gurgle escaping his lips.

He would be dead in minutes.

Rachel heard movement behind her. The two stunned men on the floor were crawling to their feet. They blinked and shook their heads dazedly, assault rifles swinging wildly in their grips. Rachel rolled off the dying man, dropped on her back, and brought her Sig around and up a second before they depressed their triggers. By the time their bullets peppered the air several feet above her head, her shots had found their flesh with deadly accuracy. They went down hard.

Her earpiece buzzed again. 'Alpha Four, this is Alpha One. Move to Alpha Two's last known location and prepare to—'

'Alpha One, this is Alpha Two. Comms room secured, over,' Rachel snapped into the wireless transmitter pinned to her tactical gear.

There was a brief silence.

'Roger that, Alpha Two. Stand by for further instructions, out.'

The voice was brisk. Rachel suspected she was the only one who heard the trace of relief modulating Alpha One's tone.

*Definitely going to have to have words with him.*

## Chapter Two

Rachel gathered the dead men's weapons and kept them close at hand while she flicked switches and entered commands into the communications systems, re-establishing vital network connections that had been deactivated by the guards. Screens lit up across the board, indicating the vessel was back online.

Thirty-eight hours had passed since the US merchant marine cargo ship *Nostradamus* was intercepted by pirates two hundred nautical miles from the Horn of Africa, in the Gulf of Aden. With over $50 million worth of prime, heavy, electrical machinery bound for the Philippines and twenty-five crew members on board, the vessel was attacked mere hours after it entered the Arabian Sea.

The ransom demand came just as Rachel's team completed a covert mission in Yemen, where they had captured the leader of a terrorist cell with affiliations to the Taliban.

Formed as part of the U.S. Department of Justice's goal to combat international drug trafficking, the Foreign-deployed Advisory and Support Teams, or FAST, were the DEA's answer to the military's special ops forces. Officially, FAST teams were tasked with training foreign narcotic law enforcement units, carrying out counter-narcotics missions, and gathering evidence and intelligence to support U.S. and allied drug investigations. Unofficially, FAST were elite tactical units capable of counter-terrorism and direct-action missions on foreign soil, similar to their military counterparts.

Two months shy of her thirty-first birthday, Rachel became one of only a handful of female DEA agents to have successfully completed the arduous selection and training program devised by U.S. Special Operations Command for FAST recruits. The operation in Yemen was her twelfth covert assignment since she joined the team in Afghanistan eight months ago.

Although the mission to rescue the hostages aboard the *Nostradamus* normally fell under the remit of Navy SEALs and Marine Special Ops, Rachel's team was called in on the action as the geographically closest tactical unit to the Gulf of Aden. Everyone knew siege situations were at their most critical twenty-four to forty-eight hours following first contact. Beyond that, hostage takers got twitchy and hostages got desperate, leading to a perfect storm that often ended in tragedy. When the DEA got wind that there were possible links between the pirates holding the *Nostradamus* hostage and a powerful and ultra-secretive drug cartel in East Africa that had so far eluded the U.S. and its allies' efforts at infiltration and intelligence gathering, it gave the FAST team an even stronger justification to be the unit to attempt the rescue.

Rachel suppressed a grimace. *Would have been nice if it wasn't mission number thirteen though.*

Although she tried hard not to fall prey to baseless superstitions, an Irish upbringing and a grandmother who was more catholic than the Pope made this a tricky goal to achieve. Still, the number thirteen was unpopular even with members of the military special ops forces.

The staccato of gunfire started to die down in the distance. Moments later, the words she had been waiting to hear came over the channel.

'Alpha Team, this is Alpha One. We have control of the ship. Helos are on the way. Stand by for further instructions, over.'

'Alpha One, this is Alpha Two. Standing by, out,' said Rachel.

A sigh escaped her lips. She allowed herself to relax slightly, the guns still close at hand.

Though they had been weary after the mission in Yemen, the chance to save lives and gather intelligence on the elusive drug cartel they suspected had been behind many attempted military coups and terrorist attacks across the northern African continent had galvanized the FAST team into action. This was the kind of stuff they lived and breathed for.

It took them less than eighteen hours to assess, plan, and execute the rescue mission in the Gulf of Aden, with the support of a U.S. Navy amphibious assault ship and a destroyer.

Fifteen minutes later, two UH-1N Huey helicopters touched down on the main deck of the *Nostradamus*. The Marine Special Ops team aboard soon assumed control of the ship from the FAST team.

Rachel handed the communications room over to the two soldiers who came to relieve her.

'You guys did good,' said one of the men. He glanced at the bodies on the floor. 'I hear there are no casualties among your team or the hostages.'

She headed for the door, a small smile on her lips. 'Our team leader runs a tight ship.'

'I hear he's got a good XO.'

The soldier's gaze skimmed her figure, admiration evident in his eyes. His companion elbowed him in the ribs.

Rachel's smile turned into a full-blown grin that caused the Marine's breath to catch in his throat.

'That he has,' she said with a humble nod.

*And this XO wants to see her commanding officer right now.*

She found Benjamin Westfield, aka Alpha One, on the bridge of the ship, where he stood in conversation with the Marine Special Ops team leader. Lights blazed through the windows of the superstructure dominating the cargo ship's upper deck. In the darkness beyond, she made out the assault ship and the destroyer on a fast approach, the waters of the Gulf parting in white, phosphorescent waves beneath their bows.

Thirty feet below the bridge of the *Nostradamus*, the hostages were being led to the safety of the Huey helicopters. The pirates who had survived the attack knelt in a huddle inside a ring of armed FAST agents and Marines on the starboard side of the main deck.

The ringleader of the pirates lay dead on the bridge. Next to him was another man. This one was very much alive and bleeding heavily from a gunshot wound to the abdomen. He was being attended to by Tom "Hannibal" Cook, aka Alpha Five, the FAST team's medic.

'Yeah, yeah, it sucks to be shot,' muttered Hannibal as the injured man groaned beneath his ministering hands. 'Shouldn't have seized this ship then, should you? Asshole.' He looked up when he spotted Rachel. 'Hey. We thought you were toast when you didn't respond earlier.' He glanced to the left and grinned. 'Ben was having kittens.'

Ben concluded his conversation and frowned at Hannibal.

'I was not having kittens,' he said in a hard voice. His gaze found her face. His eyes softened almost imperceptibly.

Rachel clamped down on the hot emotions flooding her

chest as she walked up to him, aware of the Marine team leader's curious glance from the other side of the bridge.

Ben's were the most expressive eyes she had ever seen. Normally the color of the sky, they invariably changed with his emotions. They could be as cold and as bright as diamonds when he got angry or turn the color of sapphires when he was happy. But the color she had come to love the most, the one that made her heart melt and her body tremble, was the cobalt-blue of his irises when they made love.

'Sweetheart, you and I need to have a talk when this is over,' she said quietly, her face impassive.

Guilt flashed across Ben's face. She was the only one close enough to see it.

'I was just worried about my XO.' He paused and dropped his voice to a whisper. 'My very sexy XO.'

Rachel shivered when he surreptitiously touched her hand, his fingers leaving a hot trail on her skin. Sensual images of the last time they had slept together danced across her inner vision.

*Not that we did much sleeping*, she thought, feeling the flames of desire burn through her core once more.

They first met eight months ago, on the day she landed in Afghanistan to take on the role of XO in the DEA's most active FAST team, the previous agent in that role having moved back to the agency's U.S. headquarters. The attraction between them had been instantaneous and as scalding as the heat of the battles they went on to face together. After fighting their feelings for nearly half a year, they finally succumbed to the undeniable pull that existed between them.

More than the great sex, and the sex was THE best she'd ever had, that *either* of them had ever had, Rachel soon realized she had found her soulmate in Ben. They were compatible in almost every way, not just physically, but intellectually and emotionally, with the same life aspirations and ambitions. It was worth the years of shitty, short, unsatisfying relationships she had endured in the little personal time she had had while she worked her way up the career ladder to be at the top of her field in the DEA.

Ben was the man she wanted to spend the rest of her life with. And she was the woman he wanted to grow old with.

She hid a smile when she thought of the engagement ring in the top drawer of her bedside table in her quarters back at their base in Afghanistan. Ben had proposed at the end of a grueling training day exactly one week ago, while they were both still dusty and sweaty from a ten-mile run in the desert. There had been tears of joy, followed by hours of heated lovemaking that almost broke the bed in his room.

Still, a tinge of sorrow had tainted their happy day. Rachel had applied for a transfer to Quantico, where the other FAST teams were stationed at the Marine Corps Base. Their rapidly burgeoning relationship meant they couldn't work together much longer; to continue to do so would violate the DEA and special ops' rules and compromise the safety of their team on the field. It also meant that, bar a few stolen weeks here and there, they would live apart for a good few years until Ben rotated back into one of the U.S. FAST teams or progressed into a more senior role in the DEA, something his father desperately wanted.

'Nearly patched up,' Hannibal muttered from the other side of the bridge. 'What the—hey, you shouldn't be moving around so much!'

Rachel looked past Ben.

The injured pirate had rolled onto his front and was crawling across the deck toward the bulkhead where the dead ringleader lay. An incomprehensible mumble escaped his lips. His movements grew frantic, fear evident on his face. Hannibal grabbed his shoulder and frowned at the man's garbled speech.

Rachel froze. Ben tensed. They both recognized one of the Somalian words the man had spoken.

Hannibal paled as he looked in the direction the man was pointing. From his position beside the pirate, the DEA agent could see under the table next to the bulkhead.

He turned and shouted, *'BOMB!'*

The last thing Rachel saw was Ben moving in front of her.

The last thing she heard was the explosion.

The last thing she felt was scorching pain as her body drifted helplessly through the air, skin crisping and flesh succumbing to flames and pressure waves from the blast.

Then darkness engulfed her, scattering her hopes and dreams to the winds.

Get the book now!

Mission:Black (A Division Eight Thriller)

Ingram Content Group UK Ltd.
Milton Keynes UK
UKHW041313100423
419921UK00001B/132

9 780957 282698